At first Kyle Elder can't b[...] inherits a sprawling Vermo[...] met. But soon he wonders if his inheritance is more a curse than a blessing. Why is there a human skeleton in the trunk of his car? Who poisoned one of the female guests at the inn? What's behind the strange behaviour of the nuns who have come to mark Easter at the inn?

Reviewers of Trevor Ferguson's previous novel, *Onyx John*, used words like "offbeat," "wild," "idiosyncratic," and "dazzling" to capture its particular charms. **The Kinkajou** only confirms the vividness of Ferguson's imagination and the compelling eccentricities of his characterization.

"Ferguson's strength is his skill at comic satire and irony. The characters, who look and sound so familiar, quickly belie their ordinary appearances. The plot leaves the realm of reality for wild fantasy . . . " - *The Saint John Telegraph*

TREVOR FERGUSON

The Kinkajou

M&S

An M&S Paperback from
McClelland & Stewart Inc.
The Canadian Publishers

An M&S Paperback from McClelland & Stewart Inc.

First printing August 1990
Cloth edition published by Macmillan of Canada 1989

Canadian Cataloguing in Publication Data

Ferguson, Trevor, 1947-
The kinkajou

(M&S paperback)
ISBN 0-7710-3128-9

I. Title.

PS8561.E64K56 1990   C813' .54   C89-090755-2
PR9199.3.F47K56   1990

A slightly different version of book one, chapter four, was previously published
under the title "First Flames" in *The Malahat Review*, no. 71.

The author is grateful to the Ontario Arts Council for support during the writing of
this novel.

This is a work of fiction. All characters and events are fictitious. Any resemblance
to persons living or dead is purely coincidental. The *Toll House Inn* is a fabrication
not based on any inn or other establishment; nor is it intended to refer to any inn or
other establishment which may have the same, or a similar, name. Any such
reference or resemblance is purely coincidental. No character who may hold public
office or public service position in this work of fiction is intended in any way to
resemble or to refer to any individual holding a similar office or position, either in
the State of Vermont, the Village of Stowe, or anywhere else; nor does the conduct
of the fictional characters intentionally reflect in any way on persons who may hold
similar positions.

Cover design by K.T. Njo
Cover illustration by Richard da Mota

Printed and bound in Canada

Published by arrangement with Macmillan of Canada

McClelland & Stewart Inc.
The Canadian Publishers
481 University Avenue
Toronto, Ontario
M5G 2E9

This novel is dedicated to the memories of

Robert Parkin,

Bertram Kidd,

and Marjorie Sharp

Contents

1

I discovered the bones on the morning of my departure from Tennessee. In quiet repose, the skeleton of a small human lay in the trunk of my car. Perfectly arranged, as if laid out for burial, albeit decapitated, the skull resting in the well of the spare tire. Someone had rudely planted a dandelion in the pelvis, and a spider was suturing the ribs together, fabricating new skin.

Both my hands were laden with luggage — suitcase in my right, dulcimer in my left. My fright developed a curious obsession with belongings: I panicked when I found no place to let them drop.

After spinning in circles, I stomped rings around the car.

Deep breaths helped, and I returned to the trunk to gawk at the remains, culling personality from the astonished cavities of the eye sockets and slack jaw. Transfixed by our mutual gaze, I could not begin to think straight until I had slammed down the lid.

Jesus.

Why me? Why *today*?

Skeletons had been cropping up indiscriminately around town. The phenomenon had been occurring for months now, this was merely the latest incarnation; yet I was offended to have been singled out as a recipient. Especially on this day of days when I was to be delivered, courtesy of fluke or accident or grace, from my self-imposed captivity. I consoled myself with the reminder that I had gotten off lucky. At least a skeleton had not materialized in my bath or bed, a misfortune inflicted upon others.

What to do next was an easy decision. Transport the bones to town. I elected to finish packing my life's belongings — no great chore — using the car's backseat instead of the trunk, then I'd drive into Walkerman's Creek to deposit my find with the sheriff.

Good intentions, thwarted along the way. Driving on the twisting, hilly road, cautiously, so as not to disturb the sleeping contents of the trunk, I caught sight of a police roadblock around the bend and through the trees. Slowed down. Thought this one over. To drive into town and voluntarily report a body in my trunk was an action consistent with good citizenship. To be stopped by police traditionally suspicious of me, to be seen with my bags packed, and then to claim feebly that I was on my way to deliver the cargo to the appropriate authorities was not a course laced with intelligence. I made a U-turn. Burned rubber. An alternate route through the hills ought to save the day. The sheriff would return to his office to find a noble citizen patient on his stoop (that Kyle Elder, he's such a fine fellow), his booty exposed for all the world to view, nothing concealed.

So I drove. Settled my nerves. Turned on the radio and rolled down the window. Bellowed out some forlorn hick tune. "Blue mmmoooooon of Kentucky keep on shinin'!" As my concentration drifted, the Mercury also shimmied off the blacktop. Recovering, I glimpsed the rearview mirror (reconnaissance check, to confirm that no one had seen my folly) and spotted Sheriff McGrath's car at a distance and gaining. I picked up speed. He kept coming. I broke for the back roads. The trails were my stomping-ground, but they were native to him too, and he had the superior car. The chase was on. Careening around blind corners, spinning wheels uphill, letting her rip along straightaways as bumpy as a farmer's fallow; the single-lane dirt track was moonshiner's path, ancient hillbilly horse-and-buggy links. Some ski trails aren't this daring. The ol' Merc' was blowing black smoke and screaming at me and still I kept my foot down and drove hell-bent, wheeling at every junction, praying for an absence of sheer cliffs and dead ends. When I ran right into an ancient hollow once used for distilling 'shine and after that for deflowering maidens, with no way out, I anticipated capture.

Miracle of miracles. No McGrath. That I eluded him can best be attributed to luck. The S.O.B. must have rammed a tree.

I laid low for a few hours. Then left in short spurts. Cutting the ignition about every hundred yards to listen for his ambush. The man can move with stealth, as quietly as breath. He's as devious as night. No sign of him. If he's knocked himself unconscious, don't count on me to call the medics. Maybe he was hungry and had returned for lunch, figuring he knew where to find me. Fooled you, McGrath. Today's the day I blow this popcorn stand.

A change of plans was in order. What was one skeleton lost to these old hills? I would carry on to Vermont, lugging the illicit cache behind me.

When I stopped that night to rest, safe in another State (too disoriented to name it or be certain of my direction), I checked on my companion in the rear. He or she had not traveled well. Bones were jumbled up, a shin impaled a funneled nasal cavity, toes bejeweled a jaunty hip, and a fresh hairline fracture had appeared across the skull. Sorry, stranger. But look at it this way. I'm taking you out of that loony bin to a more peaceful resting place. I could've dumped you by the side of the road, but I respect your dignity. My deliverance is yours. We're heading north, bud. Migrating with the birds to a sanctuary where I have been assured of welcome.

Where I'll lay you down in virgin soil, in a decent grave that won't chuck you back out again.

I slept fitfully that night, dreamed of headless ghosts doing a Halloween strut, and hit the road at sunrise. One thing about my choice of traveling companion: skeletons rarely complain, speak only when spoken to, and their hunger can usually be satisfied with crumbs, their thirst quenched with sips of red wine.

The ramble out of Dixie north through Yankee pastures was a subterranean journey. No sky. Blue Ridge fog, then Pennsylvania smoke overhead. Ghostly roadside figures. The landscape a visceral passion, the dust of my dislocation kicked up, forests, farms, and settlements tightly bound by black industrial belts. The weave of a drunkard's stumble home: regurgitated urban sprawl. America. New Jersey. East Orange? Another wrong turn. More back roads distinguished by their sense of intrigue. My fellow travelers should have been thieves and escaped lunatics; predictably they were military personnel in search of a peaceable motel, and husbands on the lam. Men bereft of women. And me — what was my excuse for subterfuge? Either I was escaping Tennessee on the sly or slipping into Vermont unnoticed, I didn't know which was more important. I felt furtive, a toe-length ahead of the law, and richly subversive. My trunk loaded with contraband, my purposes sinister. In dreams I struggled to be on the loose, unrestrained, set in motion. In dreams I was a hitchhiker without a skin, my bony ankles bound by chain.

I was heading home! I reminded myself, trying to be cheery. But no. That word, *home*, made no sense. I was heading north to formally inherit my father's house, as spooky a prospect as disposing of the ramshackle corpse.

Northward ho.

My preliminary view of the house bequeathed to me by my estranged father was through a fence of tall, budding maples — a first impression that vanquished, in an instant, a week's worth of artful inventions. I was expecting less. Much less. Had spent the previous seven days dreading a moldy shack, one harvested by termites as wind whistled through gaps in the floorboards and the roof sagged under an avalanche of snow. I could see it all, a gang of cheery, chubby trappers squirreled away for the winter initiating me into their revelry; together we'd emerge in the spring as lithe skeletons playing the washboard and spoons.

Poof!

Suddenly I'm confronted with the actual, tangible house. Right in front of me.

Of course, not every fabrication had been gloomy. Clairvoyant on rye I had conjured pastoral mountain retreats: a rustic log cabin, bug-free; a centuries-old stone house once inhabited by any one of Ethan Allen's Green Mountain Boys, if not by the sinewy old soldier himself. (Deduction: Vermont must be an impoverished State to have just the one hero.) But no vision, however startling or sublime, had prepared me for the jarring authenticity of the real thing. This was it. The proof that the house actually did exist.

4

After days and nights of pinching myself my bruises had at last paid off: I wasn't dreaming, I was wide awake, the house now was as irrefutable as it had been inexplicable.

"Not in a million years, I never expected this!" I had proclaimed to anyone willing to hear me out on the day a lawyer had called me with the news. "Nobody ever told me that I *had* a father — or, what's more to the point, that he owned a house." It's a bartender's job to listen, so I buttonholed the one on duty in Apps' Pickle Barrel. "Tell me, how could I have guessed that my father was alive when he never bothered to tell me that *I* was? At least in his mind." Out of courtesy, I paid my landlady her rent for April, apologized for the short notice about leaving, and, while each of us held a possessive hand on the check, said my piece. "Apparently my old man thought so little of me that he had to be dead before he could stand the thought of keeping in touch. I'm not that bad a guy, but he never took the trouble to find that out. Or did he? I dunno."

A dad.

Deceased.

I had phoned the lawyer back half-a-dozen times, long-distance, to verify that he hadn't made a mistake. "You sure you got the right guy? And my — you know, father — he's dead?"

"Is your name Kyle Troy Elder, or what?" A young man's impertinent voice, a combination of pride and inexperience. A cockiness descended from stupidity. He goofed on a regular basis, I surmised, and this instance was no exception.

"It is," I admitted.

"Your mother's name was Rose. You were brought up by her and by another woman, one Emma St. Paul. Your mother passed away some time ago, I believe. In 1970. True or false?"

"True." Who could deny the skeletal details? Still, I felt disoriented learning that they were public knowledge.

"Yes or no: you were born and raised in Montreal, Quebec, Canada."

How does he know this stuff? "Yes."

"And you've been living in Tennessee. Am I right or wrong?"

"You're right." God help me, I was still confused. What a shock

5

to discover that others — *outsiders!* — knew that I existed.

"And my, you know" — I choked on the word — "father? You're certain that he's dead?"

Ryder was the lawyer's name. "Well sir, we took the trouble to bury him five months ago. If he wasn't dead then, it's a safe bet that he is now."

Green Vermont — as promised on every license plate — greeted me robed in white. The fourth of April, Maundy Thursday, a taste of spring on the warming breeze, flavored by a winter's seasoning. In the woods, rings of sodden grass had appeared at the base of the trees, the forest blighted by these pockmarks expanding across the melting snow. Gazing up the hillside pasture to my illustrious inheritance, indicated by a weathered, arrow-shaped signboard with the name darkly stained in the chiseled wood — TOLL HOUSE — I surveyed rheumy boulders, and glanced across the backs of surface rock protruding sleepily from the white quilt. Discerned grasses on the steepest pitch like the hair of awakening, bewitched maidens yawning in the sun. An interval of hibernation coming to a close. My own had lasted fifteen years.

Onward and upward.

In light of the spring thaw, the narrow, bone-jostling road ascending to Toll House had been maintained in reasonable condition. Not that any road is smooth to my '64 Mercury. Twenty-one years old and still chugging along, but barely; I have to stop for oil more often than for gas. I don't drive in big cities because the contraption draws attention to itself and to its driver in certain neighborhoods. Cops investigating my trunk would be in for the shock of their lives. I don't drive at night because the lights won't work. I don't drive much, period, and should never drive downhill because the brakes are faulty. She made it though, to my surprise, all the way from Tennessee to fart black, smelly exhaust upon fragrant, snowy Vermont.

Steering the Merc' along twin ruts to avoid the soft, muddy shoulders required my full concentration. One slip of the wheel — mine an ornery one to muscle onto the straight and narrow — and the car would likely wallow in the muck. Or, with my luck, sink.

So much for the corporeal dangers. Metaphysical booby traps awaited as well.

Two-thirds of the way along, without warning and blatant amid the bare deciduous trees, a bright red octagonal sign stood out, with white lettering:

HALT!

Smackdab in the middle of nowhere.

Fancy that. Obeying, I braked slowly, coaxing the car to a stop, and came upon a second sign, previously hidden behind the first, this one square, peppered with dents from a shotgun blast, bold black letters on a faded yellow target:

PAY
TOLL

What was this about?

No bridge to cross nearby. No scenic trail to follow if the price was right. No available means to either collect or pay the due in evidence, only the monstrous signs. Perhaps a charitable donation of indeterminate amount was expected: coins flung deep into the underbrush for summer retrieval by bandit raccoons; dollar bills shaped into jets, floated upon the north wind to dive-bomb one's indigent neighbors.

Peculiar.

I didn't know what to make of it, or what to do with myself. Suspicious that this lunacy could prove to be the handiwork of my unknown, departed father — not an auspicious introduction to his nature — I toyed with the idea of making a run for it. Beat it, fellah. Right now. Quickly! While you still have the chance. This madness about making a new life for yourself — stuff it! Skip learning about the one you might have missed had this so-called father abducted you or won a custody battle; a little knowledge can be a terrible thing.

The trouble was, at this juncture the road provided not an inch of turning space. I could trespass, or I could pay up and proceed, or I could risk life and limb driving backward down the hill. The two things I could not do were turn the car around and flee, a perennial favorite, or drop everything and go to sleep, my habitual response to dilemma.

Thwarted, I flicked a penny into the woods, wrenched the shift into gear, and rumbled on up. Yeah, I admit it. I'm that big a fool, and that cheap too.

To counter my trepidation, I sang in a deep bass as I drove up the hill.

Dem bones, dem bones, dem dry bones!
Dem bones, dem bones, dem dry bones!
Dem bones, dem bones, dem dry bones!
Now hear the Word of the Lord!

The skeleton sang falsetto.

2

Toll House loomed into view again at the zenith of my ascent. More so at first glance than in the days since, the building appealed to me as a brooding organic structure that had clumsily expanded eastward with successive generations. Striking the somber, detached mood of a graveyard, the house exuded character: mossy and damp, a shady personality; and yet the essence of discretion.

The snowy road traced a precipice that dropped off rather steeply, then widened into a parking lot where I was greeted by yet another sign. Nothing spooky, thank goodness, not this time, simply:

CAUTION
BUSES TURNING

Buses!

I willed myself to hallucinate a fleet of Greyhounds disgorging a fifth of Boston, perhaps a third of upper-class New York. Behind them in military convoy, a battalion of armored trucks wheeled in to collect the weekly receipts. I was rich, man, *rich*! Connecticut Yankees would funnel their savings into my bank account.

Delighted, I carried on to the far end of the lot nearest the house, managing to control my euphoria long enough to pull in next to a Cherokee Chief. Flanked by a pair of rusting Toyotas, a black Fleetwood Cadillac was centered in my rearview mirror; otherwise, the lot was empty. The swarms must be arriving later.

From this side of the house, and I didn't know whether it was

9

the rear or the front, the inn was entered at the second story. Having been built squatting on the hillside, the lower level had windows on three sides only, facing the valley. Stonework had been carried to the top of the second flight, where it yielded to cedar shakes and massive, protruding beams. The severe slope of the roof, interrupted by intricately gabled, peaked dormers, suggested low ceilings throughout, while the size of the main chimney promised a large, traditional hearth.

I caught myself. And chuckled under my breath. For I had been guessing at the interior; believing out of habit that access would be forbidden to me.

As legacy of an olden days' aversion to drafts, the windows in Toll House are small, yet modern thinking shines through the skylights, and through the glassed second-floor deck which is the dining-room. The enormous extension — actually a horizontal series of growths — that I had observed from down below was hidden by the angle of my view. I presumed correctly that it had been executed with taste, for the inn — my new home! — sad and tranquil, was both a gracious and a formidable sight.

And I — I, Kyle Troy Elder — was poor no more.

Instant success fabricates friends quickly, I found that out. A nattily dressed, beanstalky young gentleman (mentally, I put him behind the wheel of the Cadillac) was advancing on me with intent. As I stepped out of the ol' Merc', I inhaled my first stinging breath of raw mountain air. Potent enough to devastate the two-pack smoker.

"Tennessee plates!" the man sang out, probably with the same inflection that he might bray "Objection!" in a court of law. I recognized his musical bark as that of the lawyer who had probated my father's will, tracked me down by who-knows-what devious devices, and telephoned. His stylish wool overcoat, opened down the front, was pushed apart by his elbows; his hands, pocketed in the trousers of a pinstriped, three-piece blue suit, no doubt fingered loose change. He was about my age, early thirties, a Wall Street yuppie lost in the north woods. "That must make you none other than Kyle Elder Junior himself!"

"It does?" To undergo a change of name was not inappropriate,

I suppose, given the recent upheavals in my life. But I balked. "Nobody's ever called me 'Junior' before."

"Really? Why not? Your father always signed himself 'Senior'. Faithfully. Damned proud of it too. Franklin Delano Ryder, sir, at your service. Your dad's attorney." I shook the proffered hand. An eagerness stimulated his features, a brash boyishness thrived beneath the knitted cap of thick, black curls. His freshness was as abundant as the hills. "Yours now too, I hope. My friends call me Franklin D., or just plain F.D.R."

"Thanks for locating me. It couldn't have been easy."

A modest shrug. "Wasn't hard, once I knew where to look."

"How'd you know where to look?" I noticed that he was guiding me away from the house.

"My old man told me. He was your father's lawyer since way back when. Hey! I guess that makes us related! In a way. How're you doing, cousin?" Before I could defend myself, Ryder had clamped an arm around my shoulders and was squeezing me with affection. "Your daddy was a sly fox," he confided, and we nearly rubbed noses. "The old coot. Left me with incentives. The sooner I contacted you, the larger my fee. Talk about diminishing returns!"

Abruptly, I was released. We had stopped behind my car. "Does this primordial relic still run?" The insolence!

"Carried me clear from Tennessee."

"Without a tow? Amazing. Feel free to junk it."

"What?"

"The Jeep is yours." My eyes must have indicated befuddlement, because he gestured to the dark blue Cherokee Chief with his chin. I'll be damned. Wheels! I could have kissed him, but I'm more reserved than my benefactor. Besides, my giver-of-gifts seemed to be waiting for me to do something. I drew a blank until Ryder generously gave me a hint.

"What's in the trunk?"

"Nothing!" I suppose I shouted a little too loudly. "Why?" I croaked, then I coughed to get the frog out.

"No bags? Whew, you're traveling light."

"Oh, sorry, they're in the back seat. The trunk's been sealed shut for years. Rust."

"Ah! I get you. So! Tell me. Be honest now, did you stop?"

"Pardon me?"

"Down below," Ryder pressed me. "At the signs."

"Oh yeah. I did, actually."

"Me too!" The lawyer laughed. "I always do! A few weeks ago I promised myself I wouldn't. Stop, I mean. Barrelled right on through like a rumrunner. A hundred feet beyond the signs, that's about as far as I made it. No further than that. Next thing I knew, I was backing down again. Then I got out and gave that 'Pay Toll' sign a kick in its gluteus maximus. I felt much better after that. Believed I had accomplished something. Don't ask me what."

"I paid."

"You *what?*"

"Just a penny."

"Jesus! You're as nutty as your old man!"

Franklin D. made a brief, valiant attempt to wrench open the rear door, driver's side, to get at my luggage. Tapping his elbow, I signalled him to step aside, then raised my foot, gave the center of the door a swift thunk with the heel of my boot, and smiled as it obediently swung open. I've spent countless hours keeping the ol' Merc' running and I know exactly how to treat her. The door has no latch and stays shut only because a twist in the metal binds with the frame, but I didn't say so to Ryder.

"The knack," he surmised. "That's all that life requires."

"Didn't my, you know" — the word continued to snag on my tongue — "father, didn't he have an explanation for the signs?"

"Nope. At least not one that he was willing to share with me. I asked him about it often enough. Inevitably he'd hit me with some cagey rejoinder."

"Like what?"

" 'Never met a man who didn't have to pay the price.' That sort of thing."

"Is that how my father talked?" For the lawyer had imitated a dusky, varnished voice; the timbre of mahogany if wood could speak.

"More or less. Don't forget, it's always possible that he erected the signs merely to suit the name of the inn. But *he* named the inn

Toll House, so which came first, the chicken or the barbecue sauce?"

A question that I had asked over the phone, but in my weariness needed to broach again, was "And this is a viable business? A fellow can earn a living?"

"Debt-free and humming. I told you that already, didn't you believe me?" With two of my suitcases strapped under his arms, a third in his right hand and my dulcimer case in his left, Franklin D. struck the pose of a smart and snappy bellhop. Suddenly he whirled, lumped all my worldly goods back on the rear seat, and I decided then and there not to tip him.

"What's the matter?"

"Listen." He wrenched my elbow and drew me close. His anxious breath moist on my cheek. "Before she comes out, I have to warn you about Hazel Stamp."

I followed F.D.R.'s panicky gaze to the side porch of Toll House. Through the large storm windows, I could see a stout gray-haired woman bundling herself up.

"Kyle, give her half a chance and she'll take over. She'll run the place and your life as well. Won't be a thing you can do about it. There is no Court of Appeal when it comes to that woman. May I suggest a firm hand right from the start? But with a gentle touch, because the one thing that you *don't* want is for her to quit. If she threatens resignation, yield. Appease her. Show her who's boss, yet bear in mind that she's indispensable. Keep her in line, but be cautious where you draw it. Have you been in business before, Kyle? Have you had any experience handling recalcitrant employees like her?"

Although his advice was contradictory, I passed on the opportunity to challenge him. The infamous Hazel Stamp was preparing herself for a major expedition — or an Arctic fashion show. She was taking extraordinary care to dress for the out-of-doors. Twice she unwound her scarf, apparently dissatisfied with the fall of the dangling tails of alizarin crimson across her mauve woolen coat. She experimented with her fur collar up, flat, up in back and down in front, and practiced knots with her viridian neckerchief. She adjusted the tilt of her fuchsia toque.

"Yes to your first question," I informed Ryder after a few moments delay. "No to the second. I had a one-man operation."

"Like me! But no, that's not quite true. I have a secretary, and she's an imperial pain in the descending colon too, so we'll have that in common. The thing about Hazel Stamp is —" and here Franklin D. turned his back to the house as the woman of his nightmares had finally emerged, fluorescent and briskly swinging her arms in a military step up the stone walk towards us in her lime boots, a soldier intent on procedures and drill, if not combat — "she has technique. She's not merely opinionated, she has guile. Rest assured, she'll do everything in her power to confound you. I know. I've been overseeing this operation since your father's death. Because of her, I can't honestly tell you what day it is. She's incorrigible! My sympathies, by the way, now that we've met in person. On your father's passing, I mean."

"Thank you." What could I say except politely acknowledge the remark? I was not convinced that I had sustained a loss. One day I'm fatherless and penniless. The next I'm comparatively rich. How do I mourn the death of a non-existent family member, except to cluck my tongue at cancer's further carnage? I could not help but think that I had gained from this shuffle of lives.

"She'll spook you," Ryder prattled on quickly, knowing by the crunch of her footsteps on snow that Hazel Stamp was within range. "She'll try to make you appear ignorant. She's not happy until everyone around her looks ridiculous. Bluff her. Pretend you know exactly what she's talking about. That'll drive her batty!"

"Never listen to lawyers!" was the small, thewy woman's greeting. Hers was the voice of a prophet issuing the first of Ten Commandments for the modern age. A few strides more and she was next to me, her hand extended to tug on my coat-sleeve. The force of her downward yank caused my shoulder to dip. I consented to stoop. And encountered verdant eyes, the opalescence of a meadow. Bees buzzed amid the wildflowers. Severe stress wrinkles extended down from her mouth like cracks in a china cup, otherwise her skin had aged well. I put her in her late fifties. "Whatever he has said about me is a damned lie. So forget it right —" she slapped one hand with the other sharply — "*now!*" I was shaken by the emphatic retort. She convinced me.

"Mrs. Stamp, *please*," Franklin D. defended. My chance to see him in action. Lord knows I needed the help. "I haven't mentioned your name. I would have soon enough, of course, but only in the most glowing terms. Isn't that right, Kyle? *Kyle?*"

Fortunately, he gave me no time either to sustain or correct the lie, adding, "By the bye, Mr. Elder, may I introduce —"

"Hazel Stamp," the woman interrupted, this time allowing her hand to be pumped once in affirmation, settling every conceivable dispute. "Either I'm hired or fired," she stated. "You're the one to decide. Eight years I served your father" she elaborated. "Faithfully. If that's not good enough for you, I don't know what is."

"Neither do I. Is it Mrs. Stamp?"

"Hazel, to you. I don't truck with interference. Your father (my sympathies) was responsible for what he called Marketing, which was a flimsy excuse for doing bugger-all."

"Hold on —" F.D.R. endeavored to intercede, in vain.

"What he called Public Relations was one of his better justifications for getting plastered. If that's what you have in mind, I'm all for it. I can run this place without you, but not with you. Nothing personal. I'm independent-minded, that's all. An improvement over this yokel here who doesn't have one to begin. So. Keep out of my hair. *Especially* in the kitchen. If it's your intention to dip your sticky fingers into my beeswax you can give me my walking papers right now, thank you very much."

"Hazel, you're not being fair," my limp lawyer attempted to interject.

"Mrs. Stamp to you, lawyer," she stipulated. "Well?" — turning her leafy eyes on me. "What'll it be?"

I laughed. At least a week's worry whistled out of me like a locomotive's blast of steam. The breathtaking view, or the lack of oxygen up there on top of the world, or the penetrating unreality of talking with strangers who knew more about my family background than I did, suddenly overwhelmed me.

I experienced a rowdy intoxication. "You're hired, Hazel," I bubbled over, enjoying myself. Franklin D. nodded his cowardly consent, which I did not particularly appreciate.

"That's settled then," Hazel agreed, failing to sound as pathologically grumpy as she had probably wished. "Now I can get down to brass tacks. We're terrible busy inside, making things proper for the nuns. They're arriving today too, of course."

"The who?"

"The nuns! The nuns! It's Easter!" Hazel Stamp ordained, already halfway back to Toll House, a spring to her step, thanks to the confirmation of her authority. Run the place for me, Hazel! I shouted after her with silent glee. My life too, I don't care! Take every little worry off my hands! All I want to do is count the loot. Suddenly, she twirled around and said, "They'll be expecting you, Mr. Kyle, to read to them." Spinning again, an iridescent children's top, she quick-marched back inside.

"See what I mean?" Franklin D. whispered. In a conspiratorial pose, he draped himself across my left shoulder. "Deliberate confusion. That woman expects you to know everything in advance. Mocks you if you don't. It's her trademark. You should have said, something like, 'Ah, yes, the nuns, of course!' *That* would have slain her. Ah well. Next time."

"What's this about reading to them? Read what?"

Ryder shrugged his lofty shoulders. "The Bible?" he suggested initially, before inspiration alighted on his brow. "There you go! If she brings up the subject again, pretend you know all about it. She'll split a gasket!"

And I wondered aloud, "Why are nuns coming to an inn in the first place?"

"It's Easter," Franklin D. explained, which only deepened the enigma. Then he laughed, and leaned on me more heavily. All he would add was, slyly, "Welcome to Vermont, pal."

3

Enter Toll House, unpack your bags, take a load off, relax; and become lost in the chambers and fables, the corridors and nuances of a dead man's mind.

The rooms are never the same, as though they continually revolve upon a lazy Susan. The fascination of Toll House, and its inherent frustration, is that the inn accommodates guests by adopting their spirit and collective personality. Send me your degenerate prisoners and quickly the rooms will appear to be as squalid as jail cells. Your executives, and observe the inn miraculously transform itself into an exclusive corporate retreat. I'm told that winter downhill skiers turn the place into a swinging joint on weekends. Mid-week it's an old fogies' home. I can believe it. Nuns arrive and my home becomes a convent.

Toll House, then, is not whatever I had anticipated, but neither is it what I sometimes think it should be, now that we are knowledgeable of one another. Its mood is contradictory, at once pervasive and chameleon.

The house is no rudimentary maze. Pity the pilgrim with a growling stomach who staggers forth in quest of a midnight salami-on-rye only to tumble onto his keister because someone had thoughtfully rearranged the furniture. *Ssshh*, and watch: a love-spoiled maiden slinking through the shadows in a wispy negligée bumps hard into a ghost. Both ghost and maiden flee, in opposite directions. Over orange juice in the morning, two friends compare remarkably similar stories and matching bruises.

Always beware when putting down a glass. In the time it takes

17

to stoke the fire a perfect stranger has chug-a-lugged your daiquiri. Abandon your bed at breakfast and you may discover an attractive woman comfortable beneath the sheets upon your return. Which could be an opportune meeting if only she was still alive.

Varnished to a tawny, warm glow, planked tongue-and-groove pine walls and the overhead dark cedar beams consecrated Toll House with a reverent sheen. The five stone hearths that I managed to locate — later I'd find seven — solidified the inn with a sense of endurance, of history, of permanence in the midst of change, while providing the denizens of this decade with tangible comfort. Entirely fenced in stone, the downstairs bar was a quaint dungeon sheltered from errant bomb blasts and featuring a raised fireplace and cushioned Windsor chairs. Pewter steins with glass bottoms. I considered helping myself to a drink. Presumably I owned the spirits and besides, I was willing to run a tab. But I failed to alleviate the sensation that I'd be pilfering. Giving myself a scolding, I returned upstairs bone dry.

On the top floor I opened doors at will, hoping to catch a chambermaid in an illicit embrace, or to stumble upon hideaway lovers in the throes of an international tryst. No doors were locked, nor could they be, yet I never overcame the sensation that I was an intruder. Someone worth arresting. I had to combat the inclination to knock. *This is my house!* I reminded myself, seeking to convince the blackguard in me who would not believe it.

Pomanders secreted scents from cedar-lined linen-closets. High, wood-framed beds were graced by decorative quilts. (So many beds! Each provoking the temptation to curl up and fall serenely asleep.) In a stroke, my middle finger proved the window sills dust-free. Close inspection judged the carpets combed clean. The community bathrooms might have been sterilized; panicky germs could not find a safe corner in which to cower. In the extension, the small rooms adhered to the sparse, dormitory style familiar to weekend skiers, though several rooms in the original house were treasures from the past, spacious lairs with interesting nooks preserved for posterity. Early American antiques personified the rooms' charm, and here and there I discovered that rare and celebrated luxury in a New England country inn, the private bath.

The centerpiece of accommodation at Toll House, the Mt.

Washington Room, was a nest fit for supine self-indulgence. A skylight over the bed evoked nights of stargazing between kisses. (I speculated on what it might cost me to sleep in there.) Dark at this afternoon hour, the room felt solemn, somehow observant of me, while the placement of windows promised sunshine for breakfast in bed.

I wanted to celebrate! Party until dawn!

Old habits linger, however. I chose to take a nap.

Up the stairs, I located the room above the kitchen where Franklin D. had deposited my luggage. High-paying customers lived well; by comparison my quarters were worthy of the hired help. A single bed discouraged romance; a desk under the window invited self-reflection. An oak bureau, shelves for books, and the final letdown, a white enamel basin, chipped, completed the trappings. Do I use the bowl for a good-morning cold-water splash, or for an emergency pee in the middle of the night? Either way, am I to toss the dirty water out the window? I'd have to investigate the stains in the snow outside to see whether they were soapy or yellow.

In spite of the certainty that my chamber would delight an ascetic, my disappointment was not severe. After all, the roof showed no signs of leaking, which had been an inconvenience at my previous abode. There I used to be up half the night shoving the bed around to temporary dry patches, rearranging buckets and flowerpots to catch the flow; in the morning I'd wash my hair in fresh rainwater stained blackish by roof tar. The diminished floor-space in my new room was tolerable in exchange for the luxury of being able to read without an umbrella.

I lay down on the bed. Bunk, rather. A trifle hard, but I could adapt. Asleep in less than an instant, I needed a few moments to discern that the knock on my door came from outside the boundary of my budding dream.

Franklin D. poked in his head uninvited. "Everything okey-dokey?"

"Fine." I sat up. "Great. The inn is way beyond my expectations." (Little did he realize that an outhouse would have accomplished that.) "Just thought I'd grab a few winks. The long trip, all this excitement, I was feeling drowsy."

"Good idea. Kyle — we have papers to sign. Perhaps on Tuesday? My office? I'm closed both Good Friday and Easter Monday, you see."

"I'll be there with bells on."

"Here're the keys to your Jeep."

I restrained myself. Didn't want to snatch them too abruptly. Easy now. Be cool. That's it, let your hand rise slowly. Franklin D. dropped the key ring with its lucky rabbit's foot into my predatory palm. I clamped my fist tight, and hid my suddenly valuable hand under a protective thigh. "Thanks a lot, F.D.R."

"You're most welcome. I'm off. Kyle, if you have any questions or problems, anything whatsoever . . ." He let his voice trail away, his offer implied, and appreciated, although he had not actually committed himself by concluding his point. He gave my shoulder an affectionate prod instead.

"There is one thing," I said. Among many.

"Fire away." His eagerness to please had more to do with his boyish vitality, I think, and his longing for good marks, than with professional manner. He sat down beside me at the foot of the bed.

"I take it that this was my father's room."

"Your daddy was well-off, but frugal. It's amazing how often those two things go together. Since you own the place now, choose any room you want."

In that case . . . but no, I'd keep a lid on my desires for a respectable length of time. "What I'm wondering is, where are his things? The shelves are bare. The bureau's empty. The sheets feel coarse, as if they're stolen government issue." I turned up a corner of the pillowcase. "Property: United States Navy." F.D.R. laughed at my little joke. "The point being, why are there no personal touches? I'm disappointed — and frankly, astounded — not to find a single reminder of him. No photographs. No knickknacks. None of his reading material. Nothing at all. Zero. Which holds true for the rest of Toll House too. It makes no sense."

Bouncing back onto his feet, Ryder offered a silent, convoluted reply with his elastic facial muscles to indicate that he couldn't help, adding, "Your father is gone, Kyle. I guess it's only natural that his belongings were removed. But take that one up with Hazel. No doubt she ordered the clean-up. Knowing her, she overdid it.

The woman's a zealot. Okay, look already, I'm off. Been a pleasure meeting you, Kyle. We'll speak again soon."

"So long, Franklin D."

Moments later, an engine's roar had me on my feet so quickly that the charge must have come from a dream. I bounded to the window, fearful that someone was swiping my Jeep. Ryder was leaving and not, as I would have presumed, in the Cadillac. His chariot was a yellow Toyota in need of a new muffler. (And he had had the gall to sneer at my car!) Mind, he did rise in my estimation, owing to his choice of vehicle. I bet myself that he'd been borrowing the Cherokee Chief for the last few months. Probably that's what he'd been doing at the house, switching cars for my arrival.

My head lay on the pillow again for no more than ten seconds when Hazel Stamp's *ratata-ta-tata* had me up once more like a Jack-in-the-box. This game would have to stop. Perhaps my first order of business as the inn's shiny new proprietor should be to supply every room and certainly mine with a "Do Not Disturb" sign. And locks. Didn't they realize I sometimes sleep for days? Wake up to find myself another year older? Hazel, at least, politely waited for me to open the door before entering. But enter she did, using her trolley as a battering ram.

A snack. How nice.

"To tide you over, Mr. Elder. A spot of tea for health and a speck of nourishment. I'm afraid that you cannot expect dinner until half-past eight, after vespers. That's when the sisters sit down and they'll insist that you join them."

"Hazel, where are my father's things? I haven't seen a shred of evidence that he ever occupied this room."

Unwittingly, by sitting on it, I had foiled her desire to straighten the bed cover. Hazel chose to tidy the perfectly arranged curtains instead. She spoke while her hands were busy.

"Your father now, his final months were difficult, poor soul. He ought really to have been in hospital. But who am I to be saying that? He wanted to die here, and no one could very well deny him his only wish." Turning, she willed her hands to be submissive, holding them still in front of her. "He'd lost control of his bowels, your father did. Vomited something fierce. We had to fumigate on a regular basis."

"My God."

"The practical thing to do was to trash everything. Keepsakes went down to the furnace room, stowed away in boxes. I'll show you through it all when we both have time. For now, be a good lad, sip your tea. It's camomile."

"Oh, Hazel — ?" I intercepted her quick stride out the door. A marked change in her disposition was apparent, now that the lawyer had gone. She was neither hostile nor insecure.

"Mm — ?"

"Do you drive?" I was worried that I might have to share the Cherokee with her, for business purposes. If I was lucky she owned the other Toyota. I wanted to ask her about the mystery guest whose Caddy was parked out front.

"Mm-hmm" was her vaguely affirmative manner.

"Do you own a car, by any chance?" Please say yes.

Incredible. She actually blushed. And studied the floor. "Hmmm," she said, a noncommittal response. The next moment she confided, "A Cadillac."

"Sheesh! What do I pay you?" My surprise and, I daresay, my annoyance, were rescued by the woman's sense of humor. She laughed quite merrily.

"A pittance!" she exclaimed. "Not enough to feed the cat! But the Cadillac was your dad's. Left me the keys in his will, he did. Truly I was shocked. Especially because that stumblebum lawyer didn't rook me out of it. Guess you knew that your father was a great one for practical jokes, he was. Gave me the car as a gag, I'm sure of that. Any time I'm behind the wheel I hear him having a jolly old time, roaring in his heaven. Evacuate the streets they do, whenever I drive into Stowe, so I'm told. Which explains why no one ever is around. Rumor has it the town's rigged up the air-raid siren to announce my arrival."

"You're not serious!"

She smiled.

"That was good of him," I simpered. "Undoubtedly deserved. You were the one who cared for him during his illness."

"Actually, no. I just mopped up. Mother Superior Gabriella did

22

the bulk of the nursing. It's her profession. She moved in for the last two — mmm, I guess it was more like three — months. Those were hard times. That's one reason why your father bequeathed his fortune — except for his property — to the Order of the Seven Veils. That's the nuns."

"Yes. Of course." I feigned knowledge. A fortune? Are we talking about cold hard cash here, on the barrel-head? He gave away his greenbacks to a bunch of poverty-embracing spinsters in funny penguin suits? What a waste! I tried not to let Hazel see my chagrin, not wanting to confess that I had never known my father, nor he me. Perhaps Hazel and Franklin D. already understood that much, but I chose to continue on the premise that they might not fathom the full extent of our estrangement. As I had interpreted the story, my father had flown the coop before my birth, an unwanted, scruffy starling in a nest of tropical fowl, leaving behind a lethal dose of his spermatozoa squirted on an unhatched egg.

A complicated position. How could I justify my blessings when I had not been present during my father's final days, perhaps months, of agony? I likened my situation to that of a novice on his first day in a yoga class, the instructor having gone home, who must figure out how to unwind from a pretzel-bend of limbs. I was stuck.

Dwelling on my posture, I never noticed Hazel leave. Suddenly she was missing. Weird. I was tempted to search for her under the narrow bunk or in the shallow closets.

Buttered blueberry and corn muffins a convenient arm's reach away, I lay down. The ceiling loomed oppressively close. Claustrophobia steeped in my bloodstream. My father's den; he had breathed the same air. All trace of him now extinguished. Who are you? I wondered in the silence of the sanctuary. Where have you been? What've you been doing all these years?

The funny thing was, my questions echoed. In the stillness they'd bounce off the walls, and I heard them asked of me. The quiet air awaited a response.

Answer.

4

This afternoon, clouds list to port. Indicating, I've been told, a dull day in heaven. Among the dead, the more curious hang out over the balustrade to mark the progress of old friends and relations fuddling down below. There are souls that weep, and souls that mourn; others yuk it up. If you care to don your spectacles, Father, and peer over the edge (always maintaining, of course, a toehold in the fluff), you are free to spy me as I am.

I have little enough to say for myself. Excuses are tiring, and I prefer to govern my grudges, keep them from taking command. Listen, thanks for the house. In death you have behaved as a proper parent. If, from your celestial vantage point, the chip on my shoulder is obvious, then the reason for it should also be plain. Forgive me, Father, but I would have preferred knowing you alive.

A solitary recollection of you persists from childhood. You may be interested to hear that your existence, in addition to your absence, had a riveting effect on me. And be surprised to learn that I spied you once, briefly, going up in smoke. In a trice you were reduced to cinder and ash. The moment for me remains both vivid and confused, in and out of focus. Of this much I'm certain: Mother, wearing a cardigan an autumn shade of sorrel, butted her cigarette in the dust of your face. Her way to illustrate a point.

I was eight years old at the time, in grade three, and in love.

Puppy love was the euphemism for what ailed me. A childhood malady more critical than scarlet fever, more disorienting than whooping cough. In the latter stages of the disease, I'd risk sneaking out-of-doors without permission to scamper three blocks and gaze forlornly at the curtains in her window. Whenever I felt particularly bold, I'd run up and touch the base of her house, dashing off again as though the bricks had been hot coals.

Waiting in the on-deck circle, I scratched her name in the dirt with my bat. I stole chalk from girls playing hopscotch and scrawled her name on the pavement, always with an exclamation point. *CINDY B!*

I had been smitten the morning the school nurse lined up the grade threes to inoculate our bottoms against diptheria, typhoid, and a Latin dictionary of diseases epidemic in the Dark Ages. Most children endured the indignities without embarrassment: shirts or tunics tucked up, pants or bloomers slipped down a notch.

Poor Cin. Unconscionable, thinking back, to excuse the event as coincidence. Not when the prettiest girl in school should be the only one to have had her floppy blue drawers yanked down below her knees by the visiting intern. Girls giggled or blushed; boys made faces. Bent over the teacher's desk, Cindy was in obvious distress, her eyes brimming with tears. And I felt sorry for her, honestly I did, Father, but my heart was overruled by my enchantment for the twin globes flexing nervously before my eyes. I lived in a household of women but this was the first one I'd viewed semi-nude. I had fallen in love.

The intern, a studious, thick-lensed over-achiever, with an adolescent's complexion, affectionately patted her skin, causing the flesh to quiver. He whispered that this wouldn't hurt, then, watching her, made her wince.

Plucky Cindy refused to cry.

Snickering boys repeated coarse words learned from their older brothers and fathers. Even had I benefited from that usual pattern of male education, I still would have been too stupefied to speak, laugh, or utter grunts as some were doing. Cindy's bottom, along with an especially roguish frame from a Dick Tracy cartoon in the weekend funnies ("Come here, baby," said the sexy slut to the detective who was shot full of holes), had galvanized my prurient interest as nothing has since.

But I mean to report a sadder day. Waterlogged in memory as though doused by the spray of hook-and-ladder trucks: the afternoon Cindy buried her father, the afternoon mine was cremated.

In honor of a fireman's funeral, class had let out early. Cindy's dad had died a local hero. Burnt beyond recognition, the wags avowed. A closed coffin at the parlor. He had left behind three daughters in elementary, a son in high school, another in diapers, and a wife in ruins. The civic ceremony included an impressive march from the funeral parlor, where the coffin was hoisted aloft a pump truck and draped in the Union Jack, to the man's home, then to the firehall and on to church. Wonderful hoopla. For some, the most fun since the five-car pile-up in the Jarry Tunnel. I got a kick out of the columns of firefighters in crimson blazers and the policemen solemnly marching behind in Prussian blue. The Legionnaires' band piped everyone outside. A fall festival. Kids had a field day with their slingshots and peashooters.

Women and a few men dabbed their eyes as the procession trudged along.

"Poor children," a neighbor of mine lamented. I was alarmed by her open grief. What's the problem here? And suddenly she appeared, my Cindy, bewildered in a tailored black suit as she marched along with her siblings, in tears, eliciting the usual comparisons to Shirley Temple.

"Poor lambs!" the woman next to me cried out. "Deprived of their father so young!" Her companions sadly nodded.

Walking home gloomy, I straggled behind my buddies. Deprived, she had said, of their father so young. Deprived. Naturally, the demography of my household had been curious to me, but never a sore point. I was conscious of being a fatherless child. Other kids were quick to point it out to me, although what they considered to be my greatest curse, that I had to tolerate two mothers, was actually a blessing. "Ugh, yuck, how can you stand it?" I never saw the problem. Anyway, I knew that my homelife was envied. Who else could boast of six tropical birds and an eleven-foot boa? If the truth be known, my one tangible disappointment about not having a baseball-hurling, I'll-give-you-a-spanking, nickels-dispensing pop was that pops drove cars. I judged that my family did not have a car because I didn't have a dad, and really (no offense, Father), it was the absence of a Chevrolet that I rued the most. Deprived, the woman had said. The word sounded ominous. Of their father so young. Entering my house by the back way, I let the door slam.

"You're late! You're late!" Bish, Aunt Emma's myna, balanced on the washing-machine wringer, cackled at me.

"I'm early, you stupid bird!" I yelled right back. I was going to explain about the funeral, but stopped myself.

Bish flew across the kitchen and landed on the fridge. "Frack you! Frack you!" he jeered, the one word he had been taught to pronounce incorrectly, so as not to offend certain audiences, but to charm others.

In my room I threw my schoolbag and my empty lunch pail on the bed, causing the turtledoves to coo and Malcolm, our macaw, to cluck. Alphonse and Neptune, parakeets, who must have been misbehaving because someone had chained them to their wooden perch, turned their sulking backs on me. Going through to the living-room, I plunked myself down on the sofa, where I was susceptible to prodding by my aunt.

Tears were immediate. "My daddy!" I lashed out. I saw his body charred; the coffin being lowered into a muddy grave. There had been no parade. "He's dead! Dead! And you never told me! I'm deprived!"

"Oh no, no, Kyle! No." Aunt Emma gave her frowzy tower of hair such a demonstrative shake that the tangled coil toppled to one side. With the shift of ballast, the tilt of her head followed. She was wearing her usual habit, patched jeans and a man's oversized plaid shirt.

"Honey, that's not true at all. Whatever made you say such a thing? You have your mother and me. You have Malcolm and Neptune and Bish and Clyde. You're not deprived."

Hiccups, burps, and sobbing. Eventually a stammered account of the funeral, the misery of my lovely Cindy taken so much to heart that I saw my own father being swallowed by a grave.

Aunt Emma's reassurances included spoonfuls of brown sugar, a glass of water sipped from the opposite side of the rim with my face upside down leaning over the carpet — dizziness and bubbles up my nose — and a horrendous unholy shriek to scare the ailment right out of me. Which it did, as well as send our flock into a dither. We heard the parakeets hysterical at the ends of their tethers. As soon as I was cured of the hiccups, Aunt Em promised to produce a photograph which, she declared, would "absolutely conclusively" prove that my father lived.

"Fantastic!" I cried. "Yahoo!"

Bish released a battle cry, and I raced him down the hall. Swooping under a hanging Christmas cactus, the myna beat me into the room and frantically circled around twice before alighting upon the swinging perch that hung next to the window. Bish settled down, likely dazzled by the parade of varicolored suncatchers (churches and cats, floral emblems, sailboats, a giraffe, a primrose koala and a pink sperm whale) refracting the fall of light into a sunburst of scorched hues across the walls, ceiling, and bedspread. As I pounce down onto the four-poster double, I'm intrigued by a glimpse of myself in the vanity mirror. My left cheek is irrevocably scarred by flaming magenta rays, my neck skewered by a dagger cast in burnt sienna.

"Lemme see! Lemme see it!"

"Hold on, young man. This may take some looking."

Aunt Emma had a talent for understatement. With me bouncing on my knees on the springy double bed and Bish oddly distracted, my aunt burrowed for shoeboxes chock-full of the black-and-white snapshots from her past. The vacuum-cleaner, hatboxes, supermarket sacks stuffed with discarded clothes intended for, but never delivered to, the Salvation Army, misplaced laundry, Yuletide lights and decorations, my old cheese-cutters and a castaway, threadbare rug were uprooted and tossed behind her. The bedroom resembled the aftermath of a gas-main explosion. Miraculously discovered safe amid the debris were the boxes of pictures.

"These aren't in any order, Ky. We'll have to sift through them."

Each male face provoked the same question: "This him?"

"No, Ky. Your father was not a lion-tamer."

"Is *this* him?"

"Nor was he a wimp."

The photos prompted Emma to reminisce about the good old days, though she did not discuss you or Mom or the traveling carnival. She paid homage instead to former companions: Eggshell, "Eggie" for short, the crested cockatoo, and Penelope the Parrot.

"Ah, look at this fellow. Isn't he sweet?" A smallish bird with a peacock's plumage. "Do you know what he is, Ky?" She handed me the snap.

"A whydah bird!" I exclaimed. (Aunt Em had always shared her passion for birds with me. When most three-year-olds were balancing on their father's kneecaps, giddyup galloping or flipping through picture books to identify the elephant's trunk, the cat, the bear, and the moo-moo cow, I was huddled for warmth next to Aunt Emma's side browsing through *her* books, reciting bobolink, chickadee, cardinal, ruby-throated hummingbird, goldfinch, singing out when the page turned onto the sooty shearwater or, my favorite, the golden plover. When I went to school, my chums were adept at recognizing the faces of left-wingers and all-star defensemen on their trading cards, but how many of them could differentiate between, say, the Arctic and the willow warbler? I had friends who went fishing with their dads, catching perch and bass and pike, but who among them had experienced the joy of snuggling down in the damp, chilly underbrush next to my Aunt Em, welcoming the return of the blackpoll warbler from its winter retreat in Venezuela? By the age of seven I had learned not to fidget, and could fall asleep standing up, leaning against an oak.) "I didn't know you had one of *these*!"

"Sure did. Someone kidnaped him outside of Edmonton. Stripped him of his feathers, I fear, then set him loose on the bald prairie. Poor Maxwell. Dessert for a hungry hawk."

"Is this my dad?" I asked, producing an ornate gentleman in a Panama hat, wearing a gaudy handlebar mustache, waxed, and supporting his tall frame on a walking-stick. A discernible sparkle in his eye hinted that he was about to break into a tapdance, or sprinkle sand on the floor and give us a coy soft-shoe. Emma studied the faded, crumpled portrait for several moments — I thought she might say yes and was planning to celebrate. But she sighed and handed the picture back roughly.

"No, Kyle," she explained. "He's not your daddy. He's mine."

"Really?"

"Yep. A carny, through to the bone. Remember, Ky, fathers aren't necessarily all they're cracked up to be. I don't know why you're so interested." She suddenly reclaimed the photo, picking the burlesque dandy out of my hands and slipping him into her breast pocket over her heart.

Mother announced her arrival home by kicking in the back door. I rushed out to greet her, transported by my expectation of a matching father soon to materialize. Barely managing to keep her cigarette ash out of the protruding celery, Mother was buried under three bags of groceries. She wrestled them onto the counter. I don't have to tell you, Father, that she was a tall woman, especially by a child's standards, a full head and shoulders above Aunt Emma. In those days she wore her fair hair cropped, cut in a style identical to my own. As she had explained, "We don't want any confusion about who your real mother is, now do we?" I was her territorial claim over Aunt Em. It never occurred to me to evaluate how good-looking she was, but walking with her anywhere I had become accustomed to hearing construction workers whistle.

"Why do they do that, Ma?" I asked her once.

"Because."

"Because why?"

"Just because. For one thing, I'm a snappy dresser. It's like this, Kyle: men whistle to a woman in fancy clothes the way that birds sing to the rising sun. Why do birds greet the sun? Because. Its light shows off their colors. A man sees a woman in vivid colors and thinks to himself that he must be the bright light making her shine. Men are backwards that way."

"Fuckit," Mom muttered in the kitchen. Upon opening the egg carton, she had discovered three shells already broken. "I wish you'd learn to eat these, Clyde."

Our pet boa constrictor slinked across the tiles. Mice and rats, which we kept penned in the basement, constituted his diet.

I was waiting for evidence of my mother's mood before saying anything, when Aunt Em sang out from the bedroom, "Here it is!"

Gliding down upon the water faucet, Bish heralded her arrival in the kitchen. "Feed me! Feed me!" He had eyed the groceries. Bish always made his point twice, then shut up.

Emma charged in waving her discovery.

"My dad!" Too excited to contain myself, I clapped my hands. "Lemme see!"

"What's that, love?" Mother demanded. The shrill note in her voice made me wary.

"Oh, Rose, honey, Ky came home bawling his eyes out."

"I did not!"

"He saw that poor slob's funeral march, that Rocky, whatshisname, the fireman? Kyle thought his daddy must be dead too. He was feeling . . . *deprived*. Look! It's a picture of the three of us together.

"Lemme see!" I jumped up and down, and made a grab for it.

Mother snatched the photo away first. She studied it, one hand on her hip, the cigarette wedged in a corner of her mouth.

"Your father is not dead," she told me plainly, sympathetically, and I was grateful for her tone of voice. Smiling, Ma tucked my head into her hip and smoothed down my hair. While I nuzzled her sweater, she reached over my head to switch on the stove's gas jet. The orange and blue flame flickered on the periphery of my vision. My mother's coffee. How she loved a coffee when she came home. Leaning down, Ma kissed the top of my head, twice, tenderly, and gave me a squeeze before she sacrificed a corner of the picture to the fire.

"Rose!" Aunt Emma gasped, her voice pale. "Don't."

The paper ignited, a green-gold flash.

"Ma!" I pleaded.

"Fire!" Bish sounded the alarm. Our automatic smoke-detector. "Fire!"

And, for a fleeting moment, I witnessed the three cryptic figures ablaze, the lank bodies curling in upon themselves, vanishing, the eyes squinting into a summer sun suddenly sibylline through a turquoise flame. Ma watched the paper burn down to her fingertips, holding it high in case I tried to blow you out, my incandescent father, like a birthday candle. She dropped you into an ashtray alongside her cigarette. Stubbed the butt into the black ash of your eyes.

Smoke lingered at the level of the adult heads. A cloud above me, the scent of charred skin.

"Your father isn't dead, Kyle," my mother repeated. Her eyes, looking down upon me, calm aquamarine. "He simply does not

31

exist." She patted my cheek swollen with surprise. "You are a child of the Virgin Birth, and I am the spitting image of the Holy Mother of God. Now run along outside and play. Be back before dark."

"Shazam!" Bish recited. "Shazam!"

I dragged my heels heading for the door. Stepped over Clyde who, motionless, was admiring the long legs of the kitchen stool to wrap himself around. Rescuing my jacket from the top of the stool, I looked back in anger. Mother was doing what she often did when Aunt Emma was mad and fuming with a sour look on her face, stepping around behind her, then reaching forward to rub her front. She blew her breath across the hair on Aunt Emma's neck. Slid a hand between her buttons.

My father existed, Ma. He owned a house. He's left it to me. It's my inheritance!

Cross over in peace, Father. If you see her up there, say hello.

5

Sumo-wrestling, in lieu of sleep, with slippery angels and demons alike.

Awakened by geese honking — but wait one minute! Hold on for two seconds. Those aren't geese, you numskull, wake up! Struggling to the window, I overlooked the parking lot and the source of the commotion. Car horns blared away. Assorted makes and sizes of automobile were being spewed out by the Toll House road to compete for space, bandying about like bumper cars at an amusement park. Still photographs would have given the impression of a demolition derby.

Abruptly, each vehicle parked. Keys were claimed from ignitions, motors muttered quiet, and the moment of peace that ensued could have been in response to a secret sacring bell.

In pairs, in fours, doors sprang open, prelude to an instantaneous scramble, akin to a football scrimmage, of exuberant, gang-tackling women, every one of them offside. Snowballs flew through the air. Then the battle escalated into hand-to-hand combat as victims were dunked headfirst into the season's last snowbank.

Laughter soon incapacitated each combatant, and a truce was declared. The women bunched together like a reunion of old classmates, hugs and kisses all around, banter and bedlam too delirious for me to interpret.

Were these . . . nuns?

Unlikely.

The style and carriage of each woman begged a different explanation. Perhaps I was to host a convention of aerobics instructors hell-bent on flattening my tummy. Or spend the weekend playing canasta with Atlantic City blackjack dealers, and on Monday I'd be the one checking out, having gambled away the inn. The few who were civil in sedate woolen coats were lambs in mortal peril amid the predatory furs. A wily white fox conspired with the erudite ermine. Conspicuous amid the denizens of this zoo, a lady in domestic black leather looked particularly lethal.

Trunks yawned open. Active hands forged for a cruise-ship's supply of luggage. (Look! There's something suspicious. Bottle-shaped brown bags. Whatever gave them the idea that this was a B.Y.O.B. inn?) No small number of the laughing women were lookers. Two caught my attention as being uncommonly beautiful. Yet my interest was diverted to a young woman apparently ignored by the others as she plodded along lugging an over-sized, over-stuffed suitcase toward Toll House.

Frequently she put her burden down, switched hands, and hoisted the load again. Tilting her body to one side, she'd jut out her hip to support a portion of the weight. Under her cerise tam, the cut of her brunette hair was quite short: a fashionable prison style. She was slender and wore a puce and white dress visible under her open suede coat. A bird of the north woods. Hers a fragile, delicate beauty enhanced by an aura of sadness.

Quietly, inspired, I whistled the migration melody of the ruby-crowned kinglet.

Unconsciously affected by my stare, the woman looked up, and I was astonished by the concentration of her gaze. I might have expected a timid or faltering look, one wary of scrutiny and mindful of entanglements, but this lady was remarkably self-assured. Neither a challenge nor a hostile reflex, her stare presumed understanding, and conveyed, in addition to a greeting, a glint of recognition. She had identified me.

My pulse quickened.

I resisted my natural inclination to lie down. Lookit, I'm the new owner of the inn, right? Shouldn't I be downstairs welcoming my guests? I can show them to their rooms (if I don't get lost) and see to their comfort. I can schlep the heavy bags of the ladies who interest me.

The full-length mirror tempered the impulse. I was unkempt. My underarms somewhat whiffy. It occurred to me that Ryder and Stamp had been generous to admit me without first turning a hose on me. Plainly, I was polluting Vermont. To make a suitable impression, a bath, a shampoo, and a shave were in order.

Toiletries and fresh duds in hand, I slipped down the hall to the sanctuary of the narrow, bone-white room that I would be obliged to share with my guests, and where I shivered in the nude.

The chamber had not been designed for its current function. What had been an ample linen- and broom-closet in a wealthy man's retreat now sheltered a washstand with restricted space to maneuver around it, and a bathtub fitted lengthways which, though narrow, squatted down to fill the floor's full width. Occupying the end of the room like a sleeping, fat madam, the tub demanded of the lithe and the daring an ambitious, broad step over its sloped back, a risky and inconvenient plunge. Bathers had no choice. They could not run their water in advance, for to reach the taps necessitated mounting the slovenly old bitch first and sitting on her chilly enamel skin.

I scalded my feet, the water was that hot. Standing on one tortured foot at a time I spun the silly dials in frantic search of the cold. Then I levitated, and held my position by crooking one leg over the side and supporting my sagging weight above the boiling surface clinging by my fingertips to a towel rack. My free toes twirled the knobs this way and that, without resolution. Soon I'd be steamed lobster-red, or I'd soak in the water as a cannibal's stew. Finally! An Arctic flow! As the heat receded, I spilled into the drink with a terrific splash, and turned blue before I fiddled again for the hot water that no doubt was heated by lava directly underground.

Scrubbed myself raw. Quite literally, as the soap was flaked with cinders. Working up an impressive lather in the soft water, I left myself with an impossible rinsing job; I now swam in a bubble bath and damned if I'd submit my head to another game of Russian Roulette under the taps. Nevertheless, I immersed my whole body and soul in the suds like a converted Baptist and felt born again pulling the plug — and mused that that's exactly what I was.

Downstairs, someone who had carried in a ghetto-blaster turned up the volume. Judging by the way the house shook, I'd say the nuns were dancing.

Being unaccustomed to the rhythms of an inn, I had neglected to bring a towel. I remembered that several hung over the frame at the foot of my bed, which did me no good at the time. So I stood dripping. Contaminated by goose bumps, I shook like a dog to throw the excess water off my skin, and let myself drain uncomfortably into a puddle on the floor. I used my shirt to fluff my hair up like Einstein's, sponge my genitals, and wipe the backs of my knees, then with my jeans mopped a patch free of condensation on the mirror.

With little else to do, I gave myself a close examination.

Confronting my visage straight-on, note that my ears aren't visible. A sybil in Tennessee had told me that ears resting flat against the scalp indicate character in a man.

"You will flower late in life," she had said. "Your youth and your middle years have been and shall continue to be a washout. God willing, you will benefit from a contented retirement."

"What do I do, sleep until then?"

Isabelle lived in a sheet-metal shack with cats on the outskirts of Walkerman's Creek. A feline herself, she took her work seriously. "I wouldn't give you two cents for your love-life," she warned me.

"Why not?"

"Your jaw. What a disgrace!"

One cleft might have been considered sensual. Two, parallel and incisive, look like surgical wounds left to fester.

"*You* are my love-life, Issy."

"I rest my case.

"Until you gain wisdom" — was her primary advice — "take what you can get." Issy was twenty years older than me. I adored her hair. She wore it down to her waist. Leaves of rust, flecked gold, riffling amid the ropes of raw umber. Lice and sweat. My favorite rookery.

A persistent, scratchy sound disposed of my meditative moment and I worried that Toll House catered to mice in the walls. Too late I saw the credit card inserted in the door jamb, working its way upward to come under the hook-and-eye latch. The lock was tripped. Before I could move, protest, or cover up — a razor in my hand raised to harvest a foamy beard — the door was flung open and I was exposed.

Their numbers were legion. Women's faces like bright, glistening stones under a watery cascade. A whistling, cheering, clapping turbulence egged on by Bruce Springsteen coming up the stairs singing, "Boooornnn in the U.S.A.! I was boooornnn in the U.S.A.!" In my haste to retrieve them I dropped my pants, and bending over to snatch them off the floor excited an ovation.

"What buns!"

Cat-whistles.

Clamping my shirt as a pathetic fig leaf over my privates, I shuffled toward the door to slam it. Two women with fingers in their mouths competed for the loudest, most piercing whistles. They and the others scattered when I charged. I hurled the door shut. It bounced open again. And in that instant before I threw my weight against it as a barricade, the woman who had attracted my attention earlier sauntered casually across my field of vision. Still toting her cumbersome suitcase. In a moment too brief to measure I noticed her glance at me, slip a peek downward at my protective patch, and smile. She looked me in the eyes again. I smiled too. She heaved her case up higher on her hip, and labored down the hall. Springsteen had sprinted on ahead of her and in the quiet I distinctly heard the woman hum. A gentle tune.

I shut the door. Softly.

Nuns?

Come *on*.

6

In my old clothes I beat a safe retreat from the bathroom, stripped and dried off in my room, and donned a clean shirt. A shirt with all its buttons gives me a high. Tucking into my dress blues — jeans free of sawdust and engine grime — inspired scrutiny of my appearance in the full-length mirror. I came across as stumpy, less lean than I remembered, slouching.

Combed, sprinkled, and suited out, boldly I ventured downstairs, not making it halfway before I was accosted by a guest.

"Welcome to Toll House!" rang the woman's war whoop. An inch or two taller than me, she was handsome in a business-like, contemporary fashion. Wavy black hair swept down to the nape of her neck. Apple cheeks and salient eyes, the pupils unusually large. Broad shoulders. Above a friendly chin her mouth opened much wider on one side than the other, crossing up her smile. This partial paralysis endowed her grin with a leathery, tongue-in-cheek attitude.

"Thanks," I murmured, conscious that our roles had awkwardly been reversed. I fought back, "Welcome to you too."

"Accept my apologies for the prank," she pleaded. Shades of a smile dimpled her face. Sincere, she also seemed unable to kick an undercurrent of amusement. "I'm so sorry. You're new here, you're unprepared, an innocent! Had I known, I would have squelched their antics."

"It's okay," I managed to squeak.

"Their excuse, I'm afraid, is pretty flimsy. Your father used to encourage their high jinks. They did it in the spirit of his memory."

"No harm done." An unforgivably dour response. I was daunted by the woman's speaking style. She bobbed her head and shoulders, a fighter's feint, with a coordinate deke of her stomach and hips. Pinned against the banister as though backed into corner ropes, I weaved slightly to stay out of her puncher's range. A moving target, I managed to smile.

"When your father died we were simply devastated. We miss him so. Of course, we were prepared . . . and relieved that his suffering had come to a close . . . still, it's hard to lose a friend." She was close enough to give me a head-butt. "One good thing — Hazel's news roused our spirits! We hadn't heard that Kyle — ah, excuse me, the elder Kyle, I mean, that is, the elder Kyle Elder — goodness! This could become confusing!"

I prefer not to find humor in names. My friend, Cindy Bottomley, had wearied of the theme. In contributing light laughter I was indulging my duties as host, a parody of good relations.

"What I'm trying to say is, we didn't know that your father had a son. Calling himself 'Senior' seemed like another of his puzzles, part of the disguise, if you follow my drift."

"I didn't know that he had a son either." Clever footwork, and I gained a measure of breathing room.

"Like father like son, I see."

"Come again?"

"You're a puzzlemaker too."

I was stunned. Similar traits to an unknown dad? The woman took advantage of my condition to land a real, albeit playful, jab to my chin. Is everyone in Vermont so damned physical?

"Bottom line — we're delighted that you're carrying on, Kyle. Where would we be without Toll House? Coming here for Easter is our tradition. Officially, by the way, I'm Mother Superior Gabriella, if anybody's asking. You may want to call me Gaby, for short."

"You nursed my father through his illness." The statement popped out by surprise. I then felt obliged to add, "Thanks."

Unwittingly I had landed a left hook of my own. The woman's eyes misted, she averted her glance, looking to her corner for help.

"I can't take credit for that — and I'm not being modest," she protested in a rush. "After all . . . he died." Although I didn't hear the bell, the round apparently had ended, and she backed off. As the victor congratulates and consoles a valiant opponent, Gaby brightly announced, "If there's anything that I can do for you, Kyle, anything at all — *ahaha*, protect your from the Sisters, for instance — please don't hesitate to ask." My foe lowered her voice to a confidential whisper, muffled to those at ringside. "You have my personal assurance that from now on you can bathe in peace."

Mystified that I was being treated as the guest while Gaby had assumed the mantle of hostess, I thanked her for her good wishes. We shook hands, and she surprised me by folding the fingers of her left hand over the crown of our covenant in a gesture of endearment. With that, she bounded up the stairs two at a time, and I, wobbly, but still on my feet, headed down.

The women had calmed themselves. As I peered in, the largest of the sitting-rooms was remarkably subdued. Conversations were muted. A log snapped in the crackling fire; the warming scent of wood smoke permeated the room. I hesitated, fearing that I might be intruding upon an ecclesiastical quiet hour — then noticed that two gray heads were bent over Scrabble, not the Bible. Rather than prayers, moving lips murmured checkers strategies. Chess wars raged in silence.

A hush.

Again, the choice of clothing did not jive. Everybody knows that dress codes have been relaxed in recent years, but designer jeans? Sweatpants? A T-shirt not only promoted a silly caption ("Property of the New York Jets") but displayed the woman as emphatically braless. Vermilion painted toes? A *peroxide* blonde?

Snippets of conversation. "I am *on* a diet. I am *not* anorexic. There *happens* to be a difference."

"Darling, it's not your body I'm concerned about. It's your mind. I mean, wheat germ on watercress?"

Standing very still and gawking, I had not attracted attention to myself. A tally of the odds confirmed their fifteen to my one, an imposing discrepancy. My probationary step forward was foiled by an unnerving screak of the floorboard, a few women glanced up, and I panicked. Resisting the impulse to cross myself and genuflect, I whirled around, suddenly busy, a million things to do, and rushed downstairs.

Whew. Safe and sound, guzzling fortifications from the bar. A rum-and-coke put me right, before I found a package of daiquiri mix and made up a batch. Behind the bar I was comfortable, secluded in the lee of a rampart. I raised my second drink to the bartender in the mirror, and poured myself a third. Kyle Elder. Your official host. Fine, but what am I supposed to do? Say? On the blackboard I inscribed, *K.E. 1 R&C 2 Dqi*, and, glass in hand, the rum awash in my bloodstream, I lumbered back upstairs to launch my diffident self upon the front room once again.

Women who had seen all of me earlier lowered sultry, conniving eyes. Two culprits blushed.

I confess that my perusal was false — a thin excuse to be nonchalant while centering my attention on the woman who had snagged my interest earlier. Lost in thought, she sat quietly by the fire, and did not react as I approached, flinching from her daze only as I sat down on the lumpy sofa beside her.

The woman tilted her head — the jerky motion of a bird — and I met her solemn gaze with my toothy, plebeian grin. I noticed her eyes, like those of a bird, showed little white.

"Lookie, lookie, Chantelle has a cookie."

"Remember those worn-out, worked-over chastity vows, Sister C.," the dummy at the bridge-table remarked.

"Guess who's coming to confession tonight."

All chortled.

Her obvious annoyance with the banter dissipated quickly, tempered by a cool head. She smiled up at me. A splendid ease and gaiety. The lift of her eyebrows indicated that needling was one of life's minor irritations, to be endured with aplomb. "Hi!" she said.

"Hello," said I. Then I coughed.

"You're dressed." Partly a reflection of the fire, the light in her eye was also a jocular glow.

"I intend to stay dressed too. From now on I'm taking my baths fully clothed. I'll drip dry by the fire."

As if we were old friends she leaned into me slightly. "I wouldn't worry. The Sisters are very creative. They're not likely to repeat the same joke twice."

"That's not wholly reassuring." The most natural position for my right arm was behind her, relaxed across the back of the sofa.

"Valid point. If I were you, I'd be terrified."

In this breezy roomful of women I was magnetically drawn toward this one in particular, who knows why. Pretty enough, but no rival for at least two of her friends. Perhaps I was responding to the interest that she had initially conveyed in me. Returning my stare from the window with a glint of recognition had simultaneously alarmed my defenses and spruced up my confidence. She extended her hand from her enfolded body, and introduced herself.

"I'm Chantelle Cromarty."

The shock of her cold palm. No wonder she had been sitting by the fire, she was thawing out. "I'm Kyle Elder."

"Sorry about your dad, Kyle." This last spoken more loudly than the partial whisper on which we had settled. In striking the serious note Chantelle guarded against a possible insurrection of frivolity among her peers.

I mumbled, "Thanks," thinking . . . if one more person offers condolences . . . .

"Hazel mentioned that you just arrived," Chantelle offered.

"One step ahead of you. I haven't unpacked. All I've had time for was a bath and then that quick striptease."

I stoked the fire. Flames leaped. In them, red flashes of Cindy, secretly amused.

Settling down again, I reached for my drink to find that my glass was empty. "That's funny," I noted.

"What is?" Chantelle perked up because I had finally initiated a conversation, maybe.

"My drink."

Giggles alerted us. An impish young woman behind my back was whirling her eyes for her audience, her voice garbled by the ice-cubes in her mouth. "They're impossible!" Chantelle exclaimed, and joined in the laughter. "They never quit!"

Obliged to play the good sport, I grinned sheepishly. "I own the bar, right? There's more where that came from."

As the tittering sputtered out, I actually felt more secure, now that the women had had their fun. Chantelle leaned more closely against me to whisper, "Do you know where the stables are?"

"Stables?" I indulged her secretive tone. "I own horses too?"

Laughter like a sudden hiccup. "No, silly. In the summer you lease the stables to a riding school." I had to bow forward to catch her urgent, hushed instruction. "Take the Toll House Road back down."

"Okay."

"Keep your eyes peeled for a path tramped smooth on your left."

"Left. Right."

"Cross-country skiers use it. Follow it along. The cut through the trees will become obvious. Stick to the trail along the top of the dam. Once you're on the other side, trace the ribbons along the ski trail. You should be able to spot the stables through the trees."

"Great. Thanks. Across the river and into the trees."

"I'll take the path down the back way, Kyle. Meet me there in, oh, say, twenty minutes?"

Shazam.

Immediately dealt an assortment of symptoms common to the romantic struck by an infatuation, I suffered weak knees, greasy palms, and a burning sensation in the esophagus. The chance that I was being victimized by another practical joke did cross my mind, but how could I risk missing out on the strategic opportunity?

"You leave first," she whispered.

All righty. I stretched, yawned, excused myself, and walked upstairs acting the role of a man in drastic need of a nap. I know the part well. Putting on my whole armor, a sweater and jacket, I wandered the corridors of Toll House to locate an alternate staircase down, so that my departure would go unnoticed. Made it outside without having to climb through a window.

On the front porch, I found a convenient shovel. Why not? As long as the bones were in my trunk I was fearful of their discovery. For the moment, everyone was indoors. I could move the skeleton to safety, to a place which would not implicate me, and then I'd be free to dig a grave at the first opportunity.

A shed attached to the house provided me with what I needed, a large garbage bag, which ended a tendency toward procrastination. I would not only meet with the fetching Chantelle and see what that was about, I would also dispose of the sad remains of my traveling companion.

Careful to collect each one, I packed away the bones, added the skull last, and began my walk.

Dizzy, exhilarated, and expectant, I quickly disappeared from the view of the house behind a stand of evergreens. Bag and shovel in hand, I fell into a comfortable downhill jog while my shadow kept pace. If she was coming, Chantelle would be behind me — yet I wanted to arrive ahead of time to seek out a temporary hiding place for my bag of bones. And I relished an urge to case the joint first, to prepare myself for anything, for anything at all.

Especially, luck willing, for romance.

Women, I was thinking as I marched across the dam. The ocher, late-afternoon sun hesitated above the peaks. The snow was soft and shallow underfoot, each step crunching an icy layer below. Women. At least, the women I choose. Rather, the women who choose me (although I heartily endorse their taste).

I have not successfully determined whether I am inclined toward lunatics or if something in my disposition and demeanor draws them toward me. As if by appointment our destinies manage to coincide.

Or collide.

Cindy Bottomley was not overtly kooky when first I pursued her as an impassioned eight-year-old, but give her time. As the daughter of the deceased fireman whose funeral had upset me, she and I had that in common: no dad in the house. A strikingly pretty girl, Cindy was pestered by boys two and three grades ahead of her, whistled at by policemen. She well appreciated her beauty, and early in life made plans to be the next Marilyn Monroe. "I'm going to be an actress, a movie star, a sex symbol." Typical ambitions for a ten-year-old, presented to the world with a cheekiness adults could neither savvy nor deny. No one would put it past her. Mechanics, as she practiced her wiggle down the neighborhood sidewalks, commented that she could hardly fail. Teenagers hanging out at Hill's Delicatessen agreed that she was too stuck-up for her own good. She could not expect to get away with that walk, not forever, not on these streets. The boys in black leather jackets, adept at threats, concealed their pimples behind cigarette smoke and tough talk, but they were more afraid of Cindy than she was of them. To complement her beguiling looks, Cindy had nurtured a saucy disposition and an untouchable indifference to her peers. She had her eyes on Hollywood.

"Show us your bottom, Bottomley!" taunted the boys, jutting their jaws and smirking.

Deaf to the world, she never missed a wiggle. Hers was the last laugh. She filled their nights with dreaming, she knew, and guessed that she was adored locally the way that Marilyn was revered worldwide. Half the male population of Park Extension, the working-class district of Montreal where we grew up, yearned for the moment when she'd magically sprout breasts, and counted down the hours to when she'd transform from being jailbait to being fair game. The other half may not have been that patient, but Cindy could handle them all with her arresting walk and button nose in the air.

Periodically, she permitted me to carry her books. "It's on the way," I'd fawn, though I knew that she knew that I would have to make a detour. Cindy took ballet, and, thanks to Aunt Em's instruction, I was the best boy-dancer in grade five. Cindy considered our routines in gym class boring, the exercise beneath her. Still, if she was forced to dance with nerds then she deserved a partner who wouldn't trample her talented toes. Those monthly whirlwind performances mastering the waltz and catapulting one another through the Virginia Reel earned me my merit badges: as reward, if she had a load of books, I got to serve as her mule.

Cindy lived near school, on Wiseman Street. Which gave me a mere block in which to impress her. Learning that she would molt, become an immobile, unblinking, scarcely breathing statue whenever a bumblebee buzzed nearby, I proved my mettle one day snatching one out of mid-flight, quickly tossing it up and away into the breeze.

Tentatively uncoiling from her whatever-you-do-don't-move stance, Cindy uncorked a bubbly, champagne smile. I grew wings. I flew. "You're brave!" she praised, a lavish endearment. What was even better, she declared, "You're crazy!"

Bragging about myself backfired, however. Cindy had a difficult time accepting that I lived in a roomful of tropical birds.

"You're fibbing me, Kyle. You don't have any."

"Do too. Ask anybody. Straight out of the jungle."

"That *talk?*" Her own budgie refused to speak, therefore she believed that the whole idea was an elaborate invention, like Santa Claus.

"Bish says my compositions for me out loud. All I have to do is write them down." (I was liable to exaggerate in her company.)

"Okay, smart guy. If you have so many birds, show me one."

"They'll fly away if I bring them outside. Come over to my house."

"Let's go." Cindy had not flippantly accepted my invitation. She had issued a challenge.

"Tomorrow," I hedged.

"What's wrong with right now?" The lift of her right eyebrow denoted victory. She believed that she had called my bluff and now had me over a barrel.

"Because. It's Tuesday. My mother's home. Wednesdays she works. My mother doesn't like kids too much. She picks on them."

"What a big fibber you are, Kyle. You're telling stories," she admonished me. "You know I have ballet on Wednesdays, and on Thursday you'd find some other excuse."

I had been reduced to the rubble of the other pretenders to her affections. Cindy took her books and headed up the stairs.

"Okay, if you want, you can come over now."

She turned. Narrowed her gaze in cool assessment. "What about your mother, fibber?"

"Just don't listen to her no matter what she says."

Surprised that my invitation had survived her challenge, Cindy mulled it over. "That's what I do with my mom," she concluded. "But if you don't have any birds — I mean *big* birds, budgies don't count — you owe me a dollar."

"Don't worry. I have lots of birds."

"That talk."

"They won't shut up."

"Or you owe me a dollar, Kyle. Hang on a sec', I'll put my books inside." She reappeared in the promised instant, her face flushed with further restrictions. "Just so's you know, I don't play doctor or hospital or spin-the-bottle."

The front door to my house was kept locked and I never had a key. My usual entry was through the back door into the kitchen. I had hoped for an early and enthusiastic greeting, and for a few dreadful seconds feared that Aunt Em had taken her birds away to entertain a convention or to cheer up a hospital congested with children. Cindy wore a triumphant smirk on her face.

"Shut the door, Cindy, or the birds'll fly out."

"You're the limit, Kyle Elder," she put me down, but did as I asked.

The neighborhood beauty was in my house! Standing in the kitchen was the girl who so frequently paraded through my day-dreams. Pride welled. I hoped that half the city had seen me lure her here. If not, I would brag of it to all my friends, and to my enemies too.

As we entered my bedroom, my confidence, and my privileged position, was restored. We were greeted by a robust flapping of wings, whistles, the parakeets in circular flight, the turtledoves in harmonic duet. Yellow-feathered (his tertiaries were green), crimson-shouldered Malcolm, flexing his magnificent cobalt head and luminescent throat, took an immediate shine to the dazzling young beauty. "Cheap pretty! Cheap pretty!"

" 'Pretty as a picture'," I corrected him. "Or 'She ain't cheap.' You were never taught to say 'Cheap pretty.' That's an insult, Malc."

Cindy stood mesmerized amid the clucks, coos, and cries, and the torrid crush of colors. "I don't believe it!" she chimed, her eyes wondrous with joy. She performed a graceful pirouette on her toes for this partisan audience. "It's fantastic! Fantastic!" she sang out with a bird's stark excitement, and ducked as Bish sailed into the room.

Drawing back his wings like an ancient prophet of the skies about to deliver heaven's proclamation, Malcolm shrieked, flapped rapidly, and managed an awkward bound onto Cindy's near shoulder. She flinched and gasped, but Malc hung on.

"Is the big parrot ever neat!"

"Malc's a macaw."

Neptune attacked. Hers a long-smoldering jealousy. Gunning for Malcolm's neck, she drove him off the startled girl, who protected her face from the frantic slash of wings and nattering beaks. The birds landed on separate perches and bickered vociferously.

"What's going on in there?" my mother called from the kitchen. I doubt that she knew I was home and was merely chastising the birds.

"Remember what I said," I warned Cindy. I lifted Alphonse onto his swinging perch and set it rocking.

Accustomed to the worship of other kids' parents, Cindy paid me no mind. Undeterred, she extended her sweatered sleeve to give Malcolm a lift, and wiggled to the kitchen to happily proclaim, "Kyle's showing me his birds, Mrs. Elder."

Mom, apparently, turned around. Coffeepot in hand. Cindy immediately released crisp staccato cries in rapid succession. The sound was thoroughly disorienting, and Malcolm took flight. Piercing ordinary eardrums, Cindy's scream grew louder, higher, putting the birds into a panic. Beaten back by the flapping wings, I was slow making it out to the kitchen. Cindy wheeled, darted outside, the door slammed, and I heard the sound of her peal for blocks as a vibrant, wailing siren alerting the neighborhood.

Neither particularly amused nor shocked, my mother's expression was strange. Impossible for me to decipher. As though she had undergone a swift transfiguration, she stared at the closed door.

"Ma, aw gee, do you always have to wear Clyde around your neck?"

Actually, the boa wound the full length of her torso; across her waist, thrice around under her bosom, encircling her shoulders, a spin around her throat and up the back of her neck to rest its head in the nest of my mother's hair. It glared out above her like a malicious sentry to an occult cave, mouth agape, fangs ready, its evil snake's eyes as lifeless and as fascinating as bullets.

My double-headed mom.

"Kyle, tell me, son," she spoke from her trance, adrift and enchanted by a spell. Her words shocked me because Mother normally took exception to the friends that I brought home. "Wherever did you find that *angel*?"

Courtship invents its own logic, rules, and obligations. Exacts its own toll. My education had commenced, and I had digested the very first commandment to bear in mind when pursuing a flame.

Rule # 1. Never, ever, under any circumstances, bring your new girl home to mother.

Over time, a second consideration would be impressed upon me.

Rule # 2. Keep your serpents, real or imagined, under a reliable lock and key.

Fortunately, my mother's presence could not invade my tryst with Sister Chantelle, and discipline kept the vipers of my mind firmly boxed. Yet the applecart had already been upset, and the forbidden fruits had spilled onto the ground. Here I was, on my way to woo a nun (a nun . . . was I serious?) who had already been met by my rarefied father. That wasn't all. The rendezvous scared me because here I was, out alone in a strange environment to meet an odd girl under unusual circumstances, and I had to proceed without the benefit of any rules at all.

Chantelle was late.

The stables were perfect for temporary disposal of the skeleton. I simply tossed the bag into a dark empty stall and shoveled on some dirt and hay. It would be easy enough to return tomorrow and bury the bones deep in the woods. I felt quite proud of myself.

I moped about the empty stables. The last whit of warmth was drawn off by the setting sun. Whirling, caliginous breezes sought shelter for the night. Damp with winter, the small barn afforded scant protection. The primeval timbers were bitter with complaint, exaggerating every creak and plaintive groan while I stomped about in cold feet.

Why was she meeting me down here? To test my catechism?

A rosy sun collapsed behind the mountains. The expanding darkness spooked around me, a mischievous element, culling whispered voices from the timbers and agitating night critters to come out for a prowl. I reasoned that this had to be another prank, cousin to the bathtub invasion and the quickly slurped daiquiri. If I returned to Toll House immediately, I'd be met by a gauntlet of howling, teasing, probably goosing nuns in penguin habit, braying at my boundless gullibility.

I continued to wait, the holy night breathing through my pores. Moonglow skated on the thin ice of the pond, and set off the shroud of dark mountains in relief. Oho! The hoax would be on them. Hours, the night, days would pass. Sooner or later they'd feel obliged to dispatch a search party and, if I had not frozen to death in the interim, the louder would be my emaciated laugh, the more vapid my snickering at their remorse.

And yet, when I spied her coming, her hurried steps creating an illusion of glide, of skiing on a swath of moonlight, I knew that coming here had been my only choice. Framed by a stable window, her movement and impending presence reached to the very quick of me, thrum and heartbeat and temperature shift. Her delicacy and bird-like wildness, her Little-Red-Riding-Hood vulnerability as she skipped through the woods to enter the den of my Big-Bad-Wolf's heart, startled my slumbering soul. She woke me up. I wasn't used to this. I was unaccustomed to joy; my infatuation was monolithic, the whole of my mind agitated with love.

In pulling back the rickety, creaking barn door, Chantelle admitted herself on a scurry of light and blown snow. Rusty hinges blasphemed. She leaned her shoulder into the door to shut it again. Then she surprised me. Kicking the floor bolts into place, she effectively locked us in. Chantelle crossed the floor to the opposite door. "Hello, again," she piped up, though I could not have been more than a shadow to her, a murky silhouette. By dropping a two-by-four into its cradle, she barricaded that entry as well.

The darkness and the bolts had thwarted the world. We were confined within our own dimension. I waited in silence.

"I owe you an explanation." As she spoke out of the darkness, I heard Chantelle walking toward me. "I don't invite every man I meet down to the stables for a confab."

And then lock him in, I was tempted to add.

"It's just that I very much wanted to talk to you." She emerged into light reflected off the snow and shining on the smeared windows. Opening a stall gate, Chantelle gripped the upper rail and wedged her toes between planks. She pushed off, swinging on the gate in a slow arc. "I wanted to explain about the others. Make excuses for them, I guess. I think it's important. You see . . . we are serious about what we do, it's just that Easter can be a tense period. Sometimes we let off steam. Keeps us loose. That's the beauty of coming to Toll House — we can be ourselves here. Trouble is" — she added upon further reflection, with a slight laugh — "being ourselves is not necessarily such a good thing."

Chantelle had changed clothes for this outing, and was now sporting a red parka, blue jeans, and tall leather boots. In trying to reconcile her costume with traditional nuns' habits, I was satisfied that at least her parka had a hood. She climbed higher on the gate and swung one leg over the top to sit astride it, riding it like a horse.

"I wanted to talk to you because I'm . . . I was . . . a close friend of your father's. Well . . . we were all very fond of him . . . but I think it's fair to say that Gaby and I were especially close. Kyle, you've been seeing our frivolous side first. I'm worried that that's neither appropriate nor fair." I could easily imagine her carrying a crop, reins in hand, feet in the stirrups, guiding her horse through the intricacies of dressage. "Despite the shenanigans —" she laughed quite gaily — "*all* indications to the contrary, we do have our serious nature." Beginning at her kneecap, Chantelle drew her thumb up the outside of her left thigh. "Given the circumstances — your father's death, I mean — it's occurred to me that the others are behaving abysmally. Do you think so? I —" she pulled a leg free and slid down one side of the fence — "am no influence on them, I'm afraid. All I can do is bitch."

Chantelle came up to me and slipped an arm around my waist. "I met you here because I needed to talk to you," she repeated. "Anywhere else and the girls would pull a prank."

"I met you here because I've been bowled over by you" was my gentle retaliation. I wanted to discover our limits. "First from my bedroom window. Then from the open bathroom door. Again by the fireplace. I felt an attraction that's very compelling. Chemistry."

"You've had a long day," she cautioned me. "And an eventful one. You haven't even unpacked yet, you told me — mmmm, maybe in more ways than one?"

"My mind is functioning," I assured her. Responding to her tentative, exploratory move to pull away, I tugged on her shoulders. Gently, she curled into me, we seemed to fit, we gazed at one another, the very sadness in her eyes dampening with tears. That was the moment when we kissed, briefly, sharing a weighted tenderness. Overwhelmed by the gesture we split apart, severed as conclusively as two halves of a log split by an ax. I felt chopped up further for kindling. Her back to me, Chantelle walked away.

"I'm sorry" was her whispered disclaimer.

"Don't apologize."

"One of us should."

"Why?"

Before daring to face me, she dried her eyes on her sleeve. "This is not what I had in mind," she stressed. "I wanted to impress you, demonstrate that we're not a crowd of ninny females."

"I think nothing of the sort. Not that it matters."

"But it does!" Chantelle was quite strict on the point. "We've gotten off on the wrong foot, Kyle. You're not prepared for what comes next. No one's thought things through. Gaby, she says it's not necessary, but I disagree. I disagree. We could scare the hell out of you before the weekend's over."

Moving slowly in her direction, stalking her, I naively believed: "It can't be that bad."

"Any bets? The girls playing tricks on you or the two of us down here stealing a kiss — golly, what was that about? — is hardly a proper initiation. Your father knew us. Loved us, too. Gee, you look so much like him. He'd get on our case whenever he thought we were out of line. Light a fire under us when we were slacking. If he thought we were too serious, he'd keep us loose. He understood us, at least to a certain extent." Pausing to catch her breath, she eyed me closely. "You haven't a clue what I'm talking about, do you?"

Within kissing range again, I hesitated, suspecting that any advance would be rebuffed. Chantelle would insist on expounding the ground rules first. "Let me in on it then."

"It's not that simple."

"Just tell me what's up."

"That's what I mean. I can't. It's not that I *will* not, simply that I *cannot*. We're not a group that can be neatly pegged. We're diverse. We can't be summed up in a few words."

"Fair enough." Intrigued, my mind was spinning. "Let's try a different approach. Give me an example, Chantelle. Or a clue, at least."

"Okay. I'll give you an example — a smidgen — of what we're

about. An inkling." On a lower stall, one probably intended for shorter farm animals — pigs or goats — Chantelle hung her crossed arms and rested her chin upon the cushion formed by her wrists. "Let me think," she requested.

I studied the contour of her body. Not a carnal inspection, for I was thoroughly involved in the wonder and oddity of the last few minutes. I had not imagined it: we had actually kissed! Right off the bat, as though we'd been pals for years. Too soon, to judge Chantelle's reaction. For her, matters had to be revealed, explained, worked out. If we were going to fall in love with one another, it had to be for a valid reason, our passports into that treasured domain officially stamped.

Her chin was a trifle pointy, her nose (I should talk) a fraction too long. When not upturned in a smile, the customary fix of her mouth relaxed into a pout. The set of her eyes struck me as austere and compulsively clairvoyant. Perhaps I had originally evaluated the significance of her features incorrectly. Her skin, once so desirable, had seemed a frail and precious membrane over her bones and bloodstream, an indication to me of her fragility. Revise that. I was sensing now that the quality transparent in her was strength, a courage that had been exercised, a fortitude upon which she had been forced to rely. Similarly, I had elected to adorn her presence with an air of vulnerability, a defenselessness in the face of treachery; my meditation in the stable, however, took note of the tiny crow's feet about her eyes and the solitary line across her brow. I thought in contrasts. That her innocence had been through the wringer, that the aura of sadness strategic to her persona had been furrowed by experience, and that the tranquility of her nature had been hard won. Chantelle was not a simple woman to measure, nor could I be confident in my own resources. Whether I was cutting through to the bone or dressing her up in the period costume of a convenient mythology was impossible to tell. My talent for portraiture was unpracticed, my hand unsteady, and she made for a difficult subject. As well, the lighting was poor. I warned myself to defer judgment.

Her eyes seemed lit by a bright idea. "Did you count us?" was her peculiar question.

"Count you? No. Why? Is someone missing?"

"Always count," she instructed me. "We're twenty-eight in all."

"Okay. So?"

Stooping, she held her knees together while her free hand smoothed the earth and straw in a patch of moonlight on the stable floor. I hunched down facing her.

"The single-digit multipliers that work out to twenty-eight are four and seven, correct?"

"Is this a math class? Am I back in school?"

"Shut up and pay attention. You might learn something." She sniffed in an affectionate way that stirred my heart.

"Four sevens are twenty-eight."

"Gotcha."

"Add the two and the eight of the twenty-eight."

"Ten."

"Add the one and the zero of the ten."

"I can do that, I think. The answer is one."

"The whole. The one God. The created *uni*-verse. Unity."

"Okay," I allowed. Given that the connection was precious to her, I was willing to grant it nominal validity. Another speaker uttering similar irrelevancies would have drawn my scorn.

"Let's start with the four."

"What four? Pun intended."

"The four in four times seven equals twenty-eight. Keep up here. A pyramid has four sides, not counting the bottom."

"Hold it right there. I'm no dummy. I've seen pictures. Pyramids are triangles."

"Each erect side is a triangle. The floor is a square, from which rise four equal triangular sides, not three."

"I'll take your word for it." A lucky coin, a copper freckle about half the size of a penny, had been deposited an inch below her left earlobe, claimed by a slash of moonlight.

"Four represents the square. The square symbolizes perfection, because each of its lengths and each of its angles are equal."

"We've found perfection and unity. We're on a roll. What's next?"

"The purpose of a pyramid is to 'peer amid'. To look inside. To look within." Chantelle sketched a triangle in the earth with her

54

middle finger. "Seven," she declared seriously. "The seven centers of being. The seven steps to heaven. The seven heavens."

"Sounds idyllic." But what did any of it mean? I refrained from asking.

At the pyramid's uppermost tip, which Chantelle constructed on its side, she gouged a small hole. "One," she said. Two more holes were dug a short distance down each side of the triangle being formed. "Two." An equal distance lower, away from my feet and toward her, she repeated the procedure, pinching the dirt between her fingers and disposing of the debris behind her. She worked with the efficiency and rhythm of a steam shovel. This time she added a third dot on the imaginary center-line under the peak.

"Three," I spoke up, a clever student and the teacher's pet. Chantelle continued adding equally-spaced dots to each subsequent line, until she had filled in her triangle down to its base.

"Seven rows," she elaborated. "Each row has one more dot than the row above it. Each row has a corresponding number of dots: row five, for example, has five dots. How many dots are there, Kyle?"

My motion to count the dots individually was cut short. Chantelle eased my hand away.

"Do the sum in your head. One plus two plus three plus four plus five plus six plus seven equals . . . ?"

My answer was a question. "Twenty-eight?"

"Precisely. In other words —"

"You're one side of a pyramid."

"In a manner of speaking, yes. A pyramid which signifies unity, perfection, and the way to God. Also, it reveals that we're engaged in the cosmic flow of circumstances and events. All things connect. Did you know, just as one example, that the sides of a pyramid are angled at fifty-one-and-a-half degrees?"

"No, that never came to my attention before."

"And that Stonehenge is located at fifty-one-and-a-half degrees north latitude, more or less? These things are not accidents. They are *occurrences*. It's to this realm of occurrences that we belong."

"I see." We stood. I did not feel transformed by these equations, and my enlightened joints and back had stiffened in the cold. "So you *are* religious," I appraised.

"Funny, isn't it, how suddenly you're no longer so keen to kiss me."

The lady had caught me out. My desire had dissipated. In summoning me to this lecture, in kissing me, and now in reading my feelings, she had demonstrated an uncanny knowledge of my thoughts and mood even before I was fully conscious of my stance. Swallowing a considerable lump of embarrassment, my throat's bob was loud in the still stable. Chantelle's smile expressed her triumph.

"I presume that you work with numbers a lot," I interjected, hoping to revert to a safer subject.

"Quite a bit. It's one of my things. The others aren't so interested. What are you thinking?" Chantelle asked me at pointblank range. Her direct, straightforward contemplation was not the sort of inquiry one should scoot around. Answer honestly.

"I'm wondering if what your friends said is true."

She furrowed her brow quizzically. "Which was what?"

"Something about chastity vows."

To study me, she cocked her head to one side. Shame put color on my cheeks. Having satisfied myself that she was nutty, a carnal interest had been rekindled. I shifted my gaze as her scrutiny intensified. Unable to bear it much longer, I complained, "What?"

"You're a funny-looking bird."

"Thanks heaps." Miffed to be compared to fowl.

"When you're old and gray you'll look exactly like a wise snowy owl. For now, you're closer to the scruffy barn variety."

"I can hoot too."

"I bet you can! Do it!"

Owls have never been my strong suit, though the effort I put into it had Chantelle in stitches.

"You're a weird guy."

"You never answered my question," I pried.

"You never asked me." I was alert to her mildly flirtatious tone. "And even if you ask, I'm not telling." Playfully, she shoved me away from her. "I have to go back, Kyle. Before the others come looking for me."

"One more kiss?" I dared.

"You're incorrigible!" She actually did sound disapproving. "I had hoped to give you more to think about than that."

"A wee kiss. The first one was very nice."

"Yes," she agreed, thrilling and astounding me simultaneously. "It was."

We gave it a whirl. Our lips tentative, testing the other's powers. Quick sips. Suddenly she pressed her lips very hard against mine, before breaking off in a flurry. I expected more apologies from her. At the door, working the bolts, Chantelle looked back at me and spoke in a voice less calm, less convinced that she had been reducing the world to its mathematical quirks. Breathless. "See you at dinner, Kyle. Never say that I didn't try to warn you about us. You will read to us, won't you?"

"Read? What's this about reading? Come back here! Chantelle!"

She did return, and in the darkness we met and kissed again, our bodies bruised by the contact as we fumbled for one another, and snared each other in a passion too long dormant in me and, I could tell, bewildering to her. She wanted and did not want this, equally. Chantelle, in spinning away again, fell back against a hitching-post, one hand to her face as she whispered startled cries.

"Chantelle?"

"My God, it's started," she lamented.

"What's the matter?"

"Nothing." Foraged desperately through her pockets. "A nose-bleed."

Kleenex flashed, a flag of surrender in the moonlight. She held tissues to her lower face like a white surgical mask.

"You all right?"

"Sure. This is nothing." She did not elaborate.

"Does it happen often?"

"Once in a while. It's seasonal. The thin mountain air. A nearly full moon doesn't help either. Please, Kyle, don't be disgusted with me."

"Don't be absurd!" I held an arm around her shoulders until the bleeding stopped. She dropped the soiled tissues into a bucket.

"I'll clean up another time." A weak, valiant smile.

"Forget about it."

"I never knew that kissing could be so dangerous," she noted, and laughed.

"You sure you're all right?"

"Definitely. Anyhow, to answer your question, one of your father's fables, that's what you should read. It'll be great! Preferably *A Kinkajou in Hackensack*, that's our favorite. That tale always gets us into a mellow, depressing mood. Will you read to us, Kyle?" I certainly had my qualms, but they dispersed under the pressure of her campaign. "For me?"

"That's not fair."

"Then you will? Great! I'll tell the others. In fact, I'll make that my excuse for talking to you in case we've been spotted. If anybody asks, say we bumped into each other by chance." She was almost at the door.

"What about my other question?" I was close behind her.

"I'm not telling!" she pealed. "Kyle, wait here a minute. Give me a headstart. We mustn't be *seen* together, I'd never live it down. I'd be ribbed to death! Besides, what hope would I have to whip the girls into shape if they knew that I was down here smooching with you? Stay a while, please, Kyle, then take the route back the way you came. I'll go through the woods. See ya!"

A glimmer in the forest, a gossamer trace adrift across my heart. God, I thought, I'm in love again. Pretty good after being dead to the world for the past fifteen years. Hey! That's pretty damn good indeed!

I waited in the barn a while, true to her instructions, my heart pumping with the adrenalin of infatuation. What a day! A house, an inn, and now the potential for love! My life really was changing, fortune had decided to shine.

That it was all too good to be accepted should have been obvious to me.

Somebody grabbed me from behind. Powerful hands. My mouth was clamped shut and a vice squeezed my chest. Breath was escaping fast, fright pinioned my legs, and I collapsed under the weight of my attacker. All I could think was, the skeleton's come back to life! The skeleton!

I was on my knees. The hand let go and I gulped immense volumes of air. Suddenly a bone, the size of a forearm, was rammed between my teeth like a horse's bit. My neck was being pulled backwards by the force. And a voice, low, guttural, almost indecipherable, whispered in my ear, "Run". Rhythmic commands. "Run." I cried out against the pain exerted against my mouth. "Run."

The moment I was released I coughed out the bone and had one foot in the blocks to make my escape: as quickly as before I was clutched by the phantom. Saw the hand reach down for the forearm bone. At least that hand wasn't skeletal. "Open" was the muttered order. I opened my mouth wide, moaning vague entreaty. The bone was brought sideways into my mouth again. My attacker gripped both ends of it to yank my head back.

"Bite."

I bit down.

"Run."

And this time I did not spit out the bone as I was released, but picked up my feet and ran like crazy, out of the trees and across the dam, along the trail and up the Toll House Road. I was almost at the parking lot before I dared remove the offending object from my mouth, holding it like a runner's relay baton as I charged up the hill.

Exhaustion set in by the time I made my car. I sat down on the rear bumper and tried to catch my breath, to make no mention of my wits and dignity. Terrified to my core. When my heart-rate calmed down and my breathing was restored, I tried to think. Should I report the mad marauder in the stables? How do I explain my presence there? What's more, how do I explain the bag of bones which would surely be discovered if the authorities became involved? If I contend that the madman, whether he is still there or has fled, must be responsible, what do I do when my fingerprints are discovered all over the remains?

Obviously, broaching the subject would have to be done with care. Maybe there was a logical explanation. Perhaps the inn was not all that I had inherited, and a legacy of maniacs was included.

At a loss, I lifted the tailgate of my new Cherokee Chief, and found a nifty rear compartment into which the bone fitted as comfortably as a cadaver in a coffin. A little weak in the knees, I stumbled back to the sanctuary of Toll House.

7

I sang for my supper that evening.

Upon my return to Toll House, I had discovered the dining-room enchanted by the warm spell of candlelight. Infinitely repeated on the facets of crystal and silverware, the miniature flames transformed the space into a starry night, a gypsy galaxy broken loose from heaven.

On impeccable white linen, the table settings were immaculate. The arrangement of chairs had been executed to an exact symmetry. Sequel to its dance in the massive hearth, the fire cast an intrigue of shadows across the frosty windowpanes, inviting the nefarious of the forest to come revel. I had been accustomed to living in casual disorder — of the sort where the major hindrance to doing the laundry was always to find it first, and where piled dirty dishes stood as an impenetrable fortress defending the sink — and yet, within the realm of that room's illuminated perfection, a single flaw annoyed me. Menus had carelessly been stashed atop a radiator. Animated by my fresh responsibilities, I scooped up the offending mess and sallied into the kitchen.

Whoops-a-daisy. Bad timing. I had neglected Hazel's rider to stay out of her bees wax. The countertops were a mishmash of flashing knives and vegetable bits, the sinks a clutter of copper-bottomed pots. Entry at this hour verged on the sacrilegious.

Luckily, each of Hazel's eleven hands (give or take a few, they were hard to count through the blur) happened to be busy. Penalty for intrusion might be to dice the culprit's fingertips, or smooth his ears flush to the skull under her marble rolling pin. Bullied by her

61

glare, I stuffed the menus onto a shelf behind my back, and retreated into a recess in the wall.

"Get a move on, girls — this isn't the slow dance. A man walks in, you've seen the breed before, no need to stop and gawk. Cassie! Are you mixing cement? Stir, woman!"

I was the vicarious victim of her tongue-lashing, I knew, the ninny responsible for unsettling their routine. Not totally cowed, secretly I felt exalted, amazed that I could afford their five salaries.

Shielded by the bulwark of the deep-freeze which guarded the demilitarized zone between us, I asked Hazel, "What's cooking?"

Her lower lip protruded to direct a defiant gust of breath upward, cooling a sweaty brow. Tufts of hair fluttered in the breeze. "Chicken," she hissed. "Something wrong with that?"

Like a cat's, Hazel's back arched, her shoulder blades bundling into a hump. Queen of her kitchen, she would not tolerate having her authority contravened by the presence of a mere wandering tom.

"Cassie!" A chunky, dwarfish girl jolted inside her skin. "I told you to stir!"

"I am stirring," the assistant feebly complained. I tended to agree with her, though her efforts were conspicuously uninspired.

"*Stir!*" The cook's command conveyed the threat that it was never too late to add the kitchen help to the broth.

"Is there something I can do — for you — Mr. Elder — *sir*?" Sarcasm misted in the air as steam from the bubbling pots.

"Yes, actually, Hazel. *A Kinkajou in Hackensack*," I put forward. "Where can I find a copy?"

"*Kinkajou?*" Disarmed, she stared at me with a wild, scatterbrained expression, as though she hallucinated and I was a ghoul.

"That's right." Franklin D.'s advice that feigning knowledge would faze her had done the trick. "You did mention that I was expected to read to the nuns tonight, didn't you? *A Kinkajou* might be appreciated. Don't you think so?"

Hazel's recovery commenced as awkward and slow, then gained momentum. In a moment she busily, compulsively, wiped a slab of butcher block clean, nearly hacking off the hands of her servile elderly assistant who offered to help. She cleared her throat to test her composure. "We packed away his things, Mr. Elder, like I told you. I'm sorry, but I couldn't possibly lay my hands on *Kinkajou* tonight."

"I see. Perhaps you can help me with something else. How shall I say this? Ah, do any lunatics live nearby?"

"Lunatics?" She waved her rolling pin in the air like a sabre.

"Crazy people."

"Half the population. Why?"

"I'm serious. Has anyone recently been annoying the guests?"

"Such a question! The answer is no."

"Mmm. Listen — never mind about *Kinkajou*! I have a better idea!"

Inspired, I promptly bounded upstairs to tune the strings of my dulcimer. If the ladies insisted on being entertained, surely I could improve upon reading them bedtime stories.

No one had bothered to frisk me upon arrival. The tricks up my sleeve remained intact.

Neither the lingering excitement of my interlude with Chantelle, nor my terror after the attack, nor even my absorption in tuning the dulcimer, deterred a rising, and inevitable, inclination to sleep. I was soon drowsy, and the bed offered solace. A quick snooze would probably do me a world of good. Rushing through the tuning, I limbered my fingers with a few practice bars, then rested the instrument snugly in its velvet-lined case and my cranium comfortably on the pillow.

Much too soon — a drastic problem at the inn — I was awakened.

Unearthly, murmured sounds disturbed me. A chant. The voices of spooks smoldering in my dream. I jerked up with a start. What *is* that? Across the beams the melody flowed while a deeper drone, like a dirge, rumbled admirably along the floorboards like waves washing up on rocks. Interspersed were high, reedy warbles ricocheting off the walls, a melancholy similar to the cry of seabirds.

A muffling of the volume's sudden increase indicated that a door opened on the music had summarily been shut.

Weird.

Dislodged by the gothic chorus, I considered myself daring, if not downright brave, to look outside the room. Immediately, startling me, the stairwell went black. Footsteps! *Quickly!* — duck back inside, wait with an ear pressed to the wood. Local noise: the molecular vibrations of pine, the constructs and demolitions of termites, the distant thunder of a furnace. Feet scurried past. Opening the door a crack, I witnessed an unidentified woman, dressed in a black robe and cowl, flick off an overhead hall light, then scamper on her toes to turn off another.

All of Toll House now lingered in darkness.

Shivery and alone, I waited with foreboding.

The chant surged loudly once again, informing me that the lamp-douser had entered the room where the women were gathered. I shut myself in for safety's sake, and stood my vigil on my knees, an eye pressed to the keyhole.

Wait!

Look.

Light!

A glowing, fluctuating amber bathed the hall's wood in gold. Through the keyhole (I realized with a start that it was nun-shaped), I spied the women slowly approaching, swaying in unison with each shuffled step. The cowls of their monkish habits cloaked every face in shadow. Each woman clasped her hands in prayer while holding the stem of a thin white candle. A multitude of flames flickered.

They were marching around the corner into my visual range. With each step, and the appearance of more dark faces, the volume of the music increased. Windowpanes lightly tinkled behind my back and a sibilant ringing assailed my ears. Theirs an impressive choir, singing in every range and sounding as one voice. The resonance was fuller and more rounded as the voices drew near, the high sopranos singing with a marvelous conviction and control. What sound! What presence! Toll House swelled with the music, and my spine quivered.

My door seemed a frail membrane against the vocal onslaught. I empathized with the inhabitants of Jericho on their fateful day. The indecipherable Latin text I presumed either denounced or convicted me.

Hips swayed. Tassels did the rumba on female thighs. Marching directly into me, the women swerved at the final moment to take the stairs down. After the last had gone by, I tripped the latch and peered out. The darkness had swallowed them whole. The procession had disappeared from view and, in a moment, the powerful chant subsided, then ceased. With the quiet, a premonition of terror surged through the house.

The collective breath of the nuns blew out their candles, and where twenty-eight voices had chanted in unison, now there was one. A Latin prayer. Choral responses thrilled the dining-room. Lighting was turned up at the prayer's conclusion, probably blinding them all, and I, having crept downstairs, peered around the doorjamb. Chairs pulled back from the tables created a rambunctious clamor. Napkins, once everyone was seated, flashed open and were adjusted on the uniform black laps.

How foolish of me not to have guessed!

It was time for dinner.

"What's that thingamajig?" Gaby wanted to know. She sipped her V8.

Having skipped upstairs to wash my hands and fetch the dulcimer, I stood in the doorway, a stranded orphan searching for a seat. Thoroughly bashful. A waitress anxious to serve the eastern flank nudged me aside; two others burst through the kitchen's swinging doors like a police tactical squad.

The ladies were flipping back their cowls, presenting blondes and redheads as dabs of color to the room, and making identification possible. Naturally, my wish was to be next to Chantelle — at least to sit at her table. She saw me, oh yes, she saw me, yet as her sad gaze crossed mine she yielded not a glimmer of recognition. She was keeping our liaison secret.

Not knowing where to go, I considered retreating to a kitchen stool to feed on scraps doled out by the grouchy cook. Mother Superior Gabriella's waving hand intercepted me.

Hers was the only table set for five. I was expected. I rested the dulcimer case against a convenient pillar, seated myself with a brave and ingenuous smile, and replied to Gaby's question, "That's no thingamajig, that's a dulcimer."

"You play, I presume."

"Keeps me fit. Playing is the best exercise I get. Cardio-pulmonary resuscitation. Gaby, I heard tell through the grapevine that you're accustomed to hearing my father read."

"Your father's talent for public reading was extraordinary, Kyle. He had a marvelous voice, he was a natural-born ham."

"I'm not, I'm afraid." I cast a quick glance at the others at our table. The grim, royal beauty on my right accorded me the courtesy of looking up whenever I spoke; her friends never acknowledged my existence.

"You needn't be shy with us, Kyle," Gaby asserted. "I'm certain that you'll do fine."

"I have nil confidence in my . . . speaking voice," I pleaded. (I had almost said "my human voice.") "Especially when I'm unfamiliar with the story."

"Hoot, nobody cares about that." Her left hand curled into a fist which she held high, guarding her chin. Her jab would be lethal. "Nobody's asking you to match your father . . ."

"I'll do something of my own instead." Refusing to perform at all was a third option, except that I had a lady to impress. Chantelle was in the audience, and she fully expected me to materialize under the spotlight.

Gaby regarded me steadily. A knot tangled her brow. Hers a boxer's glare intended to rout an opponent's defences before the bell's first ring. "You're going to play that instrument, aren't you?" she concluded in a grave voice, her trepidation apparent.

"Yes!" Sheer bravado.

In formulating a response, Gaby first glanced discreetly at the others around the table, taking a poll of their pursed lips, arched eyebrows, and shrugs.

"Please, Kyle, nothing too merry. Today is Maundy Thursday. *A Kinkajou in Hackensack* puts us in the proper mood. We become somber. Reflective. The story makes us sad. This is the night we recall that Our Lord, in the Upper Room, forewarned of His impending execution, foretold that He would be betrayed. We require a serious frame of mind and a contrite heart."

"I see."

"Do you? This is a night of perfidy."

Which was a line to kill conversation.

A gasp. From a table nearby. Then a sudden faint cry. A fork fell, but did not clatter loudly. I saw Chantelle flex backward as though in pain. As though she'd been stabbed. Companions to either side of her seized her upper arms and held her steady. She nodded to them after a few moments, apparently murmured thanks or an apology, and her friends released their grips. Unrestrained, Chantelle shook her head several times, not unlike a pony relieved of its harness, her short mane flashing from side to side, and she massaged the back of her neck. What perplexed me particularly was that not a soul had questioned her spasm; neither its cause nor its effect seemed to interest the women.

My own tableguests — not coincidentally, I fear — chose that moment to initiate conversation. Sisters Dierdre, Sophie, and Jane had been quiet to the brink of rudeness — suddenly they wanted to talk. They nattered away like machine guns, the exploding bullets of their voices distracting me from Chantelle's distress. Grudgingly, I answered their rapid-fire questions.

"Since I was a teenager," I informed Sophie, who had wanted to know how long I'd been playing the dulcimer. She insisted that that was fascinating. Dierdre leapt in with her query, and I replied, somewhat precariously, "Actually, my interest developed as a natural extension of my involvement with birds and their music. I decided that the dulcimer was the instrument most compatible with bird songs."

"Bird songs," she repeated.

To Jane: "I was raised in Montreal."

And to her supplementary: "No, I've been living in Tennessee, actually. Originally I went down there in search of a custom-made dulcimer. A few things came up, and I stayed."

At which point, when Sophie fired another volley, I chose to cut the crap. I spun a yarn for my guests, albeit a truthful one. "Tennessee's been okay, up until last Halloween. That's when skeletons appeared on a few prominent persons' lawns. Nobody could find out who was behind the sick joke. Kids — kids in general — were blamed. Trouble was, the problem didn't stop. The mayor opened the front door of his car and a skull tumbled out. That was around Christmas. The rest of the skeleton was piled on the seat, with a foot-bone lashed to the brake. No, I'm not kidding. I wish I was. Another skeleton showed up in a housewife's fridge, its spine protruding from a caramel pudding. Yet another was found floating on an air mattress in the brand new, indoor, Olympic-sized swimming pool. The swim-meet for toddlers was canceled.

"Now, if the bones had been dug up, nobody'd found out from what graveyard. Some say the dead are clambering out of the ground on their own — prematurely. A preacher said they miscalculated the end of time, but not by much because it's coming soon. I don't believe that, but it's still creepy. So, to answer your question, Soph, I was quite happy to leave Tennessee and come here. Vermont skeletons don't strut their stuff, do they?"

The women had allowed me to jaw on for my barrage well-suited their ulterior motive — to thwart questions. Sufficient time had elapsed that it no longer seemed apropos to ask what had happened to Chantelle. As I showed no inclination to pursue the matter, we permitted each other to conclude our meal under the tacit acceptance of a truce.

Gaby stood up and, prelude to my introduction, as if this was a meeting of a Kiwanis Club, clinked her spoon against a glass. "Sisters, your attention, please." The women were a disciplined lot. Each head obediently turned to face her. "Our special pleasure this weekend is to meet, and come to know, the son of our dear, departed friend and patron, Kyle Elder Senior. The good news is, Kyle Junior intends to keep the inn open, and we certainly appreciate that." Polite applause approved the announcement, and I basked in their attention.

"As you are aware, we had hoped that Kyle Junior, in the grand tradition of his father, would consent to read to us tonight. I'm sorry —" she held up her hands to revoke a second smattering of applause — "to tell you that a treat of a different nature lies in wait for us this evening." The timbre in her voice cautioned her friends to fear the worst: conceivably, what lay in wait was an ambush. Teeth clenched, I smiled at Gaby. "Sisters, Kyle Junior brings his own special talents to our humble podium. He will play for us his, umm, dulka . . . ? Oh well, his little music box."

No applause guided me to the stage. The cat-whistles that had celebrated my nudity remained dormant. I waded through the thickening silence, intending to sing from a corner of the raised hearth. Any doubts that this was going to be an awfully tough audience were dismissed when I passed Gaby's chair and she virtually growled her cursory reminder, "Remember! Nothing cheerful!"

Fiddlesticks. I had no intention of restricting myself to the rusty-hinged squeak of the grackle. Nor am I particularly adept at imitating the lonely mournful call of the loon. Nor was I inspired to create fringilline accompaniments on my "dulka", my "little music box".

The wood in my hands revived me. The dulcimer imparted its translucent powers. Manufactured to my own design, the instrument was less than a year old, my requirement having been for a lightweight, portable, hammer-variety that would provide me with soft soprano octaves. With it, I am able to complement the pitch, say, of the tufted titmouse, and in the upper register the higher strident whistles of the indigo bunting. Imitation of these sounds had not been my intention — I use my vocal chords for that — no, I was in search of a harmonious and rhythmically orchestrated sound. Plucked symphonic strings. I wanted the vocal songs to be heard against the backdrop of a mythical, melodic woods. Forest music. The essence of sunshine on the meadow, of rainfall in the glen. The wind's dulcet mew through a marsh, the percussion of bulrushes, the spirit of air alighting on the water.

Exactly what I expected to accomplish was not possible to know. Mine is a limited art form and I have had no guide. Ah well. Like any artist mindful of his skin I know how to entertain — no one detects my true intentions. Which are? To dissolve the world. To recreate matter as spirit. To sing the soul's resound, making scratchy language obsolete. To suspend the physical a hair's breadth above the imperfectly perceived void, to imperil the body over the cutting edge of the universe, where the blood of stardust shines like silver and sings to the accompaniment of golden strings.

I erred. Once settled into a high-backed chair, the dulcimer arranged over my knees on its floor-stand, I looked out over the cheerless throng. I should have ignored them. The semi-darkness revealed that the women had covered their heads once again. For all that I knew, they had blocked their ears for good measure. The overheads had been subdued for this concert, leaving only the licks of candle flames while the glow of the fire was my stagelight. I was put off. Each face watching me formed a dark forbidding sphere. Nary a muscle in Toll House moved. Throughout my career I have had to tolerate hecklers at my performances: I sorely missed them here.

To begin, a cadence of the house wren. Ah — that got their attention. They had expected the dulcimer, not my voice, to produce music. The house wren cheerily maintains a bubbling, gurgling chatter.

du du du du chichichichi titato . . .

which is ideal for establishing a rhythm. Amid the rapid notes the bird will occasionally intersperse trills, a habit I copy routinely. The male delights in singing this song with its beak full of insects he feeds to his insatiable young. In the woods the song can become monotonous — it's sung incessantly between April and July — yet it is that percolating repetitiveness that is ideal for establishing a base line and an active beat.

tu tu chidle chidle chidle chidle
tu tu chidle chidle . . .

I noticed many of the cowled heads turning to peer at one another. Great! The stoic ladies were fidgeting, wondering what in the blazes was going on. Perhaps I give myself undue credit, yet I fantasized at the time that a few were searching around the room for the bird that had flown in a window.

I averted the rhythms of the house wren by going directly into the song of the winter wren. The two jive, the winter wren slipping into a high and clear whistle, reminiscent of a piccolo.

tu to tu ti to ti ta ti teeraaaay ti ta reee . . .

At this point the dulcimer invokes the accoustical beat abandoned by the house wren, and as the two combine I introduce the voluptuous, erruptive voice of the Carolina wren. A clear, melodious whistle, rather low in pitch. The ample variety of this song propels me into the music. Thoroughly involved now, the dulcimer provides riffs of its own inspired by the birds, as well as laying down the track. My voice shifts into the guttural of the long-billed marsh wren which marks my transition into the music of the swallows. The husky squeak of the cliff swallow is followed quickly by the whistled melodies of the purple martin. Hazel and her staff, I notice, have drifted out from the kitchen to discover what the devil is happening. A medley of several species of swallow (tree, barn, bark, and rough-winged) leads my composition into a jazzier, progressive phase, which hurtles through when the crested fly-catcher performs his early-morning lullaby. Then the same bird's wild, free-spirited calls.

Striving for crescendo I work them back and forth, the harsh and raucous sounds and the windy whistle, the dulcimer crashing away, my hammers a lively blur, and I introduce the battle call of the kingbird

> *keet keet kiki keeta keeta*
> *kitta kitta kitta kitta . . .*

easing off finally into the plaintive whistle of the evening and late-summer phase of the eastern-wood pewee. The retreat continues as the dulcimer fades and I sing the weak, rather colorless song of the phoebe, further broken up by a distant, morning song, strident and raspy, of the kingbird again.

Next, I skimmed through the liquidy whistle of the gray-cheeked thrush to split into the euphoric windy whistle of the olive-backed thrush, a song rising to the heights of an unknown majesty. The particular phrase I imitate consists of fourteen notes, each connected with damp consonant sounds between them. The chorus of the dulcimer gradually grows mute. Each line begins low, the second note is lower still, but the third note is set higher than the first. The fourth repeats the pattern, and is higher than the previous sequence. It builds. Higher. Higher. Clearing the way, like a John the Baptist in the wilderness, for the song of the hermit thrush. I sense a terrible unworthiness whenever I attempt this melody; consequently, I pour my heart into it. Modesty aside, the results are frequently spectacular.

The dulcimer is silent.

In the dark my larynx, my very soul, explores the pure notes.

> *oh lalay ilalo ilalo ilo*
> *ah laylila lilalo lilalo lila . . .*

A myriad of variations. As I conclude, I'm spent, the room is ominously still, the night is pitch black and brooding, and my reputation as a weirdo is assured. I breathe deeply. For a few moments I can scarcely discern my identity, much less where I am. Descending from simple heaven back to complex earth. Then I think of Chantelle. Chantelle! Her presence makes me glad to have returned.

In another instant, the applause is thunderous.

Shazam.

8

In vain that night I awaited a furtive *tap-tap-tapping* on my bedroom door. The vocal knock of my name urgently whispered. Not able to sleep without the assurance of a goodnight kiss, would not the lady of my ripening passion come see me in the evening? I waited for you, Chantelle, I drummed my fingers incessantly on the desktop as a galloping heartbeat.

I lay listening to the pyramidal murmurings and oblong silences of my guests. They had gathered in the Mt. Washington Room — the suite fitted with fireplace and skylight. (Up to mischief I reckoned. Witchcraft, voodoo, hocus-pocus, *counting*.) The knock that shook me, unlike a lover's clandestine signal, rattled my door like a policeman's bold entry. Hazel marched in carrying tea and cookies on a pewter tray.

"Drink up," my regal sergeant-at-arms commanded, "it's orange pekoe." As protection from peeping Toms (or Thomasinas) stalking the night mountains on stilts, Hazel drew the heavy black-backed curtains across the window, an activity intended to camou-flage the grave speculations troubling her.

The wary shuffle was familiar; even close friends never knew how to take my concerts. "Don't mind me," I counseled. "I only sing like a bird, I don't eat like one. You won't have to put birdseed on the menu."

"Such carrying on!" I liked Hazel. She spoke her mind. "Imagine! You'd think you were a turkey and this was Thanksgiving. Next time I'll carry my ax."

"The nuns enjoyed my performance. They applauded — quite

warmly, I thought. In fact, I was impressed by their enthusiasm."

"Consider the source. They used to clap for your father's stories too. *A Kinkajou in Hackensack* — my eye! He never saw a kinkajou in his life, he told me so, only the bones in a museum. Know what else he told me?"

"What?" Hazel did not believe in hoarding secrets.

"You'll never guess."

"Tell me." Hands on stalwart hips, she wore the expression of a cranky mother forever lecturing a mischievous child.

"He never set foot in Hackensack! Not once! He made it all up! I had to show him where it was on the map. And the nuns, *drooling*, hanging on his every word as if a story, a make-believe *story* about some South American monkey-like raccoon-critter coming to the States and having its bones ripped apart on the streets and reset in the Smithsonian was somehow significant. It ain't. It weren't. Significance shmignificance, that's what *I* say."

"Who are these people, Hazel?" I spied advantage in her talkative mood. The solidarity previously evident between her and the nuns had developed lesions — as the attending physician this was my opportunity to probe for private knowledge.

"You're asking me? I know less about them than I do about you." She sighed the grievances of the downtrodden, and shook her head. "I don't think that it was too much to ask, do you?"

"What was?"

"I know that they're guests but we were friends, I thought."

"What did you ask for, Hazel?"

"Nothing stupendous. A small favor, no big deal. I was polite, I wasn't pushy. I asked for a few volunteers I did, to do the dishes — so that the staff might take an early night."

"What did they say?"

"Sorry, Hazel! Too busy! We have our agenda!"

"You said it yourself," I admonished her gently, "they're guests."

Pulling back the edge of the curtain that she had so carefully arranged, Hazel peered out into the darkness. "After all that we've been through in the past year. . . ." Her voice trailed off into the night's occult realm.

"My father, you're talking about?"

"Yep." During my father's illness, I surmised, Hazel had come to know the women personally; side-by-side they had endured trying circumstances, social barriers were eroded, and together they had suffered the daily demise of my unknown parent. The women had relied on her and she on them for cheering up, sharing the load, moral support — perhaps even for doing the dishes. The abrupt revival of the status quo left Hazel leashed to the kitchen sink. I felt sorry for her. After a few moments reflection, perhaps seeing only her stubborn, forlorn, lonely image in the window, she said, with a distinct note of contempt, "Listen to them."

The nuns had resumed chanting. The monotonous drone was not wholly unpleasant; I was becoming accustomed to the dirge as one grows familiar with a wind looting branches or banging like a wastrel against storm shutters.

"I thought we were friends," Hazel mutteringly repeated.

My impression then was that Hazel had not spoken the entire story regarding her dispute with the women. Her request for assistance with that most onerous of domestic chores had been double-edged. "Perhaps I can join you in your activities later" might well have been tacked on to her proposal. Unaware of the ramifications of her petition, expecting merely to be admitted to a group of like-minded friends with a predilection for Gregorian chant (but then, who's perfect?), Hazel was denied entry to the secret cabal. What did she know of the confidential values of numbers, or of the consequences of pyramids traced in the dust? What did she care? Hazel wore the effects of her loneliness as a shield, while the muffled rituals of the women assailed her stoic ramparts as distant, savage cannonfire.

Since I could do little to salve her troubles, I tried to distract her. "You were saying, Hazel, a kinkajou is some sort of monkey-raccoon?"

"Who knows? Who gives a damn? Will you please drink your tea?"

"I'm curious." I removed the teapot's cozy, poured, and sipped.

"You could have fooled me, hotshot. If not the devil himself."

"I don't follow . . ."

"Why not creep down the hall this minute, if you're so curious? Find out what them she-wolves are up to."

My chortle nearly cost me a mouthful of the orange pekoe. "Hazel! I'm surprised at you!"

"You could be sued," she intimated. An ominous voice.

True, the wise course would have been to discourage this bent. "Sued?"

"Think of it, if something goes wrong . . . if somebody gets killed . . ."

"Hazel, I don't think —"

"That's obvious. If you did use your noggin you'd find out what they're up to. Any responsible proprietor would."

"Did my father?" She ignored my query, slowly pacing the small floor.

"Drugs, I'll bet my bottom dollar. That's why they're so hush-hush. What'll you say if the police raid? 'Ohmigawd, judge, Your Honor, I am so sorry, but it was none of my business, I do declare.' "

"Be fair, Hazel. It's worship. Like going to church. It's Maundy Thursday — they're involved in their preparations for Easter. It's like getting ready for the Super Bowl. I'll guarantee that not one of them is off snorting cocaine."

"Who worships in private? The whole point of worship is to put on your best duds and go meet the folks. Like in the Easter Parade. They might call themselves nuns — I say they're witches."

"Whatever — they're still entitled to their own customs and traditions." As we were rapidly getting nowhere, I laid the main issue on the line. "I gather that you were not admitted."

Hazel punched her thigh. "I wouldn't ask! And if they dared ask me I'd turn them down prompt!" Rigor mortis seemed to be the curious effect of her outburst: she stood incredibly still. Her ears strained to cull clues from the arcane sounds. Her eyes smoldered.

Surprised, as I stood up beside her, by my genuine and unexpected affection for this sinewy brick of a woman, I wrapped a protective arm around her shoulders. Confronting the world with enthusiastic labor and steadfast opinion, her curmudgeonly style a technique to coddle grudges and tendernesses alike, Hazel was dismayed to discover any aspect of her fiefdom beyond her control or comprehension. This was her mountain, and the people who tramped up from the valley of the world pilgrims to her shrine.

Anything that she could not understand could not be worth knowing, and was easily cast back down the hillside. Except that the women kept coming, they returned annually, and she could no more figure them out than she could throw them out. Hazel was mystified. "Calm down, my pet," I placated that dented iron will. "Tell me, what did my father have to say about the nuns?"

"He told me to mind my own business," she admitted, cocking her head up at me. "God bless his soul, Kyle, but at times your father could be a fundamentalist prick."

My laughter at her choice description worked a smile.

"They're keeping to themselves, Hazel, doing us no harm. Let's follow their lead, okay? Why should a pack of nutcases worry us?"

"No harm?" Mind-boggled by my point of view, Hazel fell back a step. "Haven't you heard about cults? They destroy families and kidnap babies and extort money, they do. They *brainwash*. And I'll tell you something else you're obviously too naive to believe. Maybe, if you're lucky, you'll sleep tonight. Tomorrow night, Good Friday night, you won't. Guaranteed. The caterwauling that goes on! It's because of them I moved down to the stone basement, took the room off the bar. Down there I can't hear a thing, but I can still feel the vibrations."

"I can sleep through wars," I pointed out. Sleep was my singular talent. "And worse: domestic feuds."

"Make light, you'll be sorry." Her chin jutted out in a defiant pout. Implicit warning. Better to take her seriously than risk reprisal.

Hazel seemed loath to leave as I returned to my tea and cookies, and it occurred to me that my father had done more than remind his chief cook and bottlewasher of her place. He must have enforced a remarkable restraint upon her curiosity. If I did not similarly curtail her freedom, Hazel could prove to be a problem.

Use guile, Kyle. Whittle your wits.

Employ *psychology*.

"Now, Hazel, it's obvious that this is not the most lucrative time of year. The cross-country ski trails have melted and the downhill slopes are limited. Only the keen beans book. Soon the mountains will be mud and runoff. Summer shall take its own sweet time."

"Ain't it the truth."

"But the nuns — the nuns are regulars. Customers with a purpose. They practically fill the place. They're not fussy — except for a concert from the innkeeper — and they make few demands. If the weather turns foul they won't skedaddle, and they all eat the same food, which makes it easier for you. To be both pragmatic and blunt, I want to keep their business. Which means, dear girl, never offending them, in action or appearance. Until they actually do burn the place to the ground, we'll leave them to their own devices. If privacy is their thing, we'll be as discreet as a mom-and-pop motel. We'll learn no secrets, we'll tattle no tales. Fumigate rumors. Vacuum innuendos. At the end of their stay we'll tally the bill with a smile. Then count the loot. Agreed?" I extended to Hazel the right hand of conspiracy.

"Of course," she breezed. Her handshake was a solemn sharp yank that has since affected the free use of my elbow. By her honor, she'd behave.

I needed to broach that other, treacherous subject. "Haze, I want you to be on your toes. While I was out walking before dinner I spotted a crazy-man. Probably a transient. I expect I scared him off, but . . ."

"I'll see that the doors are bolted," she assured me, glad of a task to take her out of the room.

And I felt doubly pleased. Toll House would be made secure, and now that I had Hazel under a moral lock and key, the corridors would be free of unnecessary traffic if I presumed to walk in my sleep at night, a ghostly, ubiquitous, attentive spy.

Waiting for the night to deepen, like a stain seeping through the fabric of our lives, I maintained a vigil and through my trusty keyhole watched as nuns, two-by-two, made their way to the washrooms by candlelight. A regimented procession. Equal intervals between pairs. A nocturnal cadence of doors being opened and shut; the rhythmic flushing of toilets; pipes gurgling harmonies as sink plugs were yanked. Scrubbed and buffed, the ladies did not retreat to their separate rooms, congregating instead in the Mt. Washington Room where they rejoined the chanting.

I didn't see Chantelle.

Indifferent to my best intentions, sleep overtook me. Pity the night-watchman who despairs of staying awake: shoulders slump, eyelids droop, the chin nods forward. He lies down for a few seconds and is soon snoring. A charity of dreams. In mine I was treated to a spectrum of vivid images, followed by hula girls on an ice floe. In the frosty circle of my spyglass they were losing their tans. Periodically, the interlude was laced by brief clear screams — one woke me up in a terrified sweat.

Disoriented — what? still breathing? still living in the world, chump? — I caught a glimpse of the walls leaping away from me like hoodlums nabbed mugging. At the mercy of drafts and the night's chill I lay on top of the covers dreading lost sleep, wondering where in God's backwater this could be. Tired, stiff muscles; rousing myself to the vertical was a struggle. Drowsiness had thoroughly exhausted my subversive and romantic ambitions: a tall stretch, a mighty yawn, and I commenced removing my shirt.

As my fingers touched the third button down I heard the scream again.

Immediate. A sharp staccato outcry amid a resurgent welling of the chant. A quick retort, the impact of a pistol shot fired at random in the dark. The bullet ricocheted through the night. I do believe I ducked.

Suddenly I was wide awake, hankering for a prowl.

A seeker of shadows, as Homer said, myself a furtive shade, I stepped out into the hallway, into the blind wind of sound. Lights had remained switched off and, stark still, the inn's sensory nuance was concentrated. Listening. Antennae alert, nerves oscillating. Shot through with the fear that my attacker from the stables had penetrated Toll House, waving the skeleton's bones.

The careful courtesies lobbied me to forget it, go back to bed, Elder, you were hearing things, but I overruled their skittish counsel and crept slowly forward. Each step both urged and lamented; my stealth creaked on the hardwood floors.

Fingertips traced a wall for security. Ahead, the murmuring had faltered, seemed to be losing voices. A mutiny in the ranks? Or were the nuns sensitive to my trespass?

A door was opened. Slammed shut again by corridor draft. *Ssshh!* The soft pad of running feet! In the nick of time I quailed in a darkened corner as two nuns scurried past. I nearly gagged on my pounding pulse. Using fingertips for eyes, I hid in a tributary corridor, one step up, flattening myself against the wall. The scouts returned after a moment, dashing under my nose, then out of sight and hearing.

The volume steadily increased as the chant resumed its momentum. I cannot exaggerate the physical power of the music; sneaking down the corridor was tantamount to penetrating that writhing body of sound. A discernible flesh, sacred, solemn, wretched with lamentation.

"AIIIII-EEEE!"

Fear slammed through me, locomotive force, hooting, steel wheels clacking on the rails. My God! Hazel was right! They had to be killing somebody in there.

Allowing myself a moment to catch my breath and resummon my cowardly wits, I accused the nuns of a lesser charge: torture. Someone had broken a rule: as punishment they were stripping off her skin.

The music's intensity dramatically increased. Voices resounded in waves, abetted now by the commotion of tambourines, cymbals, rattles, conga drums, and whistles. The floor vibrated underfoot. Walls heaved. Wending my way through a mist of nerve gas would have been easier. I felt assaulted and bruised.

I moved my body forward as cautiously as a chess piece. Pawn to queen's rook five. A dark brown towel had been draped over the red exit light like a flag over a coffin, creating a macabre hue that bludgeoned the walls with the tint of coagulated blood. In this grim cavern, my will was tested. A dozen good reasons to withdraw were harvested. What business of mine was this? Take my own advice and leave them be. Maybe this was how Vermonters had a good time.

Somehow I made it to the closed door of the Mt. Washington Room. The music, or noise, or delirium, of tambourines, whistles, and voices combined as an inquisitor's tantrum. A sound that undressed me and dissolved my skin, vibrating through my bones, dislodging muscle and vein. That physical, that intense. And then, intermittently the solo suffering voice would transcend the chorus of grief, a robust pain winging splinters through the heart.

Now what? I hunkered down, providing less of a target to the savage rhythm. Candlelight flickered in the keyhole and under the door. Through the keyhole I detected a silhouette of heads positioned well back from the door. If I was exceedingly cautious, and given that the room was quite dark and extraordinarily loud, I might be able to open the door and peer inside without being noticed. I weighed the urgency of my curiosity against my better sense, and sought to devise a plan of action.

Before my intellect had a chance to contradict my nerve, my hand bravely gripped the dire doorknob. *Don't be a fool!*

It turned.

With the door open a crack, an immense surge of the chant was released. I could have succumbed to the mesmerizing effects of the relentless rhythms. Valor endured — I pushed the door open further. The beat throbbed in my temples. My nerves were electric. I hesitated, expecting to be seen. Exhaling, I opened the door a bit more, pressed myself against the jamb, and wary of instant decapitation, poked my head inside.

The noise deprived my lungs of air. In the haunting candlelight, my vision initially accommodated the semi-circle of hunched, gyrating bodies and bobbing heads. The women were squatted on the floor around the large, high bed, and most had the backs of their cowled heads to me, while others were sequestered behind the far side of the double. Torsos bucked with lewd connection to the beat, heads spun on their necks like tops. Free hands frenetic on the instruments. The few who might have spied me, faces skeletal in the candlelight, chanted and swayed with their eyes closed.

The women were in a trance. I could have entered the room on a snowmobile and not been noticed. Protected by the noise and by the darkness of my corner, I persevered, and stood inside, shutting the door behind me.

In.

A woman lay on the bed wearing a white nightdress. Her back, shoulders, and head were propped by a mound of pillows. The room was brighter than I had expected, as moonlight wavered through the skylight and shone upon the lone, stark, suffering woman as a stage light, purposefully dimmed. As I watched, transfixed, spellbound by the nuns' self-induced musical daze, the figure on the bed bolted forward, her head coming under the swatch of moonlight as she pressed her elbows into her sides and extended her hands, palms upward. She shook as if pierced by high voltage. She went rigid, and only as her body relaxed from this terrifying convulsion did she scream. Oh my God her scream. My eyes felt singed by heat, as if whiplashed my nerves recoiled, and as she heaved forward again I confirmed that she was Chantelle.

Vertical strokes stained her cheeks, a hideous warpaint. Her outstretched palms also were splotched by a dark coloring. The interplay of light and shadow on the bed was created by the moonlight glancing off the white sheets and being submerged in blackish pools. The surrounding women did absolutely nothing to comfort her, they just beat their tambourines and howled.

Sinking back against the pillows Chantelle's body curled like a wet leaf. Then her legs lashed out. Kicking.

I breathed deeply, engulfed by waves of incense. A smoky quality to the air stung my eyes, and as Chantelle lurched forward into another writhing, riveting scream, the nightmare was too much for me to bear alone in the dark. I scratched about desperately for the light switch, and flicked it on.

My recollection may not be reliable, but my impression is that the music continued unabated, the chanters likely believing that they had entered an exalted sphere of paradise as light glowed on their closed eyelids. They had leapt from Maundy Thursday to the Pentecost. And it was during that surprised gap in time that I saw Chantelle more clearly. Evidence my best efforts would be unable to refute: the nightmare made real. The dark spots on the bed were blood-red pools. No. Be specific. Accept it. They were pools of red blood. Wounds on her hands flowed freely. And her eyes — my God *her eyes!* — were bleeding.

Chantelle!

Shock had turned me to stone. I could neither think, nor speak, nor react. Would that the world was standing still. I could live with that.

Chantelle!

The first to be conscious of the overhead light, Chantelle was also the first to look at me. She shielded her eyes from the brutal glare with a wet, bleeding hand. Dark red blood wept from her lower eyelids as tears. Old blood had formed a crust on her cheeks, twin canyons notched by the free-flowing stream. In identifying me her look conveyed a grieving sustained by the deepest remorse. Abruptly I was accosted by the mob of women, arms, elbows, hands, leering faces and the mock moons of tambourines, indiscriminate alarmed voices entreating and challenging me, soldiers seeking to push me out the door but in effect liberating me from my stunned state.

I fought back, fell, and tumbled away. A forest of legs. I came to my feet on a rampage, slicing down one side of the room and across it to elude the grasping hands. With brute strength I bulled through my attackers and managed to land one knee on Chantelle's bed. Women pinned my arms behind me.

"Chantelle!"

I wanted and expected her to cry out, to hurl herself upon me, plead deliverance from the cruel pain inflicted on her. Up close, the reality of the bleeding was truly horrific, I could not begin to grapple with the agony she must have been experiencing — eyes, bleeding *eyes* — yet she did not throw herself upon me, or beg for my protection. She partially covered her face with a bloodied hand, and in that gesture I was touched by her inexplicable sense of shame.

The mob collected its full force and pulled me off the bed. I wriggled free, thrashing, stumbled, and suddenly found myself in the tight grasp of two women who easily overpowered me. "Chantelle!" I hollered once, uselessly, for I was not even capable of turning my neck to look at her again. Bent low, I was hurried across the room, then tossed out the door like a rowdy ruffian from a bar.

I lay on the floor.

Panting.

Looking up at Mother Superior Gabriella's champion form.

9

Gaby stood above me like a self-satisfied bouncer hoping that I might start something again. Staggered by the manhandling and believing myself injured, I gulped deeply for lost breath.

"You shouldn't be here, Kyle." After the crazed horror, the chanting, the cries, the blood, the wrestling match, she had the audacity to speak in a matter-of-fact tone. The woman was mad.

"I demand to know what's going on in there — right now!" The ladies who had whisked me out the door stood behind her. Reinforcements.

"That's none of your business, Kyle. It's not for you to know."

"Chantelle's bleeding!" My voice, strident with fear, rose to an indignant bellow. I did not realize just how stricken I was until I tried to move and my limbs disobeyed. My legs wouldn't function. My arms were without strength. "She's hurt!"

"Kyle, now listen." I could not reconcile Gaby's schoolmarm voice with what we had both witnessed. "I know what you saw. Or thought you saw. I can imagine what's going through your mind, but appearances can be deceiving. You must believe that things are not always what they seem. Chantelle's all right. She's not in any danger."

Seated on my rear, looking up at Gaby, rubbing my thighs to encourage them to work again, I mustered whatever defiance was possible from my compromised position. "I saw her, lady, with my two good eyes. Don't tell me that she's not hurt."

She knelt down beside me. "You don't understand the circumstances, Kyle. We'll talk about this later, but right now I have to go back inside . . ."

"I'm calling the police." With a snap as quick as a moray eel's, Gaby knocked me back against the wall as I tried to stand.

"For heaven's sake, Kyle, smarten up!"

Smarten up?

I squirmed free. I climbed the wall to get to my feet. My knees hurt where they'd been trampled, and a thigh muscle had constricted into a knot. Gaby gave me space — though her two henchwomen inched in closer. In a vivid flash I pictured myself pinioned to that bed too, my blood a more vermilion shade than Chantelle's dark crimson, my screams a squeaky falsetto beside her contralto.

Incredibly, behind the door, the chanting had resumed, in essence declaring that my intrusion had been a minor irritation to their murder-initiation rites.

"What'll you do?" I taunted my guards, backing up. I had my doubts as to how well I'd fare under prolonged torture. "Knife me too?"

"God knows this must be hard on you, Kyle," Gaby said. "Believe me, I sympathize. And I appreciate your concern for Chantelle. It's only natural. It's also noble. If this helps, let me remind you that your father knew what goes on here."

"Of course he did." The chanting was gradually resuming its momentum and volume, forcing us to shout. "How could anybody sleep through that screaming?"

"If you respect his memory, bear in mind that he would expect you to wait in your room. It's what he would do."

"Never knew the man."

"Pardon me? I can't hear you, Kyle."

"For all I know he was as sadistic as you."

"Speak up! I can't —"

Screams erupted from the room again, a searing jolt of pain that jarred me where I stood. I rammed past the three women, gained the door, thought I had made it — tackled. Ruthless and efficient, they pinned me face down, and Gaby and another woman each sat on my shoulder blades and clasped one arm. The third woman spliced my knees together.

85

"I'm going to tell you something now and you're going to listen to me."

"Get off! Let go of me! I'm warning you! Get off my back!"

"Kyle —"

"Shut up!"

"You shut up!"

"I can't breathe!" I gasped.

"Sheryl, give me your sash."

"No! Don't do it, Sheryl! I'm calming down, I'm calming down — see? Don't tie me up."

"I was going to gag you," Gaby admitted.

"Don't gag me! No gag! I'll shut up! Don't gag me, Gaby!"

"All right then," she stated calmly, albeit loudly, while I periodically bucked beneath her. "Don't interrupt. Kyle, understand this as well as you can." I couldn't believe it. My face was on the floor, squished like an orange on a sidewalk. Gabriella was giving me a lecture. "Chantelle is not in any danger. She is having an ecstatic experience. A religious experience, if you prefer. This'll be hard for you to grasp. It's hard for me to explain. Just accept it for now. God's Holy Spirit has come into that room. The wounds are not inflicted on Chantelle," she continued shouting in my ear, "they appear on their own. Kyle, they are the wounds of Christ. She's been touched by God."

"Bullshit! She's hurt!"

"The stigmata, have you never heard of that?"

Gaby's words were both incomprehensible and alarming as, under the robust, heavy clamp of the three women, I lost energy.

"What's happening tonight occurs every Good Friday night. A day early this year, we don't know why. Chantelle relives Our Lord's passion. We're sorry but we had no chance to warn you, we weren't expecting it tonight. Now, listen carefully, Kyle. Concentrate!" To emphasize the urgency of her command, she pulled my head back by the hair. "There is not a blessed thing that you, me, the police, or anyone on earth can do for that child right now. Listen to me!" My struggle to flail free was blocked. Gaby had the hands of a bricklayer. "What Chantelle goes through is what she goes through. It may appear to be agony — I'm sure that it is — but I'm also certain that it is ecstasy. Do you hear me? Ecstasy. It's pain and it's also illumination. What she does not need — ever — is public humiliation. That you have seen her is unfortunate — for you, but more so for her. Don't let her humiliation go any further."

I gurgled for breath. Gaby lifted a portion of her weight off me.

"We'll tie you up until you come to your senses, if that's what you want. It's easily arranged. Bernice is an expert with ropes, aren't you Bernice? Is that what you want, Kyle, a demonstration?"

Fake threat was not Gaby's style. The other women on my back eased up as well, and we waited as my breathing steadied. I used the time to consider both the heresy of her words and my choices. In the end, I caved in, answering her question with resignation. "Don't tie me."

"Let him up."

They pulled me to my feet. I felt both relieved and humbled.

Had my intrusion been a humiliating moment for Chantelle? Had she not turned her blood-stained face to mine — beleaguered eyes; her gaze ponderous and saddened — then retreated from my presence? I hadn't heard her contest my rough treatment.

The fever of her fury had been obvious; so had her shame, her sense of violation. Her screams were those of a torturer's victim, yet no one, when I had glanced in, had been touching her. I had seen no weapons or restraints. Chantelle had turned her back on her rescuer. If the look in her eyes had condemned anyone, it had condemned me.

"I want to see Chantelle."

"You cannot. Not now."

"Later then."

"If she's up to it. And agrees."

"That's not good enough."

"I'll come see you later. Soon as I can. I'll explain what's permissible."

"When will you come?"

"Kyle, later. You deserve that much. Poor you. I really am sorry that you had to experience any of this without preparation."

Not happy to submit, I stood still, immovable, breathing heavily. "I was in Tennessee just the other morning," I bemoaned, injured. "There the dead walk around in their bones like the living. At high noon they snooze on people's lawns. Here the living bleed to death, they don't sleep in their beds, they scream in them. Their friends call it ecstasy." A spasm scaled my back and shot through my arms. "Take care of her, Gaby. I'm holding you personally responsible."

"Responsibility accepted. Though she's really in the hands of God."

"Come soon," I demanded of Gaby, my gruff instructions a vain attempt to save face. "Talk to me soon."

"The minute I can get away."

Conscious of hazards in the dark, I returned to my room. Alternately grim, then anxious, I experienced fits sitting in my chair. Three times I rose and with my fists walloped the bed. I sat in a heap on the floor like a discarded, obsolete machine. Waiting. Just holding on. Blocking my ears to the primitive savagery of the music, trying to blot out a brain vexed by sordid imaginings.

Whenever Chantelle screamed, I heard myself groan also.

10

Pop, you were in on this? Gaby implicated you, said you knew what went down. Is this why you enticed me here with an illusion of prosperity? Irked that I would outlive you, you arranged for me to be fed to your harem of cannibals? Why? What's the grievance? I should have stayed in Walkerman's Creek where skeletons on Sundays do the Tennessee waltz.

The screaming gradually became less frequent and the chanting subsided. The nuns' batteries were wearing down. Eventually the wind outside beat more loudly and consistently than the indoor racket.

In another hour, I answered a knock.

"Chantelle!"

"May I come in?"

Exhaustion hung on her like sackcloth. In my palm I received the weight of her bandaged limb. Her eyes had dried, she'd washed and changed clothes, so that only the copious wrappings around her hands and wrists indicated anything untoward.

"I wanted you to see for yourself that I'm all right."

In white, she appeared angelic.

"Are you? What . . . what's going on?"

"Kyle . . . I'm tuckered out. Sheryl and Bernice . . ."

"My guards."

". . . they're bushed too. Please . . . trust me. Don't make any phone calls or interfere. I'm really sorry about tonight. What happened was unexpected. We had no time to warn you. I guess we hoped you'd go to sleep and let us be."

"Gaby said . . . the stigmata."

"People require a name for things." Her tone was infused with regret. "Words give them dimension, they feel they have power. Knowledge. The stigmata — yeah, okay, but don't hold on to preconceptions about that. Especially . . . misconceptions about me. I mean . . . Kyle . . . I'm no saint. And . . . I'm not such a freak, either."

Not for a second did she disengage her eyes from mine. Being angry with myself for not having a concrete response made my predicament worse; her gaze begged me not to be repelled by the memory of her ordeal.

"Are you sure you're all right? What about a doctor? Your hands."

Her strength did falter, a surface crack in her will and deportment. Ever so slightly her lips trembled. Protruding from the gauze, the tips of her fingers located the doorknob. Chantelle did not, and perhaps could not, speak again; nodding slightly, like a will-o'-the-wisp she vanished.

The silence of the night hummed in my bloodstream.

I stumbled across the narrow floor. Collapsed on the bed. Surrendered to waves of weariness. Good Lord, whatever was going on? A few hours ago Chantelle had been in torment, bridled by hysteria, her body lanced. No valid explanation or logical cause. Half hoping that Gaby might still visit and set the record straight, I willed myself to stay awake. As if sleep was a possibility.

After a while it hit me that, even though I was sprawled on the bed, I had successfully resisted sleep. Couldn't nod off if I tried. As a rule, that's impossible for me, and I had to concentrate to remember when I had last slept. Eyes wide open like a cadaver's, I feared ever sleeping again.

Isabelle, my sexy sage in Walkerman's Creek, had proffered, "Know what your trouble is?"

"Spill the beans, Is."

"You were raised under the evil spell of your parrots."

"Evil, Issy? Isn't that going too far? My parrots were okay birds, sort of."

"As birds. As role models they left something to be desired. See, the parrot is the emblem of imitation. Which is what you are: the magnificent imitator, without the colors. One day you're a swallow, the next a thrush, but never Kyle Elder, person. Imitation summons no creative energy of its own, so it's a style of lethargy that leads to paralysis. You're becoming a slumbering, petrified tree, Kyle. *You* don't whistle, just the birds in your branches do."

I told Issy that the world outside was beyond my ken.

She sympathized. "Sing to me, Kyle, before we make out. I want to be seduced by a song tonight. It's romantic."

"A *human* song? Sorry, I can't sing those."

"Yodel."

"Perfidy."

Preferring to issue her one-word indictment than knock, Mother Superior Gabriella swung the door shut behind her. Gaby's disheveled appearance suggested that she had tussled with another intruder after me, and the self-control that she had exhibited earlier in subduing my rage had since taken a drubbing.

In the faint pallor of the bedside lamp, her skin bore a whitish cheesy texture of the sort induced by an encounter with a poltergeist. Now she looked like a ghost herself. She stared toward the window.

"On this Night of Nights Our Lord warned that He would be handed over to His Tormentors. On this Night of Nights He prophesied the Fatal Kiss. This night of Perfidy. This hour of Deceit. This moment of Truth." Gaby turned and focused her glare on me. My silence incriminated me. Either that or the fearful submission of my posture inspired her conclusion. "Betrayal."

I did in fact feel guilty. My tryst with Chantelle in the stables, however innocent, adopted depraved, malevolent proportions. My secret cache of bones might as well have been under my pillow. I cowered.

In the narrow enclosure of my father's room I had no place to hide, no clear lie to incant, and insufficient energy to fabricate denials. Gaby looked down upon me with the confidence and acuity of the hawk eyeing the field mouse.

"As Our Lord had revealed, the hand of Man would dip bread with Him into the dish. The hand of His Betrayer. The hand of

Judas Iscariot was the hand of Man, the embodiment of declared human will, the sorcery of Sin."

All right already! I'll confess!

I'm the wickedest little shit who was ever flushed out to sea!

Yet I learned that a description of my sins would have to wait, for I had noticed a gesture of Gaby's that further complicated the situation.

At first I had believed that she had pressed a hand to her heart, willing the pain and suffering there not to burst her mortal capacities. But that wasn't it. Gaby was holding her left breast. Rhythmically she squeezed the heavy globe, and, while she studied a spot on the wall, one finger agitated the clothed nipple back and forth.

I watched the nipple expand under her touch, poke against the gown.

Another thought struck home. I was not the intended victim of her accusation. She had not come into this room to condemn me, easy as that might have been. My wounds she would willingly leave to fester. No; Gaby was here to arouse and condemn herself.

"Perfidy. Sacrilege. Deception," she chanted. "Kyle, I loved your father, more than he ever knew. I loved him with all my soul and with all my heart. Body too. What I did I did because I cared for him. You must believe that! God! How wicked we are! Our hands unwashed. Our lives unclean. Look!"

Her right palm thrust forward. Splotched red.

"The stigmata?" A contagious affliction? Speaking for the first time my voice was no more than a faint quaver. I yearned to be back in Tennessee, asleep in the rain, unaware of anything except the racket on the leaky roof and the appearances of skeletons on the village green.

"No! Chantelle's blood! Your father's blood! The blood of deception! The blood of subterfuge. Of . . . of . . . the blood of perfidy! Of — betrayal! How we betray each other! How petty our lives! How helpless — hopeless too — our cause."

The grief I had been avoiding since we had first met spilled over. Without warning, Gaby wildly swung out her hands and a clenched fist decked me. I sat down on the bed, holding my sore nose.

"What exactly *is* your cause?" I asked, blinking through the pain.

"What?" The sharp gasp of her response was a real scare, for it indicated that Gabriella had scarcely been conscious of my presence.

"Your cause. What is it?"

Gaby sighed, heaving great burdens. She lifted the hem of her robe to wipe her bloody hand dry on the cloth, performing the task with the alacrity and thoroughness of a criminal scrubbing fingerprints from a weapon. "Love" was her final testament. "Only that. Just love. We've failed miserably." She slumped down beside me.

"Gaby —" I stuttered, wanting to console, to end this fiasco. I was now less interested in making sense of things than I was in concluding them. Who are these people? What am I doing among them? I wanted sleep.

Without preamble, Gaby jumped to her feet and untied her sash, then pulled it through the two belt loops. Various images sputtered to mind — that she intended to tie me up after all, and would call in Bernice to secure the knots, or that she'd weave a hangman's noose. Functional macramé. I was baffled when she simply tossed the belt across the bedside chair.

Without the sash, her robe fell straight down.

"Kyle."

Despite the harsh consonant of my first initial, she contrived to mew my name.

"Gaby?" I've been around. I was wary.

Her hemline slowly lifted, revealing calves, knees, mid-thighs.

"Gaby."

The motion was protracted, but not tentative. She was allowing me to grow accustomed to the idea.

"*Gaby!*"

The white of her hips, at eye level, dominated my view. As her head disappeared under the folds of her ecclesiastical gown my attention was galvanized on the black patch of her pubis. The gown came off in a flurry. Gaby stood stone naked before me. White breasts listing to each side. Once again my astonishment left me incapacitated: I sounded no alarm. I was not prepared for any of this, neither her display nor the crucible of her request.

"Make love to me, please, Kyle."

Shazam. Double and triple shazam.

The situation was too far gone. My one hope required initiative, device, and a calculated forcefulness. "Gaby, for God's sake." I muffed it on all three counts. My voice too weak. I dared not stand, the room was too small for both of us to be on our feet without risking contact, yet below her on the bed I was awkwardly positioned. A stationary target.

"What sort of nun are you anyway?" I demurred, sparring for apology.

"A real one," she maintained. She sat down (my cue to stand), then lay down on the bed. "We're more real than the dolts in convents."

Stretching out, she arched a leg. Against will and inclination my body was responding. I'd been chaste too long. To fortify my position I turned the desk chair around, sitting so that the bars of the backrest divided us. I tried not to stare at the hand that fondled a breast again. A blue breast in the desultory light.

A hand wandered like a vagrant between her legs.

I gawked.

Both thighs inched apart, and desire moved through me like a drug. Thinking, "God, no, no. Not this too." I had been uprooted, bequeathed a mansion, elevated in social status, given a business; I had fallen in love, been deprived of sleep, and terrified to my core all in the same day. Please, not this, not desire too.

"Kyle." Her voice softened as she touched herself, her eyes glimmering. "This is the night of perfidy. Murderers, she called us. Chantelle, her mystical voice called us condemned. And she's right. We're doomed. Every one of us, forever doomed. Damned for this for all time. For betrayal. I loved your father, Kyle. I loved him. A love that made me cruel. Kyle, Kyle, for God's sake, take your clothes off, what are you waiting for? Lie down beside me. Touch me, Kyle." This last spoken through clenched teeth.

Chantelle loomed in my mind. Her image was inescapable. Chantelle in the stables. Delectable and bubbly, perplexed and daring. A chaperone to her passion. Chantelle on the bed. Bleeding.

Gasping through unreasonable pain. Chantelle in my room. White and peaceful, yet frightened and restrained. Chantelle laughing, Chantelle crying, Chantelle spinning away from me with her nosebleed. I was not involved in the nuns' games; I stood outside their precepts. Night of betrayal, maybe. For them, for Gaby, perhaps for Chantelle: not for me. Chantelle kissing me, Chantelle turning away from me, ashamed to be seen in her hour of ecstasy and distress. I would not plunder the secret, marvelous, mystifying contact our mutual attraction had provoked. That covenant was more poignant than the lolling nude woman before my eyes.

Gaby's performance was erotic and a part of me responded, but I've never put great stock in the impulse as an agent for good decisions. "Get out," I told her, more blunt than I intended to be, but somewhat out of control myself. I pulled her robe out from under her knees and threw it across her middle.

"Oh. Kyle. No. God. Please. Don't do this. Not now. Don't do this to me *now*. Not tonight, Kyle, don't —"

"Sorry, Gaby. You have to leave. It's best. Please and thank you."

"No, Ky —"

"Out!"

My uncompromising rejection of her had an impact. Indignation supplanted passion. Gaby twirled her garment about trying to locate the hem. Eventually she wrestled the robe over her head and, when she reappeared again, tears wetted her cheeks.

"Damn you." If she wanted to rail at me to disperse her shame, I'd let her.

I did my best to shore her up. "Forget about it, Gaby. It's been one helluva night. Any other time — who knows? We'll talk about it tomorrow, once we've all regained our senses."

"Is that such a good thing?" She fitted her toes into her sandals. "Coming to our senses? I think not." Grimly, she wrapped the sash around her midriff.

"The timing was all wrong."

"Maybe you're a fruitcake. Like boys? Or is sex too messy for this sensitive child who sings to the birdies? Maybe I'm too much woman for you, huh?"

"Maybe, Gaby. Good night."

"Good night, prick."

I had done the right thing.

For good or for bad, I had behaved like a goddamned innkeeper.

Sleep was a lost cause. Sanguinary images of Chantelle floated loose whenever I shut my eyes. Or I felt bones between my teeth. The thought that repeated itself incessantly was, "This place is too insane. You can't stay here either, Elder. This place is much too insane."

That indictment might be true for the rest of the world as well, but I wanted out. I even considered returning to the death valley of Tennessee.

11

An ancient ship on a forgotten voyage, Toll House creaked through its slumber, relinquishing periodic telltale snores, coughs, and, thrice, the gurgle and swoosh of a toilet. Captain of the watch throughout the night, sitting with the window opened a crack to admit fresh air and the morning banter of birds, I maintained my vigil against calamities unknown.

Dawn's song was largely restricted to the buzzy dullness of sparrows and the bullying *cah! cah!* of crows. A marked change from the Tennessee chorus which had been awakening me for the past fifteen years. The forest was limited to species that had wintered here or were migrating early, and, missing the tweet and chirp of old friends, I felt a simple sadness. I felt stranded. A pine grosbeak — a young male pilfering seeds from the feeder outside — perked my spirits, and he was soon joined by others of his family. A flock of goldfinches switched trees, the mountains were awakening, and the disquiet of my solitude seemed to lift.

Thank goodness for the early sightings, for I'd spy no more birds that day. A thick, undulating fog rolled up from the valley like a sleepy employee reporting late for work, to be joined by a derelict gray cloud that wandered across from the neighbouring hill and squatted on my mountain. A dumpy, drizzly, dreary day. A fester of grievances. I intended, after breakfast, to sleep through several eternities.

Taking advantage of the early hour and my wakefulness to wash and shave, I returned chipper and reasonably shipshape to my bedroom. Familiar routine put the night's mania at a distance, as though the occurrences had been a vivid, powerful dream now difficult to recall. "My guests will not be here forever" was the theme of the pep talk to myself. Delirious though it may be, my infatuation with Chantelle must inevitably recede. Surely, I told myself, if I can survive bouts with pugilistic nuns, I can successfully persevere from here on in. Compared to guests who bleed, guests who complain about the service will be a snap.

Confident that my prospects were secure, I rested quietly on my bunk. Alarm clocks rang at brief intervals throughout Toll House, followed by the shuffling feet of groggy nuns lining up for the water closets. When a bell tinkled like a delicate chime in a draft I thought we were due for morning prayers. The prisoner-like tromp down the staircase followed by the bump and grind of chairs indicated that I was wrong; the signal had been Hazel's.

Such a simple, glorious feast, breakfast. Bacon 'n' eggs. Toast 'n' coffee. Buttermilk pancakes, yummmm, with pure Vermont maple syrup. Scrumptidelicious. The aroma wafted into my room, into my pores, into my soul. Feed me, Hazel! Atta girl! I've been starved for food like that since the day I was born!

Up and at 'em.

At the top of the landing I was nearly run down by Sister Sophie. She'd come up the stairs six at a time, and we each performed a convoluted jig, both to prevent a collision and, more importantly, to preserve the hot tea in the cup she was carrying.

"I'll take that." Gaby spoke. She had been standing outside the washroom door with her back to me, wearing a conventional blue terrycloth robe. I had not recognized her. Sophie handed her the teacup.

"Hazel said to tell you," Sophie tacked on the reminder, and paused in mid-sentence to catch her breath, "it's Darjeeling."

"Thank you." Gaby passed judgment on me with a scornful glance.

"Are you sure that's all you want?" Sophie sounded tentative, as if she was as fearful as I that Gaby might strip down to bare breasts and boxer's trunks. Lover or fighter or Mother Superior: which was she this morning?

"Positive. Don't worry about me." Which was all the encouragement Sophie needed to head back downstairs. I started to follow her, but Gaby stopped me short with a sardonic "Good morning, Kyle".

Stuck.

How was I to respond to these people? Was I expected to forget all that I had witnessed the night before? While I'm not antagonistic by nature and prefer to avoid confrontations, neither am I adept at subterfuge; I couldn't pretend that nothing extraordinary had occurred.

"Good morning," I allowed. Nothing more than that, a cool exchange punctuated by the washroom door being opened from the inside. Out stepped Chantelle. The floor on which I stood was either a high springboard or a pirate's plank from which I leapt into an emotional sea.

Gaby's eyes switched from me, to Chantelle, and back again. A halfhearted smile emerged as a sneer. "Here, sweetie," she said to me. "Hang onto this until I'm out." She passed me the cup and saucer. "You're the innkeeper" she flung over her shoulder as she went into the bathroom; "make yourself useful." She never said boo to Chantelle.

Color, perhaps instigated by her embarrassment, had returned to Chantelle's face, which was a relief. Today she wore a white print dress, celebrated by a mauve and azure diamond pattern that, gathered at the waist, tumbled down from her hips. Her cardigan also was white, and made her bandages less obvious. Her fingertips peeked from under the gauze like spring buds from a field of snow.

"Hi," Chantelle chirped.

"Good morning." My question stuck in my throat for a moment, for it was neither trivial nor routine: "How are you?"

"Fine. Fine."

"Good," I agreed, and, in deference to her repetition, said again, "Good."

"I'm sorry for the scare last night, Kyle." To confirm her regret she touched my wrist with her bandaged hand. I shivered. "Really."

"That's okay. Well . . . it's just that . . . I wish —" Who could help me phrase the questions? How do I probe events so bizarre?

"Un-unh, Kyle. Not now. Let's just go down for brekkie."

Without speaking, I gazed into her eyes. An effort to penetrate her secrets. This was the situation I wanted to avoid, the pretense that nothing had happened, that life among these women was commonplace. I wanted the truth to be spoken because not knowing was scarier.

"Don't be disgusted with me," Chantelle stressed. Not indicating shame this time, her statement was a precise command.

Involuntarily I flexed my shoulders, releasing the spell. "Of course not," I hedged.

"Shall we descend into Hazel's lair?"

Gaby emerged from the washroom at that moment. The scrub had not improved her haggard appearance. Weepy eyes. Tufts of hair sticking out all over her head. Accepting the Darjeeling, she looked at us both with frank dislike, sipped, and trotted off down the hall.

"On one condition," I stipulated.

She smiled. "Name it."

"We sit together."

Chantelle hooked one of her wounded wings through the crook of my elbow, turned me around, and sallied, "That's easy!" Together we traipsed down the stairs.

We seated ourselves by a window at a small circular table with a view of the burgeoning fog.

"A few hours ago," I spoke, "you were screaming in agony. Or ecstasy, whichever. You were bleeding for no reason, and more than the body can bear."

She uttered a brave, self-conscious laugh. "If you think that your situation is awkward," — she saluted me with her juice glass — "imagine how I must feel."

I offered only an ambivalent gesture with my lips.

"Here I am, Kyle, sitting down to breakfast with a man who last night was singing bird songs. That's more than a trifle weird."

"Touché." I succeeded in cracking a smile. Buttered toast was placed before us in an elegant silver rack. While Chantelle may have eased the tension a notch, watching her struggle to spread jam on her bread made me apprehensive again. "Do your hands hurt?" I asked.

She rocked her head from side to side and savored her first bite, picking the crumbs away from the corners of her mouth. "Padre Pio was asked that question. Know what he said? 'Madame, the wounds are not for decoration.' Yes, they hurt. Some. Not too much this morning. I'm lucky."

"Who's he, this padre?"

"Pio. An Italian monk. He died in 'sixty-three. Imagine, Kyle — he had the stigmata for fifty years. Nonstop for all that time. I have to stand it for one day a year — really only one night a year. Pio bled continuously for half a century!"

"Mmmm," I more or less grunted.

"And from his feet too! And his side. He was a mess."

I don't know why, I suppose I was jealous, but it bothered me that Chantelle had heroes. I spooned watery strawberry preserve onto my plate. "Can you —" I scratched my head. "I don't know how to put it. Can you explain the phenomenon? The stigmata?" The jam was tasty. My coffee was poured and we exercised a discreet silence until the waitress was gone from earshot. "It's way over my head."

"Mine too," Chantelle said succinctly. Then she beamed, and speared a dollop of dripped berry off her chin.

"Everybody's upset," she whispered, leaning forward, "because last night was not supposed to happen. I normally have that scene on Good Friday night. We weren't prepared — and your intrusion didn't exactly win friends and influence people. If you come across any grumpy ladies, like Gaby, that's why. How it happened on Maundy Thursday is anybody's guess. Gaby wondered if maybe God lost track. Think of it, Kyle. Contemplate the chaos we're bound to face if God has lost His calendar!"

Love is blind, I've heard it said. A saying I doubt. For love accentuates perception, drives heart and mind to another level of seeing and feeling. Bereft of ordinary explanation, I could not resort to suspicion, I could not condemn the occurrences as a trickster's art because I was enamored of Chantelle.

That she was involved in peculiar rituals was no deterrent, for who more than I was accustomed to women who indulged in strange practices? My mother had coddled pythons; my aunt had raised birds like children and had educated them to speak in tongues. My mother and aunt slept together in a big bouncy brass bed. In Tennessee Isabelle told fortunes and slept with adolescents and mangy dogs. Having never been intimate with a woman remotely interested in a husband and family — or for that matter a straightforward business career — I no longer expected that one day I would. In a sense I was predisposed to Chantelle's aberrations, as distressing and as unfathomable as they were.

Pancakes arrived steaming. I buttered mine generously. Set them afloat on a pond of maple syrup. Chantelle sliced hers up into sixteenths, then nibbled on a single bite. After having lost pints of blood, she was fortifying her system primarily with coffee.

"Talk to me seriously, Chantelle," I pleaded.

"Okey dokey. If you insist. Let's see. I can't really give you any answers, I'm not that wise, so I'll provide you with the questions. How does that sound?" Her tone had a bitter edge, her eyes were uncompromising, and I recognized her despair as mated to my own.

"I'm not choosy."

"Very well. Ready or not. Kyle, for one hundred dollars, tell me, do I endure the stigmata every Easter because I'm an hysterical soul who seeks an outlet in God and finds one in neurosis?"

"I can't answer that. I don't know."

"Or, for one thousand dollars, would you say that I am an hysterical soul so that God can use me as His channel?"

"You're teasing me." Coffee helped rout my panic.

"You're the one who wanted a serious conversation."

"My fault! I know! I take it back. No more questions — for now."

We ate peacefully for a while, and I was cheered to note the gradual return of her appetite. Smiles were our customary form of communication. I was baffled, yet allowed myself to slide comfortably into the sinecure of her presence.

Chantelle said finally, "Had I asked your father those questions, we'd be at it until doomsday. I'm glad you're not like him in *all* respects."

Turning to observe the play of mist about the windowpanes seemed part of the ceremony.

"I inherit an inn from a father I never knew," I recapped. "Nuns arrive. They spring open the bathroom door as a lark, whistle at me in the nude. I meet one of their number who's punchy. Another throws me for a loop. The next thing I know she's bleeding from her pores on the inn's best mattress, screaming her lungs out while her sorority sisters tap their tambourines. How am I supposed to deal with this, Chantelle?"

Chantelle touched my sleeve lightly, the motion of her bandaged hand crossing the table giving me a chill. "The problem is as old as sin, Kyle," she said, in a voice more quiet than a whisper, yet resounding inside my head. "For ten thousand dollars, do the weak embrace God because they require a crutch? Or, for forty thousand, does God reveal Himself to the weak because the artificially strong, those who are self-satisfied, are too involved with themselves? The question behind the questions is only this: for sixty-four thousand dollars, Kyle, does God exist?"

Apparently I was developing tics and spasms. My right shoulder did a quick toad-hop, my left eye blinked at random, my elbow suddenly slipped on the tabletop.

"Does God exist, or do we invent Him? That's the crux of the matter. A few of my friends have their faith on the line this weekend. Am I an hysterical child? Or someone favored to have Him reveal Himself to me? Or both? Or neither? The question's come up because . . ." For the first time Chantelle revealed a measure of the strain she was under. Ever so slightly, her lower lip quavered and the skin around her eyes contracted. " . . . because up to now God has always known what day it is. He's always been able to distinguish between Good Friday and every other day of the year. Few can accuse a neurotic of being that reliable. So if we assume that God in His heaven has a calendar —"

"You're being glib again," I chastened.

" — then the problem must be with me. Which brings up the million-dollar question. The guts of the matter. Perhaps some residual childhood hysteria is all that there is to my stigmata. My bleeding hands. My tears as red as Heinz ketchup."

I — as were others in the room — was shocked when she proceeded to unravel the bandage on her left hand.

"Maybe things are changing," she incanted. "Maybe from now on I'll bleed twice a year. Or bleed forever like Padre Pio. We're all waiting to see what happens tonight. If I bleed, then God is off the hook. He's safe. We'll know that He hasn't gone senile, just increased the burden, twisted the screws another turn. If I don't bleed, then *I'm* on it. The hook, I mean. Though my contemporaries are probably more disposed to nail me to a cross, which has a certain traditional charm.''

Everyone in the room was watching the hand. Shaken by the aggression in her voice I wanted her to stop. As though she was indeed challenging heaven. Let nothing be known or proven. That's what religions are for, to fill that gap. To bridge the known and the unknown with promise. To act as a tour-guide to the mysteries but to resolve none. If her beliefs were a crutch, so what? She was welcome to them. Just don't display a palm that was bleeding for no reason.

Or one, I thought as she displayed it to me, that is not bleeding at all. Chantelle waved it before the room like a flag. Her palm was soft, white. No scabs. Scar free. Certainly no blood. She peeled off her other bandage with the same result.

A woman came up behind her, startling her as she touched her shoulder.

"Leave me alone, Barb."

"Chanty, please —"

"I'm all right." To show that she meant it she affectionately patted her friend's hand, which mollified the woman. Barb returned to her table. The room had fallen into an abject silence, a mournful, fidgety quiet in which no one ate or spoke. The waitresses looked thoroughly confounded. In the days to come I would resurrect that moment, marvel at the quirk of timing that had prepared a pervasive stillness to receive the sudden, grotesque outcry from beyond the room.

Chantelle's astonishment accelerated my own, for in that blink of time I had expected an explanation from her. Hazel was the one who broke the spell, rampaging out of the kitchen, righteously shouting, "Not in the daytime too! This is too much!"

The second scream, muffled, less loud, also from the top of the stairs, indicated, in retrospect, that the victim had come to terms with her crisis, and now merely wanted to communicate her distress. Then she summoned control, calling out, "Come up here! Everyone! Come up here!"

The initial surprise had glued us down; the second call unstuck the nuns and me as we vaulted from our chairs and scrambled up the staircase. I followed Chantelle in the crush of bodies. The beautiful Dierdre, drained of physical motion, awaited our stampede. By the time I made the top landing, she was weeping in the arms of a companion. Without luck I tried to pick my way through the mob; many of those ahead of me were dazed while others cried out. Then I realized that most of them were in my room.

Bullying my way through the crowd, spurred on by rage, I pulled one nun back by the shoulders roughly and elbowed another aside. "Let me through. Let me through!" Chantelle followed in my wake and together we discovered, serenely lying between the sheets of my bed, Mother Superior Gabriella. A floral bouquet adorned her hands which nested comfortably on her chest in an attitude of collapsed prayer. Her empty teacup had been deposited on my nightstand, the teaspoon in the saucer.

In repose, a tranquility elevated the corners of her mouth and a grimace firmly closed her eyelids. As if to facilitate identification, her wavy hair had been brushed off her face. She resembled a middle-aged, athletic Sleeping Beauty awaiting the kiss of her Prince. I did not qualify, and had last night been unequal to the task.

The blanket — my blanket — that had lain unused but rumpled overnight had been neatly folded over the baseboard. The top sheet was drawn modestly to her neck and primly folded back, as though someone had tucked her in. Beneath the sheet, we learned soon enough, Gaby was starkers. And yes, she had indeed gone down for the count.

In due course, the coroner would inform us that Gaby had been poisoned.

BOOK TWO

"The Case of The Deadly Teacup"

1   Surprise, experience has taught me, is woven into the fabric of living. Blanketing lives, routine is a dark shroud under which we suffer the illusion of predictability. As the world swirls in its arcane courses we dither with schedules and duties. Dare; step beyond the perimeter. Alter the regimen. Toss off the cloak of the usual and surprise becomes as accessible as sunlight, the unexpected a breathable air rich with oxygen, though not necessarily pollution-free.

Twice in my life I have picked up my bed and walked. Once to Tennessee; latterly to Vermont. In both instances I blindly sauntered into jeopardy, thrust into a maelstrom of events that swept me away like a twig on a fast-running stream. I'm curious about two things: how the events would have resolved themselves without the complication of my accidental intrusion, and what my life would have been like had I not been conjoined to the fray.

Gabriella's death kindled a *déjà vu* — my introduction into Tennessee had been equally traumatic and just as deadly. Unacquainted as I was with the range and power of surprise, I could not have deduced that my early days in Tennessee not only bore a similarity to my welcome in Vermont, but that the former era would shortly be actively present in the new.

Late in the morning I took a walk into the fog and rain. The mist on the mountains, ideally complemented my mood: introspective, chilled, and damp. Not a day to view the vistas, or to perceive the whole. I had been dismayed by Gaby's dying, and, affected by the reactions of the other nuns, I felt heavy-hearted.

Good thing we had Hazel Stamp to organize us all. Our center, our Gibraltar, she saw to it that the police, a physician, and an ambulance were summoned. She delegated those in control of themselves to comfort the distraught. In the main sitting-room of Toll House, grief and self-recrimination mingled with voices offering solace and courage.

Eventually I escaped out of doors.

I sloshed through puddles and listened to my boots slurp mud, and thanks to the cloud cover I rarely imagined myself on a mountaintop. Balancing on a log I could as easily have been on the bowsprit of a tall ship, plying waters through a fogbank, eyes keen for ghostly vessels and shorelines.

Twin muddy ruts served as the road guiding me higher into the mountains. I dared not go anywhere near the stables. Toll House disappeared from view. I climbed over a rocky knoll and down to a fork in the road, where I hung a left, continuing past a shed crammed with farm implements. A John Deere tractor, fitted out with snowplowing gear appeared to be the principal prize. The path continued down to a smelly dump where garbage lay scattered by the trespass of animals and scavenger birds. Returning to the junction, I carried on along the trail to the right.

The track continued at a steady decline, a roadway that had not been used during the winter. Rain flooded the footprints I made in the snow. The end of the path came unannounced: an abrupt, sheer cliff. Guests strolling this way in the moonlight would never be heard from again. I peered over the edge. The drop was about twenty feet; after that the mountain sank away at about a fifty-degree angle. Unwary hikers out birding would tumble two hundred feet before lodging against a row of substantial boulders. I hoped that I carried plenty of liability insurance.

That's odd. Look there. Arranged like tombstones speckled amid the snow. Parts of automobiles, mainly rooftops and bumpers.

Leaving the trail, I located a way down. A slippery descent over the rocks. Being sheltered from the sun in the cliff's shadow, the snow was considerably deeper here, and had probably been augmented over the winter by the occasional miniature avalanche.

Tough sledding. I made it to where a rear bumper was poking up and wiped away the corn snow. Moisture glinted on the chrome, and I quickly discerned that the bumper remained attached to a car. Further hand-shoveling revealed an aging Buick. All in all, this was not the most convenient of parking lots.

I had entered a graveyard for cars. Apparently my father and his predecessors had not believed in trading up, preferring to push their vehicles until they expired, then propel them over the ledge. Discards from neighbors also seemed to be included as three generations of automobiles lay strewn down the hillside. Small trucks and pickups, old-time roadsters and English sportscars from the fifties, family sedans and a Lincoln Continental that had been demolished in a highway collision were slowly being devoured by the earth. Brushing away their snowy blankets and icy sheets, I was soon soaked while they were baptized by the mist.

In my rudimentary fashion I meditated in this place, the remains of metal and fabric speaking of summers lost, of travel and generations traipsing across continents and down to the beaches, the perpetual unfolding of history layer upon layer over the earth's skin. My quiet moment was illuminated by a bright idea and, happily inspired, with quick long strides I headed back to Toll House.

Yet my plan had to wait, for upon my return Hazel called me in for lunch, and there is simply no denying that woman.

"Sit here," she said. Hazel had prepared a place for me in the kitchen, in a private, cozy nook. A sizable contingent of the nuns was having a bite in the dining-room, and I wanted to see if Chantelle was among them.

"Under the circumstances," I suggested, "perhaps I should be with my guests."

"Sit!" was her cross instruction, and I sat.

Hazel had set two places. "You'll join me?" I invited.

"Don't expect so." From a considerable height, she let drop a bowl of freshly-baked buns. They jumped on the table like rabbits.

"Hazel!"

As she was paying me no mind, I traced the line of her stare. A gentleman unknown to me, a merry specimen who looked as if he had something to sell, was the recipient of her venom. She confided, "Not my sort of company, if truth be told."

"Thank you, Hazel!" the man responded, oblivious to her spite. "Good of you to replenish these famished bones!" He rushed forward extending his open right hand. "She's tracked you down, Mr. Elder, sir. I've been looking for you high and low. How do you do? Isaiah Snow, at your service, young sir. I'm honored to make your acquaintance."

In a wink he sat down across from me, demonstrating a remarkable agility for so portly a figure. His pudgy fingers foraged amid the warm buns, which he broke apart and buttered with zeal. He was clearly going to keep quiet until his hunger was fed. Leaning out to catch Hazel's attention, I asked her pointedly, "Is something the matter?"

I was relying upon her plain talk to forewarn me if this intruder was a nuisance. In sharp contrast to her sensible calm that morning, Hazel stiffened her shoulders and allowed her body language to hurl invective while she kept busy at the stove.

"Salt of the earth," this Isaiah Snow whispered to me. "Don't mind Hazel. It's my fault. She'll get over it."

"What happened?" I helped myself to the bread before it disappeared.

"My sense of humor. Won't be the first time it's run amuck. Hazel's dandy, she can usually take a joke but there are limits. I suggested to her that her Darjeeling tea this morning might have been a speck too potent. She took offense."

"I'm not surprised. Excuse me, but who are you?"

"An old friend of Hazel's, for one thing. We go back. School-days, Hazel?" he asked loudly. "We go back to schooldays? Are you willing to own up to that?" Then he resorted again to the hushed tone. "Not to worry. She'll forgive me. She always has."

Hazel carried over a bean-and-barley broth. The aroma was enticing, and I figured that if she was still willing to feed this jovial yokel, the level of her discontent could not be overly severe.

"Thanks, Haze," my visitor proclaimed in a transparent attempt to restore his standing. "This'll hit the spot."

"I'm surprised you have the guts to taste it," Hazel put in. "If you think my tea's a killer, the soup could be twice as strong."

"Mr. Snow was telling me that you and he are old friends," I interjected.

"*Inspector* Snow," Hazel judiciously informed me, and I noticed the man wince. He had wanted to keep that tidbit secret. "He's police. He *has* no friends." The victor, Hazel resumed her labors with a noticeable swagger.

Snow chuckled under his breath, chiding, "That woman. Always wants the last word."

Though I was annoyed by my defensive tone, I felt that I had no alternative but to attest, "I spoke to the officers this morning."

"Local," he said, waving mention of them away as if they were bothersome flies. "I'm State." He produced a shield, and gave me a moment to gaze down upon it as though cherishing a prized snapshot of the grandchildren. He stuffed the badge away in his front trousers pocket.

For all the wrong reasons, I was wary of this man. "A sorry mess," he commiserated. "What a way to spoil your arrival. Not to worry though, young sir. We'll get everything straightened out. All will be forgotten licketysplit." He blew across his soupspoon.

Admittedly my prejudices hindered acceptance of this man. I prefer my law-enforcement officers to look like cops. Weathered by snowbound stakeouts. Wizened by a decade of traffic control, chiseled by the elements. I like to see them disheveled at the end of their shift through close proximity to riffraff, whereas when they had come on duty they could be spotted for The Man a mile away: ludicrous suits, absurd ties. I like my cops to smell dirty, to have spent so much time scrounging around in back-alley garbage for murder weapons that they had come to enjoy the stench. Rousting derelicts has given them bad breath. I like my cops to look tired around the eyes, to be divorced, to relish a double scotch at noon, and to play touch football with their kids whenever they have weekend visiting privileges. Cops ought to be weary of life, sinister and cynical, still bitter about the solitary letter of reprimand in their file, which had been a crock, and guilty forever about the two or three times a bribe seemed like a reasonable resolution to a conflict. I like my cops to be curmudgeonly and foul-tempered, to affect bad manners and atrocious language. Courtroom formality makes them puke. At their career's end they advise their supervisors where to shove the gold watch. I like my cops to be barbarous beneath a sheen of discipline, to be fair, nine times out of ten to play it by the book, but when circumstances merit they will segregate a hardcase for a facial. I like my cops to have a soft spot for whores, to sleep with barmaids, to play poker with the boys, and to scratch their balls when rising from the dinner table. I like my cops to wear hats indoors.

I do *not* like my cops to smile like Rotarians, to be as cheery as insurance salesmen and comfortably plump, to have capillaries florid on their flushed cheeks from an excess of fine French wine, to wear glasses — I ask you, glasses? — to be well-dressed and well-heeled, or to pronounce with utter glee, "Young sir! I knew the second I laid eyes on you that you were Kyle's boy. My condolences on his passing. Be that as it may, it does happen to us all. Please, call me Isaiah, sir, and welcome to Vermont."

I presumed from his dumb-bunny mannerisms that he could be handled by politeness and false interest. "Have you formed your conclusions about the case, Inspector?"

"Case? Case? Why the melodrama? There is no case. The coroner will formulate his report, a routine inquiry will follow, and the file will be closed. It's a sad business, suicide."

"Then she killed herself."

"Yes. Yes, she did. Suicide is so hard on the bereaved. As a society we really ought to take preventive measures. Any time there's a suicide the family should rejoice, hold a party, dance on the deceased's grave. I think we'd see a dramatic reduction in such occurrences. Take away the aspect of belated sympathy, and you take away what for many people is the major incentive."

"Do you think so?"

"I know so. It'll never happen, of course. We live in a namby-pamby world. So! Since I've bumped into you, might as well seize the day and fire a few questions. Don't mind do you, sir? Routine. Strictly."

A minor warning-shot volleyed through my head. Snow had not "bumped" into me; by his own admission he had arranged this minute apart from the others. I let the premonition pass, having no choice, saying, "Ask away. I'm at your service, Inspector."

"Thank you! Dr. Tanner — who incidentally will be appointed coroner, he always is — he's speculating that the woman was poisoned."

"That's the general consensus. What else could it be? An overdose, maybe?"

"Poison. Which she may have ingested mixed in the tea. The famous tea that Hazel prepared." He had lowered his voice further to stay out of her eavesdropping range. "The teacup was passed from Hazel to Cassie Baxter the waitress to a woman known as Sophie. She brought it upstairs as had apparently been requested by Gabriella Deschenes, and she says, Sophie says, that you were there. Is that true?"

"Everything happened as you say, Inspector."

"Call me Isaiah. We're not so formal in Vermont. So you did witness Gabriella receive the teacup. Did she drink it right away?"

I thought back. "A sip or two, maybe. I think she found it too hot."

"Or not yet to her taste. Were you chatting, Kyle? 'Good morning, how are you, did you have a good night's sleep?' Innkeeper talk. You must do that sort of thing, you know, if you expect to run an inn successfully. How did she seem to you?"

"Seem?"

"Look."

"Tired," I shrugged, recalling her melancholy, but not wishing this talk to go too far. I considered last night to be off-limits. "All right otherwise."

"But not overly distraught, or, shall we say in hindsight, suicidal?"

"I should mention that she gave me the teacup."

"She gave you the tea." The news was received without surprise, indicating to me that he had already spoken to Chantelle.

"Gabriella was waiting for Chantelle — or rather, she was waiting for the washroom, and when a woman came out —"

"This Chantelle?"

"Right. She came out and Gabriella asked me to hold her teacup while she went in."

"Why you, Kyle?"

"I was there."

"Why not Chantelle?"

I shrugged again, dismissing the question as irrelevant. "Gabriella went into the washroom. When she came out she had tears in her eyes."

"So she *was* distraught," Isaiah Snow noted. I had managed to contradict myself. "And you gave her back her tea."

"I did."

"Then what?"

"I went downstairs."

"With Chantelle?"

"She preceded me. No, on second thought, we went down together. I remember that now. We had breakfast together as well."

"Yes, of course. Excellent!" Isaiah cried with undue excitement, as if happy to fit the pieces of the puzzle together and glad to see me prosper as a businessman. "Good corporate relations! You must dine with your guests on occasion. And then?"

I had nothing more to contribute. "We heard a scream during breakfast. We went upstairs —"

"— and found a woman dead in your bed."

"It was quite a shock, Inspector."

"A humdinger! Did you have a big breakfast?"

"What?"

"It's the timing I'm trying to nail down."

"Yes. A large breakfast. For me. I didn't have time to finish it."

"A pity. And why did this woman choose to die in your bed, Kyle?"

"How should I know?" I lost my cool for an instant. "I don't even know the woman."

"Give me an educated guess. You did speak to the woman yesterday, did you not?"

"Yes, I believe I did," I hedged. Not sure how much he had been told, I did not want to open the door to self-recrimination. "But I spoke to a number of my guests."

"Bully for you. You sat with Gabriella at dinner, no?"

"Right. I did, now that you mention it, Inspector."

"Call me Isaiah."

"Isaiah."

"And during the night, did you have occasion to speak to the dead woman then?"

"She was very much alive at the time." What had the nuns revealed? Had an errant spy reported Gaby's indecent exposure in my bedroom?

"So you did speak with her."

"Oh, perhaps. Briefly."

I was running in circles in a quest for answers. I did not want to have to explain that one of my guests bled from her eyes, that others whistled and stomped, or that I had allowed myself to be a prisoner in my own quarters, a meal for a madwoman's lust.

"In the middle of the night, Kyle? Do you intend to wake up your guests for conversation in the wee hours on a regular basis?"

"No, Inspect — Isaiah. No. We simply passed in the hall. Near the john. I can't remember what was said. Pleasantries."

"You seem to spend a lot of time hanging around the john."

"We don't have private baths, Inspec — Isaiah. This is an old-style country inn."

"True. But according to our friend Hazel, considerable cater-wauling was going on. What was that about?"

"Beats me. I was asleep. I'd had a long day, driving up here and all."

"You were awake going to the john, weren't you?"

"The house was quiet then."

"Then?"

"Maybe Hazel had a nightmare" was my foolish conjecture.

"Salt of the earth, that woman," Snow censured me, a sharpness to his tone reverberating in our nook. "And you can't speculate on why she chose to die in your bed?"

"Haven't a clue."

"Good grief!" he shouted, as if the possibility had dawned on him for the first time. "Maybe we do have a case! 'The Case of The Deadly Teacup'! What do you think?"

"I thought *I* had an overactive imagination." I now feared this jocular potentate.

"Six people had opportunity to poison the tea. Hazel, the Baxter girl, Sophie, you, Chantelle, and the victim herself. Crikey, I feel like Sherlock Holmes!"

Timidly, I laughed along with him.

"I guess you have your work cut out for you, Isaiah."

"All thanks to you, Kyle." The suggestion made me flex backward with alarm. What had I said? "Listen, I just had a nifty idea. Oh! This is wonderful."

"What?" Aware that he was playing games with me, I found keeping up an amiable front difficult.

"We're trying out some new-fangled polygraph equipment in town. The manufacturer sent it to us on spec'. I'm under orders to try it out. This'll be our chance to give it a whirl! Service in the field! We give the machine a thorough shakedown and you get to clear your name."

"What's wrong with my name?" I demanded, boisterous at last, believing that it was time to get my hostile back up and to quit trying to ingratiate myself.

"Oh. Nothing at all. I put it badly. I don't suspect you of a thing, but you know how it is. We're insular folk beneath our genteel surface and you're the stranger. Rumors might fly. Bad for business. Kyle, we can cut the idle slander off at the knees. Will you do it, young sir? You and your guests, and your employees, have pretty well related the same story. The pieces fit. Better I drag you in than inconvenience them. In a sense, I'll be using you to test everyone else. Really, we need to experiment with the equipment and the result will convince my superiors that this matter is open-and-shut. Prove to the community, Kyle, that your story holds water —"

"What story? What's going on here? I don't *have* a story! I'm not involved."

"Exactly! Let the polygraph confirm it! Some people call them lie-detectors; I call them truth-verifiers. More positive. It'll be the ideal test for our machine, Kyle. The truth of the matter is" — and my inquisitioner had lowered his voice to the most confidential level, even though Hazel had not returned and we were alone — "some people accuse me of being an old-fashioned codger. I'm trying to prove that I can stay in step. I actually have a computer at home. Haven't used it, of course. But it's sitting there."

Nodding, I munched on a wedge of rye bread served with onion, cheese, and bacon. When I met my interlocutor's eyes again, I elected to dispense with the charade. "I'll take your test," I informed him.

"Marvelous." He had engaged my stare.

"Because I have nothing to hide."

"Of course not. Although you are defensive about something, that's obvious. Everyone else is too."

"I also intend to call my lawyer."

"That's perfectly acceptable," the inspector remarked. He thumbed through the pages of an agenda to come up with a suitable date and time, and added with an intensity equal to my own, "And not altogether unwise."

I also like my cops to be less audacious than Inspector Isaiah Snow.

In anticipation of difficulty, I brought along a shovel on my excursion after lunch. Likely I drew a fair amount of attention to myself, for to ascend the first small hill in my old Mercury required six attempts. Tires spun in the muck. Black smoke belched from the exhaust. The engine sputtered, spat, and the valve-clatter was horrendous. Finally the motor roared as if cottoning on to the circumstances: this was its last journey. I was putting the wretched brute out of its misery. Skidding, churning, slipsliding and cackling, we made it up that first slick rise.

The next stretch was more easily accomplished. In low gear with one hand on the shift to keep it from jumping, the car accepted my guidance without serious complaint, soon mastering the gradual slope. Sorrow welled through me, for I was dispensing with a considerable chunk of my life. That's how I felt. This token ritual necessary to enter fully into my new world. Junk the car. Add it to the pile of rusting relics. Combine my history with my father's. Say goodbye to the old and defeated, welcome the coming age riding a Cherokee Chief.

Ahead, a steep grade afforded minimal traction, and I stopped to evaluate the situation. I memorized a map of the deepest puddles and the soft shoulder, and calculated exactly where I should zig, accelerate, and zag. Having walked the course, not unlike an equestrian before a horse trial, I returned to the Mercury and strapped myself in. That was the moment that I spied Chantelle in my outside mirror. Coming my way. After discovering Gabriella, I had been unable to segregate her from the others, and had taken my walk in the rain. At last she was alone. I stepped out of the car and, harboring a brave smile, Chantelle came into my arms.

"I'm so sorry," I consoled her, "about Gaby."

Her distress showed in her damp eyes and trembling lips. "I can't bear it right this minute, Kyle. Please let's talk about something else."

"Sure." The other issues on my mind would not concur with her mood either, I suspected. "What?"

"I don't know. Anything. Something." She walked away from me to think. Spinning, her skirt flared above her knees. She asked, "What on earth are you up to, Kyle?"

I told her, she offered to help, and under the circumstances we had a wonderful afternoon, sustained by the fresh air and the mountaintop's foggy peacefulness as we pushed and shoved that automotive dinosaur, muddying our feet, legs, and hands, marinating in the heavy humidity. The perfect excursion to kill a few sad hours.

My mental gymnastics and motoring skills failed to prevent the ol' Merc' from finding the deepest gully in sight in which to bury both right tires. We exhausted ourselves trying to dig, push, and cajole it loose. Eventually, we rested for a breather and a chat.

"Own up, Kyle. Spill the beans. How did you ever become a singing bird?"

"I was raised in an aviary," I explained at the outset. "My Aunt Emma, who wasn't really my aunt but that's a whole other kettle of fish, she put on shows with tropical birds that could talk. You know what I mean: they had a vocabulary, stock phrases. I was part of her act."

"So you started in show business early," Chantelle deduced.

"If you want to call it that. I grew up talking English to birds, so communicating with them never seemed to me like an outlandish thing to do. At a certain point in my life that changed. An incident occurred, one which drove home the understanding that speaking their language would be a greater feat than being a straight-man to their humor. I mean, aren't we humans supposed to be the intelligent species?"

Taking our ease, we sat on the trunk of the Mercury. The rain had ceased, mist scudded about the treetops, and clouds wafted upward or were deflated in immense waves. I was wearing the heavy, steel-toed workboots that had served as my feet for the last five years, while Chantelle wore cowgirl boots, tall brown leather with a floral filigree. Dampness further chilled the cool air, and we had assumed matching postures with our arms wrapped around ourselves and our hands sheltered under our biceps. The cold had stiffened my lips, so I slurred my words. My biggest disappointment was a runny nose that I was obliged to mop with my jacket sleeve.

"What happened to precipitate the change?" Chantelle inquired. An awkward formality. We remained unsure of one another. The question she asked of me I wanted Chantelle to answer about herself. She must have known that. I was inspired by the belief that to reply to her query first would help her to grow accustomed to the idea of revealing herself, that she needed that sort of encouragement to be intimate with me.

"Not a happy day," I remembered. "Mom, or my Aunt Em, one of them was out back hanging laundry on the line, while I was playing in the yard. Suddenly, we heard a terrible cry. A purple martin got caught in the wheel of the clothesline, at the end away from the house, high up on a pole. The poor bird was crying out and flapping its one free wing. Neighbors came out for a look, but nobody knew what to do. They didn't want the bird injured more than necessary. Pulling back the line seemed reasonable to me, but the adults contended that that would damage the wing further. Better if someone climbed the pole and pulled the line away from the pulley. I was eager to do just that.

"Anyway, here we are, arguing like mad, me saying that I could do it, my mother telling me not to dare and swatting me whenever I wander too close to the pole, and someone else running off to find an able and willing teenager. While we're waiting — and it's a dreadful scene, my Aunt Em is hysterical, the bird is practically ripping off its own wing — a cat, a bloody cat, goes up the pole. Now we have no choice. Mom pulls back the line, which does sever the wing. As predicted. The bird falls on the ground on the other side of our fence, and before I can get to it, the bloody cat has scampered back down. It's the same bloody cat who usually can't get down a pole without help from the fire department. This time it snatches the half-dead martin away. I chased the cat up a tree, but I could only watch it maul the bird. I guess I was nine or ten at the time. A susceptible age for learning important lessons."

Chantelle rubbed her eyes to relieve a residual soreness, whether from crying over Gaby's death or from bleeding the night before I did not care to ask. She nodded, saying, "I can see where that was a startling experience, but what's the lesson?"

"The cat enjoyed its snack, but I noticed that other birds were making a racket. The purple martins nested in a crack in the wall of a garage, close to the tree, and they began to harass the cat. I'm not kidding," I defended against her skeptical expression, "they dive-bombed that bloody feline. Before long they evicted it from the tree and they were pursuing it down the lane. Martins are fierce fighters. They're fearless! They're incredible fliers. They pestered that cat to distraction. The cat was humiliated, confused, and, by the time they broke off their buzzing, utterly depressed. I thought that was great. I shot off home; my mother was calling. I stepped into the kitchen and Bish, our talking myna bird, said to me, 'Shazam! Shazam!' One of his favorite expressions. I was too young, of course, to articulate my instincts, but it struck me that I felt a greater affinity with the birds out back who lived bird lives and sang birdsongs, than I did for the birds in the house who chatted in English and sang 'Amazing Grace', but who knew nothing about birdlife and were never really accepted as being human either."

Amused, Chantelle wrapped both her arms around one of mine, a gesture full of grace and affection. "So you decided to talk bird."

"Something like that. I decided that I had more in common with the birds outside than I did with my indoor pals, even though the birds indoors spoke my language. Bish was a complete idiot."

We were quiet a while. I waited for Chantelle to speak about herself. That expectation hung in the air, I figured that I had jumped through enough hoops, but the focus of her thoughts remained on me. "I wonder if there wasn't something else to it as well, you know?"

"Like what?"

"I'm never satisfied with one-dimensional explanations. Life just isn't like that. Meanings are arrived at in layers, don't you think? Onion skins. Peel away one, there's another. Each layer makes you cry a little more. Each layer hints at the layer beneath it."

"Yeah," I agreed. "I know what you're talking about."

I did, too. The evidence was everywhere. The sky layered in cloud and mist, in shades of gray. The woods detailed with snow, ice, water, and last year's leaves. We were sitting on my car which had twenty years of misery ground into its paint. The finish was beyond Turtle Wax.

"I can imagine," Chantelle continued, "that your birds drew a lot of attention. More than you did, let's say. So perhaps your child's mind ascertained that you could get your share of attention — love, that is — if you sang like a bird, the same way that the birds talked like humans."

I took some time to mull over her words before answering. "I can't deny that what you're saying is valid. But the thing is, I became more keenly aware of birds after the purple martin incident. I saw birds as courageous. I envied their freedom and sympathized with their problems. And it's true that by then I was adept at identifying species and could whistle a few tunes. Singing their music came more naturally to me than, say, arithmetic, or hockey. So, yeah, maybe I had sensed, even before I ever thought it out, that behaving like a bird might float me through life on the smoothest breeze possible. Maybe that's true."

I believed at the time that I had passed one of her tests; my willingness to accept difficult truths about myself and hone in on another level of possibility convinced Chantelle that she could reveal something of her own self to me. Tit for tat. Except that her profane tale engulfed mine, and I felt silly to have confided nothing more than the unfortunate suffering of a bird.

The pivotal occurrence in Chantelle's youth had been horrific. She related her skimpy knowledge of the event without embellishment or accent, keeping herself under strict control while my imagination reeled from the grotesque possibilities.

"What I do know for sure is limited," she told me. "I was eleven. An only child. I remember the motorcycles, the violent gunning of the engines while I tried to sleep. Today I still cringe at the sound of one. I remember hearing my father outside demanding that they be quiet. He was usually gruff with other children and that was the voice he used. I remember that we were in a small trailer, by a lake, on summer vacation. That I had been swimming that day. My dry skin felt itchy. I remember my mother's smile in the sunlight as she lay on the beach and my father charred the hamburgers and then said that that was how they were supposed to be cooked. About that night, I remember the moths against the glass, and the coming of the motorcycles."

"What happened, Chantelle?" She had seemed to be drifting away from me. I was not impatient with her story, I merely wanted to remind her of my presence, and evoke a note of sympathy. She briskly rubbed her upper arms, and bundled herself up tighter against the chill.

"The next thing I knew, Kyle, it was no longer night. That's what scared me most of all — at least, that's what I hung my fear on — the disappearance of the night. As though day had arrived by switching on a lamp. Little did I know then that many days had passed, that I had been both delirious and sedated. I was also terrified by the intravenous tube in my arm, I thought it was sucking the life out of me."

She offered a grim, affectionate shrug. "I didn't know what had happened to me, only the pain. Now of course I can figure it out. The funny thing is, that doesn't mean anything to me. Tell me that I was raped, that my parents were butchered — as an adult I went back to the newspapers of the time, my mother was axed, my father was hung from a tree and tortured with burning coals before he died —"

"Oh God, Chantelle —"

"But no," she insisted, clutching my arm, "this is my point. Even hearing the facts means nothing to me. I feel no emotional connection. I remember none of it. Just the moths. The motorcycles. The tinge of anger and superiority in my father's voice. Knowing the facts doesn't make them any more real to me. They're not. They're not real. My brain just won't permit them access. Nothing's remembered. Nothing."

"Chantelle . . . God. I'm so sorry." A huge part of me did not want to hear this. Yet I asked, "What happened to you?"

"I had no family. The authorities discovered that my mother had had a brother who had died. That was it. My mother had been in her late thirties when she married; my father forty-five. I had been their miracle baby. My last grandparent had died when I was about eight. I was taken to a sanatorium to convalesce, but don't read anything into that. It was simply a quiet place in the country with excellent care. Local communities were footing the bill as my situation had aroused widespread sympathy. I know all this because I later researched it.

"In a month's time it was Easter and that's when I began to remember who I was and what I was missing. The Easter eggs set me off. I was Mommy's and Daddy's miracle baby. I had been a religious girl. Bad dreams woke me up in the sanatorium. I screamed and cried out, made the other patients mad at me. On Good Friday morning they were teasing me as we filed into the chapel. During mass I menstruated for the first time. I was so embarrassed, I hid the fact, I didn't know what was happening to me, but the connections to be made were obvious. My parents had gone away. Secret parts of my body had been damaged. Now I was bleeding from the inside out. I was dying.

"The nuns visited me in my bed at a bad time. I'd been mopping up. My hands were all bloody. The four of them immediately dropped to their knees as though they had seen the Holy Mother Herself. A nurse came in and she didn't buy the mystical razzmatazz. She cleaned me up and found the problem, and shooed the silly women on their way."

I placed a hand around Chantelle's shoulder, rubbed her neck lightly, my sympathy enfolding the young child still breathing inside her. "Did the nurse explain things to you?"

"Oh sure. The doctors and the nurses were exceptional, they were very tender and circumspect. I'd never have made it through without them. I was their special case. But what I came to understand consciously and what I believed deep down may have been two different things."

"I can imagine."

Standing, Chantelle worked out a kink in the small of her back. "I was placed in a convent school that year. I liked it there. When Easter rolled around again I went hysterical, the unknown memories broke to the surface as these white, blazing screams. The nightmare of blood, the unspeakable things done to me and my parents — my subconscious mind erupted, a doctor described it as a volcano. In my dreams I'd hear my father lecturing, telling me not to play outside, and the motorcycles would race through my bedroom, and I'd yell at my father, telling him that I didn't, I didn't, I didn't go outside, that I did what I was told. I'd wake up in the worst sort of blind panic."

"No wonder." Really, I wanted her to stop. I'd had enough. This was not a story of a bird's wing severed before my eyes and imbued with a child's mythic sensibilities. Ashamed of my cowardice I let her go on, believing that the least I could do for her was to survive the weaving of this tale.

"How can I put this? Madness was beckoning to me. I could feel myself slipping into this morass, this madness, which terrified and enticed me simultaneously. Yet on Good Friday morning, for no reason, I felt sane again, under control. I felt peaceful. At the mass my hands began to hurt. The sharp pain was a stabbing one, like a needle, I felt faint, I kept rubbing my hands and I grew increasingly dizzy. One of the Sisters made me stop rubbing. I did for a while, then started again. I was praying to Our Lord to take the needle away, to stop my hands from sweating so much. The nun grabbed my hands and held them apart. That's when we both saw that they were bleeding. She brought me outside the sanctuary, hauled me down to the washroom, where she washed my palms. They were unmarked. And the bleeding stopped. I asked her if this was supposed to happen, a normal extension of the woman's curse. The nun kept staring at me, as if she couldn't decide between the strap or giving me a hug. She compromised. She brought me down to the infirmary. The nuns there whispered about me. Then I said to them, "I'm sorry that Mommy and Daddy are dead," and the nun cried, "Holy Mother of God!" She practically screeched. All the nuns jumped around me and two or three fell to their knees. I looked in the mirror. I saw the tears of blood before I felt the pain. Then I was screaming too, because the pain was unreal.

"Stigmata, that's what they told me," Chantelle said. "I was a celebrity in the convent and at school, which was okay with me, frankly. Papal envoys cross-examined me. I don't think I impressed them with my piety. The priests tended to be harsh with me, I was scolded as though I'd committed an indecent act. The nuns would try to soothe me, but the episodes with those insufferable men marked the beginning of my disaffection with the church.

"Ever since I have lived with the occurrence. I know that I have the stigmata because I love God absolutely, and in my suffering I understand that I must love Him more. I also have the presence of mind, and the education, to accept that mine are hysterical stigmata, a direct result of my experience. Which led to my leaving the convent when I came of age."

"How come?"

"The Holy See was angry with me." She nudged me with her shoulder and I noted the twinkle in her eyes. "The church prefers their saints to be dead. Living ones are a nuisance. Witness the fact that a living saint is never recognized as such. Not that I am or ever was a saint, but some of the nuns held out that ambition for me. My Holy Sisters would accept only that the marks were a manifestation of Christ's crucifixion. Any other possibility was blasphemy. Doctors said it was because I was psychologically wounded, nothing more. Neither side could accept both explanations.

"Either the wounds were holy or they were psychological, they could not be both. One would cancel out the other. The only real peace I have known, Kyle, came to me the day — I was about seventeen — when I accepted that I am both an emotional refugee *and* someone singled out by God to be a visionary. I'm both. That is my contradiction and my freedom, and on that contradiction this society of women was formed. We are women of the world, with all the encumbrances, devices, and benefits that that involves, and we are women serious in our relationship to God.

"I've never been the leader of our little group, merely the catalyst. Gaby, chiefly, has kept us going through the years, and your father helped. How can I put this? . . . Gaby ran into a crucial contradiction in her life. She couldn't deal with it. None of us could help her and the more we tried, the worse the situation became. I'm at least partially at fault, unfortunately."

For a few long moments, prelude to confronting me with an unusual challenge, Chantelle gazed at me without remorse. "Like you, I'm a selfish person, Kyle. In terms of how I deal with this world. Also like you, I live in the realm of the unknown, a place where birdsong makes more sense than argument. My wee birds are advising me that I've screwed up again. Maybe, you and I, being the people we are, maybe we were meant to meet. Do you think that that could be true? That God manipulated you into coming here when you did? What I really want to ask is, do you think that you and I could be good for each other? You know, friendly?"

"I think so, Chantelle." To break the mood, I jumped down from the car. "Now! Do you think the two of us can push this cantankerous old wreck up a hill?"

Like glass breaking, Chantelle's voice tinkled in the moist air. "Kyle, I think that you and I can do just about anything."

We managed, and had a high time careening down the opposite side. The brakes may have been functioning in their usual half-hearted style, but the snow and muck yielded to the car's momentum and we went sloshing down the steep slope with only random control. The ditch at the bottom gobbled up the front wheels whole. The rear wheels whirled uselessly in either direction, hurling mud a mile. We heaved and rocked and fretted and became dirtier and wetter. I had a brainwave and fetched the John Deere tractor. Hours on a similiar machine in Tennessee stood me in good stead, I showed off to my girl, and she held on alongside me as the Merc' was released from the sucking mud with immense obscene noises, and we hauled her up the next rise.

The tractor hearkened to this labor as I maneuvered the machine into position behind the car. I gave the vehicle a discreet nudge, then backed up to straighten the tractor's angle of attack. All too much for the ol' Merc'. She would not endure this final indignity. The old buggy gave up the ghost. Seeing the end so near she decided to die with dignity, class, and a touch of flair. She chose to leave this corporeal world under her own steam. Without a second bump from the John Deere, she hobbled forward, and began to roll. She picked up speed. Reaching the cliff's edge in stride, for an instant she appeared to be in flight. Spreading her wings. But no. She tipped forward, succumbed, took a nose-dive into the auto that had had its roof dented several times previously. We were amazed to see the Mercury yaw in the air, perform a handstand, balance like a slab of Stonehenge. She tottered. Crashed down with the hard clamor of a foundry, falling away from the cliff's face bounding off cars, metal on metal, glass on stone, and skidded beyond the other vehicles. She hit a rock deposited by a glacier in eons past; she rolled, lay down on her backside, shifted, and spun her tires one last time as she raced on to automobile heaven.

Exhausted, exhilarated, Chantelle and I celebrated the crotchety old dame's last ride, we hugged each other, and I managed to evolve that contact into a kiss.

"I feel like I'm burying an old friend," I confided in her.

She looked at me quizzically for a moment, then nodded casually. We continued back to Toll House, warm in one another's company, buoyed by our intimacy.

As we reached the parking lot I remarked, "I wonder who owns that yellow Toyota?"

"Pardon me?" My question had startled her.

"See that rusting Toyota? It was here yesterday before you came. One of my employees must own it, but no one took it home last night. Maybe I have a mystery guest."

"Maybe," Chantelle agreed at first. There was a pause, which puzzled me, then she said, "Believe it or not, Kyle, the Toyota's mine. It's *finito bandito*. I left the car here the time I came up when your father was dying. For all it's worth, we might as well bury it too. Let the old buggy die, like another dear friend."

A day to bury companions.

Chantelle had just one more thing to say to me. Perhaps the whole purpose of her walk with me had been to emphasize, "Kyle, you know I don't want to be a side-show, don't you?"

"What do you mean?" I turned to her. I loved her. I wanted to smother her skin with kisses and snuff out her pain.

"You won't say anything about me to the police, or at the inquest. Nothing about last night. I can count on you?"

"Tweedlelee-dee, Chantelle, what do I know? I slept reasonably well last night, heard little, saw nothing at all."

"Thanks."

We entered Toll House together.

2

Thank Providence. At last I was permitted a few hours of peaceful rest, although not before Hazel Stamp put up a fuss. She was kind enough to locate an uninhabited room for me, and, more importantly, guide me there, only to discover that the help had been remiss in its duties. Stains from muddy boots soiled the floor. Cracker crumbs infested the lower bunk.

Cassie Baxter was drawn and quartered while insisting all along that the room had been cleaned; nor had it been rented in weeks.

While the two of them went off arguing I curled up on the upper bunk. Not yet ready to sleep in my own bed, I feared Gabriella's lewd ghost. Nor did I want to disturb the evidence. Alone at last, I tumbled into my dreams in a fashion similar to my Mercury vaulting over the ledge into pastoral oblivion.

After dark, Cassie woke me, and I made my groggy way through the second-story labyrinth down to supper. The nuns were in their somber habits. I cannot say that I was charmed to discover that Gabriella's seat had been left vacant for me.

I moved through the hushed room and the candlelight as a breeze through a temple. Flames flickered in my wake. Expecting me, Sister Sophie passed me a card as I sat down on which she had inscribed a single word:

Silence

Fine. Pass the spuds.

Eating was an ordeal. None of the masticating females was more than outwardly calm. As a gesture of goodwill I had planned to read to them if someone could present me with a copy of my father's story about the kinkajou; in light of their silent treatment, no way.

Not that I did not sympathize with their predicament. Having passed the day in grief, the ladies were anxious to learn how the night would unravel. This was Good Friday, the nominal sadness underscored by a death more recent than the one two thousand years previous. Each woman wondered, as did I, whether or not a woman would again bleed from the free-flowing wounds of Christ.

I reprimanded myself, without noticeable effect, for idly speculating on the possibility, and silently denigrated these women whose faith hinged on a peculiar piece of evidence. What mattered to them was an ostentatious exhibition of suffering. Bad enough that Chantelle had to bleed, to endure extraordinary pain and in the midst of her delirium perceive ecstatic visions, but they expected her to bleed on cue. If she succumbed to her agony and passion again, the nuns were willing to conclude that God had upped the ante. For some mysterious, holy cause, the term of her tribulation had been increased. On the other hand, were Chantelle to survive Good Friday without visible suffering, the assumption would be that God in His glory had goofed. Failure to demonstrate the required wounds tonight would suggest that Chantelle's agony was merely a fallible psychological quirk, an ailment to be treated with sedation, counselling, or electric shock therapy.

Nor would the matter end there. Retirement to an institutional meadow was a possibility. A specialist in lobotomies could be put to work. The world's order was seriously contravened when hysterical women bled from their pores. Desperate measures had to be invoked.

An acrid air permeated Toll House.

Now that I was on to them, I could expect to be watched. Access to the halls would be denied me. After the women had doused the lights and retired to the large room upstairs, I absconded to the sitting room to mind my own business and snooze by the fire.

Finished with her chores, Hazel joined me. Her darning needle flashed. She had been into my dresser drawers! Those were *my* socks she was mending. Such service!

Our ears were tuned to the eerie stillness of the night.

"What will you do when they begin to shriek?" Hazel asked without looking up.

"Come on, Hazel."

"Come on what?"

"Don't give Toll House a bad reputation. Granted, people have such a good time here they find it necessary to commit suicide, not a great advertisement, but let's leave it at that, shall we? I don't want the whole town to know that we're a den for religious freaks."

"The whole town knows already," she pointed out.

"The State, then. I don't want the whole State to know. There's to be an inquest. Do me a favor and downplay the ruckus last night."

Hazel pressed her darning into her lap. "You want me to perjure myself?"

"No, Hazel, of course not." The dexterity of her fingers, as she resumed her labor, was as mesmerizing a performance as the flames cavorting in the hearth. "I wouldn't dream of it. All I ask is that you not exaggerate."

"On account of that won't be hard, I consent."

"Remember, sounds carry at night. The same noise in daylight probably would go unnoticed."

"Stick to that story, Mr. Kyle. You'll go far."

I gave up. "How about a brandy?"

"A cognac would suit, thank you." Before I headed downstairs she called after me, "The cupboard above the sink is handier." She evidently maintained a private reserve.

Comfortable again, I probed, "What do you know about Isaiah Snow?"

"What do you want me to know?"

The chicanery of her reply made me hoot. I enjoyed Hazel and valued her company.

"Is he a good cop?"

"Honest as the day is long. He's tough. Never cross him. He has no use for the bad guys. The innocent have nothing to fear except his infernal machines."

"What machines?"

"Isaiah tinkers. He spends most of his spare time trying to expand the capabilities of his lie-detectors." Hazel looked up at me while pausing to sip her cognac. "Isaiah makes them in his basement. He's always looking for fresh guinea pigs to test them out."

"He told me he calls them truth-verifiers."

Hazel laughed out loud. "Rooked you in, huh? Probably strung you a line and you tripped right over it. Oh well. You might have a fun time, who knows?"

Upstairs, the nuns had commenced their dour chants. "Here we go again," Hazel scorned. "Did you bring earplugs with you?"

Precious little was said over the next hour as we listened to the calls and responses, the rhythms of the women thrumming through the ancient, heroic timbers of Toll House, the singular corporate voice surging in the cool night air as a draft self-immolating on the fire. I listened for a strident cry, but heard none.

"Hazel?" My rapid heartbeat encouraged my nerve. I had to trust someone.

"Mmmm?" Finished with my socks, she had embarked on the creation of an iridescent shawl.

"That room they're in, the Mt. Washington Room. It has a skylight."

"A bubble." She continued working. "That's right."

"Tell me, is there an easy way to climb out onto the roof?"

Ever so slowly, Hazel's fingers ceased their craft, and she let her hands fall to her lap. Watching the fire, she stated, "That depends on who's going. What's easy for some is treacherous for others."

Silence truly is golden in the glow of a fire. I weighed the pros and cons, but without much discrimination, for I favored my compulsion over the few dregs of commonsense issuing dissent. "You and me both," I agreed, and Hazel rewarded me with the brightest smile that I have ever divined on the face of an adult.

"Follow me," she said.

Caution to the wind. Clearly the move to Vermont had cost me the better half of my senses.

In Hazel's room, I leaned against her bureau while she wrapped herself up in the vivid colors of the rainbow. If she were to slip, slide from our rooftop and cascade into the valley below, she'd light up the night sky, be mistaken for Halley's Comet. Next we hurried to my room, where I was forced to don a sweater and a jacket. Approving of the treads on my mud-caked boots, she ordered me to change out of my shoes. "The roof'll be slippier than a greased sow after all this rain," she warned.

I was having second thoughts. "We'll probably kill ourselves."

"That's not funny," my escort admonished. "Not today."

"Sorry."

We were spotted in the corridor. A spy stood guard to report on our comings and goings. The volume and cadence of the chanters was swelling behind her, though still without the extraneous screams.

"We're off for a midnight stroll," I placated the guard.

Not about to alter her nature for discretion's sake, Hazel frowned, and advised our watchdog, "We're desperate for a little peace and quiet!"

The nun smiled thinly, and Hazel and I went downstairs.

"Now what?" I wanted to know, chickening out.

"This way," she whispered. "Quiet as a mouse."

To have a guide familiar with the terrain was essential. We had to wend our way through blackness. I swear that woman could see in the dark. We passed under the solemn choir and mounted stairs at the opposite end of Toll House from my room. On the upper floor, Hazel popped open a window where the corridor turned, and we climbed feet-first onto an iron fire escape. From there we had to stretch to gain a foothold in a niche in the wall, not so difficult for me but demanding every inch of stride that Hazel could manage. We held onto each other for balance. Perched on a dormer, the odd angles of joinery created convenient hand-holds as we prepared to scale the peak.

A safe, rudimentary ascent. Crawling on our hands and knees across the ridgepole of the rooftop, our way was lit through the night and fog by the few exterior lights which illuminated corners of the parking lot and paths to the front and side doors. Our destination glowed in the dark: light through the plexiglass bubble shone on the mist.

"Anytime we have summer droughts I come up here to wipe the bird-goop off the glass."

"How will we get down there, Hazel?" Suspecting that I might not want to hear her reply, I had delayed asking the question.

The drop to the skylight was about a dozen feet. The slope on this side of the house, steep.

"Very carefully," she advised. But I should have known that Hazel embarks on no task for which she is not artfully prepared. Confused as to why we were leaving our destination behind us, I continued to shuffle along on my seat after her. Until we reached a roof ladder.

The ladder consisted of two lengths, one short, one long, hinged together. The hinge lay at the roof's peak, with the longer length running down the side of the roof opposite the skylight. Working cautiously in the darkness, the two of us managed to turn it around. Designed to act as an anchor, the shorter length bites into the shingles with metal claws. We were facing one another and grasping the ladder between us, so that our progress back to the skylight was comical and slow. I would bump my behind backwards, then Hazel would hop her bottom forward. We must have looked like nitwits cantering on a double-saddled, two-headed horse. I'm glad that we weren't spotted.

We finally made it into position when the rains came.

Pouring.

In buckets and pails.

Cats and dogs.

Someone had pulled the plug on the sky.

Both Hazel and I were blinded by the torrent. We could do nothing more than shelter our faces. The rain passed on as quickly as it had begun; we heard it marching like an army through the forest. We proceeded down the ladder, our clothes sopping.

I went first, and supported Hazel's thighs on my shoulders when we reached the skylight. Ever so carefully, we leaned over and peered through the shining globe.

Our crystal ball.

Three incomplete concentric rings of candle flames faintly lit the room below us. Distinguishing the forms was impossible. The black-cowled women appeared as creatures sheltered in the dark, their fur camouflaged in the undergrowth. Each semi-circle of light was interrupted by the bed, while on the bed, in white, like a fairy princess lay Chantelle. In this light, I could not see if she was bleeding.

I asked Hazel to please remove her shoes from my fingers.

"Thank you."

"You're welcome."

Peering into that depth again, I discerned that we had come at an opportune moment. Chantelle sat up straight. In a meditative position she either stared into the abyss or, eyes closed, explored inward. In a minute she stood up on the bed, catching her balance on the bouncy springs. Looking up, she gracefully raised her hands overhead. Both Hazel and I pulled back, stricken, guilty, then reminded ourselves that we were invisible in the night. We peered through the enchanted glass once more.

Chantelle dismounted from the bed. She strolled among the kneeling worshipers, the candles casting her shadows into grotesque shapes. In a moment she stood above one of the slumped, huddled, anonymous forms. Chantelle swayed with the rhythm of their song, performed an intricate Polynesian-style dance with her hands. The woman she had selected shed her clothing before our startled eyes, and magically ascended into our view.

As though she floated on thin air.

The woman, whose name I knew to be Emily, was a beauty readily identified by her flocculent blonde hair. Companions beside her had raised her vertically to the heights, a practiced maneuver, and now lowered her onto the bed. Emily lay with her arms and legs parted in the manner of a child carving angels in the snow. Hands swarmed over her, kneading and caressing her, a licentious, unbridled massage. As Emily, hidden beneath the hands, began to writhe, she was lifted on high again, this time parallel to the floor. The hands that had been above her, now supported her from below.

Her body wobbled at shoulder height as more women squeezed in beneath her. On cue she was raised as an offering to the heavens.

Emily lay still. Nor did the women move. In the twinkling of lights in formation on the floor, Hazel and I recognized that her body was being rotated, as slowly as the minute hand of a clock.

A tedious procession.

Uncomfortable on the ladder, I was growing stiff and achy, and shifted to relieve strained muscles. My movement caused the ladder to jump slightly, and the wood creaked with boisterous complaint. Scorned for my fidgetiness by Hazel's scowl, I leaned back over the magic window.

After being rotated once around (in fact, it *seemed* like an hour, but was more like ten or twelve minutes), the floating woman began to sway as the hands below her moved in a coordinated pattern. I heard for the first time the chanted accompaniment, likely because the wind and the distant rain were quietening, and I assumed that within that room the music was moderately loud. To and fro she was rocked on the human mattress. Early on her motion was contrived by the spectral beings beneath her; she appeared endowed with no more power of animation than a hand puppet. But she came alive. Aloft, eyes closed, she commenced to squirm. Wiggle and lash out. Flex and jolt. Raising up her knees she flung out her arms, and the rhythmic nuance of her hips became decidedly sexual.

Hazel covered my eyes. "This is where you stop watching," she teased. She was as mesmerized by the macabre dance as I was. "What do you have to say about their so-called religious customs now?" she taunted me. "You call *this* going to church?"

A noisy retort rattled the ladder, disturbing our espionage. "Are you sure we're safe?" I demanded of my accomplice, my nervousness showing.

"No problem. Be brave. I've been out here at least twenty times before." Brash confidence.

Another frightening creak and stretch of the wood.

"Hazel? I don't want to belabor the point, but if you don't mind my asking . . ."

"What?"

"How many times have you been out on this ladder with a second body?"

My assistant and co-conspirator gazed down upon me, and in the dim afterglow of the candlelit skylight I could see in her eyes that my question had merit. We stared at one another in a moment of suspended dread. Then the supporting overhang of the ladder flipped up under the stress of our combined weight, something snapped, a gunshot, and for an instant we wavered above eternity like a pair of cartoon characters who had scampered out over a cliff, the realization dawning. We commenced our swift, perilous crash down.

My life and Hazel's stout bum flashed before my eyes. Convinced of my impending doom, I had time during that awful, clamorous descent to regret a few choices in my life.

The catastrophic sound that signaled our rescue shredded the night. Hazel and I and the ladder came to an abrupt, lurching stop. Saved by the drainpipe. Our momentum tore most of the eaves-trough away from the roof, a horrific alarm, and the pipe now veered outward like the drawstring of a bow. The ladder was the arrow about to be launched into the vacuum of the night sky. A moonshot.

A window jumped open beneath us. An occupant poked out her suspicious head. "There's people up there!" she announced, for the moment more amazed than raging. Hazel and I scrambled up the ladder, praying between steps that the few remaining fastenings on the eavestrough would hold. On our bottoms we scooted across the peak, then slid down to the next level and hurled ourselves through the secret window.

The hall light flicked on.

A trio of nuns, their faces concealed in the shadows of their cowls, glared at us. Our hair plastered wet upon our scalps, our breathing heavy, our bulky clothing in disarray, we stood convicted. Wallowing in our shame, both Hazel and I cowered.

"We found them!" one nun shouted to her friends. No time to implore her, plead mercy, or offer a bribe. In a wink the corridor filled with the black creatures.

Chantelle pushed through to the front of the line, followed by Emily, whose nakedness had been exhibited moments ago. Had I been alone in this subterfuge I would have retreated to the rooftop, murmured my final apologies, and leapt into the dark vale below.

One small mercy: Chantelle was not bleeding.

Having robed in haste, Emily did not wear her hood. Her eyes flashed hatred, even as Hazel stepped forward and sought to assume full responsibility. "Sorry, Miss. My fault, Miss." Neither I nor the others were having any part of that.

"Nonsense," I scoffed.

No need. The women only had eyes for me. They focused their outrage on the degenerate target: me, the household's lone male.

My eyes fixed on Chantelle, I implored her to forgive me, to comprehend that my invasion had been borne of a curiosity that, under the circumstances, ought to be considered admissible. Estranged from the woman I loved in her time of crisis, what else could I have done, stuffed my ears?

Sadness in Chantelle's eyes. Nary a hint of reprieve.

I switched my attention to Emily as she pushed in front.

Had she been a woman who honored a different moral code I might have had my eyes scratched out, my cheeks shredded. Lucky for me she was an adherent of non-violence, for she vented her perfect wrath instead with a single, cursory dismissal: "Get out of my sight." Her breath was warm on my lips, she was that close.

I hung my head. Disgraced. Shame wound a stranglehold around my neck. Let me die, here, this instant. Let my body be zapped into cinders and dust. I had not merely spied her nude, I had blasphemed a sacred ceremony, and thereby deserved her deepest contempt.

I had humiliated the woman I loved.

Chantelle wouldn't even look at me.

Slinking away, Hazel and I dolefully trudged down the stairs, the scorn of our accusers stinging like whips across our backs.

3

Ill-prepared, but willing, to pit my word against the misanthropy of modern technology, I drove into town on Tuesday morning to challenge Isaiah Snow's hobby-machines to a duel. It was unfortunate that events over the weekend had contrived to distract my thoughts from the contest ahead.

That only three days had passed since the nuns' departure was difficult to fathom. Time drags slowly when you're sick at heart. Promptly after breakfast on Saturday morning the women had packed up, an austere procession compared to their arrival. Ghetto-blasters filed past but none were switched on. The ladies paid individually, which gave my right arm a workout on the credit-card machine.

Chantelle passed me her American Express card.

"I left home without mine," I deadpanned, hoping to chip away at the ice. "What else could I do? The infidels have never seen fit to give me one."

"Will you add up my bill, please?" was her surly response.

"Yaha! Now comes my appointed task," I boasted to Chantelle. "All I do is zap it through the machine. Spring training. I'm getting my arm in shape for the season."

"That's about all you're good for," she countered, accepting her card back with the receipt.

"It's not mystical, but it's a living."

"You bastard." She stomped away, trampling my hopes in the process.

"Come again some time!" I called after her. "Don't be a stranger! We have weekend specials!"

A moment later I was mortified by my behavior. Which is nothing new. I could challenge Chantelle for sainthood if ever I conduct myself according to my regrets.

"Hold down the fort for a while, Cassie."

"Yes, Mr. Elder."

"Chantelle!" I hollered, giving chase, bounding upstairs, though I knew as well as anyone that it was too late.

I found her in her bedroom. Not in the expansive chamber where she had screamed blue murder and revelled in her mystical visions, but in her official sleeping dorm, a tidy, functional lair with bunkbeds. Chantelle was folding black robes into a gigantic suitcase, her duties in the order not limited to being the resident visionary, stigmatist, and numerologist — she was the valet, too. Talk about being exploited.

"Go away, please," she commanded.

"Are you always so polite?" I was groping for a fresh start.

"All right then. *Fuck off!* How's that?"

"There's something to be said for being polite. Look, Chanty —"

"Don't call me that. Only my best friends call me that. *You* don't have the right."

"Let me apologize, at least."

"Feel free. But apology will never undo your action." She was working at such a furious pace, folding and stuffing, that her forehead had begun to perspire.

"I'm sorry, Chantelle. I don't know what possessed me. I — I was concerned."

"What a cruddy thing to do, Kyle. Spy on me. You're a crud."

Under the circumstances I considered her choice of appellation to be mild, and took heart. "That's common knowledge," I confirmed. Without looking, I had become aware that nuns had gathered behind my back and, obliged to whisper, I asked, "Forgive me, Chantelle? Look. Can't we be friends?"

My distinct impression was that Chantelle, in turning, spied her bodyguards, and that their proximity altered her attitude. "Please,

Kyle. We thank you for not charging us for the duration of the weekend. Otherwise, there's nothing to say."

"At least tell me where to send flowers for Gaby's funeral."

"You're not going to find out where I live that way. Put flowers in the room where she died if you want. Now please, go away."

Her buddies required no further instruction. They barged into the room and I was hustled out.

"Hands — off!" I let it be known. They released me, though a few begrudged me my freedom. I smoothed my shirt, rolled my shoulders, and summoned sufficient dignity to walk away unmolested. Nor did I deign to watch the ladies drive off. I lay in bed and in my awakened misery went to sleep. My only consolation was that I would see Chantelle again at the inquest in a few days' time, and by then she might have had a change of heart.

That Sunday I took my Cherokee Chief for a spin along the mountain roads, and in the evening phoned Franklin D. Ryder at his home. I delivered a summary of key developments, notably Gaby's apparent suicide and Inspector Snow's request that I take a polygraph. "Don't do it, Kyle. Cancel out." Something in Franklin D.'s character makes him a far more decisive man over the telephone than he is face-to-face.

"Nope, I've given my word. Besides, I think it'll be a lark."

"Not a smart move, Kyle."

"I have nothing to hide, Franklin D.," I insisted.

"I'm advising you, as your attorney, to cancel out. I can't make myself more clear than that."

In the background at F.D.R.'s place, another embezzler was taking it on the chin on "Sixty Minutes". "I'll go through with it," I told him. "I've got nothing else to do. Besides, it'll look bad if I chicken out."

"Don't fall for that old ploy. At least let me call Snow. I'll have him commit to writing that the lie-detector's opinion cannot be admissible in court without your approval, and that the result cannot be made public without similar authorization."

"Fair enough."

"Nor will the machine's advice be grounds for arrest."

"Stop talking as though I'm guilty of something," I chided

him. "I haven't *done* anything, so what can I be arrested for?"

"Standard precautions," my lawyer stipulated. He was wiser than I gave him credit for being. "Also, I want to be there. I don't believe in trusting your life to a cop's folly and a computer's mood."

"Keep my innocence in mind, F.D.R."

"Think liability" was the gist of his concern. "Think public innuendo. Think bad publicity. It was your inn, Kyle. Your tea. Did I hear right, it was your bed too?"

"That's just the point! I have to clear my name. Never mind the law, it's the gossip that worries me. I have to live in this town. People will believe a computer long before they'll listen to me. Unlike a lawyer or a stranger, a computer's trusted. Even one built in Snow's basement. Incidentally, you should know that I don't cough up professional fees on demand. I'll expect a fully itemized account for your services."

Don't take it personally, I wanted to add. I'm lashing out at everyone. Ticked off with me, he returned my volley, "So why was the dead woman in your bed anyway?"

"Who knows? Goodnight, F.D.R."

The time had come. I had been foot-dragging long enough, although always shackled with a valid excuse. Pinching a shovel from the tool shed I made my way down to the stables. On the night that she had met me there, Chantelle had taken an alternate route; I located that path, a ski trail marked with ribbons, glad for the chance to move invisibly among the trees.

In conversation with Hazel, and later with Cassie Baxter, I had learned that the inn periodically had problems with drifters, hobos who would camp on the grounds and be discovered in the equipment shacks, the stables, or scrounging through the garbage pit among the grackles. I hoped that mine had had the presence of mind to beat it after our encounter, for most victims could be expected to inform police, friends, or to return with a shotgun. Still, I was wary. Maybe he was an intuitive bum who realized that he could hold the bones over my head. The shovel was intended to dig a proper grave, but, should the need arise, it could also serve as a weapon.

And upon entering the stables I carried the spade overhead like a club poised to crack craniums. That the stables were unoccupied and showed no signs of having been inhabited recently was an immeasurable relief. I was relaxing with that good news when I investigated my mound of dirt and hay, only to discover that it had been invaded. The skeleton was gone. Every bone unearthed. Again.

At first I was jittery, wondering where in God's green acre the remains might show up next. But I urged myself to be calm. The bones were now beyond my jurisdiction. Whoever might be caught with them, it would not be me. The only scary thing to consider was that — who knows? — given its history, maybe this skeleton really was mobile, a restless, grave-hopping wraith.

Shouldering my shovel, I marched back up the grade, watchful for spooks.

Hazel had directed me to call upon a contractor in Stowe and arrange to have the eavestrough fixed. Not only was it an eyesore and necessary to channel the spring rains, but it was a reminder of her indiscretion. She wanted it repaired fast. With time to spare before my rendezvous with the "truth-verifier", I ran Hazel's errand first, asking for the boss by name. Vince. Emerging from his office like a bear from hibernation, the man stretched, yawned, and glimpsed the sun through the curtains, measuring its height. Vince was as woolly as a bear too, with chest hair fluffing out his shirt and curling about his collar. Indoors all winter, he was feisty, anxious to be busy again.

"You Kyle Elder's boy?" he quizzed the moment I introduced myself. He was squinting up at me as though the power of my intellect shone down upon him like a five-hundred-watt bulb.

With trepidation I conceded, "Yes, I am."

"Yeah, I heard about your first day up at the inn. What do you feed your guests, arsenic?"

"An unfortunate occurrence," I lamented seriously, chagrined that my misfortune (and Gaby's) had become the town joke.

"A restful holiday is one thing, but dying? I doubt if that's what your guests had in mind. How can I help you, Kyle?"

My turn to get even. "Part of the eavestrough at the house has separated from the roof. Poor installation, I imagine," I decreed with a straight face. "Go on up whenever you can, Vince. Hazel will show you the damage. And do me a favor. Don't fall off your ladder. I wouldn't want you to be the butt of people's jokes. I'm sure folks would laugh for weeks if you happened to bust your skull. I have to run. See you!"

Matching wits with townspeople was good practice for my showdown with Snow's mechanical judge.

"Am I plugged in yet?" I beat my inquisitors to the punch with a query of my own. Inspector Snow was ably assisted by an immaculate technician in a white laboratory smock, the prim, prissy Miss Windicott.

"All set," the lady with the wires and computer terminal confided.

"I didn't kill the nun!" I blathered defiantly, hoping to browbeat the machine with conviction. "I didn't kill Mother Superior Gabriella!" Flat out. No preamble. Straight to the point. My voice echoing with credence in the small, sparse room.

"Young sir, please, we must follow a recognized procedure," Isaiah Snow stressed. He didn't want me to foul up his invention. "Wait for our questions."

"Let's do it. Let's get on with it."

Their very first question threw me into a dither.

"Is your name Kyle Troy Elder Junior?" the technician inquired breathlessly. Seated opposite me behind her desk, Miss Windicott seductively wiggled on her bottom. Her voice, amplified in our small enclosure, was brittle and caustic, yet I sensed that our rubber and copper-wire connections aroused her.

"Yes. No! No. Yes!"

Inspector Snow was miffed. He wiped the wrinkles off his forehead, frowned, and let them fall back into place. Having removed his glasses he swung them back and forth. "Mr. Elder, sir —"

"Kyle."

"Kyle. This isn't a game. Please answer yes or no. Not both."

"I can't. There's a complication. Let me explain." Perspiration commenced to chill my brow. The wires, the straps, the electrician's tape on my arms, the diodes registering the sweat factor of my palms, a recollection of poor Gaby's austere dead face — I felt bound to the chair, harnessed, captured, doomed, anticipating a faulty connection that would short-circuit my measly life. I resented my interrogators for adding a blithe "Junior" to my name without my consent.

"Yes or no. Are you Kyle Troy Elder Junior?"

"I don't know. I — "

"Young sir — Kyle —"

"That's a trick question!" I was terribly claustrophobic. Our torture chamber was a converted washroom, bleak, slate-gray walls and high windows.

"Mr. Elder, Kyle, believe me," Snow vowed, "it's nothing of the kind. Calm down." He misinterpreted my meaning, thought that I was merely paranoid. "Initially we test the machine with easy questions to determine your compatibility range."

"I don't want to marry the silly thing. It's not my type."

"Routine procedure, I assure you, sir. We have to run a check on the machine's performance, in case it was jostled out of order during transit."

"Who's under suspicion here, Inspector? Me or the machine? Or the delivery truck?"

"Oh not you, sir. We know that you must be an innocent man." I searched his eyes for a sparkle shining on his sarcasm. This one was a poker player after all. "Remember, Kyle, don't think of the unit as a lie-detector. It's a truth-verifier, and a highly sophisticated apparatus."

"Who's the builder, Isaiah?"

"Is your name Kyle Troy Elder Junior?" Miss Windicott called through from behind her contraptions.

"Own up, Inspector!"

"Answer the question, Kyle."

"What do you do in your spare time in your basement?"

"I'm asking the questions. You're answering."

"All right already! I'll try answering yes. See how that goes down."

"Then say it," Inspector Snow counseled.

"Yes." But I wondered, do I believe it? And is the machine

144

convinced? I heard the needle on the graph scratching away, observed the attendant's itchy pencil adding a comment. "So? What did it say?" My interest was genuine and urgent: did I accept that I was my father's son? "Am I or am I not this guy? I really want to know." My hands perspired into their sensors. I grew panicky, tried to control myself, suffered the impression that my liquid palms had been cut and were bleeding.

"Can we proceed?" Isaiah was becoming testy.

"Okay, but no more trick questions."

In good conscience I managed to regulate my breathing and respond affirmatively to the next items on their list. The date and city of my birth were confirmed, and we agreed that my hair is brown and that my eyes are a warm shade of walnut. That I'm male. Then came the shocker. Miss Windicott's voice was barely audible when she asked completely out of the blue, "During your lifetime, Mr. Elder Junior, have you ever committed murder?"

"What!"

"Have you ever killed another human being?"

"What kind of dumb question is that!" I was furious.

"Yes or no, please, sir." She was on the brink.

"No!" I yelled as loudly as I could while maintaining my composure, but I heard the needle hysterical on the graph, threatening to gambol off the page. "Yes! I mean no! I mean I don't know! Who does, really? I won't answer that question. I have to explain. It's another trick question!"

"Mr. Elder, young sir, Kyle! Please control yourself. We only ask that sort of question to elicit your reaction, to study your range on the graph, not to insult. Don't take our questions so seriously."

"I will *not* control myself! This is not what we agreed to do!" I yanked out wires, peeled off patches — *ouch!* — taped to my hairy arms. Snow ran over to the machine to validate the exact course of my response. "I didn't kill that mother-superior nun!" I hollered once and for all. "You have no right to ask me about anything else!"

"Whom *did* you kill?" Snow asked me, graph in hand.

"Eff off!"

"What was the woman doing in your bed?"

"Who knows? Maybe she wanted to die in peace. Have you

thought of that? Away from the other nuns. Why don't you electrify her corpse if you're so good at tinkering with machines? Raise her from the dead, Isaiah, I'm sure you could do it! Ask her if she committed suicide! If your machine is so smart it ought to be able to accomplish that!"

"You're not doing yourself any benefit, Mr. Elder, sir."

"What if I was in the army, in Vietnam," I grilled him. "I wasn't, but what if? How do you differentiate between what is killing people and what is murder? Mmm? You should have thought the issue through before asking me that trick question."

"You weren't in Vietnam, you just said so. We ask the question to check your response to murder. Yours was rather excited."

Swinging open, the door behind me spanked my rear end. My lawyer had arrived, uselessly late. His client's stormy temper was readily apparent.

"We agreed not to start without me," he reprimanded Snow.

"Mr. Elder gave no indication that he preferred to wait."

Go ahead, blame the entire fiasco on me.

"They've been asking trick questions," I informed my defender. "Like what's my name and whether I ever killed anybody before. Answer yes or no, they said. But it's not that simple, F.D.R. They wouldn't let me explain a thing."

"I take it the interview has not gone well," my counsel deduced.

"*Interview!* Whose side are you on anyway? *Interrogation* is more like it. In another minute they'd've been zinging me with high voltage hooked up to my privates. I thought I was in Vermont, not South America."

Isaiah delivered his biased assessment. "Your client has been deliberately disruptive."

Franklin D. was nonplussed. "That's his prerogative. There is no official sanction —"

"How can you say that, Isaiah?" I interrupted. "We agreed on my hair color. We didn't go into details, like what I'm going to do to keep from going bald, but still. Now if you'll excuse me . . ." and I burst past both Ryder and Snow, out of police headquarters, to speed home and await my imminent arrest on some trumped-up charge.

Abysmal conduct. Snow had not only provoked my natural

defence mechanisms, but his wires and questions had stimulated centers of memory long suppressed.

Had I killed anyone in my life?

How am I supposed to answer that question?

Mom? Cindy? Any ideas?

4

Winters were bitter in Park Extension whenever Arctic winds pilfered the south. For a while I had a newspaper route. Froze my cheeks on a Monday, Tuesday my fingertips were speckled with white spots, the next afternoon my toes went numb. Were it not for Thursday's relative thaw I might have been reported among the missing. Back then, snow was not removed from the streets; plowed against the curbs, huge banks grew as the winter progressed. A lost child who had plummeted through a soft spot might be revealed come springtime, keeping company with a bushwhacked hooligan stored away since Christmas.

Made brittle by winter, we children sweltered in summer heat. Beneath the narrow shade of buildings we sat dripping after a romp. Summers are most prevalent in my mind, individual and decisive, while winters all seem to have been the same. Winters were endured. Summer — the suffocating heat, the dust like history's glaze, the rampaging thunderstorms articulate with bombardment, lightning, and torrents — was a time for adventure.

And in Park Extension few hot-weather entertainments could generate larger audiences than a fire. Early in 1970 we enjoyed a rash of outbreaks that left the neighborhood frenetic. Fire, primeval, chimerical, was the favorite topic of street conversation. Pumping gas, the owner of the Esso station fretted that the city was a tinderbox. "We'll be razed to the ground if we don't get rain." Still gullible at sixteen, I contemplated whether homes required periodic showers to maintain their good health.

Contributing to the ferment, street toughs high on mischief

yanked fire alarms to wake up the neighborhood, or they'd tele-phone the operator to report a blaze out of control. The game was to scream in the poor woman's ear as if flames consumed their bodies, and be convincing enough to get her to ring the fire depart-ment. Daily, moronic red trucks raced down the congested streets, chased by children and teenagers, the bells and sirens paging the hordes.

I, too, listened for the wail of fire engines and scampered along their routes, less interested in the excitement of fires than I was compelled by the sexual awakening of adolescence. I had penetrated a cogent mystery. Where there was fire, sure enough, there was smoky-eyed Cindy Bottomley.

Before too long I learned that the opposite was true as well.

"Nice fire," I ventured, stepping out from behind her. I had been admiring the jauntiness of her bum. Hands in hip pockets, elbows and shoulders thrust back, spine askew, Cindy's attitude of deceit and defiance intimidated me a trifle. Over the years I had wandered in and out of her favor. Subject to an elaborate system of merit and demerit marks, her reaction to me depended on her mood of the moment. The weather also came into play, the clothes I wore, the clothes she wore, with consideration to the vagaries of chance, protocol, and who was watching.

"It's already out," Cindy commented about the fire. Great bil-lows of gun-metal smoke had clouded the Park Extension sky for a few minutes, blotting out a hot sun, but we had not seen flames. The two-story house dripped with water, miles of hose lay strewn about the street like leftover spaghetti.

"How did it start?" My lame attempt at friendly conversation.

Cindy, the expert, said, "Space-heater. You can tell because the smoke came out the middle. Not from the kitchen in back, so it wasn't a stove fire, and not from a cigarette in any of the front rooms."

"It's summer," I pointed out. "Who has their heat on?"

Scowling, she thought me dim. "Look at her." With a nod of her chin she presented the burned-out tenant as Exhibit A. "Her hair's in curlers. Bet you anything she wanted to dry her hair fast. The heater exploded."

Too stubborn for my own good I persisted in my cross-examination of her testimony. "She could've dried her hair in the sun."

The witness of my dreams rolled her eyes heavenward, thoroughly rankled by my stupidity. "What woman wants to come outside in curlers? Only hags do. You're not too swift, Elder."

(I could have argued the point. Before the advent of the hand-held blow-dryer women of all descriptions appeared in public barbed in wire like warriors.)

A fire marshal led the shabby tenant up her outside staircase to survey the damage. Her furry slippers splashed on each step. The firemen had drowned everything that didn't move. Just before she reached the top step, she emitted a long and harrowing shriek, an exhibition of terror that cannot be rehearsed. The two climbers whirled and hurtled back down, chased by huge licks of orange flame that burst from the windows and doors. The firefighters had been rolling their hoses prematurely. The crowd surged together once again, ooohing and aaahing in tune like a choir. Cindy pronounced, "I told you it was gas."

She smiled her pleasure at the flames' performance.

Twenty minutes later the fire was out for good and I invited Cindy back to my place.

"What for?" she challenged me.

"To see my birds if you want."

"Won't your mother be there?"

"Naw. She's out. She's working days now."

"What about that repulsive snake?"

"I'll lock him up. Come on. What d'you say? We'll get something cold to drink."

On this occasion, Cindy acquiesced.

"Ugh, yuck, gross!" she complained upon arrival. Clyde was the problem.

He had draped himself across the kitchen counter for a languid siesta in the sun. His head moved, causing Cindy to bound four feet. She scaled my back, riding a horse, my neck the pommel she frantically gripped. "Sheeee-it!" she exclaimed. "Get it out of here, Kyle!"

"Hang on." I galloped over to the basement door, where she dismounted. "Follow me down," I instructed, and we descended into that dusty cavern.

Noticing the cages, Cindy quavered. "More snakes?"

I put on a gauntlet and selected a big, juicy rat. "Food," I enlightened her, "for Clyde."

"Keep it away from me!" she warned. Borderline hysteria. With my advantage squirming in my fingers I chased Cindy in a circle around the basement and quickly cut her off at the pass. She squealed in a pitch not dissimilar to the cries of our doomed rats.

"Ky-yle!"

"I'll stop if you kiss me."

"Stop it now!"

"Kiss me first."

"Never!"

Cornered, she screeched, and immediately capitulated as I dangled the rat by its tail near her face.

"All right all right!"

"Kiss me."

"Get rid of that icky yicky thing first! Then wash your hands *pour cinq minutes*! You're a rat yourself, you know that, Kyle Elder? A rat and a snake."

I gave her fair warning upstairs. "Don't freak out, okay? I mean, don't tear off down the street chanting like a Zulu warrior."

"I was a little girl then," she protested, taking offense. Yet when I fed the rat to Clyde and he spread his jaws wide to accept the morsel whole, and the lump of the rat's body appeared behind the boa's eyes, Cindy nearly swooned. "Gross, gross, *gross*," she declared, blotting her face in her hands.

"That's life." My machismo statement for the day. "The big feed on the little. The sun rises in the morning. Birds sing." I broke into the sunrise celebration of the eastern meadowlark. And added, "Boys kiss pretty girls."

"Forget it." Cindy slipped loose from my attempted full nelson and adroitly put me in my place. "Wise up, Kyle. I'm not going to kiss you."

"Next time" — was my solemn promise — "I'm feeding *you* to Clyde."

"Hey, Kyle, where's your birds?"

A careful reconnoitering of the house turned up only two parakeets and the young myna, Bish — our fifth Bish. On the fridge door, a note explained the disappearances. "Gone to Shriners' Hospital with birdies — Em." Emma loved to act solo, and especially for children.

"The parakeets don't talk much," I told Cindy. "Sorry about the others being gone."

"That's okay. These are my favorites anyway. They're so beautiful."

"Like you. Want a Coke?"

"Any beer?"

"Sure." I cracked two open, nervous about it because I was not allowed to drink alcohol. Cindy had wandered through to the living-room and was sprawled sexily in a large, comfy armchair, one leg slung over the side. I pulled her beer back before she could reach it. "Kiss me first," I teased.

A serious frown. "Kyle, you are the ugliest boy I know, and poor on top of that. Why would I ever want to kiss you?"

"Charity?" I surrendered the bottle and sat across from her. "Think about it. It's good for the character to be kind. Millions desire you; nobody in their right mind would want to smooch with me. That makes us the perfect match. Beauty and the beast. I'll get what I won't have otherwise and you'll build your character." Perfectly reasonable to me.

"No sale. I've already built my character." She swigged her drink.

"Is Jimmy Durante ugly?" I pressed on.

"As sin."

"Would you kiss him?"

"Why not? If he's still alive. Is he? He's ugly-cute."

"I'm ugly-cute. Look, if you bumped into a Durante look-alike on the street, and he's not rich, he's not Hollywood, would you kiss him on demand?"

Quenching a rampant thirst brought on by the fire, Cindy swilled her drink while thinking it over. "He'd have to pay me plenty," she concurred.

"Exactly. The only reason you'd kiss Jimmy Durante in person is because —"

"He's in show business."

"That's right." I raised my glass to her. "*I'm* in show business."

"Wise up. Playing the ukelele and whistling like a robin ain't show biz."

"Oh yeah? My aunt and me have an act. We almost made it on the Ed Sullivan Show except that he retired. And it's a dulcimer, not a ukelele."

"Tell me another one." She absentmindedly twitched her toes, twirling her shoe like a baton.

"I'm serious. For your information, we're doing a show this Friday night."

"Where, the kitchen?"

"Downtown. It's a private club."

"Can I crash?"

I choked on my mouthful of beer. I should have known that Cindy would be quick to challenge any boast, and from past experience I knew not to put her off. "If you can stomach the place, I can sneak you in. It's a little weird though."

"Weird how?" Sitting up, Cindy kicked off her shoes and folded her legs beneath her. She was keen.

"It's a private women's club."

She leaned forward, simply staring; then she stretched back. "I've heard those rumors," she muttered. A delicate lift to her eyebrows denoted conspiracy. "I heard my mother say it on the phone."

"Say what?"

"Is it true? You know, is your mother queer?"

I did not reply. I did not defend or attack my mother. I was mute. Something lay on the coffee table, magazines or a newspaper, which I nudged further away from me with my toes. I guzzled my brew, not knowing how to reply.

"What do they do together? Ever spy on them, Ky-ky?" Hers a wicked, incisive laugh. "How do they know who's who? You know what I mean. Do they flip a coin?"

"Cool it, Cindy."

"I think it'd be *neat* going to that club. I'd like to catch your act. Check out those weird women."

"They'd skin you alive."

"Yeah. While you're safe, I bet." On her feet, Cindy was advancing on me barefoot. "Smuggle me in there, Kyle. I'll kiss you if you do."

"I'm not that big an idiot, Cin. I'm going to take your word for that?"

"I'll kiss you right now then."

"Promises promises."

Arching her arms over her head, she unfolded into a delicate ballet movement. One foot came up under my chin. Her toes drove me back into my chair as they traced a line from my forehead, nose, Adam's apple, and chest, moving downward to plunder my belly. She ceased at my belt buckle — a disappointment that was short-lived. Commencing at my earlobe, ascending to my brow just under the hairline, Cindy bequeathed a light fluttering of her lips across my skin. She plunked a kiss on the top of my nose. Another smack between the eyes. Blew my left eyelid shut while my right eye strained to watch.

"Will you take me, Kyle?"

Foolish question. "I think I can swing it."

And she consented to kiss me on the lips, a quick and forceful lunge. "You're a sweet guy," she informed me, singlehandedly restoring my self-esteem. "You're always okay with me. You don't maul. You don't yank out your wang. You don't paw my tits. I like that. Meet me tonight, Ky-ky, nine-ish? We'll take a walk in the moonlight. See what's shaking."

"Sure. Yeah. Sure."

"Great. Pick me up at Andy's, okay? My mom won't let me hang out with you. You know, on account of the time with your mom and the snake and I came home a nutcase. Maybe also because your mom's queer. Don't let it bug you, though, don't take it personally. My mother has it in for everybody else too. I'm only allowed to talk to relatives, half the time that's what it seems like. What she doesn't know is, three-quarters of my relatives want to catch me with the lights off anyway, so what's the difference? See you later, Elder."

That speech sounded suspiciously as though she intended to be my girl. *Cindy B!*

Loitering was not permitted at Andy's, the delicatessen at the corner of Jarry and Querbes, so it failed as a hangout. I would not benefit from the swift notoriety that could follow a public date with Cindy. She was meeting me on the sly, in a place where we'd go unnoticed, terms I was obliged to accept.

Cindy had never achieved the great promise expected from her beauty. She was short, under five feet, and her breasts were tiny. Her reference to boys rummaging around inside her blouse stemmed from wishful thinking, not from experience. I'd learn much later that sometimes she'd go downtown in her Marilyn Monroe figure — lightbulbs in her bra — but only on Saturdays. Midweek, boys were apt to snicker about her being "flat".

Still, she was extraordinarily pretty and looked terrific in jeans. Her major problem was that she had cultivated her beauty to suit an overtly glamorous age; she had been weaned on her mother's movie magazines. In an era of tie-dyed T-shirts and patched jeans, Cindy coveted mink stoles and diamond necklaces.

Cindy waved as I approached, sipping Seven-Up through a straw.

"Hi-hi," she said.

"Hi, Cin."

"Ready?" A large red satchel swung from one shoulder.

I was eager for anything. "You bet."

We strolled down Durocher, one of Park Extension's oldest streets. The buildings were crammed together, many were three and four stories, with spiral outdoor staircases leading up to the individual flats. On Saint Roch Street, she guided me east into the hinterland between the railway tracks and the defunct sheds attached to the endless row of duplexes and apartment buildings. "This is a good spot," she confirmed.

Perspiring, I sat down beside her. That Cindy did not immediately snuggle up and neck I put down to modesty. Her eyes scanned the backyards and balconies to make certain that we had not been spotted. This is it, I believed, staggered by the moment, we're going to go all the way.

Cindy removed a folded newspaper from her bag, then wedged it into a crack in the wood of a shed. Intrigued, I watched as she sprayed the paper and the wood with what appeared to be a nasal mist. I sniffed the cool evening air. Gasoline? Cindy struck a match and quickly rolled clear.

"What — ? Cindy! What're you —" In trying to blow out the fire, I inadvertently fanned the flames, and Cindy pulled me away.

Daring and frantic, the flames licked gas from the rotted timbers, scouting about with a thirst for more of the delicious fuel. They retreated. The bright orange and blue flames were replaced by a small red fire. The wood crackled. Snapped. This stage of the fire was patient, methodical, warming the wood for the pyre. Cindy clutched me to her side and I was torn between the urge to snuff the spark or to remain in the glory of her heated embrace. Her eyes were luminous and questing.

Satisfied that the shed was properly lit, Cindy fled with me nipping at her heels. "You're crazy!" I exhorted her. "You're nuts! What did you do that for?"

"I felt like it." The rationale of a generation. She pulled the fire alarm on Saint Roch. I was glad of that. The broken glass tinkled on the pavement. Then we took off, and huddled in a laneway.

We heard the bells clanging, that familiar refrain, the jeremiad of sirens mournful in the gloaming. All smiles, Cindy expressed her pent-up excitement with a comic arabesque as though she herself was a flickering flame, a match.

People were emerging onto their balconies, called by the sounds. Whirling lights, children singing out. Cindy held back from observing the activity until the trucks had clamored past us, the neighborhood kids in tow. We joined the melee. For a while, the danger increased that the firemen would leave, putting this down to another reckless false alarm that had disturbed their evening poker hands, when a voice screeched onto Durocher Street. The fateful words, the terror since time immemorial, homage to the great god, "Fire! Fire!"

Firemen scampered up the stairs and soon discerned that the outbreak was in back. Cindy and I tagged along with the hundreds who circled the block to witness the blaze.

I watched her as she observed the minor inferno. Cindy was rapt. Comtemporary firefighters who survey the spectators with video cameras look for exactly her expression.

The gallant men had to work over the rooftops and trail hoses through people's flats to reach the source. The shed could not be saved, but the fire was blocked from spreading. A Niagara Falls was created; homes were soaked.

I led Cindy away as the burnt timbers smoldered, protecting her with my silence and complicity from the retribution of many families. She was our friendly neighborhood pyromaniac, and I felt the burden of that knowledge as a special responsibility. Cindy had admitted me into her life.

We journeyed down the railway tracks: the further away from the scene the more she became herself again. Safely distant, she grew sad. Either she regretted having burned the shed, or she was disappointed not to have ignited the adjacent homes. I dared not ask which.

"Come, follow me," she said, indicating a well-trodden path down from the grade. We crawled back under the fence and into the sweetly-scented, grape-heavy vines of a secluded backyard garden. There, she made love to me with one hand, and I gasped in that fragrant orchard, helpless under her fingers, traumatized by this ruthless combination of ecstasy and pain. The experience was odd, for of course I was seething with desire for this my first touch from a woman, but I worried that this would be the price, the due, that to have sex with Cindy we'd have to burn villages, intercourse would be earned by razing cities, anything kinky had to be purchased by consigning the world to flames.

Cindy let me kiss her, and I walked her home.

My first real date.

"Kyle, will you get off your lazy butt and feed Clyde!"

Believing that my mother was less interested in the welfare of our boa constrictor than she was in evicting me from the room, I did not leap to do her bidding. "I'm busy, Ma."

"He's slithering around like he's hungry. Go fetch a mouse, I don't want him busting up the furniture."

I took a look. Clyde was indeed indulging in the motions of a hunter, carving the carpet, practicing deep folds of his length to glide forward with unusually long strokes. He rarely exercised this much.

"A *small* mouse, please," my mother tacked on. "I need him smooth."

"Later," I procrastinated. "When I'm finished."

Alongside my mother and Aunt Em, I was applying my makeup. Bemused, Cindy waited with her chin in her hands, her elbows propped on the vanity where I labored. I applied mascara in broad strokes to highlight my white-face, and carefully contoured my eyelashes to be thick and long. Though I looked ridiculous, the theatrical preparations excited my girl.

Food made Clyde tranquil and passive, and thus more manageable on stage, but in the flurry of the hour I forgot to go mousing for him. I forgot. I plumb forgot. We all make mistakes.

I helped Aunt Em carry the bird cages through to the front room instead. Mom emerged and loaded Clyde into his traveling box, folding him into three-foot lengths and wrestling with his head and tail.

"Behave yourself, Bish," I cajoled, mad at the myna. The latest in our long line of gabbers, the bird often suffered nervous breakdowns, mindlessly murdering his entire vocabulary. Our most talented and least disciplined myna ever, he was going berserk in his cage.

"O Christmas Tree, O Christmas Tree!" Bish sang.

"Shut up!" I shouted.

"Don't take it out on Bish," Emma cautioned.

"What? The bird's cuckoo, and you're on my case?"

"O give me a home!"

"You know what I mean."

"Where the buffalo roam!"

"Do I?" I hated Emma's pose, arms folded across her chest.

"And the skiiiiiies are not clucky all day."

"Cloudy," both Em and I corrected simultaneously.

"She might tie one on tonight, Kyle," Emma warned.

"Bish? I don't think so." In her heavy makeup, Emma looked preposterous. Her cheeks were a shiny crimson, her lips like neon. In that light with those eyes she looked ghoulish.

"Don't be smart. I'm serious. She's bound to get drunk."

"Mom's just hyper."

"Why do you insist on arguing with me these days? Is this what having a girlfriend does to you?"

"Feed me! Feed me! Shazam! Shazam! Frack you! Frack you!" Bish ranted.

"Leave Cindy out of this."

"I wish I could. Why didn't you? Kyle!" She grabbed me as I tried to brush past her. "Listen to me!"

"And the skies are not clucky all day!"

"Cloudy!" we yelled in unison.

"My mother is about to get plastered. Fine. Let her. She deserves it. Maybe I will too. Maybe we should *all* tie one on."

"You're not allowed to drink!" she panted, in her rage looking like a haggard shrew with all the paint.

"Auntie — look. Stop worrying. Will you please call the cab?"

"O give me a home!"

"Bish, *shut up!*"

"Now you've hurt his feelings, Kyle. I hope you're satisfied. Bish only has the butterflies, the same as you."

"Us." I didn't want to be singled out as being nervous.

"Oh — my — God!" Aunt Em, looking over my shoulder, whooped. I whirled to see Cindy's smile under a streetwalker's mask. Gold-spangled eyelids and blackened lashes, lipstick to stop cars, an amber powder on her cheeks like yesterday's bruises. Next to her, Mom squeezed Cindy's shoulders. "Well? Well? What do you think? Is she a fox? Is this girl a vixen or what?"

"Abominable," Emma whispered, though not so loudly that Ma could hear.

Bish was less circumspect. "Ugly duckling! Ugly duckling!"

Cindy broke down laughing, pointing a finger at me.

"Okay. What?" I demanded. Irritated.

"You look like the city fool!" she gushed, swept up in the giggles.

The four of us took a good look at ourselves, and immediately we were laughing out of control. Soon we were hugging. We were careful not to smudge faces, and dabbed tears from our eyes before our careful preparations were damaged.

"This is fun!" Cindy confided.

"With you here it is."

"O Christmas Tree, O Christmas Tree!" Bish was happy again too.

With our costumes and makeup, our boa constrictor and wise-cracking birds, we struck genuine fear into the heart of our cabbie. Emma consoled him with a generous tip.

Affectionately known as "Skinhead", an aging black man was proprietor of the St. Antoine Street bar, the upper story of which had been rented out to Mom's sorority for a night. Downstairs at Skinhead's, the serious drinkers compiled their litany of woe, exchanged stories and coarse jokes, and ordered another round.

The upstairs portion was normally segregated as a strip joint, though one night a year the strippers stayed home, yielding the space to Mom and her friends. The T-shaped ramp on which ladies strutted their sequined wares in a traditional bump 'n' grind, twirling glittering chains attached to their nipples, provided the ideal stage for assorted entertainments. Complete with multicolored lights and a wild audience, this room represented the big time for our daring troupe.

On such a night, I was the only male admitted upstairs.

Alone, I ventured onstage to the catcalls, whistles, and slanted boos of a hundred or more invisible voices. Clownish in tails, a tie, and no shirt, I saunter to the rim of the stage and nervously peer over the edge. Obscenities escalate. I resemble a nutty diver contemplating a leap into that sea of writhing, darkened, female forms. I wait for voices to shush. Finally, as sufficient quiet is restored, I begin to sing like the Lincoln's sparrow. First surprise, then delight, sweeps over my audience; I turn their derision into cheers. In this climate any man is to be vilified: but a man who sings like a bird, encouraged.

The crowd is still for my plaintive call of the whippoorwill, and they applaud the high, sweet music of the solitary vireo as I stroll to the rear of the stage. Bathed in blue light, I reach behind the curtain and pull out Bish upon my sleeve. I quickly lock the wrist bracelet that is affixed to his leg. Those seeing this act for the first time are quite amused. They applaud the bird. Sitting down upon a park bench, I open a newspaper and start reading the want ads in the Montreal *Gazette*, an unemployed Charlie Chaplin with a bird on his arm.

My aunt enters stage right.

Vamping for the crowd, she thrusts her pelvis forward as she walks, while manipulating her hips in an exaggerated wiggle.

Bish missed his cue, my whispered prompts do not suffice, and I'm forced to imitate the bird's rasping human voice, concealing the movement of my lips behind the newspaper.

"Sex-y! Sex-y!" I (as Bish) call.

Huffy, Aunt Em returns. Hands on broad, padded hips, she is affronted by my colloquial tongue. "What did you say, young man?"

I chirp like a summer tanager who has landed in a fruit tree.

Pik-i-tuk-i-tuk . . .

The crowd roars.

"*Don't* whistle at me, blockhead!" Aunt Em retaliates. "I'm warning you!" She slinks away.

Bish finally cottons on and accepts my cue. "Cutie pie! Cutie pie!" The women have noticed the difference between my voice and the myna's, and go wild.

"Say that to my face, knucklehead!" she sneers, returning.

I whistle the flight song of the bobolink.

"You insolent little dunderpuss!" My aunt scowls and, tossing her mane, turns to stomp away in her fury.

Bish rises to the occasion. "Gimme a kiss! Gimme a kiss!"

Aunt Em continues her spin. Coming full circle she gives me a smack across my face. Unfortunately, the backstage sound effects are a little off, so the echo of the blow resounds long after her assault. I respond with the attack song of the scissor-tailed flycatcher. As Em marches away with her back to us, Bish recites, "Nice ass! Nice ass!"

Again, Emma whirls, charges. Bish scrawks. I scrawk. I run and Bish madly flaps his wings as Aunt Em chases us around the stage. The audience howls at the burlesque, Bish cleverly ad libs, "Frack you! Frack you!" and around we go again.

Pointing to my temple to indicate that I've been inspired by a brainwave, I unload my cargo and my nemesis, tying Bish to the park bench before I escape offstage. Frazzled, exhausted, Em sits down, then lies down, on the bench. The lights dim. The women grow still. I'm behind the curtain urging Bish with his cue. Finally he spits it out. "Sex-y! Sex-y!"

Aunt Emma's eyes pop open, her head jerks up, and the ladies in Skinhead's Bar go wild.

An erotic waltz followed. A brief interlude, the idea being that the two women would return often to the stage throughout the evening, each time wearing less clothing. I had seen their act before and always stuck around for the finale, when the line between what was dance and what was sex, and between what was simulated and what was real, was indecipherable.

Ma's snake dance was next. Aunt Em and I were busy preparing for our second skit, a kind of bird-land operatic ballet. We would traipse about the stage sporting our beautiful tropical birds, singing birdie serenades and arias while trailing colorful silk wings of our own. Very campy. I've been told that the spectacle is beautiful, even captivating, and we were usually rewarded with the utter attention of our audience.

Cindy came over to me with a mammoth grin on her face. She gushed with praise congratulating Em on her acting, but for me she had only a surly admonition. "How can you let yourself be treated like that?"

"Treated like what?" I was hurt.

Just then Cindy spied Mom through the curtains. Half-nude, Ma was obliged to improvise her dance, for Clyde was not cooperating. He was more rambunctious than usual. Rather than dance with a passive boa, poor Ma practically had to wrestle with him. I suddenly remembered that I had forgotten to feed him.

My mother usually wore provocative costumes, and on this occasion the flimsy material had ripped, and the swimsuit had been stretched out of position, exposing a bobbing breast. Under the lavender floodlight, the elaborate syncopation of the nipple absorbed my whole interest. Down writhing on the floor, Mom was having extreme difficulty lifting Clyde off her. Tantamount to rape. The crowd of hooting women loved it.

A real trouper herself, Ma concealed the extent of her troubles, but I knew that she would survive her ordeal as cross as razors.

Cindy stood beside me, watching Mom less than she did the cheering, drunken orgy of women. She looked up at me with doleful yearning. "Sorry, Kyle. But your mother won't be able to complete her act tonight."

"Don't worry about Ma. She can handle Clyde."

"That's not the point." She smiled with peculiar guile. "I set the cloakroom on fire."

I darted off in three different directions and wound up directly in front of her again. "What? Cindy! What!"

"It'll take a while to really get going."

"Cindy! Jesus! You have to stop doing this!" I scolded her.

"Relax. We have plenty of time to get the birds out."

Overruling Emma's frantic objections, I put the birds in their traveling cages, then ran out onto the stage, my silk wings flowing behind me, to rescue Clyde from mother's fury. "Smartass snake!" she was muttering. And continued swearing royally under her breath while bowing to her cheering admirers. Ma made the most of her exposed boob by cupping it with one hand and giving it a lewd, merry shake. The barroom shook with laughter and applause. "Damn fucking snake," Ma hissed, not at all displeased by the rescue, and she helped me pack Clyde away in his box as the curtain crossed in front of us. We made it offstage.

"No curtain calls tonight, Ma. Something's come up."

"What?"

I leaned into her to whisper. "Don't panic. Do as I say. The house is on fire. If we're not the first out we'll have to leave Clyde and the birds behind."

My mother looked around anxiously, but was quick to hoist her side of Clyde's crate. With Emma and Cindy managing the birds — except for Bish who rode on the box between Ma and me — we paused at the head of the stairs where I sounded the general alarm.

"Fire!" I shouted into the darkened bar. "Fire!"

Seconds later, smoke crept under the cloakroom door.

"Fire!" I shouted more urgently. Bish joined in the call. "Fire!" the myna resounded. "Fire!"

Soon the cry ricocheted throughout the nightclub, upstairs and down. Our little band managed to be among the first to escape.

Pissed off with Cindy, I forbade her, as punishment, to hang around and watch the place burn. Women were fleeing into the dark night down the latticework of fire escapes and bulging through the main doors. Some jumped into the arms of others. They swarmed together for mutual consolation as the sirens of fire engines converged. We hailed the first taxi passing, and although the cabbie was more inclined to be a spectator, I took charge, cajoling and coaxing, and finally the sheer rage in my voice propelled us home.

I lost control at our door. Emma tried to arbitrate our dispute, discover its cause, but I was no squealer. Without courtesy or limit, I was mad at Cindy. Equally indignant, Cindy decreed that she wasn't coming in. "Fine!" I proclaimed. "Good riddance!"

Mom was the one who insisted that Cindy be escorted home, and she elected herself for the task. Probably because she noted the consternation that this announcement produced in both Emma and me, Cindy consented to the plan. Flashing her cruelest smile my way, Cindy linked arms with my mother, tucked herself in close to her, and the two of them, still made up as ghouls, headed into the night.

Aunt Emma hit the bottle. A double scotch vanished, chased by a triple. "Bitches!" she hollered to the world at the top of her lungs. "The bitches!"

Responding to a loud and angry thud, I opened Clyde's box and allowed him to squirm free.

"Exactly how naive are you?" demanded Aunt Em.

"Exactly?"

"Do you honestly believe," she continued, "that your dearly beloved *mother* is so all-fired concerned about that child's welfare? Do you?"

"Take it easy," I protested.

"What's she doing with her right now, Kyle? This second. Mmmm? Tell me. Do you know what your *moth-er* and I are, Kyle? Or do you still believe that our crowd is a branch of the YWCA?"

"I never believed that," I told her. "I just let you think I believed it." We never spoke about such matters.

"Oh. Smart guy. He knows. He's always known. Man-of-the-world, he knows. Genius, you know so much, why haven't you figured out that your *moth-er*" (spoken again with that sneering inflection) "is patting that sweet girl's bottom —"

"Shut up, you!" I warned.

" — that right this minute your *mother* is trying to slip a hand inside that child's blouse, maybe work a finger down her panties?"

"Cut it out, Auntie. I mean it. You're way out of line."

"That's supposed to be your job, smart guy. Aren't you supposed to be fussing with girls this time of night? Does your *mother* have to do *everything* for you?"

"Stop it!" I lashed out, losing my cool. "Just shut your damn yap! Don't say a thing about Mom! You always sound off if she's not here, never to her face. You're a fucking coward!"

"Do you think she's unclasped Cindy's bra yet? Or her own?"

"*Shut up!* Cindy can take care of herself, see. Believe me. Better'n you think. Besides, who in the hell are you to talk? You're not even my aunt, remember? You know what you are, eh, Emma? Eh?"

"I'm dying to find out. You're such a smart guy."

"You're my mother's live-in whore. Yeah. We shouldn't even be allowed in the same house together, you're a corrupting influence. You're a goddamn corrupting influence."

I had never hurt Aunt Em so brutally before, and these many years later I still try to justify my outburst. No one, male or female or bird, was closer to me than Aunt Emma. Yet her spree had damaged a raw nerve. I hated to think of my mother as a lesbian. The world had only begun to enter an era of liberal mores, and I knew of society's contempt for my mother's behavior. I was secretly angry with her for being different. I wanted her to succumb, conform, marry. Set Emma free. The way things were was unfair.

I viewed Emma as the innocent coerced by love. In all my images of her, I could never accept that she was equally responsible, that she lived with my mother because that is precisely what she desired to do. Instead I saw myself as the battleground between oppressor and victim; I was the prize to be won, or ripped asunder.

Reacting to my assault, Emma did not strike back at me. She spoke my name, an attempt at reconciliation, her voice frail with pleading. "My dearest Kyle."

"I'm nobody's Kyle," I taunted. I did not believe myself independent, but denied the mantle of allegiance. At that moment, in her customary style of physical overkill, Mom stormed home through the kitchen. Doors slammed, and our birds screeched against the racket.

"Kyle!" Her shout verged on a snarl. Momentarily stunned, Emma and I offered no clues to our whereabouts. "Kyle! Where are you, you snivelling bastard."

Such affection.

I cringed as she vaulted into the living-room, made more desperate by Emma's enemy posture. The two women were not only anxious to go at it, but they had been primed for the contest.

"What did you do to that child?" parried Em, choosing to get her licks in early. Her rancor, and particularly her defiance, shocked me.

"Oh, so I'm a molester now, am I? Listen, bitch, don't insinuate a goddamn thing. I never touched her. Kyle!" She aimed her forefinger between my eyes.

"Yes, mother?" I battled for appeasement.

"I never want to see that girl around here again."

"Hah!" stormed Emma triumphantly. "She turned you down flat!"

Mother's half-turn was methodical, cruel. "You bitch, Emma. You — If you had eyes you'd see she was a tramp."

"Slap your face, Rose? Did she? I think I see the red marks." Emma was stewing for a brouhaha. Courage from the bottle.

Wisely, my mother altered her tactics. Emma could win a punch-up. Instead, Ma sat down beside me, and steeled her emotional visage. She draped a conniving arm around my suspicious shoulders, tugging me close to her. She kissed my right temple. "Why's Auntie-poo so upset, Kylsie-wylsie?" she inquired in baby-talk. "Has she had too many drinkie-winkies?"

Clyde slid out of the room, he'd had enough, his long form crossing over the toes of my shoe like an army's scorched earth retreat. I admired his freedom. I should have followed him out.

"You don't deserve a son, you fatuous cunt," Emma yelled, "so take your fucking hands off him right this fucking minute."

Ma just laughed at her. "But Auntie-poo, I have no intention of releasing my son. A mother is allowed to hug her son."

I did my level best to squirm free. Her claim an iron vise around my shoulders, Mom would not let go. Pulling me against her, she suddenly slurped a wet kiss upon my ear. Noisy and comic. I ducked. Emma's glass, thrown like a football, a perfect spiral, crashed against the wall behind us. I had no time to recover from that bombardment when my mother bit my earlobe between her teeth.

My aunt crawling into bed next to me after Ma had flown off the handle was customary practice. She reeked of booze, as though she was secreting scotch through her pores. Wide awake, I reluctantly accommodated her shape with a huffy shift of my weight. Turned away from her rancid breath. Emma's mouth hovered close to my ear — warm breath and spittle — as she mewed, "Rose is not your real mother."

"You're drunk, Auntie. Try and get some rest. And for God's sake, quit breathing on me! You stink worse than a distillery!"

"Rose is not your real mother, Kyle." She let her words hang, as if from one of the perches above us.

"What do you mean?" I spoke to the ceiling. My question rose on the air of my breath, descending back down upon us. Dust settling.

"I am."

I was not terribly alarmed. In her stupor she wanted to make some claim to my life, some vague assault against my mother. "Auntie —"

"I *am*! I am your real mother." Emma bounded to her knees, tossed off the sheet, her head butting against the canvas overhang, and she cried out, "I am! I am! Dammit! I am!"

Stricken, I stared up helplessly at this madwoman in her underwear. The birds nervously shifted about, made nighttime noises, clucking their worry. Streetlamps glared vacuous light on the curtains of my window.

"You're drunk," I rebuked her, with effort maintaining some sense of decorum, of balance.

Inexplicably, Emma, gently, tenderly, touched my cheek. "You poor child," she demurred, the effect of her inebriation being to run the three words together. I tried to sit up and push away from her, feeling claustrophobic, smothered, but her weight now held a knee of mine for ransom, and I couldn't budge.

"Your father," Aunt Em commenced, which was the trick that made me want to listen, "was married to Rose, that's true. He wanted a child. He was that type. Whether through conspiracy or nature, Kyle, I do not know, but Rose did not conceive.

"We were working in the carnival then. Your mom was the Snake Lady. I was the Bird Lady. After he fell from the high wire, your father was a clown. I'll be honest with you, Kyle," and she seemed more sober than I had ever known her to be, solemn and genuinely contrite, not the least bit dippy, "I desired your father. He wasn't a handsome man but he had something. I was a young woman alone, I had feelings, I wanted to sleep with him and one night when I was plastered I told him so. I made myself available. Your father was a simple, happy man, Kyle. Affairs didn't interest him. His marriage to Rose was stormy, at best — to this day he's the only person who ever stood up to her — but he was not the sort of man to seek solace elsewhere. At least, not with me. Your father was a strong man, Kyle, a faithful man, you could do well to emulate him. That's the blood that seeps through your bones. Your mom — Rose — and me, we corrupted him."

Confident that she had my attention now, Emma freed my pinned knee. I sat with my back against the wall, engrossed now in this first telling of my creation, this long-awaited revelation of a paternal connection.

"Rose saw through me. She's the one who engineered your birth. In that sense, she is your mother. She put your father and me up to it. She planned that he and I would make love. Rose would, as she put it, assist in the proceedings. She said she wanted to keep everything kosher.

"The deal was this. If I became pregnant, I would carry the child as a surrogate mother. Then your father and Rose would raise the baby. Everybody had a job to do. We wrote the details down on paper. Your father insisted that any male child be named after him. I presume he was skeptical that he and Rose would last forever, he wanted to make sure that he had dibs on you. I agreed in writing to bear a child from your father's seed. That's exactly how we worded it. I loved him, and wasn't about to refuse the chance to be with him. Bearing his child was a special bonus."

"Rose, she was giving her husband a baby, fulfilling his princi-pal desire, and could do so without having to endure the pain. Of course, that's not all that she had in mind. She was out to get what she wanted, too."

Emma paused, shuffling through the images still prevalent from that period. I had drawn my own conclusions. Exhaling a deep breath, I said, "You."

"Me," Emma confirmed. "She wanted me. That was her scheme under her scheme. We three went to bed together, Kyle — I know that sounds sordid. It wasn't really . . . I don't think. Your father showed up for the big event in clownface, with that stupen-dous frown, big red nose, and painted tears weeping down one cheek. He wore his costume too, but of course he had to undress. All my birds were there, and I had a lot more back then, and Rose's snakes. Her idea. By making a big production out of the event she hid her true intentions.

"I can't lie to you, Kyle. With the three of us in bed I was flattered and aroused too by your mother's attention. She said I had to be excited to do it right, to conceive properly, but that she'd be jealous if your father enjoyed me too much. So *she* enjoyed me too much. She seduced me, Kyle, but was I unwilling? Unlike your friend Cindy I didn't have the brains to rebuff her, I didn't slap, I preferred to go along for the ride.

"I liked it. It was so unreal! The birds were reciting gibberish. The snakes were slithering on the furniture and crossing over the bed. Your mother was crazily made up doing strange things to me and here comes a sad-eyed clown, intent on making babies. God, what a kick."

Revulsion washed through me in waves, I felt nauseated, as though I was to blame for their behavior. Apart from their conniv-ing and lust, I was beginning to perceive also that unbridled truth. I was not my mother's son. I was Aunt Emma's.

"After you were born, Kyle, I stayed on. Your father left, shunt-ed aside because your mother — Rose, I mean — and I had fallen madly in love. And I stayed on because I loved you so. You were my baby, my precious, flesh of my flesh, blood of my blood — to remain as your aunt was the alternative Rose permitted. You were her possession. Rose possessed me because she possessed you. And also because I loved her. She stuck to the letter of our written agreement because that piece of paper was her power, her authority. So she named you Kyle Troy. She kept the name of Elder. But that's past. I've been waiting for you to grow up. For years I've been waiting. Now you know the truth: I am your mother. Sorry to spring it on you after all this time. I cannot bear that woman any longer, Kyle. We . . . together . . . the two of us . . . we have to tell her to go. Kick her out like she kicked your father out. Tell her to scram. Beat it. Get out of the house. I'm your mother, Kyle."

Lethargy camped upon my brow, suspending the minutes in a motionless daze. I spun off the bed, fresh adrenalin and venom raging through my bloodstream, and I struggled to put my jeans on. My hands shook so much that I could barely manage the buckle.

"You're nuts!" was my futile rebuttal. "You're lying! Why are you lying? You're not my mother, you coot, you're not even my aunt. You're just a, just a, a fucking *lesbian*." I spit the word out as though it represented sufficient insult.

"I'm a lesbian, that's right," Emma declared, her voice resonant with a conviction uncommon to her. "So what? I am what I am. But you should know by now that I would have left her a hundred times if it weren't for you. I would never abandon you."

"Oh sure. Blame me. Did I tell you to go to bed with a gang? Did you have to sleep with practically the whole goddamned carnival? With who knows how many birds and animals too? Now I know why you're always so nostalgic for that time."

"Kyle! Oh God, Kyle. I don't blame you. I knew I had to tell you someday, I knew it wouldn't be easy. Please accept at least that I'm your real mother. We'll go from there."

"My mother *shit!*"

I threw on a shirt. I wanted to run until exhaustion hauled me down, or sprint forever into another world. Nothing could be said to stall my flight, at that moment the very sound of her voice would ignite my momentum to flee, my white-face a visible scream in the darkness.

Except that Emma was wise.

She did not speak.

She sang to me instead.

Not a lullaby. She tweeted the afternoon thanksgiving of the eastern bluebird, and combined it with the evening devotion of the wood thrush. At that moment my denials crumbled; I believed her conclusively. Emma was my mother.

We stared at one another, Emma and I.

A haunting examination.

A desolate impasse, like looking in a mirror and seeing your own life trapped within a foreign skin and bones.

At that juncture then, a ruling from heaven. Ordained. We heard a startled cry and a heavy thud.

Then more quick, frantic cries. Squeaks.

Slow to react, we raced out and across to Ma's room. Barricaded by the lock. Now she was screaming with chilling terror, unable to surface from the horror of her nightmare.

"Ma, wake up!" I was yelling. "Wake up!"

Our combined weight failed to dislodge the latch. Again and again we drove our shoulders hard into the door until the wood cracked and we fell through. Mother — she would always be my mother to me — lay on the floor, gagging.

Wrapped around her, squeezing tight, was Clyde. Her pet boa. Peeling him off her was impossible.

Craven sounds emitted from her dying lungs. Her eyes rolled back.

I ran to the kitchen and returned with a knife. The only sounds I remember now were Emma's despeate pleas. I slipped on a scatter rug and was sent flying. Damaged one eye badly. Unsure if I was even conscious I scarcely hesitated, falling on Ma and slashing Clyde with the butcher knife.

I hacked and stabbed and worked the blade deeper and still the beast would not let go. Mom was silent. Limp. Her eyes now glaring back at this world without a blink. I plunged the knife into the snake, down through that crisp tough hide, down into tissue and realm, plunged again into fluids and bile, blood and membrane and despair, the knife slipping deeper and into the very flesh of the woman I called "MO-THER!"

I gouged out the snake's deadly eyes. The beast expired and I continued my assault, carving one dead form free from another, scalping the reptile's hide glued to my mother's in an embrace of eternal damnation.

Emma attempted to pull me away. Half my strokes now merely glanced off the boa and etched my mother's skin. But I would not quit until the creature was off her, freeing her corpse from the indignity, and freeing her soul from the candor and grip of this evil sphere.

Expiation. I was setting my mother loose.

Emma and I held one another. She wailed with pathetic lament, breaking away to try and resurrect my mother with her kisses and tears and the pain of her grief.

Considerable time passed, I think, before we could function. We both passed through a veil of lunacy to which we might have succumbed. We persevered to the shelter of our shock and sadness. Emma dialed, and I spoke to the police. We agreed to wait for them.

Requiring fresh air, a glimmer of life perhaps, I walked through to the back porch. At once I heard the beating of wings, like a scurry of angels. I had no reason to fear what the coroner would eventually determine. That Rose had died of abdominal strangulation administered by her pet boa constrictor. That her son had tried to save her. That the sixteen knife wounds on her body were not the determining cause of death. I had tried to save her, yet I could see her blood on my hands in the dim backyard light, and I questioned where the impetus for each of my blows had come. I felt my life was vile and unworthy, condemned.

Emma joined me on the porch. She tried to touch me. I recoiled from her. From our complicity. I despised her at that moment. For bringing me into this world. For not getting me out. To announce my despair and to revile all of humankind, in the danger of the moment I revealed to her that "Bish escaped."

My aunt could scarcely comprehend. "What?"

"Bish. He escaped. Others too."

And from the depths of her numb, distraught condition, she studied my choice of words. Her lips hardly moving, she murmured, "Escaped?"

"Shazam," I breathed in the cool night air. "Shazam."

5

Now, cynics might theorize that choosing to be driven to the inquest as a passenger in Hazel Stamp's Fleetwood was a clinical manifestation of a death wish, when really I was anxious for a morning pick-me-up. Some choose caffeine. I prefer to career down mountainsides. Having perceived that my best interests would be served by being awake for the proceedings, I wanted to have my adrenalin pumping.

Hazel drives her car in a fashion similiar to cowboys riding bucking broncos. She opens the gate and hangs on. Apart from her evident inability to control the vehicle's speed — she tends to slam either the accelerator or the brake pedal to the floor — the most harrowing of her habits not only shook me to full wakefulness, but I cannot declare for a certainty that I have had a restful night's sleep since.

Hazel's technique in negotiating curves is to enter them from the wrong lane. Blind hills require that she drive down the middle of the double-line as if the car was on rails. Let others swerve to safety. On the high-speed straightaways, she compensates for on-coming traffic by steering the right-hand wheels along the shoulder of the road, even when there isn't one. I thought I heard the air-raid siren alerting the village of Stowe to Hazel's impending arrival.

She braked.

I fended against the dash.

Surfaced.

We had made it alive.

"Ah, Hazel —"

"My pleasure, Mr. Kyle. No need to thank me."

"Okay," I said. "I won't."

In the Town Hall parking lot, I found Chantelle waiting for me. I clunked the car door shut, heard another door open nearby, turned and there she was, dear Chantelle. She had been sitting alone in the backseat of a Honda Accord.

I derived a virtuous pleasure from the sighting, as I would from identifying a rare species of bird, or one flying beyond its customary geographic limits. I approached her cautiously, mindful that any reconciliation would require renewed confession and atonement. Hazel went on ahead without us.

"Hi, Kyle. How are you?"

"Fine, thanks. How are you?"

"I'm fine."

"Good! That's good. We're both fine."

"Great."

My chin bobbed with fake confidence as I searched for a way to penetrate our joint awkwardness and civility.

"I guess you're attending the inquest," she said.

"I think I'm the star witness. You're not alone?"

"There's quite a few of us inside. I —"

"How many? Exactly?"

Startled by my interruption, she looked at me with guarded interest. Hard to imagine red tears caked on her soft (and in this breeze, pink) skin. "I'm not sure. Why? What difference does it make?"

"Always count. That's what you taught me."

My attempt at humor, and my wish to revive the camaraderie of our early hours together, was scooped up by the wind and borne away, out of sight, out of mind.

"Sorry," I retracted.

"I stayed behind because I wanted to talk to you first."

Foolishly, always the lame-brain, I continued to resort to flippancy. "No tampering with my testimony," I joked.

"I had precisely that in mind," Chantelle answered seriously, and for the first time that morning honored me with her familiar searching gaze. Attentive and penetrating, her look exhibited no self-consciousness, as though I was being examined through a lens.

"Okay," I allowed. "What gives?"

As she spoke my expectations plummeted like a barometer before a tropical storm. My lady had not undergone a radical change of heart. Our floundering relationship was not Chantelle's concern; she was interested only in the welfare of her cult and the maintenance of her good name. She desired peace between us merely to assure that my testimony would be neither damaging nor provocative. "I can't go through life being labelled a freak, Kyle. And anyway, it's none of the public's business what I or any of us do."

"So far I haven't breathed a word, Chantelle. If anyone wants to know, you and your crew were as quiet as church mice."

"Thanks, Kyle." Even her smile disturbed me. Was it not calculated to bind me to my oath? I had lost rhythm with Chantelle; I distrusted her.

"You don't have to worry," I reiterated. "If anybody's in the soup today it's me."

"You! How come?" We strolled toward the Town Hall building.

"Racial prejudice. I'm the stranger, the new kid on the block, the prodigal who never made it home in time for his father's funeral, only to reap the blessings of the will. Ergo, I must be guilty of something, and there are those who are determined to find out what."

Chantelle smiled, perfectly naturally this time, an indication that she might actually be enjoying my company. "Are you always this paranoid? Or only on special occasions?"

"Always." I swung open the door for her, and she passed under my outstretched arm. "At heart I'm a big-city boy who's a fool for small-town politicking. The police inspector is mad at me, the assistant district attorney's assistant is seeing red, I suspect, and my own lawyer has his knickers in a twist. All because Gaby chose to lie down in my bed."

As we climbed the staircase to the second floor, Chantelle advised, "Tell them the truth."

"What truth?" Did Chantelle know about Gabriella's licentious visit to my room?

"I gave it some thought. It occurred to me that Gaby didn't die in *your* bed, Kyle. Tell them that." Chantelle expected me to lie? Or did she possess restricted knowledge? Had Gaby died elsewhere and been planted in my bed along with the floral bouquet she grasped? We stopped in the corridor.

"She didn't?"

"Gaby died in your *father's* bed. That it was yours for one night is incidental. She and your father were famous friends. We heard hints of a romantic link. She nursed him through his illness, and, well, Gaby never wholly recovered from his death. She brought the poison to the inn because she planned to die — at a certain time, in a particular way, in a special place. In choosing suicide, I think she was seeking to be close to him again. Dying in his room was probably symbolic for her." Chantelle clutched my elbow to turn me around, and we headed for the open door. "Not to worry, Kyle," she encouraged, patting my hand. "You'll do fine."

Crossing the threshold, I did experience the uncanny sensation that I had been prompted, given my script. My lines had been carefully rehearsed. Seated beside her, I did feel safe, as though Chantelle had woven her magic to protect me from any defamation, and her close presence routed innuendos. The nuns and I were friends, as everyone could plainly see. They did not view me as having contributed to their leader's demise. Let the court take note. Armed with an answer at last, I eagerly awaited my turn to testify. I do have a flair for performing in public.

"All rise!" sounded the bailiff, with a voice like a French horn.

"Sit sit sit sit sit," contradicted Judge Dwayne Pearson as he flew into the room, robes fluttering as wings, and sounding remarkably like the Tennessee warbler feasting on its afternoon lunch. In his early fifties, the magistrate was a much younger man than I had expected, with none of the wary furrows etched in his brow that I had feared. He slept nights. The ghosts of condemned men did not drop by to haunt him. Anyone he had sent up the river was still paddling.

The inquest was not taking place in a courtroom. Instead we were gathered around a massive oval table in need of varnish. In the spacious four corners of the white, rectangular room, chairs accommodated the excess witnesses. Chantelle and I were seated there. Not one to be daunted by formality, Hazel had chosen to sit at the table with the bigwigs. Her expressed purpose was to defend against any allegation concerning the strength and flavor of her tea.

Opposite me and uncomfortable amid the scrutiny of nuns sat my dim lawyer. The women had deemed Franklin D. Ryder attractive. He had no function at these proceedings, and was here to observe.

Judge Pearson commenced with a formal reading of the obligations and purview of this court, although his tone shifted after his reading of the required text. "Hi, Dave! How're the kids?"

The assistant district attorney's assistant smiled brightly. They were in cahoots! "Terrific, Your Honor."

"Dave, if it's all right with you, I'd like to begin with the medical testimony."

"That's fine with me, Your Honor."

Physician, heal thyself. Dr. Lewis Tanner was a pallid, emaciated individual who wore literary leather patches on the elbows of his tweed jacket. His bald spot was notable for its glossy shine. He spoke from his seat, which happened to be next to Hazel's, repeating at gruesome length the extent of the autopsy and relating his conclusion without resorting to drama. Technical names for everything, translated to mean: Gabriella Deschenes had died of deliberate poisoning. Prompted by the A. to the D.A.'s A., he conceded that the poison was consumed with a cup of tea. "The deceased, Your Honor, was a registered nurse who worked in a hospital in Manchester, Massachusetts. One would presume that, if the drug was self-administered, it was acquired through improper means."

"Thanks, Lew," Judge Pearson said. "How's the golf swing?"

"Been practicing in the backyard, Dwayne. It ought to be in shape this year," Tanner bragged.

"Your Honor," Dave Mathison suggested, "I'd like to follow the path of the teacup through Toll House, from the time the tea was prepared, until it was drunk by the accused."

"Why? Did some of it spill?" Judge Pearson asked. I zeroed in on him, amazed, and somewhat relieved, by his whimsy.

"Not to my knowledge, Your Honor. I'm more concerned with what might have slipped into the cup than with what might have spilled out."

"Sounds like a tempest in a teacup to me." Being judge seemed like a nice gig. Holding an audience is a snap, and everyone is too respectful and fearful not to laugh at a jurist's jokes. Hecklers can be sentenced to hard labor, which is handy, and the curtain can't come down on your act until you say so.

"Something like that," Mathison allowed.

"I see. Well, I'd rather hear from the friends of the deceased. I want to know Miss Deschenes's — or is it Mrs.?"

"She was divorced, Your Honor. She used Mrs."

"I'd like to know her state of mind close to the time of her expiry."

The nuns were universally boring. Each one repeated that Gaby had given no sign of her depression, and added that she had always been an intensely private person, a woman difficult to read. They sounded prepared. Rehearsed. Sister Celia, whose gray hair in a bun and placid composure constituted a blatant imitation of a traditional nun — and I was shocked to learn that that's what she had been most of her adult life "until about six years ago, when I switched to a less orthodox order" — was asked to field the inevitable and difficult, question.

"Did anything occur, since your arrival at the inn, that might possibly have precipitated Gabriella Deschenes taking her own life?" Mathison probed. "Some sort of dispute or argument, for example."

Intent on the reply, I leaned forward slightly. Chantelle did the opposite. She touched her lips with an index finger, then tightened her grip on the narrow aluminum arms of her chair.

"No, sir. Not to my knowledge. When she died, all of us, all of her friends, we wondered what we had done to hurt her. But I don't believe that any of us were directly involved. Gaby — Gabriella Deschenes — brought the poison with her to the inn, didn't she? I mean, it's not the sort of thing you carry around in your purse. So I think that she planned to do it ahead of time. She chose where and when, and the rest of us just happened to be there."

"And why do you suppose she chose to die at the Toll House Inn?"

Shaking her head to indicate that the answer was beyond her perception, Sister Celia took a stab at it anyway. "The one thing that occurred to me was, she didn't want to die alone. But I can't untangle her thinking."

"Would you hazard a guess as to why she chose to die in the bed of Mr. Kyle Troy Elder Junior?"

"You may answer the question if you wish," Judge Pearson put in, "but guesswork is not really the domain that we wish to investigate."

Celia shrugged, looking at the judge with the meekest of expressions. "I just don't know," she said.

When Dave Mathison asked Chantelle Cromarty to come forward, Judge Pearson expressed his impatience with the way things were progressing. "Dave, we haven't learned very much at all about the emotional state of the deceased. In fact, we haven't come up with a thing."

"Miss Cromarty is a neighbor of Mrs. Deschenes, Your Honor. Perhaps she will be able to shed some light."

"Let us hope so."

Chantelle sat at the oval table, facing me more directly than she did the judge. She was sworn in. Asked about her friend's emotional status, Chantelle noted that she had seemed stable. The courtroom collectively sighed. Boredom reigned. In the next breath, she added, "However . . ."

"Yes, Miss Cromarty?"

"There is one thing."

"What's that?"

"About five months ago, Kyle Elder Senior passed away. Gabriella was at his side to the end. They were close friends. I don't honestly believe that Gabriella ever overcame her grief, or recovered from the loss."

Chantelle did not return to my side. She chose a chair among her companions.

Mathison made his pitch. "Your Honor, I would like to trace the movement of the teacup —"

"If you must."

"I call Mrs. Hazel Stamp to be sworn in."

"How're you doing, old girl?" the judge asked my housekeeper.

"Not bad, young sprout. You?"

"Alive and kicking."

Hazel's testimony was straightforward. Sister Sophie had requested an extra cup of tea. "That's what they call each other, Dwayne: Sister. You know how things are nowadays."

"Indeed I do. I have daughters, remember?"

"How are they doing anyhow?"

"I'm paying for their education, Hazel. I'm not convinced that that's what they're getting. Let's go back to the tea, though it grieves me to say so."

Hazel had made the tea. She passed it to her helper, Cassie Baxter, who handed it to Sister Sophie. Dave Mathison could not bring himself to ask the imperative, and impertinent, question, so Judge Pearson took the daring plunge.

"Old girl, you weren't experimenting with weird concoctions, were you?"

"It was Darjeeling!" Outraged, Hazel's fist slammed the table as judiciously as a gavel.

"Thanks, Hazel. We appreciate your dropping by."

"Your Honor," Mathison announced, "the State calls Cassie Baxter."

"Oh, for heaven's sake, Dave!" the judge objected.

"Well, Dwayne, what else am I to do?" pleaded the assistant district attorney's assistant.

"Cassie!" boomed Judge Pearson.

"Yes, sir?" squeaked the timid girl.

"Did you spike the teacup with poison?"

"No, sir, I didn't."

"There!" Pearson triumphed. "That's that. Who's next?"

"Sophie Buchwald."

"Are we going to follow the teacup up the stairs?"

"That's my plan."

"Why?"

"To ascertain that others, not merely the deceased, had opportunity to —"

"Look," Pearson stood and addressed the room. "Did anyone put poison in Gabriella Deschenes's otherwise delicious Darjeeling tea?"

Nobody confessed.

"There we have it, Dave," Pearson summed up. "What else do you want to know?"

Humbled, the young man barely made himself heard as he put forward his next request. "Could I at least talk to Kyle Elder?"

"He's dead, Dave. What do you want, a ouija board?"

"Junior, I mean. His son. Kyle Elder Junior."

"Is he here? Sure. Kyle Elder the Younger — ah! There you are! Hey! You look just like your dad. He and I were great pals, Kyle. His only flaw was that his right hand was a mite too liberal with my wife's derriere. All in jest, of course. I'm pleased to meet you, Kyle, and" — I knew what was coming — "welcome to Vermont."

"Thanks."

"Be seated. Anywhere."

My chair at the table gave me a clear view of Inspector Isaiah Snow, which unnerved me somewhat.

"Mr. Elder, Junior," Mathison commenced, shuffling papers as though in hunt for my life story which he had scribbled down somewhere, "did you in fact receive the teacup prior —"

"Dave!" Judge Pearson sounded positively outraged, which I appreciated. "I thought we had finished with the damn teacup!"

"Well — I —"

"Forget the teacup, Dave."

"Yes, Your Honor. Ah — Mr. Elder, Junior, that is your name?"

I looked at the judge. Who looked at me. We both shrugged. My eyes crossed Snow's. "Apparently," I said.

"Yes. Well. Could you advise the court on how the deceased came to be in your bed?"

"I really don't know, Dave," I answered, delighting in my familiarity. This was Vermont, after all.

"I see."

"I can speculate, if you like."

"Be our guest, Kyle," Judge Pearson invited.

"Well, as I see it, Gabriella Deschenes and my father were very close. We've already heard that she was upset by my father's death. Now, we're calling the bed mine. And so it is. But at that point I'd only slept in it the one night. You see what I'm saying here,

Dwayne? Could it not be that she chose to die not in *my* bed, but in my father's? Really, it's *his* bed. I'm only a newcomer in these parts."

"How about that, Dave?" Pearson asked. "The young Elder makes sense. I'm prepared to close this case unless you have something further to add." The judge turned to me. "I believe in judicial efficiency. Justice delayed is justice that denies me a round of golf. Do you play?"

I shook my head in the negative.

"Pity. Very well: this inquest finds that Gabriella Deschenes died by her own hand. Does anyone here dispute the verdict?"

The courtroom was silent. Mathison and Snow exchanged looks, and shuffled their feet; no other dissent was registered. F.D.R. winked at me, unnecessarily I thought.

"Well and good. I'll write it up after lunch. In the meantime, ladies and gents, we are adjourned."

In the tumult of the exodus, I was keenly interested in isolating Chantelle from her peers. It appeared that she was equally intent on eluding me. The nuns stampeded from the room, using the benefit of their sex, as the men, like the waves parting across the Red Sea, permitted the women passage, then closed in behind them as though I represented Pharaoh's army.

Someone was tugging on my elbow. Dr. Tanner was pressing me for a word. "Just a second, please." I squeezed out the door, but Chantelle was long gone. Dr. Tanner coughed into his shoulder and pulled me aside again.

"Infernal cold," he attested. His wretched illness demeaned the potency of his arts, an embarrassment. "Can't get rid of the damn thing."

"What can I do for you?"

"A word. Perhaps lunch? Yes, let's have lunch. I promise not to sneeze too much."

"I don't know," I demurred, and checked my watch.

"It's about your father," Tanner said quietly, tipping the scales.

I gave the good doctor my most enterprising smile while steeling my defense mechanisms against his germs. "Lunch," I agreed.

Any number of fine restaurants flourish in Stowe (anyone dining out in the area should not forget Toll House), yet my anemic physician chose a simple lunch counter where sandwiches constituted the feast-of-the-day. The coffee was exceptional.

"Your testimony today interested me." Dr. Tanner began. "I was particularly intrigued by the connection you drew between the poor dead woman —"

"Gabriella."

"Yes yes, and your father. I think you should be told, Kyle —" he followed a sip of coffee with several deep, life-saving breaths, a rattling gurgle down his windpipe — "that that woman's was not the first mysterious death to occur at Toll House."

Dr. Tanner had my whole attention. Instinct told me he was not talking about deaths in antiquity.

I could feel the blood draining from my face. "Who else?"

"Your father's," he said.

"I don't understand," I postulated. "He died of cancer."

Tanner poured a murky gravy over his fries, and transferred his napkin from his lap to his collar, wearing it as a bib. He fed himself the messy fries with his fingers.

"I was treating him for cancer, that's true. His case was terminal, that is also true. Your father suffered terribly. His decline was rapid. The morning before he died, I paid him a visit. His struggle was a valiant one, Kyle, his heart was in good shape. He looked like a corpse, but frankly, barring a sudden stroke, I expected him to linger another month or two. He had a strong fighting will."

"I see."

While he spoke, Tanner would wave a french fry in rhythm to his words; he'd punctuate his sentences by popping one into his mouth and noisily chewing. "When I was called back the next day, I wasn't altogether surprised. These things are not easily predicted. Certainly not by me. Kyle, I was surprised to find your father looking well. His cheeks were bright and rosy, the first color I'd seen in him in months. I almost said hello to him."

"Almost?"

"He was dead, Kyle. Rosy in death. In life, he'd known only a pale pallor."

"What does it mean?" I asked him.

"That rosy complexion . . ."

"Yes?"

"I'm not an amateur, Kyle. I recognized his condition right off the bat."

"His condition? He was dead!"

"I've viewed the dead before, Kyle."

"And?" I pressed him.

"Carbon-monoxide poisoning."

I stared him down in silence.

"Most of those so-called nuns were at Toll House at the time," he added.

Shaking off my surprise, I found a voice. "It wasn't Easter."

"Nope. You're right, they don't usually go there, except at Easter."

It was left to me to articulate the understanding we shared. "A mercy killing?"

Dr. Tanner neither agreed nor disagreed. He preferred to elaborate on his own role as an accessory to the crime. "I chose to let it go. Your father's agony wasn't easy to bear. He refused strong painkillers and stuck to the mild. More than anything, he cherished his consciousness. Told me himself that he wanted to looked death squarely in the eyeball, if death had the nerve to face him. He couldn't remember being born, he said, and next to that occurrence dying would be the most important day in his life. He wanted his mind free of encumbrances. His repudiation of the hospital was part of his thinking, though we both knew his life would only be shortened and made less comfortable. When the time was near, and the pain too much for even him to bear, I suspect he bullied the others into it."

"Maybe he did and maybe he didn't," I said. Specifically, I wondered, who? Who did it? Who put my father down, out of his misery as though he was a pet dog?

Tanner burped and exhaled. "I wrote down natural causes due to cancer on the death certificate. Why make a fuss? I've done things in my life that pester my conscience more. When I learned that the Order of the Seven Veils had inherited a substantial sum . . . yeah, I suffered twinges. Worried about it. I mean, they could hardly collect if they'd done him in. Maybe the money was a greater incentive than mercy. But I maintained my peace. Until now. This second death . . . let's say that I'm concerned."

"What do you mean?"

"Your father was killed, and the event presented as natural causes. Today we declared that Gabriella Deschenes killed herself, but who really knows for sure? You understand, don't you, Kyle, that I'll deny saying any of this? Please don't repeat it. But I thought, as Kyle's son . . . I thought you should know. In the end, his mode of dying was more peaceful than it might have been."

"I suppose that's true. Listen. Thanks for telling me. I — I appreciate it."

"No problem. Hey, glad to have you with us, Kyle. Welcome to Vermont."

Walking away from the sandwich shop I was walloped by intuition as though I had slammed into a lamppost. Intuition? Or the obvious facts? I now knew why Chantelle had discarded her yellow Toyota at Toll House. Run a hose, did you, girl, from the exhaust to the back seat, where my poor papa slept? What's the matter, woman, nervous? Can't bring yourself to slide behind the wheel again of your death machine? Afraid his ghost might suit up for the ride?

Like it did with Gabriella.

I trudged most of the way home on foot. My mind in a quandary. I had allowed myself to be manipulated at the inquest. I had chosen to be circumspect to protect Chantelle. Done with me, she had fled immediately afterwards. No thank-yous. No good-byes. Vanishing into the thin air of mountainous Vermont.

When my heels blistered I stopped off at a motel restaurant and called a cab.

Swollen feet, and a headache to match. I was not in the best shape for my next discovery. How could I have known that the closet skeletons of Tennessee were indeed alive and well and living in northern Vermont? Stowed away on my property. Awaiting my return to Toll House.

1

The afternoon that I returned from the inquest into Gaby's suicide, I endeavored to nap. When I, the master of sleep, cannot catch forty winks while the sun's up, something dire must be wrong with my system. Time to see a shrink, or invest in term insurance. Tired of my fitful tossing, knotting my limbs into a macramé wall-hanging, I decided to take a walk. Perhaps the mountain air would either revive me or mercifully knock me unconscious.

I dressed for the occasion with Band-Aids on my blisters.

Missing Chantelle, I had an urge to return to the stables; perhaps my mood could be remedied if I relived our few happy moments together. From a distance, I thought I saw a wisp of smoke waft upwards from the stables' chimney. That stopped me in my tracks. My fear, and skittish imagination, made me angry with myself, but I have little difficulty choosing between discretion and valor.

Besides, Isaiah Snow was coming up the Toll House Road.

Three uniformed officers accompanied him in the unmarked Ford. "Howdy, Kyle!" As friendly as sunlight and rainbows. "Glad that mess is over with!"

"How do you do, Inspector?"

"Call me Isaiah." He switched off the ignition, and stood beside the car with his arms resting on the roof. "What a view!" he blathered. "I'm a mountain man at heart, Kyle. Does me no good to live out my days down in the valley."

"Book in for a week or three, Isaiah. I'm always glad to take a guest's money. Bring your wife."

"No can do. She gets a nosebleed at high altitudes."

The news bolted through me like an electrical charge. Alarmed, I said in a faint, cracked voice, "What can I do for you, Inspector?"

He had not noticed my fleeting distress. "This is very much routine," he indicated, a disclaimer that made my hair stand on end. "Before the inquest, Kyle, I was obliged to run a check on you. No offense. It's my job. You are a stranger hereabout."

"Listen, Isaiah, I don't know what got into me. Nerves. Weariness. I'm sorry about the lie-detect — sorry again, the truth-verifier test. Okay? I apologize."

"Accepted. Think nothing of it. You'll accept my apology in exchange, I trust, when I tell you that I have a warrant."

I looked at his three accomplices to determine if he was joking. "For my arrest?" I bleated.

"Mercy, no!" The boom in Isaiah's laugh bounced off the mountains like a rubber ball. "It's a search warrant. Just routine."

One man's routine is another man's trauma.

"Want to tell me what you're looking for?" I inquired.

"We've had a tip."

"A tip. Cute."

"Telling us where to look. We don't know for what. We want to look in your car, Kyle."

More strange by the second. "The Cherokee?"

"No. The Mercury, if you please, sir."

"Isaiah? What the heck is going on?"

Coming around from his side of the Ford, the inspector slapped the warrant on to my shoulder. I steadied it. "Just routine, Kyle. We'll be out of your hair in no time. Where you parked?"

"I buried it," I told Isaiah Snow, and stalked up the hill with the silly damn warrant scrunched in my fist.

Isaiah had come prepared for a minor archeological expedition. Shovels, crowbars, and pickaxes advised me that most of the northern half of the State now knew that I had sent my car over the edge, and that Snow was merely acting on common knowledge.

The appearance of an oxyacetylene torch was another matter.

"What're you here for really, the scrap-metal?"

Embarrassment tinged his answer. "I heard that the car might be banged up a little."

The task set before them was not an easy one, requiring the dexterity of mountain goats and considerable human muscle. They worked their way down the rock face to the buried automobiles, slipping on the springtime muck and burdened by their heavy tools. The men panted and cursed trying to pry open the trunk of the upside-down Mercury.

Above them, on solid rock, I practiced the evening outburst of the orchard oriole. Periodically the laboring peace officers shot looks at me, obviously wishing that this was hunting season and that they had brought along their shotguns.

The assault with the crowbars succeeded only in punching holes in the metal and further gouging the chrome. The car's trade-in value depreciated by the minute. An officer lit the torch.

I stopped whistling and Isaiah climbed up to my eyrie. "The keys should still be in the ignition," I told him.

"Doubt if they'd do much good. The car is pretty battered."

Like a virus, nervousness had infected my bloodstream. A suspicious agent of the law may have interpreted my unease as a sign of guilt, but my symptoms were generated by the circumstances. That anyone would want to investigate the jalopy was odd. I knew very well that I had left the trunk empty, but my fertile imagination easily filled the space. I expected bags of cocaine. Tennessee moonshine. The lost loot from the Great Train Robbery.

"What are you looking for?" I demanded again of Snow.

"You tell me."

I remained mute. Suddenly the trunk lid sprang open, striking the ground. A burly officer, not the welder, peered up into the yawning cavity. Poked his head back out.

"There's a sack in here, sir," he called up. "Wedged in."

Somehow, I was not wholly surprised.

"Remove it, please," Isaiah requested, in a tone suitable for addressing a distracted child. "Any ideas?" he asked me. To admit to the contents now, his tone seemed to indicate, would spare me a hardship later.

"Beats me," I told him. "Honest, Isaiah, I don't know what's going on."

The "sack" proved to be a familiar-looking plastic garbage bag, and it spilled out of the trunk with a hideous clatter. O God. No. The officer ripped it open with a penknife. The first article he withdrew, and held up to the waning rays of sunlight for our perusal on the hilltop, was a gray, thin bone about a foot long. I had one just like it in my Cherokee Chief.

The second item was a human skull.

The empty black eye sockets stared mournfully up at me.

The next moments were confusing. I remember that I plunked myself down on the cold damp stone. I was stunned by the return of the skeleton to the Mercury, by the manner of its discovery, and by my estimation of the probable consequences. I'm in trouble now, I told myself repeatedly, perhaps out loud on occasion. I'm up shit creek now.

Isaiah Snow read me my rights. "Come on," he said, in conclusion. "We'll contemplate the charges on the drive into town. I guess I will be searching your Cherokee after all. Your room and Toll House too. I'm disappointed in you, young man. I am very disappointed in you."

2

The jailhouse to which I was moved in Burlington, Vermont (the lockup in Stowe being judged too piddling for a man who carted the dried bones of his victims around in the trunk of his car and then buried the car) was a superior dormitory to some motels I've frequented. Splash color on the gray walls, hang plants by the barred windows, modify the steel cot with a mattress and springs, remove the open toilets from view and elevate the level of graffiti: a clever decorator could subdivide the place into attractive condominiums. A prestige address, and I was comfortable, harboring only two complaints. One: I could not fathom why I was having so much trouble sleeping. The cold steel slab was downright cosy compared to some of the beds I've inhabited. And two: I was lonely. Apparently Burlington was experiencing a spring thaw in the crime rate.

I was pleased to see that my lawyer had come to visit me, though his greeting was less bubbly than usual.

"How're you managing, Kyle? The food okay?"

"I'm allowed to order out. Greek, Chinese, or American standard. My choice. So far I've stuck to hot chicken sandwiches and steaks. I'm in enough trouble, I don't want anybody thinking I'm unpatriotic."

A lethargic nod. F.D.R.'s expression had lost much of its usual spontaneity. He slowly, repeatedly, wiped his chin with a meditative, downward stroke, finishing the gesture by pulling the skin above his collar away from his Adam's apple, then letting it snap back like an elastic band. Something was troubling my legal beagle, and he was not sufficiently courageous to come to the point quickly.

"Haven't you made bail yet?" I pressed.

"Hmmm? No. Not yet, Kyle. I've asked my father to meet us here." His voice carried an uncharacteristic tremor.

"Good thinking, Franklin D. It would be difficult for me to meet him anywhere else. Is this a social visit?"

"He was your father's lawyer." F.D.R. beamed, taking pride in the fact. I couldn't see the point.

"I recall you mentioning that earlier. I take it that he's retired."

"Yes, I — it behooves me to consult with him now and then."

"Behooves?"

Franklin D. looked down. Astonished by the floor's grime he looked up; shocked by the thickness of the high cobwebs he looked left; appalled by the sexual scribble he looked right; mesmerized by the forest of steel bars he looked over my shoulder into the stained bowl of my toilet.

"Kyle, ah, I should tell you —"

"Yes?"

"I'm not a criminal lawyer."

Vigorously he rubbed his palms together, and I suddenly feared that he was trying to wipe clean the stain of our handshake.

The danger of the situation allowed me to manage an assured, implacable calm. With conviction I reminded him, "You're not dealing with a criminal, Franklin D."

"I'm not?"

"I'm an innocent man!" I exploded. "Remember?"

"Oh yeah. Right," he apologized.

I imposed an unforgiving, forthright glare, and F.D.R. avoided looking at me for as long as his conscience would allow. His face was flushed with shame, his cowardice had caused him to run a temperature. "*What*," I barked, "are you trying to tell me, Franklin D.?"

"I'm under enormous pressure, Kyle."

"And I'm not?"

"I realize that."

"Are you bailing out on me?"

"My father . . . he thinks I should dump you. He holds a rather low opinion of you, I'm afraid. And . . . I . . . I value his judgment."

F.D.R. coughed his embarrassment. Echoing amid the steel and cement, the sound was slow to decay. Like a man clutching a lifeline I gripped one of the bars that separated us, and squeezed, squeezed hard. "Come on, F.D.R. What gives? I've never met the man, how can his opinion of me count?"

That a certain interest appeared in Franklin D.'s eyes was satisfying. At least he was not looking at me askance any more, attempting to shelter his discomposure. Genuine curiosity focused his attention on me, and for a moment, for a change, I was the one who had begun to squirm. "That's odd," was the only clue to his thinking he divulged.

"What is?"

"That you don't remember meeting him."

"Who?"

"My father. He remembered you. Told me where I could find you. Hazel was the one who told me to ask my father where you lived."

"Hold it. Your *father* knew that I was in Tennessee?"

"And yet you say you've never met him. With all that money involved —"

"What money? Franklin D., what are you talking about?"

"Perhaps you're more callous, Kyle, than even my father believes. But of course, you would have to be, to kill, and carry the skeletons of your victims in your trunk."

"Franklin!" I tried to grab him, my arm impotently stretching between the bars. He was safely out of range.

"My father," he declared, "is more experienced than me. I've invited him down to interview you. If you can pass his scrutiny, if he thinks I should take this case, then I'll defend you. Otherwise, you're on your own."

"I don't believe this!" My anger popped. Lucky for F.D.R. that the bars divided us. "What the hell is the matter with you? Don't you have a mind of your own?"

"What do you mean?" He seemed perplexed.

"You're telling me that my fate resides with a man who has already prejudged me! You're telling me that my lawyer is incapable of making a decision on his own, but needs his daddy's permission first! You bastard! I'd be better off with a trained seal!"

"Fine! I agree! That's settled then." He made a move to escape.

"No! Stay where you are! I'm not letting you off that easy! You're defending me, Franklin D.! I don't care if you're the worst lawyer in New England — you're defending me!"

"Who says I'm capable of pleading your case? And even if I do defend you and by sheer fluke happen to win, I'll probably lose my business as my reward. I'll be known as the bastard who got you off. I'd bungle it anyway. No matter how you slice it, I'm not brilliant like my father."

His words served to conjure the devil's agent. The great locks rattled as the bolt slid free, admitting a stooped, harsh, elderly, limping gentleman to our row of cells. The man's studded heels echoed violently off the walls, his cane measured each step with brutality. I detected F.D.R. disintegrating into a cauldron of fears and, while he was bent forward, I finally managed to grab him by the lapels.

"You stand up to him, Franklin D.," I hissed. "You hang in there."

Yet I confess that I, too, was diminished in the old man's presence. Perhaps F.D.R.'s fear was contagious, but I recall bowing in slight self-effacement before the autocratic eye. Anticipating ruthless interrogation, I was unprepared for the man's snap judgment.

"You twirp," he began, and I assumed that he was addressing me. But lanky F.D.R. was the recipient of his rebuke. "This isn't even him. You incompetent boob!" The elder Ryder raised his cane and threatened to swat sense into his idiot son. "Bad enough that you defend a homicidal maniac, the very least you could have done was to ask for his identification!" The blows did rain, two swift cuffs across Franklin D.'s right shoulder. "Just think! You were going to give Toll House to this imposter! Numskull!"

F.D.R. braced both his arms to deflect any slash to the face.

"Swindler! Pervert! Degenerate!" I was thinking that the old gentleman had an extraordinarily low view of his son when I realized that he was finally addressing me. He waved a finger under my nose. "You'll have to wake up a damn sight earlier in the morning to pull the wool over the eyes of Theodore Ryder!"

A last malicious glance at his offspring. Burdened, the old man soldiered across the cement floor and rapped his cane against the door to be let out.

Feeling sorry for Franklin D., I was startled to discover that the episode had perked him up. Jovial, he appeared to have won a critical indictment.

"What're you grinning about?" I demanded to know. "What's so funny?"

"You're not him!" he practically hooted. "You're not Kyle Elder Junior! You're not him!" He was positively ebullient. "Which means that I don't have to represent you for another minute because I don't even know who the hell you are! I'm off the case!"

Triumphant, F.D.R. retrieved his briefcase from where it leaned against a wall. He wiped away the contaminating dust and prepared to leave.

"Bullshit!" I recovered. "I don't know about the 'Junior' part, but I'm Kyle Elder!"

"No, you're not. My father knows you. I mean, he knows Kyle Elder Junior, and you're not him."

"I am so him! I'm me, dammit!"

He was about to rap on the door to exit.

"Franklin D.!"

"Adios, amigo."

"F.D. fucking R.!"

Turning my way, he inquired out of passing interest, "So who are you anyway?"

I gripped the bars. "Franklin D.! Please! Come back here! We have to talk."

Perhaps he detected the desperation of my appeal, for he returned. "So who are you anyway?" he asked again. "Tell me. Just for fun."

"Get the keys, open the cell, come in here and sit down. You and I are going to have a long chat."

He consented to a compromise. "I'm comfortable on the stool

here." Being on the same side of the bars as a madman went against his sense of caution. "Okay, mystery man," he directed me, "talk."

3

Had the hills been smoking, the day might have been sublime. The sunshine brightened our spirits, the wind buffeted our high hopes as we lay on sacks of oats in the back of a Dodge pick-up. We had hitched the ride out of Washington, D.C., ecstatic when we noticed the license plate.

"Tennessee! Here we come! Yahoo!"

An open-air view of the Smoky Mountains.

Breaking loose for the first time in our lives, we were finally putting the miles behind us after a wearying trip down from Montreal via New York City. Tennessee was my ultimate destination; Cindy was along for the ride on condition that we hit the hot spots along the way. Broadway. (To gawk at the theatres.) Harlem. (Harlem? The meter was running on our cab. Then I got the idea. Cindy was evaluating abandoned buildings to torch. "Driver, step on it and don't look back.") On to Philadelphia. And Washington. We were seeing the world. The sights had stimulated Cindy to come away with me and I had no illusions: once we crossed the Smokies, keeping her at my side would become more difficult.

In the middle of the afternoon, with no clue to our bearings, we were dropped off in the dead center of nowhere. A desolate, pastoral countryside devoid of human intervention. Our driver and his wife waved good-bye and disappeared through the dust, their route an unpaved track.

Cindy pulled a face. In case I needed help to interpret it, she added, "We gave up New York for this?"

"At least we're in Tennessee."

"Kyle, we are in the backwater of Hicksville. On the outskirts."

"I don't know about that." My grumble could not alter the obvious: things looked grim. I didn't carry a map, and the nearest settlement could be miles away. "We must be closer to where we're going."

"We've stepped out of time," Cindy deduced. "At least you could have given me the roaring twenties, Kyle, not the depression."

"All right already, I'm sorry. How did I know where they'd dump us?"

Cindy sighed, stretched mightily to work the kinks out of her muscles, and fluffed the dust from her hair. Done with complaining, her mind turned to practical solutions. "Which way out?"

"We came from there." I nodded to the east. "Can you remember the last town? I guess we go thataway, west."

Cindy slung her backpack over her shoulders.

"What're you doing?"

"Walking."

"Get serious."

"Kyle! Look around you! You don't actually expect another car to come down this donkey-trail during the next half-century, do you? We are in the backwoods, sonny boy. Wise up. The only people who'll find us here will shoot us for being northerners. They haven't heard that the Civil War is over."

"Come on, it's not that bad." But I knew that she was right.

"Whatever you do, don't tell them that the south lost. You don't want to rile those farm boys. As it is, I'll be raped."

"You wish."

"I'm a change from their sisters and barn animals."

"Dream on," said I, but followed her lead and hefted my clumsy satchel.

We would have walked until the cows came home, except that they never did. On occasion I would point out a bird to her and listen to its song; otherwise, we walked. The thought crossed our minds that we could die on that deserted stretch of roadway, that delirious under the sun we'd collapse in our footsteps, our lips too chapped to enjoy a farewell kiss. In the sense that a man may crash his car, fracture both legs and his pelvis, lose his teeth and half his marbles, then count himself lucky for not being killed, we considered ourselves fortunate that a vehicle came puffing over the hill, weaving slightly, raising dust storms where the wheels ran onto the shoulder, bearing aggressively down the steaming blacktop flattening fragrant cow patties.

"Terrific," Cindy acknowledged as she raised her thumb. "A drunk. A farm boy who hasn't seen a chick since puberty."

Still, she was sufficiently pragmatic to raise a leg, teasing the driver with her daring and shapeliness. That dust-smudged knee did the trick, for the car, well past us, plodded indecisively to a stop. Exhilarated by the rescue, united in adventure, we raced down the road to catch it. We had to scamper a fair distance, and both of us were disturbed the nearer we approached. The driver was putting himself through unusual contortions. His head disappeared behind the front seat; a moment later his feet came into view, flailing away.

We stopped running. Caught our breath as we reconsidered.

"What do you think?" I asked Cindy.

She wiped the perspiration from her lips. "If he's getting undressed we either skip him, or bonk him on the head and take the keys. If he's putting his clothes on . . ."

"We take the chance," I concluded, and we resumed our lengthy sprint.

We shared a what-choice-do-we-have shrug before accepting the man's invitation to hop in. He had still to put on his shoes and socks and tuck in his shirt.

A white car. Chrome-studded. A gas guzzler, not that anybody cared in those days. Yankee extravagance, a '64 Mercury.

"You two passin' through?" Generally he kept his eyes on the road and had only vaguely looked us over.

Cindy and I contradicted one another simultaneously. She answered, "Yeah," while I claimed, "No." The driver whapped the steering wheel.

"Hoho!" he cried. "A lovers' tiff! I can dig it. Where do you reckon you're off and bound then, pretty miss?"

"Hollywood." Cindy's terse accent defended against my opposition to the idea, and as a barrier to the usual scoff her ambition received.

"You're going to be a star," the stranger remarked, without irony.

Pinched between us on the front seat, Cindy gave him close scrutiny. "That's right," she ventured, not wholly convinced of the man's sincerity.

He nodded with frank conviction. "I believe you. I can see it. You have star quality. You'll make it." He conferred his assessment without a second glance her way. His opinion had been sealed by a single glimpse and, while he took the curves too tightly and leapfrogged the pointy hills, I seethed.

"Where you headed if yer not passin' through, young fella?"

I hummed, hawed, explained that I played the dulcimer. "The best ones are handcrafted in Tennessee, I heard." Passionately, I elaborated on my favorite subject. Cindy yawned. "I'm looking for craftsmen. I've heard there's a few in the Cumberland Mountains."

"No way," the man said emphatically, giving me a start. "You want Monroe County, boy. You don't have to go no further than Walkerman's Creek. We're not talking craftsmen here, we're talking artisans. Yes, migawd. Artisans."

Delighted with this odd fellow, I asked him, "Is that near here, Walkerman's Creek?"

"Twenty minutes. Happens to be where I'm headed."

I had done it! I had traveled to Tennessee on speculation, and now my dream was unfolding with ease.

"By the way, my name's Dakota Hats," the man said, holding out a hand as large as a broom. "What's yours?"

The contents of Dakota's trunk would explain his name. He brought Cindy and me to a commune of long-haired, psychedelic creatures typical of the era, who crowded around us like a remote, primitive tribe curious for news of the alleged outside world. The massive trunk stretched open, and Dakota displayed hats for everyone. Hats, hats, and more hats. Leather hats and straw hats, feathered hats and fedoras, jaunty caps and villains' black hats and bowlers and rainbow-hued *chapeaux*, even a Garden of Eden hat that grew raspberries around the brim. Summer sun hats, rain hats, fishermen's sou'westers, plastic hats, lace hats, and First World War helmets. Any outrageous headgear on earth had found its way into the trunk of Dakota's Mercury.

We helped distribute the hats among the forty-odd individuals who had come from their workbenches, kitchens, and fields to greet Dakota. Praise abounding. I was surprised, then, when every hat was returned. No sale.

I clued in. Mr. Hats was not here to sell. He had come here to buy, and to acquaint his suppliers with styles currently in vogue. In turn, Dakota was invited up to the barn to preview some of the group's new designs, and Cindy and I tagged along.

Our high-spirited meander towards the barn and its satellite sheds was halted by the appearance of a police cruiser speeding onto commune property. The crowd turned quiet, waiting for the car to stop in a whirlwind of dust. A thickset, slack-jawed officer stepped out, adjusted his gun belt, pushed his shades up higher on his nose, and crossed to where Dakota waited for him. An atmosphere of menace pervaded the quiet air. From the corral, a mare whinnied.

"Afternoon, Everett," Dakota said. Conscious of the tension, and puzzled by the stillness of the community, Cindy and I surreptiously tried to slide out of view.

" 'lo, Dakota. Heard mention y'all were back."

"A drummer's life, Everett. If I'm not coming I'm going. In the end it's all the same."

"Now yuh know, Dakota, we been having troubles here in Monroe County —"

"Damn sad," Dakota Hats commiserated.

"What I heard was, y'all weren't alone drivin' down the road. I like to keep track on who's comin' or is on their way out."

"Just a couple of our own people, Sheriff," one of the hippies spoke up, and I experienced the protective net of this community enfold around Cindy and me. We were grateful.

"Show me them," the sheriff commanded. I do not believe that anyone pointed, nodded, or twitched. Yet The Man had no difficulty picking Cindy and me out. We were dusty enough, but not nearly as ragged nor as stylish as the others. I regretted my relative cleanliness and unpatched jeans.

"Is yer name Elder?" the sheriff asked me. I'd learn later that his name was McGrath.

Without opportunity to conceal my shock, I wondered aloud, "How did you know that?"

"Make it my point," he bragged. He spat, without expression, and bulldozed the spot of mud with his boot. "So tell me, what do yuh do here?" His badge sparkled in the sun and made me squint. "Contemplate yer navel?"

"I play the dulcimer," I told him. "I also sing like a bird." To wit, I offered him the rasping, tripthongal twitter of the long-billed marsh wren. Laughter, and a smattering of applause, toasted my shenanigans. McGrath made obscure noises with his lips, as though he was trying to speak the language, and gave Cindy a cursory examination that managed to be a blatantly sexual probe at the same time. Knowing that he'd been upstaged, he put on an insipid grin and tipped his cap to us all.

"Just checking," he said, as he backed off.

"Can I interest you in a dandy white Panama with a green silk band, Everett? They're all the rage in Knoxville. Catching on in Memphis. It's more popular than westerns, some places," Dakota pitched.

The sheriff winked and politely declined. "That's okay, Dakota. I got what I came for." A remark that baffled us all.

A frail, redheaded chap with a thin beard, who was rummaging through the deep pockets of his coveralls, ambled over to me after McGrath had gone. He pulled out a tin of snuff, and stuffed a mound under his upper lip. "You really interested in dulcimers?" he asked me.

"They're my life."

"Come on over to my place. Take a look at mine."

The campfire that night was as peaceful a place as the earth allows. Away from the flames, the night sky revealed the Milky Way in its stupendous glory. The galaxy gathered lights to itself — fireflies and errant sparks. I was stoned on good weed, and perceived with the full tyrannical ardor of youth the universe as my rightful home.

By the fire I asked Dakota Hats, "What did the sheriff mean today when he said there's been trouble in Monroe County?"

Dakota cracked open a beer. He had had quite a few (the empty bottles were accumulating behind him), while religiously abstaining from the roving weed and hash pipes. His discernible nod in the firelight seemed to affirm private thoughts. "I was going to tell you about that. You listen to this too, Cindy, this is something you both should know. It never pays to be unwary."

I lay with my feet close to the fire. Snuggling back to back with me, Cindy rested her chin on the shelf of her knees. Others around the fire had also taken an interest.

"Kids have been disappearing, Kyle. Including, over the months, three of our own."

"Kids are on the move everywhere," Cindy pointed out.

"This is different," spoke a voice from the opposite side of the flames.

"We're not talking about kids hitting the road," a girl swaddled in an Indian blanket mentioned.

"Sometimes their bodies are located," Dakota told me. "Sometimes not."

"They're being killed?" The chill in Cindy's voice propelled a shiver down my spine.

"Knifed," Dakota said.

"Across the throat," the girl in the Apache blanket elaborated. "From ear to ear. That's what happened to the ones that've been found."

God knows I don't need this, I thought. Blood and knives.

"Girls or boys?" Cindy piped up.

"Both."

"That's the main reason I picked you up," Dakota put in after a solemn silence. "You might not have made it through Tennessee otherwise."

I considered the people who had dropped us off on that barren highway. They had put our lives at risk, but once they reached home, conscience had evidently urged that they telephone Sheriff McGrath and have him monitor our journey.

"Thanks, Dakota. Appreciate it."

"Yeah, thanks," Cindy agreed.

"Don't mention it."

What conniving scum I am. The distressing news gave my spirits a lift. Now Cindy might hesitate before embarking for California, stay with me a while.

To dispel the somber mood that talk of the killings had precipitated, more logs were added to the fire. A blaze. Cindy was entranced by the gyrating leaps of flame; every time the fire shot higher she'd scrunch herself up, perfectly content.

"This is how you're supposed to enjoy fires," I lectured.

"It's okay" was the limit of her concession. I kissed her on the bridge of the nose, in the glow of the bonfire, a peck to express my love and my heart's swollen ache. Cindy beamed.

And yet, "I'm never going to be a Hollywood star" was her plaint as we lay down to sleep in the barn's hayloft.

Seeing the opportunity, I took it. "Why not stick around here? I bet there's professional summer stock in Tennessee. You can gain experience. You could latch on."

"Yeah," she conceded, grudgingly. "Maybe."

We churned together. Adolescent lovemaking, a maelstrom of urge and blunder, wonder and desperation. I was mismatched. She was far more sophisticated than I was, on the surface of things. Afterwards I stroked the backs of her thighs as we nestled together.

"All this straw," she teased, licking my ear. "This dry old barn. If someone lit a match — *whooof!*"

"Cindy Cindy Cindy," I admonished her, squeezing her tight.

We slept wrapped in one another's limbs. I dared not let her go.

"G'morning, Kyle!"

"Good morning, Dakota. Have you seen Cindy?"

"Matter of fact, I did. Before breakfast. Hey, you're going to have to rise a lot earlier if you expect to be fed around here!"

"Where'd she go?"

"Into town. A few of the other girls invited her along. That's women for you, always shopping!"

Dakota's broad smile revealed teeth as white as country snow, each one perfectly shaped. Either they were false or expensively capped.

"Her belongings are missing," I informed Dakota.

"Took 'em to the laundromat. Kyle, come on my rounds with me," he invited. "I'll introduce you to the finest guitar and banjo pickers in the county. Grab a loaf of bread out of the kitchen and we'll eat on the way."

Members of the commune were engrossed in their morning chores, tending animals and laboring in the fields. A pretty girl in the kitchen gave me a loaf warm from the oven and a bottle of milk.

We drove through hardship countryside. Dakota honked his horn at a few tenants, who waved back. He often drove with his elbows resting in the spokes of the steering wheel, supporting his chin in his hands. On an empty stretch of highway that followed the river, he pulled over.

"What's up?" I asked. I didn't like the loneliness of this place, the billowing dust from our wheels like the smoke of ancient battles.

"Kyle, I'm sorry to tell you this. But I took the trouble to drive Cindy across the county line this morning."

Comprehending and at the same time confused, I stared into my hands. Devastated. Dakota passed me a note.

"Honest to God, I haven't read it. We didn't have an envelope to seal it in. But I've respected your privacy, you can count on that."

I unfolded the neatly quartered sections, and recognized Cindy's miniature scrawl. Today her words would probably be an embarrassment to her, a testimony to the passion and idiocy that comes with being young.

If I stayed any longer I'd be trapped. I know it. You know it too because that's what you want. I'm going to Hollywood to find my destiny. I really do love you, Kyle. I'm sorry about your Mom. Sorry I burned the club. I didn't mean it. I couldn't help myself. Thanks for being my friend. You had to come down here to Tennessee and I've tried to understand why. I think it's just to get away and I don't blame you for that. I have to go to the coast and I hope that you will understand why. Look for me in the movies. If you go back and you see my mother before I do, tell her that I'm okay. Not that she'll care much. Love and all kinds of kisses in all kinds of crazy spots. Cindy.

"Because of the troubles," Dakota explained apologetically, although there was no need, "I gave her the ride. Didn't want her hitching through these parts without a friendly driver."

"How come you didn't tell me back at the farm?"

He patted my shoulder. "Thought you might prefer to be alone. Back there, nothing's done alone. Folks even use the three-holer at the same time. There's no privacy, they don't believe in it. No way they'd let you suffer on your own. My guess is, that's not how you'd want to play it."

Against my best efforts, tears flooded my eyes. My chest began to quake.

"Let it come, son. Ain't no use trying to stop it. Now, you see that linden tree yonder? Marks a trail. Takes you down to the finest ol' swimmin' hole on Walkerman's Creek. Go on down, son. Set awhile. I'll be here or maybe I'll join you later."

He knew that a good bawl was the best prescription. I staggered, blinded by tears, as I hobbled down the steep, rocky path. I loved Cindy and now she was gone, and what sense, what use, could the rest of my life have?

The gurgling brook helped. And trout jumping in the pool. I cried myself out and, under the sun, slept.

Dakota Hats nudged me awake. Stood above me glimmering in the nude. I squinted into the bright sunlight, gazing up at Jack-in-the-Beanstalk's giant's head, leering down from the clouds. The race of fluffy castles quickly made me dizzy, as though the earth was sliding out from under me.

A pertinent fact that did not go unnoticed was that Dakota's tan was uniform and unbroken.

"Let's take a dip, Kyle. Afterwards we'll feast and soak up the sun. There is only one cure for a broken heart."

"What's that?"

"Life! Life! *Life!*"

A confirmed nudist, Dakota claimed nature as his habitat. I followed him into the swimming-hole created by damming the riverbed and dredging a wide spot. The pool was large enough to accommodate Dakota's length. Soon he was somersaulting beneath the surface, doing handstands so that only his pink toes broke the surface like fish darting at flies. I warily dogpaddled around the perimeter, keeping my head out of the water.

"City-boy, are you, Kyle?"

"That's right."

"Thought so. Know how I know?"

"Easy. I'm not tanned."

"Nope. That's not it. Country boys tend to keep their shirts on too. It's the city lads who find the time to lay around on a beach somewheres and fry. Nosireebob, it's the lung capacity. City-boys are shallow breathers."

I followed him out, not an easy maneuver on the smooth, slippery rocks. Dakota seated himself on a round boulder, his legs outspread.

"Ah, this is the life, Kyle. The primitive country life. Nothing else comes close. You did right by coming to Tennessee. Here, I have something else to give you." He pinched a piece of notepaper from his trousers bundled on the ground, holding it out to me.

"What is it?" Tentative.

"Addresses. I'll take you 'round to the instrument craftsmen in Monroe County, but here's a few names of ateliers elsewhere in Tennessee. I suspect that I know all the good ones. I enjoy keeping in touch with the young folks."

I braved a few steps forward, and at arm's length reached across for the list. "Thanks."

"You wanna eat? Sure you do, you missed breakfast. You're a young and growing boy!"

Sufficiently dry to put my pants back on, I sat down fairly close to Dakota and received the benefits of his picnic basket. He stretched out in the sun, rolling over to direct the curative rays onto his brown fanny. He did not give me an apple of my own, preferring to slice portions with his hunting knife and feed the two of us alternately. Slow nourishment, but the meal did not intrude on conversation.

"I used to be in haberdashery," the man told me. "Small town, South Dakota. My store was ruined by a shopping mall taking the bulk of the business. A shopping mall! On the prairie, where there ought to be cattle grazing, they put up a mall! I had to rely on friends feeling guilty, who'd buy a tie from me after they purchased a suit and shirt at the chain store. Decline, my friend, in any form, is a terrible thing to experience. So I started traveling. I hit the road, as they say. Eventually, I got into hats. How come you're so conventional, Kyle?"

"I'm not. I whistle bird songs."

"That's true. But your appearance, pardon the pun, is old hat."

I shrugged, not wanting to take it any further.

Dakota's knife glittered in the light, and after three apples we started on a hunk of cheese.

"Sing me a birdy tune."

I rendered the afternoon serenade of the Tennessee warbler. While the Tennessee is not aptly named and is rarely seen in the State, the riverside, forest environment was an appropriate setting. On concluding, I listened attentively for a response from real birds.

"That's excellent!" Dakota enthused. "You have a remarkable talent!"

We spoke about my affection for birds and about my joy with dulcimers, and he confided a portrait of his youth in South Dakota. From his earliest remembrances, he had had difficulty keeping his clothes on. As a boy he'd strip in the wheatfields, on the long jaunt to church, during school recess. For his industry his bottom was paddled on a regular basis. "The teenage years were the toughest. Muddled by sex as every teen is, I did actually become a pervert. I exposed myself on streetcorners in Fargo. My idea of courting a girl was to catch her behind a tree and unzip my trousers. Not the best tactic. For a while I'd stroll through public places with my fly undone and hope people would notice. But those years were a passing phase, nothing permanent. My nature is no longer licentious. I merely enjoy the out-of-doors, preferably in the buff. What on earth can be wrong with that?

"I keep south now so I won't freeze my dick off in winter. I'm a paid-up member of a half-dozen clubs, scattered through as many States, where I can frolic to my heart's content without being arrested. And I know a zillion spots like this one where I can relax and never bother a living soul."

"You were nude yesterday, driving your car!"

Dakota offered no apology. "That does get me into hot water on occasion. Most of the time I mind my manners."

He flipped over. Grass and dirt clung to the dramatic length of him. To avoid the creeping shadow cast by a eucalyptus tree, he wriggled slightly away from me, then, from the depths of his basket, withdrew a package of lemon-cream cookies. Again his knife was active, separating the cookies' two halves. He doled out a side with filling, then one without, alternately. The meticulous distribution opposed the careless ambiance of his naked, sprawling limbs, and I began to feel drowsy again.

"I almost forgot!" Intruding upon my grim silence Dakota bounded to his knees. "Cindy gave me something else for you."

Fumbling through his pockets. Soon he plucked out a book of matches. "Why didn't you give me these before!" I exploded. Snatched it out of his hands.

"Sorry. I forgot. Is it a kind of code?"

Though the booklet identified a seedy restaurant on Jean Talon Street in Montreal, its significance was not lost on me. Cindy was telling me that I had no cause to worry. I would not be able to follow her, as I had once joked, by looking to the horizon for smoke. She would no longer burn buildings. Dakota's knife pried off a side of another cookie which he passed to me.

"Everything all right?" he inquired gently.

Accepting the cookie, then looking down, I said, "I'll live."

And having no sooner received that statement, the forest around me exploded. I froze inside my skin, my mind blasted numb. I had seen the white flash. My body flapped about like a fish yanked from the river onto hard ground. When I looked back at Dakota he was already dead, a perfectly round circle of blood forming between his open eyes. His pecker stood straight up. In one hand he held his hunting knife; in the other, his half of the cookie. Stunned beyond reasoning, my skeleton seized by the incomprehensible violence, I stared into the underbrush, into the sniper's lair. I expected to die that instant.

Sheriff Everett McGrath stepped out from the trees. He strode up next to me, where I sat as rigid as Dakota, his pistol still smoking.

"Got him clean," he said, as if surprised. "y'all were lucky, boy. Another second and he'd have opened up yer throat like the smile on a punkin. Yer damned lucky, boy."

In my shock, I forgot that I could talk. The strangest feeling. I wanted to fall asleep and wait for the world to carry me away to another place in time.

Fifteen years later, that's exactly what happened.

4

In the dreary confines of my cell, I also talked to F.D.R. about my relationship with Isabelle Dravecky.

I felt wistful for my early days with her: the stretch of time that followed Cindy's disappearance and the shattering death of Dakota Hats. Wistful in the sense that soldiers sometimes are nostalgic for their war. Dangerous days. I feared snipers in the woods and guarded my back. Not wholly convinced that Mr. Hats had intended to carve me up as he had the apple, cheese, and lemon-cream cookies, I worried about daggers still prevalent in the night or twinkling in the light of day. But the killings ended, I was at loose ends, and I enjoyed that counterfeit of freedom.

Despite his gruff manners and his comical insistence on emulating the persona of a redneck highway patrolman, Sheriff McGrath proved to be a valuable acquaintance. At his suggestion I took possession of the Mercury Monterey. The car would sell for next to nothing at auction, he said, and given the circumstances he could square it with the town fathers. Around the county I was known as the lucky kid who had cheated death. McGrath was a hero. My savior. Unable to thank him properly, I followed his advice instead, and didn't object when he offered me the wheels. The car was the last place where Cindy was known to have been alive, and that was as important to me as being mobile.

I wrote to Cindy's mother, explained that her daughter had gone on her own to Hollywood, and asked to be notified if she had any news from her. Cindy's mom had too many other children to care for to be distressed. Although I reported Cindy missing, another name in a ceaseless list of runaways, no search was made for her.

The best that I could do was to watch movies as they came to town, to see if she showed up on the screen.

We had no way to confirm that Dakota Hats had dropped her over the State line as he had claimed, preferring to sharpen his knife on me, or whether he had successfully slit her throat. The torment of not knowing inspired me to get blasted one night in Walkerman's Creek. I fell in with a few good ol' southern boys and we raised holy Cain. Took our act out on the road when the neighbors complained. The boys were noted ruffians, and one of them, Dupree, even had a record. I was having a good time, feeling no pain, so I was doubly upset when my new friends suddenly jumped me from behind, and rolled me for my last nickels and dimes.

"What else did they take?" Franklin interrupted suddenly.

"I didn't have anything else to lose."

"Your wallet?"

"Yeah, but it wasn't worth much."

"Driver's license?"

"I suppose so. Actually I didn't have a license, only a learner's permit."

"Go on."

I had fought back, letting fly the anger stockpiled over recent months. Which earned me the booby prize. I was summarily pummelled. Left to rot in a ditch. I had never felt so miserable; every movement hurt. I was bleeding, I vomited, I pissed my pants, and I cried forlornly for my dead mother. I was all set to die. Isabelle discovered me there in the morning — led to me, she claimed, by one of her cats. I was susceptible to her kindness. She took me in.

Lovemaking was neither art nor science with her, neither strenuous nor relaxed. To make love was a reflex, as symptomatic as a sneeze. She of the occult habits subscribed to the great mystery religion of our times: "If it feels good, do it." And we did.

Long before our alliance broke apart, I had learned that I was the most recent adept in a vast line of succession. Issy would accumulate boys and shelter them in her shack just as she did stray cats. I could stay so long as I made proper use of the litter box and politely made room for other incoming strays.

I drove her cats loony with my bird calls. They looked for openings to attack. From the cats I learned how to sleep often and for great lengths of time. I lounged around the clock, stirring only for food, bodily functions, and fleeting romps of passion. Issy did not seem to mind.

"How did you survive, Kyle? Did she keep you all this time? What did the two of you live on?"

Isabelle set me up in business. In the sweet denouement following an invigorating tussle in the sack, she explained her idea. My problem with locating quality custom dulcimers was probably a universal malaise. "Economy hinges on the middleman," she lectured me. "Why not connect local builders with buyers around the nation? All you'll need is a brochure to distribute to music stores. Maybe advertise in the classified section of a folk-music magazine. After that, you process orders, you job the work to the most worthy craftsmen for the price, see that the product is delivered, and we'll eat fruit in winter. Otherwise it's macrobiotic rice. You won't get rich, but you'll have your health. And me." With little adornment, that is how I'd earn my living for the next fifteen years.

Coming home late one night, I encountered Issy bouncing on the mattress with two boys, both of them younger than I, who had been walking their dogs across her property. The German Shepherds were also on the bed, tongues lolling, their puritanical backs turned to the proceedings. My entry was announced with considerable barking from the dogs, rhythmic grunts from the boys, and Issy's impassioned groans.

"Excuse me? Isabelle? I'm home."

She had a difficult time with my objections. Mind, I was circumspect. I did not venture to explain my aversion to three in the bed and the triggers that that scene fired in my brain. I did not explain to Issy that I had been conceived under similar circumstances. We would always remain pals, and occasional festive nights would reunite us as lovers, but the next day I moved out and rented a shack even farther out of town.

At times the sheer unadulterated laziness of my life nagged me, and once I panicked. I realized that I hadn't been out of bed for a fortnight except to poke my pecker out the window for a pee or to crack open a can of Spam. Everything I ate came out as water. I was dying. Benzedrine helped, the pills keeping me awake and kicking for days. In the end I'd collapse, sliding into lethargy and inertia as though returning to the sanctuary of the womb. Apart from being limp and sleepy most of the time, I'm sure that I passed through moments when I was clinically dead.

An attentive F.D.R. lapped it up, taking it all in as though he was a father confessor waiting for the baser sin. In the end he sighed, contorting his face on the free side of the bars into a variety of indecipherable expressions, then he slapped his knees and asked, "And you know nothing about the bones in your car?"

"It's like I told you. They were coming out of the earth in Tennessee. The saints were marching in in Walkerman's Creek. Returning without their flesh, just this clatter of bones. Whatever was going on, it was epidemic in Monroe County."

"Hmm. I see. For what it's worth, Kyle, I believe you. And I believe you are who you say you are. Nobody would invent such a shitty life for themselves. I believe you are Kyle Elder."

"Junior," I added. "Thanks, Franklin D."

"I'll arrange for your bail."

"What about your father?" I reminded him.

"That's the real mystery. That's what has me guessing." Mystified, instilling no confidence whatsoever in me, he walked out.

Alone among my employees, Hazel Stamp had stayed on at Toll House, the others having seized the opportunity to leave alive and collect pogy. Hazel had seen fit to cancel all reservations, and had arranged for our guests to be comfortably ensconced elsewhere. "What else could I do, given the situation?" she asked me.

"You're top-notch, Hazel."

The "situation" to which she referred was the likelihood that the new proprietor of the Toll House Inn was a lunatic, "a murderous madman," she elaborated, and, carried away with herself, she proffered this gem, "He's a carnivorous crocodile who feeds on human flesh."

"I beg your pardon?"

"It's in the papers."

Vermont journalists know how to condemn a man without ever mentioning his name.

"Brave of you to stay," I said, "with a crocodile lurking in the house."

"It's your reward" was her enigmatic response.

"For what?"

"You know," she said shyly.

"Remind me."

"For taking me up to the roof. Your father kept me out of things. I could have throttled him sometimes. Any time something really interesting happened, he kept me in the dark he did. What do you suppose those women were doing?"

"Making babies. It seems that no one has ever showed them how."

"Are you serious?"

Revived by the chummy atmosphere, and by the hallowed, cloistered walls of Toll House, I was cognizant that the inn, source of many troubles as it was, had begun to feel like home. Like refuge. In a serious vein I asked my housekeeper, "What's the damage, Haze? Is Toll House kaput as an inn?"

"Goodness gravy, no. Locally," she replied bluntly, "you're dead. It won't matter what the courts decide. But who's heard of this mess in Boston or Montreal? None of your guests come from town, you have that to be thankful for." She rapped her knuckles on my kneecap. "Not to worry. Time will pass and you will become a legend, nobody will have an accurate recollection of the facts, twenty versions of your exploits will circulate through Stowe, and tall tales make for good advertising. Long term, you've got it made. Mark my word. Hazel knows."

I went upstairs to sleep in the Mt. Washington Room under the stars. This could be my last night of freedom, and I wanted to be comfortable.

My previous experience with the machinations of Vermont's quirky judicial system had been false preparation for what lay ahead. Proceedings into the death of Mother Superior Gabriella had been characterized by their down-home, folksy informality. Back then the result had been a foregone conclusion, and the simple sport of the legal beagles was to bark with conviction, and to roll over and play dead on command.

The bones were a different story. Something wicked here. Something sick. The inquiry had been upgraded.

F.D.R. led me into an honest-to-goodness courtroom, properly fitted out with flag and judge's bench, witness stand, and solid oak tables for the contesting attorneys. When bored, Judge Thurman, a gray-eyed, white-headed fossil, would chew his enormous, protruding lower lip, wiping away the juices on the sleeves of his black robe. The inquiry had all the earmarks of an authentic trial, minus the jury, and the demeanor of the judicial adversaries was suitably correct and grave.

The prosecution commenced the deliberations by reciting a litany of items that he intended to demonstrate were incriminating. He assured the court that medical records would identify the body, and that I would be implicated not only for possession of a corpse, in itself a heinous crime, but that sufficient evidence would be presented to commit me to trial for murder.

An ebullient grim reaper by the name of Norman Bowles, the prosecutor reminded the court that a recent death had occurred at Toll House under unusual circumstances, and that he would present evidence to have that case reopened as well.

"Come on, F.D.R., this is getting out of hand!" I whispered.

"Relax, Kyle. Let him blab on."

Bowles questioned my right to life. Serious doubts had arisen, he stated, as to the true identity of the accused, and that this issue also needed to be broached.

In his opening remarks, delivered in a carefree, colloquial manner, my lawyer — the attorney I had insisted upon as the only human I could trust to defend me — declared that I was "as innocent as the first day of spring," that I could no more be discredited "than the blush on an apple blossom could be considered impure," and that the charges against me would be cut down "like freshly mown hay." Resting my head in one hand, I leaned forward over the table, and felt the grass that so moved my defender growing luxuriantly above my carcass.

"Are you all right?" Franklin D. asked me upon retaking his seat.

"Plead for gas," I bargained. "Spare me the rope. I've thought it over and I don't want the chair."

The first person called to testify was Inspector Isaiah Snow. He described unearthing my Mercury, and discovering the treasure of bones.

"What did you do next, Inspector?" Bowles inquired.

"We searched his new motor vehicle and his home. In his Cherokee Chief we found a bone."

"And then what did you do?"

"I arrested Kyle Elder Junior."

"And have you investigated Mr. Elder's background since taking him into custody?"

"Yes, I have, sir." Isaiah was looking as though he had trouble at home. Bags sagged wearily under his eyes, and his was a tired voice. The man's usual perkiness was only habit today; he was working too hard to put me away.

"And has the accused ever been convicted of a crime?"

"No, sir."

"Has he ever been charged?"

"No, sir."

"Has he ever been investigated for criminal activity?"

Franklin D. objected. Thank God he was still alive. "Being investigated for a crime is not in itself criminal. Your Honor, this is a court of law, not a clearinghouse for rumors and innuendo." I was pleased that he had stirred the visitors' gallery to titters.

"Your Honor," argued the prosecutor, "the State wishes to determine something of the psychological effects of Mr. Elder's history which may give insight as to how he could commit such a crime as murder."

"Objection sustained," Judge Thurman pronounced. "Rephrase, Counsellor, and bear in mind that this is a preliminary hearing, not a trial. We need to determine the extent of the evidence against Mr. Elder, if any, and have no business delving into the psychological subtleties of his mind."

"Yes, Your Honor. Thank you." A regular brownnoser, this

Bowles. "If the accused proves to be Kyle Elder Junior — and I have already indicated that will be a matter for conjecture — can it be said, Inspector Snow, that he killed his mother?"

The gasp, the murmur, and the hush occurred with such rapidity, that the judge had time only to locate his gavel and to raise it. He never needed to strike a blow for order. Satisfied that the room had disciplined itself, he waited for an objection from my table. Franklin D. was asleep at the switch, but consented to rise to his feet. "Objection, Your Honor." A weary, uninterested voice, as if he had overextended himself.

"On what grounds, Counsellor?"

"Your Honor, the prosecution cannot have it both ways. If the assistant district attorney does not believe that my client is Kyle Elder Junior, he cannot bring evidence concerning the real Mr. Elder into this court."

"This is a hearing, Your Honor, and not a trial. Whoever the defendant claims to be, we must present evidence to bring him to trial."

"Objection sustained," the judge ruled. Hey, we were winning! Two in a row! But the jurist also decided, "You may answer the question, Inspector Snow. We must assume that Mr. Kyle Elder Junior is on trial until such time as the defendant wishes to deny it, or evidence is brought forward to the contrary."

Isaiah replied, "Kyle Elder Junior's mother was strangled and/or asphyxiated by a boa constrictor. She also suffered knife wounds inflicted by her son."

There it was, my past, revealed for perusal by the cruel and curious of the world. Scribes behind my back scribbled furiously. This time, Judge Thurman did pound his gavel to interrupt the bedlam.

"The court ruled —" Snow endeavored to continue.

"That'll be all, Inspector," Bowles noted. Brimming with confidence, he thanked the officer for his testimony.

"What did the court rule?" asked my dull and stalwart knight.

"That the boy had been doing his best to rescue his mother from the snake."

"Quite right." Franklin D. adjusted the vest of his suit as he stood up. He smiled. Shuffled loose a paper on his desk. Unable to shake his interminable fascination for the natural habitat, he asked Snow a question about the weather. "What sort of day was it, Inspector, when you discovered the bones in the Mercury?"

I sighed.

"A misery, sir," Snow replied. "Cold up in the mountains."

"Then you were not out for an afternoon stroll."

"I beg your pardon, sir?" Snow definitely had not been sleeping nights. He wasn't sharp. Conscience or lower-back pain?

"Your Honor," Bowles objected, "surely this line of questioning is irrelevant. The climate has no bearing on this case, nor do Inspector Snow's recreational pursuits."

"Sustained." The judge tapped his gavel to silence giggles in the gallery. I turned to see who was laughing and spied Chantelle, though she was not among those stifling a paroxysm.

The cautious, quick glances that she permitted in my direction were unfocused and vague; the sort of sidelong glimpses a lady on a bus might grudgingly bestow on potential tormentors who were acting up. Turning back to confront the courtroom, I experienced a bright, game eagerness for life's next jolt. Chantelle is here!

The judge asked Franklin D. to come to the point.

"Inspector Snow, whatever brought you to that car? Why had you come to Toll House? Do you usually visit your neighbors carrying an oxyacetylene torch?"

"Your Honor," the prosecutor jumped up, "may the witness have the privilege of answering one question at a time?"

"I had a warrant, sir," Isaiah Snow replied without waiting for an official ruling.

"And why did you happen to have a warrant?" Franklin probed further.

"We . . . the police department . . . were fortunate to receive a tip, sir," Snow concluded.

"Ah, I see," F.D.R. acknowledged, enlightened. "A tip!" Then he abruptly sat down. I could not believe his nonchalance, his lack of aggression. I made a mental note to find out conclusively whether or not this was a hanging State.

Half-expecting that she'd be gone — or hoping? now that's a

puzzling one — I turned to study Chantelle once more. How the mere sight of her shredded my defenses! I had not expected to see her again, and so had not prepared myself for the staggering effect that her proximity had on me. Primly seated, she was ostensibly intent on the case, but the fact of her presence exclusive of her cult opened all variety of hope and opportunity.

"See that girl in the pearl-gray business suit?" I confided to my attorney as the prosecutor rose to fill the void left by F.D.R.'s abrupt conclusion.

"What about her?" Franklin D. asked.

"Inspector," quizzed Bowles, "who gave you this so-called tip?"

"She's one of the nuns." I whispered to F.D.R. "I think I'm in love with her. Check that. I *am* in love with her."

Franklin D. twisted his back more deliberately to give Chantelle a closer look. "Probably a prosecution witness" was his cryptic evaluation.

"Get serious!"

Suddenly it hit me. Chantelle could only be here to see me through my ordeal. I had not been abandoned. Let the court find me innocent, and she'd be around to help me pick up the pieces again.

Isaiah Snow had answered, but being intent on Chantelle I had failed to catch his words. His evident fatigue had subdued the volume of his voice. I asked Franklin D. to repeat his reply.

"He said the police in Tennessee gave him the tip. He called them because it was your last known address."

"What police in Tennessee? The only cop who knew me was totally baffled by the bones. Ask him. Object. Do *something*, F.D.R."

Other than tap my wrist and again advise me to relax, my lawyer did nothing. The prosecutor sat down looking as though he had swallowed a mockingbird, burped, and Inspector Isaiah Snow was dismissed from the stand.

"You've convinced me," I said, leaning into Ryder. "You're incompetent. I'm relieving you of your duties."

"Let's wait until we get to trial to decide that. I have a hunch you might think differently by then."

I might have continued to argue the point, except that the

prosecutor chose that moment to call Miss Chantelle Clarissa Cromarty to the stand.

The ramifications of her betrayal were slow to sink in.

Once I understood that she was here to speak against me, I was impressed by her malice. To travel here, to regurgitate an inconsequential remark in a tone laden with hidden meaning, to repeat to these local infidels that trashing the Mercury had been, for me, "like burying an old friend," was intriguing for the strength and vindictiveness of her malevolence. Had I hurt her that much, spying on the communal dance through the bubble?

No one had sought her out. Chantelle had volunteered her information. She had phoned the authorities and willingly — gladly — enthusiastically! — related her memory of my words, careful to make even the inflection in her voice sound incriminating. Chantelle had come to testify against me: which was why she dared not look me in the eye.

I despaired.

Here to defend her little group, Chantelle discredited me in order to nullify anything that I might divulge about the nuns. Though why she'd be worried about it at this late date bewildered me. One thing was for certain: to malign my name with such ease and generosity, she had to be convinced of my guilt.

The prosecutor came away from his one-minute chat with Chantelle gloating. I slumped back in my chair, in shock, feeling the noose tighten. But no, I was not going to the gallows. I would be moved to a prison where I'd eke out my days. That was real. That was potential. I couldn't kid about it any more.

Rising, F.D.R. conferred his usual perfunctory smile and repertoire of gestures on the court. He appeared to be prepared to discuss old times with Chantelle before the gavel struck. He smiled merrily at the magistrate, and said to her, "My Toyota is rusting and the clutch is slipping. Sounds like a tank. Were I to junk it, Miss Cromarty, would that, in your eyes, make me a murderer?"

Mr. Bowles objected, the judge sustained his viewpoint, F.D.R. was advised to pose questions germane to the investigation, and, ever so briefly, Chantelle's eyes crossed mine. Franklin D. vowed to rephrase the question.

"What if I were to take my Toyota and trade it in?" Which created another welter of protest and further reprimand. Behaving as though he was in earnest and taking this criticism to heart, the slump of his shoulders proof that he was contrite, F.D.R. asked Chantelle, "Were you aware that Mr. Elder had inherited a relatively new vehicle, his father's Cherokee Chief?"

"Yes," she admitted. "I attended the reading of the will, if you remember, Mr. Ryder."

"I do indeed. How would you describe the condition of the Mercury that he sent over the cliff?"

Chantelle's voice was quiet in the large room, which obliged everyone to be mute, leaning forward to hear. "It was very old."

"Yes!"

"Rusty."

"Yes!" F.D.R.'s booming affirmations sounded like vocal exclamation marks.

"Banged up a little."

"Yes!"

"Very run down."

"Would it be too extravagant, Miss Cromarty, to describe Mr. Elder's car as a wreck?"

Chantelle whispered, "No."

"Thank you, Miss Cromarty. And might I add that it's been great seeing you again." As he sat, he said to me, "That wasn't very damaging. I don't know why Bowles bothered."

"He probably couldn't hold her back." But Franklin D. had no idea how wrong he was. Chantelle might be self-controlled, her testimony inconsequential, but I bled internally.

The ubiquitous Dr. Lewis Tanner was summoned and sworn in. While Bowles asked the usual cursory questions to establish the man's credentials, I watched over my shoulder as Chantelle walked out of the courtroom. That she never looked back was demoralizing. She counted me among her enemies. I was expendable. But why, Chantelle? Why take the trouble? I swear there was no knowing this woman, no way to comprehend her motives.

I stared at the door that had closed behind her. Hoped that she would reappear in the gallery, but she did not. So. She did not even care about the verdict.

I heard Dr. Tanner talking and considered what he had told me. Chantelle and the others had killed my father. Had they collaborated on Gaby's demise as well? Had I fallen in love with a monster? Could the bones in my car have been Chantelle's handiwork? Part of a macabre ceremony? Had one of their number spotted me removing them, and chosen to put them back in the Mercury? Then I caught myself. How easily I accused Chantelle of wrongdoing; she had been equally swift to denounce me.

A question posed by Bowles snapped me out of my reverie and earned the whole of my interest.

"Dr. Tanner, after these various scientific investigations and the gathering of data which you have detailed for us with such precision, what have you concluded as to the identity of the skeletal remains?"

I wanted to know the answer to that one too. Tanner spoke in a decisive, careful voice, and I was pleased to see that he had recovered from his cold. "The medical and dental records are conclusive. The collaborating evidence, such as bone size and age, offer no contradictions. The bones are the remains of one Cindy Anne Bottomley, formerly of Montreal, Canada."

Bowles faced me. He informed the court, "The bones of the victim found in Kyle Elder's trunk" — now he pointed an accusing finger right at me — "are those of Kyle Elder Junior's childhood sweetheart."

Too late for F.D.R. to object. The damage had been done. And I was too shocked to utter a denial.

5

Caring for me as one would a recently bereaved widower, Franklin D. led me to lunch. At Jack's Restaurant, I consented to his choice of the spaghetti-and-meatballs special with an apathetic nod. We were served promptly, and between bites F.D.R. chased journalists and the curious away. I chewed several mouthfuls and swilled half a glass of Coke before I found my voice and range. "Did you know, F.D.?"

"About what?" Polishing his lips briskly with a napkin.

"About what! About Cindy, about what. Why are you so dense?"

Although F.D.R. deigned to look at me, the sympathy evident in his eyes made me squirm. "Yes," he admitted.

"You bastard." Knife in one hand, fork in the other, both utensils bloody with a spicy sauce, I stared back at him. "You could have warned me at least! I had a right to know!"

"Actually, it would have been unwise to tell you," Franklin D. answered. "I wanted the court to appreciate your surprise, your genuine shock. The judge noticed, by the way, and so did Bowles. For that matter, so did I. I'm sorry, Kyle, but we're in this for keeps and we can't pussyfoot around. It was critical that your facial expression reflect the fact that the prosecutor was telling you something that you did not already know."

I sat back to digest this argument. Did my lawyer really possess a brain? "That's the first intelligent thing you've said all day."

"Thanks."

On the walk back, I asked him what was likely to happen

during the afternoon. "Or does that have to come as a shock too?"

Ryder was surprisingly well-informed. "Bowles will try to prove that you don't exist. He'll have to do it by pulling rabbits from hats, because Thurman has already determined that he won't entertain that line."

"I don't get it."

"He wants to trap you coming and going. He wants to prove that if you're Kyle Elder you're guilty, given your history of slaughtering your mother and your kinky devotion to your girlfriend's bones. Sorry, that was unkind. If you're not Kyle Elder then he'll allege that you killed him too."

"Who?"

"You. That you killed yourself, so to speak. It's his job at this hearing to cast aspersions, so bear up. Try not to take offense, and trust me."

Ryder was on the mark about Bowles' plans. To demonstrate that I was an imposter, the district attorney called F.D.R.'s father to the stand, and the old man shuffled in, wielding his cane. Obedient to the district attorney's example, courtroom eyes surveyed the senior Ryder, then his son, and back again. My lawyer blew a bubble in his cheek, then popped it with a poke of his middle finger.

Judge Thurman paid obsequious compliments to the aging legal warrior, and Bowles, with a flagrant smirk directed at F.D.R., commenced his questioning.

"Mr. Theodore Ryder, what is your occupation, sir?"

"I'm a lawyer, retired."

"In your capacity as a lawyer, did you have as a client the late Mr. Kyle Elder Senior?"

"I did."

"And in your capacity as his attorney, did you ever have occasion to meet his son?"

"Once," the legal patriarch announced. My attention was well concentrated. I knew beyond a doubt that, prior to last week, I had never laid eyes on the man.

"And when was that, sir?"

"Nineteen-seventy. I've taken the trouble to check my files."

"What was the occasion for that meeting?"

"Mr. Elder had learned through a friend, one Emma St. Paul, that his wife — from whom he was divorced and who was the mother of his son — had passed away. This court has already alluded to the bizarre circumstances of that death. Once it was legally established that his son was in no way responsible, Mr. Elder Senior wished to make what he called 'restitution'. The difficulty was that the boy had left home, ostensibly for Tennessee, according to Miss St. Paul, in the company of his girlfriend. I wired a communication to the various counties in which he might be expected to appear, explaining the situation and offering compensation for information. Through that effort, we managed to locate the boy.

"The young Elder came to my office. I remember him well. Not a pleasant lad. He declined to meet with his father, and the senior Elder did not push the issue. The elder Elder seemed to understand why his son felt the way he did. At any rate we had offered the option of refusing to meet his father as an incentive to come, which the boy had accepted, and he also accepted his father's token of fifty thousand dollars."

Someone in the courtroom whistled. F.D.R. periodically peeked my way, measuring my reactions. All I could do was look baffled.

"Bearing in mind the passage of time, do you see that boy in this courtroom today, Mr. Ryder?"

"No. I do not." In the witness stand, Franklin D.'s dad leaned forward on his cane.

Bowles feigned surprise. "Mr. Ryder, please look carefully at the defendant. Is that man Kyle Troy Elder Junior?"

Hardly glancing at me, the old man scoffed, "No sir, he is not." To drive the knife deeper, he embellished, "I don't know who my boy thinks he's defending, but it's not Kyle Troy Elder Junior."

Bowles sat down in the terrible silence of the courtroom. Everyone appeared to be mourning my death.

"Good afternoon, Father" was F.D.R.'s hapless beginning as he rose to his feet. "How are you?"

"My God, Franklin, get to the point."

"All right. Thank you for that direction. I shall." Tittering echoed behind our backs. "Tell me, Father, when you met Kyle

Elder Junior in 1970, and handed over to him a cheque for fifty thousand dollars, what identification did you require?"

The old man rummaged about and came up with a look of mild cantankerous surprise. From him Franklin D. had inherited, and expanded upon, his flourish for facial expressions. "Well, I don't know. It was fifteen years ago. I don't remember."

"I remember, Father, that you always taught me to interpret the phrase, 'I don't remember,' as meaning 'I'm not telling and you can't make me.' " The audience loved it. "I accept your challenge, Father, to jog your memory as best we can. Did you ask him for a driver's license perhaps?"

The courtroom was stirring. This was the first indication that Ryder the younger had gumption, and was capable of combating his father's authority. The senior Ryder scratched his chin, and I was fascinated by this confrontation between father and son.

"Actually, no, Franklin D. He was very young, and did not have a permit. No — hold it. I'm wrong. An old man's forgetfulness. I believe he had a learner's permit."

"Excellent, Father! Your memory is sound enough to recall that detail. What about a social security number? In Canada they call it by another name, I believe, but did you see anything like that?"

F.D.R. was pacing now, the onlookers' heads following as though they'd been filmed in slow motion at a tennis match.

This time the witness scratched his nose. "Like I said, I can't remember exactly, but I believe he was too young for that too. He had never worked. I do wish you'd come to the point, Franklin D. These questions are useless."

"What identification did you ask for then, Father? I recognize as well as anyone that you are old and not as alert as you once might have been, but please do your best. After all, if you can differentiate between a learner's permit and license, you must have a grasp of the details."

"Objection, Your Honor," an amused Norman Bowles spoke up. "The defense is badgering the witness."

The courtroom laughed heartily.

Even Judge Thurman smiled as he struck down the jocularity with his gavel. "The defense shall remember to honor thy father."

"Yes, Your Honor."

Under the merriment, F.D.R.'s father seethed. Small wonder. My own chin had dropped an inch. The old man's reddening neck marked the rise of his blood pressure and fury; his eyes flashed. F.D.R. would get it when he reached home, but for the nonce his father was obliged to answer the question.

"There was, yes, I remember now, an identity card, yes. Are you satisfied?"

"Not in the least. An identity card from what source?"

Flustered, the gentleman blew out a gust of wind. "If I remember correctly, and it has been over fifteen years," he reiterated, "it was a student identity card, issued by a school. His Montreal address was printed on the back, and that checked out. Oh! I remember! He also carried a picture of his mother."

"A picture of his mother!" I was overwhelmed.

"I showed it to Elder Senior," Theo Ryder protested. "For confirmation."

"A picture of his mother?" F.D.R. had miraculously switched gears, speaking now as if addressing the senile. "And this I.D. card, did it include a photograph of the boy?"

"Not that I recollect, but it had his signature."

"Whoop-dee-doo!"

"What do you mean, 'whoop-dee-doo'?" At my back, people were cracking up. In the periphery of my vision Hazel Stamp was bent in two, clutching her side. "Benny, are you going to allow these ravings to go on in your courtroom?"

"Objection, Your Honor," Bowles called from his seat. "I fail to see the relevance of this line of questioning."

"It's about time you spoke up!" Theo chided him.

Benny's gavel rang loud and true. The courtroom came to order, and he stated simply, "Objection overruled."

Pointing a deliberate finger into the face of his regal old man, F.D.R. shouted, "Father!" so loudly that the judge, myself, and a majority of sightseers jumped in our seats. "You gave fifty thousand dollars to a boy without conclusive identification. Did it never occur to you that the real Kyle Troy Elder Junior" — and he now pointed directly at me — "might have been drinking in a bar one night, a bar that turned a blind eye to juveniles; that he might have been mourning the disappearance of his girlfriend, not to mention the recent loss of his dearly beloved mother; that his new-found friends in Tennessee might have taken him for a ride; that, far from home and alone, he might have been beaten, robbed, and left bleeding in a ditch? Is it beyond the realm of possibility that that robbery was a set-up, a deliberate ploy to abscond with his identification?" F.D.R. was shouting now over Bowles' repeated objections and Thurman's ringing mallet. "Did it never occur to you, Father, that you had notified half a State that a large inheritance was due to any lad who showed up *claiming* to be Kyle Troy Elder? Did it never occur to you, Father, that the youth who presented himself to you may well have been an *impostor*?"

"How could an impostor know to come to me?" Theo fired back with equal hostility, a lifetime of disappointment in his son charging his invective, for what transpired between inquisitor and witness now was really a boisterous enactment of their relationship, with all the old grievances flying home to roost.

"Who sent him to you?" Franklin D. roared.

Judge Thurman had decided to let them fight it out.

Theo wetted his lips before answering. "A policeman," he said. "His name . . . on the tip of my tongue . . . I know it . . . McGrath! A sheriff."

The exchange had left me rapt and giddy, but the swift mention of a name out of my past clobbered me as surely as if I'd been pitched into the strike zone of a clean-up hitter's mighty swing.

"McGrath," he repeated, almost triumphantly, saying the name as his son stalked the perimeter of the witness stand. "How's that for an old man's memory, mmmm?"

Franklin D. did not choose to smile on his father's charm. Instead he delivered a one-word sentiment. "Shoddy."

Theo was stunned. "I beg your pardon?" He had lost his bluster. His request sounded more like a whine.

"Your practice of law, Father, was shoddy."

"You little —" What began as a bellow receded. The old man was unaccustomed to defending himself, and lacked the appropriate vocabulary.

The folks in the bleachers had grown rowdy with conversation.

Bang! went the judge's busy hammer. "Order in the court! Order in the court!"

"I'm through with this witness," Franklin D. announced, turned his back on his father, and marched across to our table.

The courtroom was silent as the elder Ryder staggered back to his seat, scowling, but not looking at his son.

Norman Bowles stood and stared into my eyes for perhaps the first time. As though he wanted to see a condemned man squirm. "The State calls Sheriff Everett McGrath to the witness stand."

Would all the denizens of my past be paraded through this room? McGrath was the last man I expected to see here, and one I certainly did not welcome. He sauntered to the witness stand, wearing his khaki uniform. For the first time that I had ever seen, his tie was neatly knotted at the collar. He gave me a wink as he passed my table.

Sworn in and comfortable in the chair, the sheriff sat holding his Smokey the Bear hat on his crossed knee.

"Thank you for coming, Sheriff. You are a long way from home."

"Glad I could make it on time."

"We were hoping that you could help us out here. We're confused as to the identity of the defendant."

"Who, Kyle? Kyle Elder, that's who he is."

"Thank God for that," I muttered to F.D.R.

"Fifteen years ago, Sheriff—"

"Objection," Franklin D. noted. "Have we not indulged the State's mania with fifteen years ago long enough? Can we not keep this hearing current? My client does not need to have every aspect of his past dredged up."

"Your Honor, the State would like to clarify the matter of identity, and then move on to a different line of questioning."

"I share the defense attorney's impatience. Please get to the point, Mr. Bowles."

"Did you, Sheriff, fifteen years ago, send a young man to Vermont to receive a payment of fifty thousand dollars from his father?"

"Nope."

"You didn't?"

"Nope. Dunno what yer talking about. I can tell yuh one thing, Kyle Elder's never had no fifty thousand dollars."

Bowles, who clearly had not had an opportunity to speak to his witness at length beforehand, seemed only mildly agitated. He had more pertinent matters to consider.

"When you were contacted about this recent case, Sheriff, what was your reaction?"

"I was pleased. Been looking for Kyle Elder myself."

"Since when?"

"Since early April, about. That's when he run off. Him and me, we had ourselves a car chase, but he gave me the slip, I'm ashamed to say."

"Why were you chasing him?"

"Wanted a look in his trunk."

"What did you expect to find?"

"Bones. A skeleton. Got a tip that a skeleton been dumped in his trunk. Wanted to check that out. Yuh see, we been having a real problem back home. Bones showing up all over the place. In the trees sometimes. On a kiddies' swing at the amusement park. In the dryer down at the laundromat. Seventeen so far."

"And you suspected that Kyle Elder might be behind this phenomenon?"

"Mister, I been suspecting everybody. I would've suspected you if I'd seen yer face. A case like this one, yuh don't leave no stone unturned, know what I mean?"

Bowles gave the back of his neck a rub. "But you did suspect that Kyle Elder, that man sitting over there, *might* be linked to these occurrences?"

"Well," McGrath conceded, and I appreciated his reluctance, "I did set up a roadblock to inspect his car. But he gave me the slip."

"And did you advise Inspector Snow, when he telephoned you for information, to check the trunk of Kyle Elder's Mercury?"

"I was out of town when he called. But yeah, when I got the chance to talk to him, that's what I suggested he do."

"No further questions at this time, Your Honor."

Franklin D. was on his feet in a flash. He seemed more agile than usual, more confident. "Sheriff McGrath! You're a legend! I'm delighted to meet you."

"Dunno about that legend part."

"Oh, but it's true. Didn't you break a major case fifteen years ago? Didn't you, in the course of your duties, shoot a serial killer? Did you not save the life of Kyle Elder, just in the nick of time?"

"I guess I did."

"Now you have new troubles down there, we hear."

"Better believe it. Damnedest thing, those bones."

"Do you think the two cases might be related?"

"Do now. Didn't before. I heard that doctor say that Kyle's girl was one of them skeletons. That's the first real lead we've had in this case."

"How so?"

"Kyle's girl disappeared way back. This is the first anybody's heard of her since."

"Do you think that Kyle Elder is somehow responsible for your current problems, Sheriff?"

"Nope. He might know something; we'd like to talk to him down in Tennessee. But I don't think it's him."

"Why not?"

"Because the problem didn't stop when he left the State. Eight days ago we found a skeleton in the barber shop, like it wanted a trim and a shave. Where was he eight days ago?"

"Kyle? He was in the Burlington lock-up, minding his own business."

"It occurred to me that maybe Kyle got nervous if he found the bones in his trunk. Took off. I wanted to get in touch with him to let him know that he was off the hook."

"In other words, Mr. McGrath, you consider my client to be a victim of your troubles in Tennessee, and not a perpetrator."

"That's about the size of it."

I could scarcely believe how well things were going. McGrath was saving my skin once again.

"Why do you think Kyle brought the bones to Vermont, Sheriff, and not to you?"

McGrath shrugged. "Maybe he didn't know they were in his trunk. Or maybe he was afraid of me. I know I saved his life but he never seemed particularly grateful. We didn't get along. But he kept his nose clean and I never meant him no harm."

"So it has all been a giant misunderstanding," Franklin D. summed up.

"I think so."

Spinning on his heels, F.D.R. said to his adversary, "Thanks for the witness."

Bowles waited for the sheriff to be seated before rising to his feet again. "That concludes the State's evidence, Your Honor."

Jumping up, Ryder demanded, "I move for dismissal, Your Honor. The State has failed to produce any proof that is not circumstantial or easily contradicted. There is no evidence to bring my client to trial."

"Your Honor," Bowles fought back, but I could tell that he was on the ropes, "the skeletal remains were covered with the man's fingerprints!"

"My client was the *victim* of a demented prank. One victim among many. Discovering the bones, he put them into a garbage bag and then buried them with his car. He may have been negligent as to his full responsibility in this case, but the circumstances were highly unusual. He did the best he could."

"He did not bury all the bones, Your Honor. He kept one back, the one that was found in his Cherokee Chief."

"An accident! He put the bones away under cover of darkness. One fell out. As a temporary measure he tossed it into his Cherokee for later disposal. Evidence, Your Honor, there is no evidence."

And the two men stood waiting for Thurman's decision.

"As you are aware, Mr. Bowles, the burden of proof, both in a trial and in this proceeding, lies with the State. You have failed to carry that burden. It does seem to me that Mr. Elder has knowingly and illegally been in possession of a human corpse. No more than that on the evidence. This is a serious offence, but I suspect that Mr. Elder would be willing to plead guilty to such a charge and pay a suitable fine."

"He will, Your Honor," Ryder said on my behalf.

"You, Mr. Bowles, are privileged to press that charge. Further charges, however, including the serious crime of murder, cannot be brought forward at this time, and cannot be brought forward without new evidence being submitted to another hearing of this nature. I declare this hearing closed."

Judge Ben Thurman's words and the bang of his gavel were as sweet and as ethereal as a vireo's whistle.

I clapped my defender's back. "Way to go! You became your own man today, Franklin D!"

His vast smile conveyed his inner thrill, the adrenalin rush. "I hope it's worth it, Kyle. I probably just wrote myself out of my father's will."

"Not to worry. In my experience, wills are double-edged swords. Anyway, you won't need it. Not with your future in criminal law." His smile brimmed below his excited eyes, and he jabbed my shoulder playfully. I stared at him. "My God, you really are going to do it!"

"No more divorces. The hell with contracts. Forget estate planning. From now on I only defend the scum of the earth."

F.D.R. need not have fretted about his father's will. Belligerent and still fuming, Theo nevertheless could not restrain a twinkle of admiration directed at his son. I like to think that that's how I would have gotten along with my father. The animosity, the scars might never have healed, but in my fantasy I see us becoming friends, acknowledging with sympathy our errors and laments, struggling on, bound together less by blood than by a common love.

I accepted congratulations from many, a kiss from Hazel and a strong handshake from Isaiah Snow. When we had another minute to ourselves, F.D.R. said, while packing up his papers, "Isn't it sinking in? You're free, Kyle. We won."

"Maybe that's what bothers me," I said.

"What's that supposed to mean?"

The courtroom was all but empty now. Visitors had gone home. A few reporters were hanging around in the hall waiting for me to come out. "He put on a show, Franklin."

"Who did?"

"For almost as long as we've known each other McGrath has been trying to nail me to the cross. Why the change of heart?"

"He's a man of integrity, Kyle. You know, he phoned me a couple of days ago. Of course he had to, I had a right to screen the

State's witnesses. But he was more than cooperative. He let it be known that Bowles had him pegged all wrong."

"That doesn't solve anything for me. That only makes it worse. He had me where he wanted me. Why the hell did he let me go?"

And I suddenly noticed that F.D.R. had turned glum and solemn. "Don't you get it, Kyle?" he explained. "McGrath didn't save your hide; he was protecting his own. He stole your father's money. It was him. He was a bigger enemy than you ever realized. And, who knows? Maybe he still is."

McGrath?

BOOK FOUR

A Kinkajou in Hackensack

1   Subsequent to my legal adventures, I wrote letters dank with bitterness and bile. Yearning to thrash things through, in these private epistles I harangued Chantelle for her testimony, vilifying her for her most grievous defect of character, her willingness to imperil love for the sake of mere prudence. I mailed my ardent accusations straight into the wastebasket, and daily Hazel would incinerate the residue of my heart in the outdoor pit.

The days went by. My vindication ought to have left me high and giddy, but I was distressed that Chantelle, through her betrayal, was confirmed as my adversary forever. Try as I might I could not forget, forgive, or exclude that woman, though I assumed that I would never see her again.

I had chosen not to accompany Cindy's skeleton on the train back to Montreal, although I did see her coffin onto the north-bound Amtrak out of Burlington. That was her proper grave. A moving train, the continuing journey, the young girl in search of the stars, the boy in me who had loved her waving goodbye.

I've said it before: God bless Hazel Stamp. While not in the best of moods herself, she did a yeoman's job trying to cheer me up. Toll House offered no guests for us to entertain, and I put off her queries about reopening. With only me to feed and boss around, she was frequently surly, though she divined that I required space in which to recuperate and endeavored to oblige. Nightly, Hazel trounced me at chess, clucking her tongue after each checkmate to imply that my defenses had been wishy-washy, my offense rudimentary. I took my repeated shellackings with aplomb, though I told her once that she was a sore winner. She thought that that was very funny coming from me.

One morning, she conscripted me into traipsing down to the furnace room and going through my father's things. I was, in spite of myself, keen. Boxes of clothing articulated a man with a variety of interests. Hip-waders and a cap emblazoned with feathered flies bespoke of angling the mountain streams. A predilection for heavy plaid shirts in winter and gaudy Hawaiian frippery whenever the weather was warm gave me an inkling into his at-home leisure hours. The liquor-stained, worn smoking-jacket suggested that he was willing to put on airs whenever potted. He also had an unfortunate fondness for ugly plaid jackets and bow ties.

The majority of his books were practical guides — carpentry, household repair, architecture, horseback riding, tapestry weaving, antique collecting, staining wood — including one that must have been anathema to Hazel — on diet. A few massive tomes, the histories of Russia, ancient Rome, modern Europe, evinced a bent in that direction, and the volumes were well-used.

Another box contained a treasure of pipes and various tobacco blends, an assortment of colognes, six different ivory-handled straight-edged razors, paperclips snapped onto a sheet in ascending order for size, Topps' Baseball Cards for the years 1948, 1957, and 1961, with complete sets of the Boston Red Sox for seven consecutive years, ending in '67; maps of Vermont, one of which had the highest peaks circled in red, so add mountain-climbing to his sports; a nail file, four penknives, a stapler shaped and colored like a frog, a shoehorn compliments of a New York hotel, a Cross pen with his name on it, and a rosary; packets of Doublemint chewing gum filled with thumbtacks; one empty shotgun shell, an electronic calculator, and the miscellaneous junk that one is likely to accumulate in an untamed desk drawer. No photographs. No notes or letters. No diary.

Nothing substantial could be culled from these artifacts, except that he was easily imagined as rotund (note the waistline of his trousers), physically active, and gregarious. He also worked hard. Business reports revealed that the inn was one sideline among innumerable ventures. From my conversations with Hazel I had deduced that my father had migrated to Vermont shortly after the end of his carnival days. Thirty-odd years ago. He started out as a handyman. After building his own home, he expanded that into an inn. His natural ease with people helped make it a successful venture, and one he never relinquished, although he also kept busy renovating and constructing homes. In time, his wealth was garnered in the State's booming condominium industry. The money he had left for the nuns had been considerable, many times that which McGrath had conspired to steal from me. Oh well. Had he left me all that loot my sleep might have remained sound. At least he woke me up.

Included in the subterranean archives were three opened bottles of wine and a collection of apple cores. I decided against telling Hazel that someone among the dismissed was a closet drunk.

What I also found down below propelled me out of there. I came across my father's writings, including the chapbook, *A Kinkajou in Hackensack*. Yet I did not open the cover, I did not read. As though in the presence of original scripture unearthed from an antediluvian cavity, I dared not touch the pages, lest they crumble in my hands.

I had to get over Chantelle first. My unmailed letters to her let off steam; the last thing I needed now was to revive my association with her through reading my father's fable. And I ran upstairs as fast as my wobbly legs would allow.

Strolling through the woods, engrossed in a satisfying mope, I noticed a ruby-crowned kinglet alight on a branch up ahead. The small bird flared its red spot chiefly for my benefit. Not overly common in these parts, the bird's appearance allowed me to feel privileged in its company.

It crossed my mind that on the day I had first met Chantelle she had been wearing a cerise tam, and to honor her I had sung a melody of the kinglet's. Right then I knew that Chantelle was on her way to see me. I sang to the bird and he flew about the trees, searching for his mate.

Naturally I disputed my intuitive belief as I emerged from the woods. Wishful thinking. Be real, Elder. She's gone from your life and you ought to be thankful. Imagine, with her bleeding by rote, what her doctor's bills would be. Ambulance drivers would abduct her routinely. We could never take a holiday in case she'd cause a scene. "Excuse me, sir," bows the maitre d', "your wife is dripping on the carpet."

Before I made it safely into Toll House, I heard a car laboring on the steep road. Tourists suck. It's amazing how many will expressly ignore the "No Vacancy" sign, believing that the impediment exists for others, and if I'd only take the time to meet them I'd change my tune.

This particular driver could have run me down and I would not have budged to defend myself. I froze.

Stopping the car, Chantelle stepped out. She wore her cerise tam. I experienced the dislocation of the sleepwalker awakened on a distant avenue. Sporting a half-smile and a tremulous, halting expression, Chantelle walked toward me. I quivered, then stood my ground. Once I accepted that this was really happening, I welcomed her wholly into my arms.

Between kisses we murmured apologies as carefree lovers might convey declarations of fidelity. "Kyle, my God, Kyle, I'm sorry sorry sorry." For speaking against me. For doubting me. For putting the interests of her group ahead of our union. She recited her litany of betrayals and I awarded each transgression with a kiss. I kissed her neck, her ears, her forehead, thinking confess! *confess!* You killed my father too! Reveal that one and I shall love you all the more. Don't hold back now! I held her tightly, thinking, I killed my mother and you killed my father and here we are, chained, neither of us can move. She punctured my skin, stabbing me with kisses.

Shackled together, bound by limbs and by remorse, somehow we burrowed through the entrance into Toll House. Our bodies were glued fast. My quick glance sighted Hazel in her adept disappearing act, leaving the way clear.

"Chantelle, you're here. I can't believe it. God. Chantelle. You're here!"

"Kyle, oh, I'm sorry. Sorry."

"I can't believe you're here!"

With stealth, I guided her upstairs. We were intruders. I had neither checked her in nor run her American Express card through the clicker. At the top of the stairs I kissed her with greater straightforward passion than perhaps I honestly felt, for I needed a moment to make a decision. Which room? That's a problem when your house has forty-two beds.

For its intimacy, my own small chamber would suit. But it had been a deathbed for both Gaby and my father, and we did not need to cope with those reminders just now. The Mt. Washington Room, where I had been sleeping lately, presented ample comforts: we could hide in there for weeks and never feel confined. But I feared that the room could prompt a recurrence, that by the witching hour she'd require a transfusion. So I led Chantelle into a room I had never entered previously.

Tidy, of course.

The bed covered by a checkered, dark quilt.

A wedge of sunlight slanting through the window.

I cannot report that we caught fire. An extraordinary coolness regulated our actions, as though the ceremony was deliberate and premeditated, not the comet's tail of passion. I opened the top button of her blouse, she started on the bottom ones, our fingers met at her breasts. Everything done in small measure. A code of courtesy informed our undressing. Our first touches impertinent. When I moved to kiss her nipples my thirst was unquenchable, yet I accepted only a polite sip. We never fumbled; I snipped away at her skirt and, with patience, she was revealed.

Chantelle lay down.

She spoke my name.

A gentle coo.

I had imagined this differently.

"Are you sure?" I begged to know, holding back. I clung to her like a man to the side of a mountain, clung to her and felt her slide. My feeble protest remains an embarrassment, but I was unhinged by love and wracked by mortal concerns.

Hesitation will doom us all.

Clinging to my neck, Chantelle pulled me down on top of her.

We wiggled about to make ourselves fit. Her plea, pressed to my ear, rang a bell of havoc throughout my soul. "Baby. Kyle. Yes. Oh baby. My baby, yes!"

What struck me as strange? I suppose that, with her arrival predicted by a bird, I was giving more credence to intuitive force. My qualms caused me to botch our simple joining, and I pulled away from her slightly.

"Chantelle?" Her name a question.

A forgiving lover, she pulled me down again. Spoke sweet endearments in my ear. Infuriated by the delay our hips sought allegiance. "Yes. Kyle. Oh. Darling. Yes. Now. Baby. Please."

And I bolted upright once more. Bewildered with myself. Overwhelmed by my clarity of mind. I felt prodded by an electric stick.

"What's the matter?" Chantelle's rhythms subsided.

"Is that what this is all about?" I demanded, my tone both firm and tender. "Baby-making?"

She swung up one leg, gathered herself into a more modest pose.

"Kyle. Come on. What's gotten into you?"

"I'm confused," I confided.

"About what?"

"About what we're doing. About why you're here. Why you went away. What brought you back. Are we talking about fatherhood here today?"

"I guess if we make love that's a possibility." Chantelle gently stroked my penis.

"No, what I mean is, are we going to have a baby *here*, in Toll House, do we give it a home? Or do you have something else in mind?"

"I don't believe this is happening," she lamented. "I don't believe we're having this conversation. It takes a lot for me to come into this room, Kyle, and you want to talk? I, for one, did not come here merely to jump in the sack. I —"

"No? Why not? When *did* you make up your mind? When did you consent to come to bed with me, Chantelle?"

"Why are you sounding so cross? When we met outside —"

"When did you start thinking *baby*?"

"What is the matter with you?" she sang out in anger, her outrage entirely justified.

I was looking at the world on a slant. The horizontal plane was tilted. Being psychic was a burden; reading her mind was scary. I sat back, leaning against a corner post, hoping the earth would level out.

I spoke quietly, directly. "I need to know what this is all about. Why you're here. Is this lovemaking, Chantelle? Or an injection of sorts. My sperm into your womb."

Spinning around, Chantelle stood on the floor and dressed. "God, you're disgusting!" she chastized me, weeping.

"What the hell else am I supposed to think? Is this your surrender, Chantelle? Is this what I am to you, your compromise?"

"Why are you tormenting me?" she wailed, standing defiantly in her underwear, her fists combat-ready.

I grabbed one of her flailing arms. "What you and the others were doing here last Easter, that was baby-making, wasn't it? An attempt, admit it, to produce a virgin birth. That's what this is all about, right?"

Chantelle wiped a tear on her thin, bare shoulder.

"Are you quitting?" I asked her gently. "Is that what I am to you? A substitute god of some kind? Come on, Chantelle. I don't fit the bill, even if I do have my father's genes. I can only make love the old-fashioned way. Bump and grind. In and out."

"Why are you doing this?" A scornful, tearful question, her voice frail.

I sighed, oh so wearily. Looked down and noticed my penis misbehaving, remaining as rigid as the bedpost. Which said less for my desire than it signaled my love for her, my need for her, with a nod to many months of enforced celibacy.

"No one in your group, Chantelle, has been able to conceive by the Holy Ghost. Now you want to give the secular world a whirl. Is this your compromise?"

She had slipped her blouse on; her long fingers were nervously doing up the buttons. "What's wrong with that?"

Tension elapsed with her concession. I exhaled a deep breath. "You could hate me forever. Today I'm the vessel of God's holy seed, tomorrow I'm the demon of carnal pleasure. Can't we learn to keep the gods out of this? They're not interested anyway. Can't this be between you and me, just you and me, no outsiders? It's this crowded bed that's put me off, this orgy of kin and ghosts and your tribe and our offspring. Can't we leave the future generations out of this too?"

"You conjured them."

"I know I did."

We held hands after we finished dressing, and lingered by the window. I kissed the top of her head. That was nice. Chantelle was sacred to me, and yes, that was part and parcel of my withdrawal too. It's hard to be lecherous with the sainted.

"I'll ask Hazel to set a table. We'll have dinner. We'll talk. We'll see what we can salvage, all right?"

Chantelle nodded. Mopped the tears that flooded her eyes with her pinky. She could not speak to me without weeping, and so she maintained her silence.

Hazel's surprise was to stick to our simplified menu, in this instance a light, tasty tuna casserole and basic tossed salad. In effect, she was treating our visitor as a friend, not a guest, and that was a nice touch. Eating in the center of the dining-room and not the kitchen was the only change to our routine. Being alone in that expanse in candlelight created an aura of opulence. We looked out over the black fluid of the mountains under the scant illumination of the stars, our drift through expanding space a restful one. Welcome to the Starship Toll House.

Hazel would not hear of our helping with the dishes — if she had a problem these days it was with the dearth of work to do — and Chantelle and I retired to the side of the hearth. Soon Hazel carried in coffee and Drambuie. And in that magical way of hers, she slipped out of sight unnoticed.

"So," I asserted.

Chantelle concurred. "So."

Our manifest discomfort stemmed from Hazel's absence. In her vicinity our conversation benefitted from the customary social controls. Once she was gone, difficult subjects were impossible to avoid. In the electrified atmosphere of our reunion we had mentioned swift apologies, yet being sorry for past events failed to nullify their importance. Eventually I breathed in deeply, tapped my heart to keep it still, and stated, "I'm really, profoundly, sorry for spying on you, Chantelle. I don't know what possessed me — check that, I do know. My great concern for you."

"And your curiosity," she butted in.

"And my curiosity. For what it's worth, it won't happen again."

As lovely as the touch of her lips on mine contrived to be, as honest as her forgiveness proved to be, in my heart I was wretchedly disappointed by her response. I suppose that my apology had really been a ploy. I had expected her to redress her own sins, to reveal that she had hooked up the exhaust pipe of her Toyota to my father's lungs. Chantelle, however, was content to kiss me and smile, and suggest that all was forgiven. I returned the kiss.

"Chantelle."

She tilted her head as though to contort herself into a question mark. "What is it?"

"Tell me how my father died."

Quiet a while. Her eyes never left mine, while I stared into the fire.

"Don't you know?" she asked. A tremor in her voice.

"That's the point." I found the courage to face her. "I do know. I mean, I know the truth."

"I don't understand, Kyle." Looking up at me. Pleading. Her eyes begging to be let off this hook. Yet even pushed to this limit she was not going to blunder, and reveal private truths. Chantelle would not budge an inch until she was positive that I already knew everything.

"Dr. Tanner had a word with me," I revealed, and watched as her shoulders collapsed. A hand went to her mouth, seemingly to block the swift expulsion of all breath. "He signed the death certificate one way, but he knew better. He knew that my father's rosy cheeks could only have been caused by carbon monoxide poisoning."

I had dreaded the consequent silence. Chantelle was making her choices. Self-defense was probably her instinctive option, one that would surely doom us to separation, our love ground under the wheel of life and lies. The other was to speak the truth, own up, confess, and face the equally difficult mill of intimacy.

Chantelle spoke. She was regarding the floor, the carpet, her feet. I sat down close to her, to hear her quiet voice.

"We drew lots. My little yellow Toyota was chosen. We chose to draw cars instead of people because it was less personal that way. We swiped Hazel's vacuum-cleaner without her knowing. Then, late one night, we bundled your father up. Crazy, but we didn't want him to catch a cold. It was funny, Kyle, he was as happy as a lark. He was going on a journey — more than a trip, an expedition — and he was tickled, you could tell by the look in his eyes.

"He kissed each of us. That was hard to take. That was so . . . hard. The kiss went inside each of us and twisted, you know, like a knife in our hearts. There wasn't a dry eye among us and we had to take turns going to the bathroom, washing our faces, composing ourselves.

"We trooped outside. It was crazy because we weren't down in the dumps anymore, like we expected, this wasn't the funeral march each of us had imagined. Someone even giggled. That might have been the only honest expression because we felt, I don't know — I do know, I just don't want to admit to it. I, for one, felt a wild sense of . . . of exultation. I was light-headed, almost euphoric. God knows, I don't know why.

"Since it was my car, I had to turn the key. That was the deal. We had chosen cars because it was less nasty than choosing executioners, that's what it came down to. Gabriella hooked up the vacuum hose from the exhaust into the car. Your father sat in the back seat. We stuffed the gap in the window where the hose came through with a pillow.

"Everyone stood away. I walked forward. I could scarcely feel my feet touch the ground. I got into the car. Kyle, I was trembling. It was crazy. Every part of me was excited and sick and happy and mad. I just sat there. Then your father put his hand on my shoulder. I jumped in my seat. I was crying, I think, but who could tell, I was sweating so much. 'I have never been so happy,' he said to me. He knew I was having trouble, and even at the precipice of death he was concerned about me. 'You do me a great service. Start the car, Chantelle,' he said, 'that I may begin my travels.' "

Sitting back, remembering, Chantelle watched the ceiling and wiped away her tears.

"I started the ignition. I looked back at your father. He smiled and took a deep breath, as if he was inhaling the cleanest air. A little joke. I got out and closed the door. An incredible feeling, as if I had no legs, as if there wasn't any ground beneath me. I walked away from the car. We let the engine idle on. I was the one who eventually shut the motor off.

"In a way, Kyle," — she was looking at me now — "it was good to see your father's cheeks flushed, rosy with life again. It made us feel for a while that we had done the right thing, that our choice to permit him a dignified dying had been the loving one."

"Only for a while?" I asked.

Chantelle nodded. "Complications. On this smelly old planet there are always complications. We had decided beforehand that, once your father was buried and a grieving period had passed, we would announce to the world what we had done. The act had been a deliberate and a communal choice. Let society put us in jail, if it had the will. We were taking a moral stand, you see, wrestling with a worldwide dilemma, which, I suppose, justified our action to a certain extent."

"So what happened? Why did you keep silent?"

Having to clear her throat, Chantelle turned away from me. She dabbed at an old tear still moist on her cheek. "Can't you guess?" she challenged. Her tone had turned bitter.

I thought about it. I recoiled when the answer came to mind, but there was no way to duck the obvious. "My God," I said. "The inheritance."

She shook some of the tension out of her shoulders. "Suddenly we could accomplish projects that had only been dreams. We could meet together more often. Build a place for ourselves. Make plans. Personally, I resented the change. I'm a stickler for moral standards — I didn't want us to abandon ours. Gabriella, she was in favor of the new plans and the issue divided the two of us. In a sense I became a misfit within the very society that had come into being to keep me from being a misfit. I was the troublesome nutcase whose hands bled, the medium who had made the group jell and given it a focus, but that was all I was. At best, a catalyst. At worst, I don't know, a mascot? Many felt that God did not want us to hinge our faith on this one sign of His presence. He wanted us to be active in our communities, workers devoted to social justice. Our group became divided between those who believed in accepting the world for what it is and aspiring to the spiritual dimensions, and those who were committing themselves to changing the world's systems through direct involvement. The first effect of our turmoil was that we never confessed to assisting your father to die. We could never come to a consensus on the subject."

Chantelle stewed in the political turmoil of her group. I had no pertinent words of assurance to dispel that silence or cure her obvious pain.

"In my state — in my ecstasy — I accused Gabriella and the rest of us of murder. Of a crime against God, not against the laws of man so much. That, and the fact that I bled on the wrong day, mix-ups in our personal lives, other things . . . she committed suicide. Since then I'm the heavy. Gaby was the one who most dreaded easing your father into death. She's the one who devised the automobile lottery to keep the stain off our hands. Originally, she was to bring a poison, and she did, only she refused to let us use it. That method placed too much of the responsibility squarely on her back. Gaby was the one worried and upset about it, but I'm the one who pushed her over the brink. Did *I* carry the poison around with me ever since? Did I mix it in her tea? No, but I'm the one who wouldn't adapt. I'm the one who resisted the changing times, the new order. I'm the one who only thinks of her own position, who's in a rut. As if this group was not formed for *my* protection! Yet *I'm* the one who bled on the wrong day, meaning I'm out of favor, out of rhythm, or simply out of my mind. And *I'm* the one who called us murderers and maybe that was the voice of God, and then again, maybe it wasn't. Maybe I was just expressing a personal opinion. I'm the one who testified against you if for no other reason than to prove to myself that I didn't want you, that I did not remotely desire you, that I still loved God more."

I was holding my head by the time she finished. The tempo of her words marched on through Toll House, the very cadence reverberating from the foundation like a drumbeat to buttress the walls.

"Quite a rival I have."

She giggled. Added, "I'm sorry, Kyle. For everything."

"Me too." I kissed her. "For everything."

We padded off to prepare for bed. When we met in the hall our kiss was gentle, with neither spite nor expectation.

"I've booked you into the Mt. Washington Room, if that's all right."

Chantelle frowned at first, but recovered. "As long as you don't leer down at me through the skylight."

I wagged a correcting finger before her eyes. "I've been forgiven, remember?"

"So you have. So you have." Cheerily: "G'night, Kyle!"

"Good night, Chantelle."

The way my system had been functioning in recent months, I did not expect to sleep, and yet I nodded off very quickly. It was not too much later that I was awakened by Chantelle's screams.

I flung on my jeans. Raced down the hall. By the time I burst in on her she had begun to calm herself, surfacing from her nightmare. I flicked on the light and was considerably relieved to see that she was not bleeding. Rather, she was having trouble breathing.

"What's the caterwauling about?" Hazel's stern demand shook me from behind. She hadn't yet been to bed, and had probably been baking bread in the kitchen, one of her common nocturnal habits.

"She's hyperventilating. Fetch a paper bag."

I sat with Chantelle on the bed as she tried to catch her breath, her deep, rapid gasps frightening me with their panic. Hazel, ever efficient, was soon back and the paper bag trick worked, reviving and calming Chantelle. She breathed evenly.

Hazel did not object, now that the excitement was over, to the slight hint with my head. She departed the room quietly, closing the door behind her.

As I caressed her back, Chantelle held onto my other arm. I soothed her anxieties with softly whispered endearments. "It's only a dream. There now. It's over." Though I doubted my own wisdom, I persevered with this comforting chatter. I kissed her cheek. Her nightdress had bunched up and although I had my qualms I allowed my fingers to brush across her thighs. Taking advantage. Chantelle clutched my bare back, her nails digging in; she uttered inviting murmurs adjacent to my ear. When I moved against her she whimpered and sighed. She accommodated me. Taking advantage. I stood up, and the parting made her gasp.

I turned off the light.

Chantelle disrobed as I approached her, pulling the gown up over her head. Her neck caught and I had to undo an ornery button. I touched her lovely small breasts. She undid my buckle. I lay down beside her and this time we kept out mouths shut, confirming our seal with kisses urgent and warm. Where previously we had been exploratory and cool and tentative, now we were desperate, embattled, and bold. We rolled together and snapped, she cried out, tugged me to her, pushed me away, punched my back, pulled my hair, kissed my mouth to silence my rhythmic grunts. Her pain was as sharp as my brutal, ecstatic release, she was unaccustomed to men, I was her first lover since her childhood terror, and suddenly she moaned once, crazily in a bizarre and horrid voice, her mouth opening wide to expel a hideous vowel.

Then, with a burst of violent, piercing wails that awoke the dead, Chantelle drove me off her.

Punching and slapping me, she escaped from the bed. She hurled herself against the door and pounded on it, her small fists flailing like hammers. I tried to restrain her, she whirled like a dervish, scrambled away, and sank into a corner of the room behind the dry sink.

I switched on the light again and she screamed, screamed her terror at the top of her lungs and Hazel was back, wanting to prevent a murder.

She saw Chantelle in the corner. Naked. Her eyes wild and panicked. Biting down hard on fingers thrust to the back of her throat, she bound her free arm around her legs. Hazel and I were both terrified.

"Better let me handle this. Somehow," I said.

"Put some clothes on first. What were you doing to her?"

"Hazel?" I held the door open for her. Again she was willing to leave.

"Chantelle, it's me," I said, approaching her with extreme caution. "It's me. I'm Kyle. Chantelle. This is now. We're not back then. You're not a child. You're a grown woman now. You're

Chantelle Cromarty. You're alive. I won't harm you. Chantelle?"

"Kyle?" Her voice was a frail squeak.

"Yes, Chantelle. I'm here. You're all right."

"Oh, Kyle." She clutched me and I was stunned by the strength in her hands. "I'm remembering. Oh God, Kyle! I'm remembering!" She wept in great convulsions and I held her to me. When the fits subsided she'd jerk her head away and dry her eyes, then face me, her expression haggard and forlorn. Sometimes she caressed the surface of my palms, other times she'd squeeze my hand so tightly that it was all I could do not to let loose a yelp of my own. Her weeping would recommence in earnest. Out of control. In the midst of her sobbing she would call to her father and to her mother, whose destruction was now visible before her eyes.

I had awakened the memory. Or the act of sex had. For the first time she relived the carnage of that night, her parents slaughtered, a bloodbath, while she was vilely abused. And at times her weeping would cease, she'd break into a holy smile, her eyes radiant as she recalled being lifted out of there, alive, taken far away, free and untouched. For she had departed the scene of her subjugation, her brain blocking out what it could not bear to record. When that part of her mind that had refused to suffer recast its memory, admitting images of the savagery, Chantelle would sway and rock through a rage of impulses and the glut of bloody deaths.

Chantelle could not talk through the rest of the night. The torrent of remembrances were too quick and too dreadful to recite. Dawn found us asleep in one another's arms, still bundled up in a corner of the room.

Chantelle was level, though not necessarily lucid, when she left Toll House after breakfast. "Once more," she insisted. "We've got to try it one more time, if I can only convince the others."

"I can't pretend that I'm with you on this. Frankly, Chantelle, I think the whole idea is ludicrous."

"I know you do." She dumped her suitcase into the trunk of her new Chevette. "A newspaper — a rag — wrote about me once, when I was still an adolescent. Wrote about my hands. On the same page there was a story of a little girl, pre-puberty, who had had a tumor in her womb. The cancer had taken the form of a fetus, with hands and legs, a head and even eyes. The cancer was growing a human body. The fetus was aborted, of course, but the news inspired me. If a cancer can create a child of sorts, why can't its opposite? Why not purity? Love? God's Holy Spirit? Why not a thought, or beauty, or holiness, that would quicken the womb to fashion a child? We've been told that it's happened before, and I'm not so sure the event was all that rare. And the more I thought about the idea, the more I became convinced that it can happen, and happen fairly easily."

"Chantelle," I said carefully, unsure of these treacherous waters, "what happened to you as a child, you know that that's not all there is."

She shushed me with a finger to my lips. "I know. But for me, maybe that is all there is. I need time to find out, Kyle. Who knows? I want to try it one more time. It's not that I want only God as my lover, but that I have to be convinced that He doesn't want me. I have to know that first."

In Chantelle's mind, we had cuckolded God. I felt a little queasy.

"When will you be back?" I closed the trunk for her; held her in my arms. Restless, she squirmed free.

"Soon. I'll have to check with the others, see how their schedules are set up. I also have to study the numbers and consult a star-and-planet chart. Not to mention find out the whereabouts of the fertility moon. I'll pick a date and let you know. You will let us have Toll House, Kyle?"

"Yes. Of course." I had already acquiesced to this request. And to another — that everyone, Hazel and I included, would vacate the premises. The others would only consider a return if the expulsion of the spies was absolute.

"Please, Kyle, don't think ill of me. Don't sour on me. I feel truly, wonderfully, incredibly inspired. It's as if what happened last night, the remembering, broke down the last barrier that's been obstructing me all these years. Now that I've broken through, there are no limits."

Heavy of heart, I watched Chantelle drive away. I feared for her sanity. Turning, I saw her old Toyota sparkle like a tombstone in the morning light. Light and life, death and darkness, permeated the shadowed woods, the sky, and my new, ancient home. Chantelle had slept with me, and obviously that experience, while jarring her equilibrium, had not measured up to the ecstasy of her mystical raptures. Armed with that knowledge, as if our carnal experiment had proven her previous course to be truly exalted, she was returning to her group to renew their faith in one desperate gamble.

To my mind, Chantelle depended on virgin birth to redeem herself, to deliver herself from her wounds and the revived memory of her childhood rape. She considered herself as vile as the perpetrators, contaminated by them, and to be delivered from that corruption she required a singular proof of her own purity. Bleeding profusely at Easter was not enough. To demonstrate that her womb was not plagued by evil, she required that it be impregnated by holy seed.

I walked back to Toll House, these matters brooding inside me. Feeling combative that morning, I challenged Hazel to a game of chess; and, lo and behold, I beat her.

2

Fact: Hazel Stamp is one of the three or four truly heroic people currently dwelling upon the earth's crust. She's indefatigable, indestructible, independent, indisputably divine, and in the inn whenever I need her. She's titan, a tyrant, a tank, a tyrannosaurus who dresses like a tropical parakeet and speaks with the complaining nasal wheeze of the tufted titmouse. Hazel has the mercurial knack of floating about Toll House like a phantom, unobserved, observing all, though she can also stomp around like a Clydesdale if and when she wishes her anger to be known. I must check her hooves for the talaria — Mercury's winged sandals. Her housekeeping is fanatical, her cooking unexcelled. Best of all she swings a mallet like a Viking. Let me shout it out: *Hazel Stamp saved my life!* I adore her. I fully intend to give her a raise.

In the time between Chantelle's leaving and her anticipated return, numerous requests collected dust on my desk. I had enough trouble making decisions on the matters I could not defer. The gentleman who operated the stables through the summer months sought permission to graze his horses. The same pasture was coveted by an ancient widow with goats; she laid claim to the mountain's first tall grass and clover of the season which flavored a special creamy cheese. I did allow the horses and the goats, drawing the line at the Boy Scout troop from Indianapolis who requested permission to pitch their tents. They were traveling through to the coast. I offered them Toll House rooms at double the regular amount to cover the cost of camp-fires in the sitting room and bed-wetting in the dorms, and they chose to carry on. As well, applications had been received from college students expecting summer employment. Several of this new generation let it be known that their future prosperity and well-being rested in my hands. No job, no education. No education, no Lincoln Mark IV or Mercedes Benz. A job at Toll House would either make or break these fragile souls.

To top it off, the customary requests for reservations from the inn's faithful clientele continued to mount.

"Are we open for business or are we not open for business?" Hazel would harp. I'd shrug. The peace, the serenity of occupying the mountain-top alone, with only my housekeeper to ruffle the stillness, was a benefit difficult to relinquish.

"Soon," I'd tell her. "I'll let you know soon."

Bills were accumulating. Economics would shake my lethargy, I hoped, and encourage me back to work. But I delayed the inevitable. I was waiting for Chantelle. We were already in the middle of June.

Then danger.

In the nadir of a muggy night, I was jostled from my sleep. Even at this altitude the climate was tropical, the residue of a Texas drought that was making the valley-dwellers molt. Awakening, I was conscious of my body's dampness, of the air warm on my lips. A shadow converged across my eyes. I bolted upright.

"Who's that? What?"

My intruder flicked on the bedside lamp. I stared up into a skull's hollow eyes.

"Hello, sunshine," said the voice behind the mask. He moved the death's head out of the way to reveal himself.

"My God."

"Yer close. Yer in the ball park."

"McGrath."

"Shitface Elder," he called me. "How yuh doin', boy?"

McGrath hauled me out of bed and bent my back. His arms were incredibly powerful, my stunted frame a Raggedy Andy under his manipulations.

"Yuh never said good-bye," he chastened. "Run off without saying a word to yer good friend, Sheriff McGrath. Made me chase yuh down. Why'd yuh do that, Shitface? I thought we were buddies. I saved yer shitty life!"

I was wrestling against him, panting, my shock grunting with futile bursts. The skull bounced on the mattress.

"I just wanted to warn yuh, Shitface, not to take a corpse across State lines."

"*Aargh!*" I cried out as he wrenched my arm behind my back. The fight went out of me as the pain lanced my shoulders.

"Y'all were my ace-in-the-hole, sweetheart. Didn't yuh know that? Weren't yuh aware of nothin'? I had yuh fingered for an arrest. Illegal bones in yer trunk. Know what the good folks of Walkerman's Creek would've thought? They'd have thrown away the key for good, boy, thrown it clear across the Blue Ridge. Y'all would beg me to lock yuh up if folks found out."

Over the past fifteen years I had had little enough to do with McGrath, although he had always taken a passing interest in my welfare. We'd been cordial. I was his star witness, after all, the one who would report a nude Dakota Hats brandishing a hunting knife behind my back. I had helped make him a State hero. When skeletons cropped up last Halloween on the lawns of the elite like a batch of stubborn, stiff weeds, and later at Christmas the bones of a man tumbled out of the mayor's Cadillac Seville, McGrath had questioned everyone in sight. The pressure was on to find the culprit, and he paid special attention to the local riffraff, which included myself and my old friend Isabelle.

As a witch, Isabelle aroused the town's suspicions. A fire on a Friday night. Odd because it started about twenty minutes after the bars had closed, an unlikely hour for the lantern to fall but prime time for a drunkard's brave vindictive match. Issy wouldn't stay on. I put her and her fourteen-year-old lover, a runaway from Chicago, on the bus north. The boy was taking her home to meet his parents.

Townsfolk were cheerful. Their problems had been solved. I hated them so much that inwardly I clapped when a skull was found in a child's bicycle basket. A leg-bone protruded from a rural mailbox. Arms hung from the coatrack in Apps' Pickle Barrel. A traveling drummer opened his door at the grotty Dixie Motel and was greeted by a whole skeleton, taped together, watching the

N.B.A. on television. A housewife discovered human ribs, meatless, in her deep-freeze. The town was panicking.

McGrath was hounded to find a solution, and now he was telling me that I had been it. That I had made it out of Monroe County in the very nick of time. He twisted my back again and I cried out.

"Now," he told me, "I can break yuh in half, or y'all can promise to behave. What's it gonna be?"

"You won't have any problem with me," I assured him.

He threw me to the floor. Released. "Put some clothes on. Then yuh can serve me a tall cool one downstairs."

"So, Kyle, Shitface, buddy! How yuh been?"

I served him his beer. Complying with a second command, I built a fire in the hearth. He wanted to experience the ambience of Vermont. "Good, McGrath. Been finding a few things out."

"Like what?"

"You stole money from me. Fifty grand."

"I swear to God, I never planned that. I called the lawyer up to say I found yuh. Something had been mentioned about a finder's fee. Wanted to get that straightened away and maybe negotiate for a little more. Before I knew it he was telling me the whole business, the whole story, it was like he was begging me to go in there and take the money. Yuh remember Dupree?"

"Only too well."

"It was him. He was in on it. He pretended to be yuh."

"That figures. He beat me up. Left me in a ditch. Stole my I.D." A log crackled in the fire.

"I saved yer shitty life. Yuh owed me. So I collected. No hard feelings, I trust. Yer set up pretty well right now."

McGrath was sitting with the skull in his lap, taking long swigs of his beer. Although he was not a young man and the exertion upstairs had caused him to perspire, I didn't think that I could take him in a fight. He had had too much experience at restraining people, and he was much stronger than I was. "What do you want, McGrath?"

"This is just a friendly visit, Kyle."

"I bet. Who's your friend?"

He held up the skull, laughing. "I call her Gladys. Pretty, ain't she?"

"Did you kill her?" The thought had occurred to me before. I had liked Dakota Hats, and could never get it out of my mind that he had been slaughtered without provocation.

"Naw. Hats must've. Know what? I found his graveyard. Fancy that. After all these years. I figured he had scattered the bodies all over Tennessee, but no. He had a graveyard across Walkerman's Creek from where I shot him. Found it last fall when I was out hunting. Been looking for that site since '70. Finally found it. There ain't no end to the bodies, Kyle. It's amazing."

I needed a moment to let the importance of that news sink in. "*You* found the grave site?"

"That's right."

"Then you're the one. You've been scattering the remains around."

"Been good for a laugh. Figured I'd go out with a bang, yuh see. Planted skeletons to upset the big shots. The mayor and his cronies. A few other prime assholes. Finally figured out a way to get rid of all the scumbags too, like y'all and that witch. But yuh had to get rich, get money from your dead daddy, inherit an inn! I was planning to stick yuh with the crime anyway, but yuh forced my hand. Heard yuh was leaving, so I put the bones in yer trunk. Damned if yuh didn't slip loose!"

"I'm sorry to have inconvenienced you."

"Don't worry about it," he said, and held out his glass for a refill. In the kitchen, I could not help but feel that McGrath was looking for some excuse, that it would be against my best interests to flee or to emerge toting a butcher knife. "Matter of fact," he continued when I came back, "I like the way things have worked out. I'm retiring soon. Think maybe I'd like a steady pension from the fucker who owes me his life."

"Get serious."

"If yuh had more respect for me, Elder, yuh'd know that I'm always serious."

"Is that your problem? Respect? You figure I should grovel at your toes because you saved my life? You figure Walkerman's Creek owes you the crown jewels because you're about to retire?"

"Yeah," McGrath said, tapping his chest. "I want my share. I want what's coming to me. I was a damned good cop—"

"You stole from me!" I interjected.

"So what? I had that coming. I saved yer life. Did I ever hear one word of gratitude? No. Never. Did yuh introduce me to yer women-friends? No. Never. I've been hanging around here lately, Elder. Like yer place. Y'all owe me yer life. Is it so much to ask that I get a share of your good fortune? Hmm? Say, fifty per cent?"

A cold draft had roused my senses. "What do you mean, you've been hanging around lately?"

He leaned forward in his chair, flashed a sinister smile, and held up the skull for my perusal. When he spoke he disguised his voice, but the sound was all too familiar. "Bite," he said. And added, "Run."

"You were in the stables."

"Imagine my surprise when yuh brought me that bag of bones. It was like Christmas!"

"*You* put the skeleton back in the Mercury."

"Right where it belonged. How was I supposed to know yuh'd go and bury yer car? I wanted yuh to find them, Kyle. But when that cop called, I thought to myself, what the hell."

"I don't get it. How did Snow call you if you were here?"

"I phoned for my messages. But hey, I was commuting. I had a job to do, yuh know. I'm no goof-off. I'm a responsible officer of the law. I couldn't waste all my time on yer shitface."

"What do you want, McGrath?"

He rotated the skull in his hands, clearly fascinated by its austere countenance. "Told yuh. A cut of the business, but we can discuss that."

"There's nothing to discuss. Believe me."

"How well do yuh think yuh'll prosper when yer guests find skeletons sleeping in their beds? Or when the word gets out that yer cook adds human bones to the broth? Mmm?"

"We'll catch you."

"Yuh didn't before, and I've been sleeping here, eating here in the cellar, the stables — yuh never saw me once." McGrath tossed the skull at me; my reflexes caught it. Immediately I put the skull behind me on the sofa, while he stepped over to the fire. He opened the screen. "Maybe I should just burn this place to the ground," he said casually, "with yuh in it."

"McGrath, *why?*" I was suddenly very frightened. "I'm nothing to you—"

"Exactly!" he exploded. "Nothing! I saved yer damned life and yuh never so much as thanked me. Yuh lived a shitty life, doing nothing, sleeping all the time, singing like a bird, and what happens? Y'inherit an inn. A fucking New England country inn! And what do I get? Bugger all. Work all my life and I can't get laid. Y'always had some woman or other for being nothin'. The best I can do is Gladys there." He pulled a log out of the fire. The flames danced at one end.

Watching the flames gambol, I was seeing Cindy and the fires that she had started, seeing her father's death by fire, seeing my father's photograph set ablaze by my mother. "This is my turn," was the only coherent thought that sustained me. "That's all this amounts to. This is my turn." And I experienced something inside me resurrect itself from its slumber and become integral, awake; I was revived; on the brink of my death I saw not the misuse of my life, but its sudden ripe budding. I was alive. I was living, thrust into a current of living, charged with spirit, reborn, alive, God, love, a child again with one knee on my wagon, the other leg pumping for speed, Chantelle, Cindy, sheer hopeless joy flying with the birds in flight, gargantuan mountains below like sand castles — Chantelle! Cindy! Ma! Aunt Em! We're living fleeting surrender chatter push and Holy Shit! I've never been so alive and God! I'm about to die I'm dying and okay that's okay too—

McGrath was advancing on me with his flaming torch, a bright burning branch. "What d'yuh think he saw in it?" he asked me.

"Pardon me?"

"Hats. How come yuh think he liked to kill so much? Was it like a sickness, or was it like a sport?"

He laid the flaming wood near my shoulder, as if knighting me with a sword. Then waved the fire above my head. I could all but hear my hair being singed. "Did he enjoy it, take his time? Or was it something that he just had to do?" McGrath moved away from me, almost dancing with the fire and smoke. "What do you think, Kyle, the sofa? The log pile first? How about the bookshelves?"

I wanted to beg him no; but knew that was his real intention, to humiliate me, just as he had humiliated and frightened so many with his bones. Instead, inspired from I know not what source, I leaned forward and whistled the melody of the hermit thrush.

oh lalay ilalo ilalo ilo

Momentarily confused, McGrath stepped back from me.

ah laylila lilalo lilalo lila

My song did not disarm my foe as I had hoped. It did not bring him to his senses, or penetrate him with either beauty or humor. Rearing back, McGrath aimed the torch like a lance at the center of my heart. Rather than feeling my strength escape I felt it swell, and I burst forth with the battle cry of the kingbird,

kitta kitta kitta kitta!

the best that I have ever sung this charge, my courage my soul in full attacking flight as McGrath raised his weapon to silence me, lunged forward — and at that instant his skull cracked.

His head wobbled to one side.

He collapsed in a heap.

Behind him, a soldier from heaven's troop, stood the wonderful, the magnificent, the victorious Hazel Stamp. In her two-fisted grip she wielded her marble rollingpin, the instrument of so many fine pastries and pies, and the weapon of my deliverance.

McGrath's torch scorched the carpet, but Hazel was on it quickly, stamping out the fire.

As bold as she had been during her moment of action, Hazel quickly withered with a serious backlash of nerves. We hugged each other with the abandon of lovers. I almost regretted my salvation, for I could feel myself returning to ordinary life.

McGrath still lay like a ruined statue on the floor. Breathing. I held onto Hazel until she calmed herself, although a delayed spasm nearly caused her to crack.

"Would you like a cup of tea?" she asked me finally, a signal that she was all right. I dared not refuse.

"Yes, please, Hazel."

"What kind?"

"English Breakfast will do nicely, thank you."

She was not that calm. Her own cup rattled in its saucer. To help temper her distress, I asked with mock seriousness, "Tell me, Hazel. Before you knocked his block off, did you check to see if he was a registered guest?"

While she laughed she began to cry. I love Hazel. She's beautiful. She saved my life! Suddenly she yelped and her tea spilled across the carpet. She had sat back against McGrath's pet skull.

3

Nobody's perfect. Certainly a germ of deceit meanders through me. I wish that I could blame that infection for every misjudgment of mind, frailty of character, and calumny of heart that I have communicated to an already diseased and infested world; sadly, the most that I can defer to the ubiquitous bacteria is my bent for subterfuge. I'm a snoop. A nosy Parker.

I had arranged with Chantelle to evacuate the inn when she returned with her gaggle of nuns. She believed that I had complied. Trouble was, the same impetus that had goaded me onto the rooftop to peer down through the bubble skylight compelled me to squirrel myself away in the basement with a bag of nuts, a few apples, and three hundred bottles of Californian chablis.

It did occur to me then that the women might grow thirsty over their stay and raid the wine cellar, so I removed to the furnace room, carrying in my grub and random vintages.

Hazel, meanwhile, was off recuperating from her adventure at her sister's home in Winooski. (She's become quite the local celebrity. Her rolling pin has been auctioned at the Church Bazaar, fetching a princely sum, and she recently pinch-hit at the Volunteer Firemen's Annual Charity Slow-Pitch Game, against the State Police. She struck out, but her swing, as advertised, was mighty. State Police won the game, incidentally, on a two-out, ninth-inning smash up the middle by Inspector Isaiah Snow, redeeming himself for his three fielding errors. I cheered while Hazel scowled.)

McGrath, second meanwhile, is convalescing in the Burlington General Hospital, while F.D.R. prepares his defense. (Drunk on the elixir of criminal law, Franklin D. has been rollicking about town in high spirits. Friends concur that it's great to see him vigorous. He's confided to me — a gallant reassurance — that he has no intention of winning the case, that his main purpose is to build his reputation among the criminal elite, his well-heeled future clients.)

Attention to detail is the key to my subterfuge. I packed a bag and departed Toll House in my Cherokee Chief, abandoning it in town and taking a taxi back. The nuns were coming, and this time I was prepared for them.

Curiosity alone was not my motivation. I was not merely an unregenerate spy. I was also Chantelle's friend and lover. Concerned for her safety and well-being. Enough nuns had tucked themselves into bed in my inn never to awaken again.

The quiet furnace, the hot-water heaters which occasionally would stir, my sustenance both liquid and solid, my father's possessions, and a smelly bucket that I routinely emptied down an open drain constituted my grim subterranean quarters. Upstairs, the nuns had gathered. I checked my wristwatch. They'd be finishing dinner soon, and this time they'd be stuck with the dishes. Afterwards, I expected, they'd get down to it.

I took another swig from my bottle of wine, a playful, sprightly surprise from the vineyards of Paul Masson. Chomped on a Spartan. And kept my ears attuned to the dreadful fall of night, when those who would woo God would scream.

Kin to an ogre emerging from the bowels of the earth after a lapse of several centuries, I ventured from my lair at midnight. Besotted, unshaven, dishevelled, my clothes rumpled and (a consequence of foul air) my mind out of phase, I crept from the furnace room and crawled up the steep staircase to budge the trapdoor open a crack. All ears, I listened. Virtually a soundless night. I rose up out of the earth, a phantom set loose upon an unsuspecting planet.

Closing the trapdoor behind me, tentatively I waited in the kitchen, attuned to the stillness. No chants tonight. No blood-curdling howls. Though I myself had risen from the black coffin of the cellar at the stroke of midnight and lifted the casket-cover of the trapdoor as my secret entry onto the earth, no vampires prowled the corridors of Toll House anticipating pretty damsels whose necks never required a bite, who bled freely due to passionate, ecstatic appreciation of their god. It was a quiet night.

The kitchen was vacant. The dishes drip-dried. The dining-room also was dark and empty. I moved with stealth.

In the social room, two women lay strewn across the floor, their limbs in such a languorous, haphazard moment that my first glance depicted them as slaughtered, as human debris. But the hand of one moved, raised a cigarette to her lips. The red ember glowed as a distant flare. As I watched, the second woman pushed herself up slightly to facilitate sipping her drink. Her free hand traced slow concentric circles around her companion's kneecap. I fell away, stricken, and headed upstairs.

A light at the top of the stairs showed a trio of women in a desultory clump. I was discovered, and stood still. What a surprise to hear no alarm! No battle cry. No accusatory fingers thrust under my nose. Their most pronounced reaction constituted a slight lifting of their chins and narrowing of their mutual gaze. A martial pose. Mere reflex. My old ally Sister Sophie was in this group, and she had no words of either censure or rebuke. I was homefree. Climbed over the threesome, and pressed on down the dimly lit hall.

My back to the wall, I paused by an open door. Conversation concerned a summer business on Narragansett Bay. I peered inside. Two women were smoking and a third cradled a bottle of beer between her thighs. No mystical hysterics here. No thrashing, no crying out.

Similar scenes were observed in several rooms off the corridor. The society of nuns had splintered into partisan sub-committees. Little migration occurred between the rooms, and I was challenged only once. "What are *you* doing here?" pestered Sister Jane. A dour, obsessive individual, she'd scold a child for smiling.

"I own the place," I reminded her. Apparently, on this occasion, that was the only justification necessary. Jane shrugged, and I plodded on in search of Chantelle.

Clearly, the nuns had disintegrated. In the morning they'd disperse, and years from now would wonder what had possessed them. For the nonce, sadness pervaded their company. To conform to another's logic holds no pleasure, not when that change is viewed as capitulation, the surrendering of dreams and vision. Defeat breathed among the slumped bodies. The time had come to reorganize their lives, to adopt the quests and nuisances of ordinary living. Tomorrow they would journey down from the mountain, frolic with the gods no more. Tomorrow what counted were career choices, making the right moves, curtains for the den, patio furniture, men. Tomorrow they would abandon one another, to meet again over bridge tables or for drinks on a Friday night. Many were seeing one another for the very last time. Their zealous, impassioned, fanatical union had been dissolved.

How Chantelle was adjusting to this change worried me as I prepared to knock on the door to the large bedroom where I assumed I'd find her. No answer. Light shone through under the crack. Adopting the custom of the inn, I simply opened the door and admitted myself.

Seated at the foot of the bed with a pillow in her lap, Chantelle was alone. Her feet didn't reach to the floor. Dangling. She was looking upward through the skylight, although the light in the room would prevent her from seeing out. Wearing a pale yellow nightdress, she seemed angelic to me, and quietly rapt.

"Hello, Chantelle," I said, hoping not to startle her.

She did gasp, taken by surprise. But she adjusted to my presence as quickly as had the others. Hers a cynical smile. "You're not supposed to be here," she chided me gently.

"I know. I'm incorrigible. I'm also concerned about you. Forgive me." I interpreted the shake of her head to mean that nothing really mattered any more. I might not be welcome, but I'd be tolerated. "What's happened here, Chantelle? Why are you so sad? Tell me." I sat on the edge of the bed beside her.

Chantelle had been weeping. Before speaking, she had to wipe her eyes once again and give her nose a courteous blow. Kleenex was handy. The litter of tissues on the floor indicated that she'd already been through half a box. She scrunched each piece in her fist before tossing it away.

"I told them, Kyle. My loyal and true friends. My . . . betrayers. I might as well tell you."

"Please do."

"I'm pregnant. Six weeks."

My brain performed the rapid calculation, rechecking it twice before I dared gloat. "Chantelle! I'm the father! That's great! That's great! Let me be the father, Chantelle. I've always thought it'd be neat to be a proper pop."

She was shaking her head categorically no.

"Chantelle! Why not? It's my baby too!"

"No," she contradicted, and in that instant a healthy portion of my love for her, I don't know why or how, deflated. "The baby is mine. It's mine, Kyle. Mine and God's."

"Chantelle." Rising, I loomed over her. "Don't play games. We made that baby. You and me. Right here in this bed. It never happened the way you planned it, I know, everything went wrong for you. Your memories interfered. Still. It was you and me. If God was here His name was Tom, and He was peeping."

Chantelle wiped her eyes once more with another Kleenex.

"I know it, Kyle," she said. Stern. Defiant. "I told *them*, didn't I? They know how it happened. You probably are the father –"

"Probably?" I quizzed.

"There's no other man, if that's what you mean. But who's to say? Who's really to say –"

"The child you're carrying, Chantelle, was *not* conceived by the Holy Ghost."

"Who's to say? Nobody knows that for a fact."

"Oh no? Well, what I do know for a fact is that no child should be raised carrying virgin birth around as a trophy."

"So I've heard said."

Her words struck me. The disturbed tone caught me off-guard. I circled the room to regain my composure. Decided that if I ever did reopen the inn I would make this room my personal quarters, and forgo the higher returns. This was a room of blood and stars, of conception, an atmosphere of conflict and reconciliation, of love and distress, and afforded me a dramatic sense of passion, of retreat, of battle, and of regeneration. I had conceived a child in this room! I knew a grain of what my father must have felt conceiving me, knowing that my subsequent fate most likely would be beyond his influence.

"So that's it," I said. "Your nuns won't buy it. You told them about the night you spent here with me, and now they won't accept your surrogate god. They'll accept a human baby, maybe, preferably a girl. For all I know, some of them already have children of their own. Kids who were brought into the world through tussling with a man, through nurture and morning sickness and ultrasound. Through labor, pain, and rejoicing. They accept their own kids and they'll accept your baby too. But they will not accept your virgin-birth scenario, not when they know that a minute's rub-and-tickle did the trick. Body-to-body stuff. Sweaty procreation."

"Stop it." An emphatic command. Not looking at me, she gritted her teeth, stared dead ahead. A defiant jut of her chin.

"Right you are, Chantelle, it's a miracle. Not the miracle you were after, that's true. Not a miracle that proclaims your womb pure, that proves to you it's been cleansed of the obscenity committed against you, that declares that God has scrubbed you raw and exonerates you for any complicity, real or imagined, in the death of your father and your mother. Clears you of killing my father too. It's not that sort of miracle, which forgives you, not for your sin but for being a victim of sin, which is what you've never been able to forgive yourself for being. Isn't that right, Chantelle? I know that scene. We live with trumped-up charges against ourselves to match the damage that's been done to us. It puts the universe right, it gives meaning to our punishment, because that's the way the fucked-up human mind works. But it's a miracle all right, Chantelle. You're right to treat it as such. Just think. A fast roll on the mattress in this holy room and you're impregnated with the seed of God. Nice work. Much easier than your previous fuss. And you're right as far as it goes. But I'm not God, Chantelle, and I've never aspired to be. Neither will your child be a god."

She suddenly railed against me, flinging out her pillow which crash-landed across the room. "What the *hell* do you think happened here? Don't you remember what happened to me? The earth cracked apart for me, Kyle, not the heavens, I wasn't merely remembering things, horrific things, what they did to me, again and again, nonstop. I was *experiencing* it again, as if it was happening right this second. My mother hacked to pieces, my father tortured and made to watch — 'Want to try?' That's what they said. 'It's fun.' " While Chantelle spoke, she held her right wrist in her left hand and stabbed the bed. " 'You don't need your mommy,' " she chanted, " 'You don't need your daddy,' " stabbing the bed, stabbing repeatedly, one hand holding the other, and I saw it and was repelled and was seized with amazement, my knees buckling with this knowledge, this uncanny attraction of spirits which had brought us together; saw her hand forced to grasp the weapon, forced to swing down into her parents' own flesh.

I grabbed Chantelle because I could not take it any more. I rocked her in my arms. No matter what became of us we were intricately linked for life. We wept together and a long time later we mopped up our faces with Kleenex and blew our leaky noses like trumpets.

"Barbarians," I said.

"God," Chantelle contradicted.

I looked at her cautiously. This time, bewildered. She got to her feet and patrolled the room.

"Why not?" she questioned. "Didn't He send His Son to bleed and die? Didn't His own Son submit to having His body pierced?"

"God, Chantelle."

"Please. Forget the religion. That's what you wanted. God and I have had a parting of the ways. We're divorced."

Speechless for a time, I followed Chantelle's angry pace about the room. She resembled an animal caged. As did I.

"I don't get it. What do you mean?" I asked, sensing that my one hope to bridge the gulf between us — and the terrible chasm that she had created within herself — was to keep her talking. A scant hope, at best.

Chantelle threw her head back and laughed. Her hair had grown longer over the months, and the cut bounced low on her neck. "Don't you know? Can't you guess?"

The sadness that had pervaded her eyes since I had known her was trampled by a vivid enthusiasm. Chantelle hugged herself, rubbing her hands up and down over her bare biceps.

"The night your father died. Excuse me, the night we killed him. Oh, our intentions were the best. He wanted us to end his misery. We were doing him a favor. The crunch came when I watched the car fill with exhaust, I experienced a — I don't know how to express it — a woven, tingling excitement. I was actually *enjoying* committing murder. That's when I started to see myself. That's when I started to lose my faith. It's also when I started to remember my parents' deaths, too. Glimpses. Flashes. So it wasn't only you, Kyle, it wasn't only sex. Murder, also, I think, jarred my memory, brought me back to certain things."

It seemed to me that she tried to level her gaze, but her eyes would not focus, as if she was stymied by her own surprising madness.

"I used to be willing to allow for contradictions, Kyle. I told you that. I was willing to subject myself to the warring psychological and spiritual fictions. My faith lay with the spiritual, I wanted God to win out, I wanted God to transform me completely, to grant me a life made new, in effect to restore my virginity, and for that matter my innocence, and bring about the miracle of virgin birth. I wanted God to prove to me that I was forgiven. In short, I wanted God. But it didn't happen. I know the comeback: the girls have repeated it often enough. I have to forgive myself. But for what? I didn't do anything. So I need forgiveness, but have precious little to be forgiven for."

"Chantelle, look," I struggled, out of my depth here, quartered by her madness and bound to her by love, "about our baby –"

"God's baby," she corrected me.

"You've got me spinning. One second you're talking virgin birth, the next you've lost your faith. Now you're carrying a holy child again."

"In the end," she cautioned me, placing her hands on her hips, "it doesn't matter. I'm going to make it so it's all the same."

"What do you mean?"

Chantelle caressed her stomach, twice raising her hands as high as her breasts.

"Chantelle?"

Inwardly I recoiled as she smiled faintly, inexplicably, at me. I stood, stunned.

"No, Chantelle. Please. No."

Her smile broadened. She had found the way to cleanse herself, to purge herself of all that had been done to her, and to divorce herself — once and for all — from the God she had honored for so long.

"Oh shit, Chantelle! Shit!"

"Now you know why the girls aren't talking to me any more. Now you know why we're no longer nuns."

Reeling, I hid my face in my hands. Looked up at her, looked away, the torment ringing in my head like the echo of the women's frantic chants. I understood, and I could not condemn her, though simultaneously I held her in contempt. She had attempted to cleanse her defiled womb, her whole body outwardly menstruating, the center of her soul profoundly offered to God and Christ; but that course had not bestowed the cleansing she desired. Nor would the abortion, of course. Yet her pain, her despair, her rage, her inner terror so long dormant, deformed her judgment. What had entered the child's womb, what had held her hand armed with a knife and forced her to plunge it rapidly to annihilate her family, dwelled inside her, she believed, placed there by her rapists, and would now be expelled. Chantelle had gone mad.

I could not blame her, I could not condemn her, even my contempt abated under the budding of renewed compassion, and I felt the load of an earthly sadness compress upon the mountains and Toll House so that any enthusiasm, hope, expectation, or way out seemed cruelly frivolous. I was in despair. Warning signals gonged, and I shook my head. If I surrendered now, not only would Chantelle be lost, but I too would never surface again. If anyone could help Chantelle, it was me, for who else could speak about plunging a knife through a mother's skin, but me? Chantelle and I shared that bond.

But what to do?

For the first time in my life, perhaps because I conceived of no alternative, I really prayed. Prayed hard. My prayer sweating through my pores. As Chantelle's faith was abandoned, mine was picked up.

"Stay here!" I shouted out, suddenly inspired.

"What?" My outcry startled her. She had not expected to hear again a voice from heaven.

"Just promise me you'll stay put. Don't move."

"I'm leaving in the morning."

"I'll be back in five minutes! Just don't move!"

Faith makes for thrilling commotion. I had absolutely no logical assurance that my plan would work. Yet I believed in it. Like a fire truck I raced downstairs, careening around corners, barging through stop signs. I tossed up the trapdoor, located the light switch, and returned to the earth's innards. Positively giddy. I tore through my father's junk. And found it.

I returned more slowly, conserving breath. The majority of the women had gone to bed. I found Chantelle, when I stepped back into the bedroom, slumped in an armchair. I pressed my father's chapbook, *A Kinkajou in Hackensack*, against my heart. "Here goes nothing," I said. My last shot.

Faith is having hope in hope itself.

So I did it, read from my father's self-published booklet, not knowing what wisdom or folly it might contain. I read while Chantelle stewed in her chair. I read because I desperately needed help from somewhere; this was not a predicament that could be resolved by a marble rolling pin or other overt act. What was required was magic, or something more than that: grace. I prayed that whatever had enchanted the nuns about this story in the first place would remain sufficiently potent to inspire this lonely, scarred, troubled woman once again.

A Kinkajou in Hackensack
by Kyle Troy Elder Senior

My name: Horace Blumquist. I live where I have always lived, on a quiet, comfortable, tree-lined avenue in Hackensack, New Jersey, in the good old U.S. of A. In times past, my street was considerably quieter and more comfortable than it is today, but that's progress for you. There were more trees back then too.

I am now an old man. I concede that much. Wish it wasn't so hard, though, to convince the younger generation that that was not always the case. I was young, once upon a time, and had adventures. I courted pretty girls. Some not so pretty.

Married one of the latter. And after that our family was young. My children were not always grown up and moved away, though nobody believes that now either.

We've hit on what I want to discuss. I am an old man and I'll be dead soon, but the same as I don't want to be thought of as always having been an old man, when I'm gone I don't want people to think that I'd always been dead. People believe only in what's in front of them, never in what's forward or behind. "Living for the moment," they call it, which has a lot of practitioners today and I can't really argue against them. Try as we might, there's no point living in the past. Only a danged fool would try dwelling in the future, though God knows, there's plenty of those folks around. There's folks who put every penny aside for a retirement on Easy Street, then croak at the age of sixty-five. That's not for me. Seems to me more each day that time is just the space you're living in, I think Einstein said that. If he didn't then I'll take the credit. I deserve credit for something in my life.

Enough philosophizing. Rumination never did a man no good except to put his inner ear out-of-whack and to sponsor various obscene disorders pertaining to the alimentary canal. I want to keep my balance now because I have something on my chest that I want off, and I won't be able to scribble it down if the room starts to totter and I'm flat on my backside farting.

I've been a nice fellow most of my life and by that I mean I've been good to folks. I've fed tramps on my stoop. Supported churches. Sent money to Africa and looked after my neighbors in need. Today I want to change all that. No more Mister Nice Guy. I want to be mean. The plain truth of the matter is I'm close to the grave with a grievance constipated in my belly and I'm not going to be a sweet old codger no more stinking up the room. I want to fart it out! I want at least the northern hemisphere to hold their noses.

Twice, sometimes three times, a year, I go visit this here Smithsonian Institute you've heard tell about. I'm a regular patron. I pay my way in, I don't hold a lifetime pass, and that's what's raised my hackles. The dogcatcher — the god-damned dogcatcher! — right here in Hackensack, New Jersey, U.S. of A., he's got a lifetime pass, and the sonofabitch has never used it! That lifetime pass rightfully belongs to me. It's mine. I ain't holding my peace no longer. If I hold it another minute my colon will split. That lifetime pass ought to be mine!

And here's why.

Chantelle had moved from the armchair to the bed, and had made a comfortable backrest for herself by fluffing up the pillows. Her hands lay folded together in her lap, her legs stuck straight out in front of her. Whether she was listening attentively or daydreaming was impossible to know. She probably had this story memorized, and she gazed up at the plexiglass bubble or down at her toes which were frequently busy scratching one another.

I read on, heavy of heart. The reading was an enigma to me. So far I had glimpsed nothing which might rouse Chantelle out of the doldrums.

But first, before I tell you about the lifetime pass I do not have, I must tell you about Luis Salazar. Luis was a genius automotive mechanic and a bigger genius real-estate whiz. Luis is dead now so no doubt many believe that he was always dead, but that is not true. He was a young womanizer when I knew him and he could fix anything. He built a garage in a gap between two apartment buildings on one of the busy streets of our town and that is why he was a genius realtor. Luis never bought that property. He sold it, but he never bought it. He asked the owner of one building who owned the property next door, and he was told it was the man who owned the other building. He asked that man who said it was the first guy. Luis did not get to the bottom of this problem. He just built his garage without asking anybody's opinion right in this narrow gap that was too small to be called a lot, and for the next twenty years everybody assumed that he owned the property. When one building was sold the new owner discovered after a survey that he also owned the eyesore garage. He wanted to tear down the garage, but Luis, who lived in the back, now had squatter's rights. A deal was struck, the garage was demolished, and Luis retired comfortably on his squatter's rights.

The knack. That's all that life requires. And Luis had it.

I would always bring my taxicab to be repaired by Luis Salazar. And Walter Chernick and Jerry Moirs always brought their small trucks to Luis, what today we'd call vans, only then they were the life's blood of small business and not motel rooms on wheels. (That's what kids do today, they drive around and pick up chicks, lay out on a mattress in the back. They don't need lovers' lanes or river views anymore, don't need the moon or luck or beer, they just park on any streetcorner and get laid. They think I'm too old to know that, too far gone to be envious. What I wonder is, what do their parents think when they see that mattress? Don't they wonder why their otherwise slovenly son is changing the sheets in his truck?) Walt and Jerr owned a pet shop on Hammond Street, and I have to tell you about that before I tell you anything more about Luis, or about how I came to lose the lifetime pass that is rightfully mine.

Jerr and Walt were the best of buddies and they were thieves. You don't see good buddies like that anymore. Only fags. (You think I don't know? You think I haven't *seen* with my perfectly adequate eyesight? I may be old but I'm not blind, not yet.) Maybe it's because Jerr and Walt were thieves is why they were such good buddies. I don't know. I don't mean they were thieves with their business, their pet shop was above board, they liked pets and they liked kids, they were two strange characters, but by night what they did for entertainment was steal. Everybody knew about it. I knew about it. When I wanted a new toaster or a better radio, I didn't go to a department store, I went to the pet shop. Jerry and Walt always had a great selection and their prices were the best in town.

People have said that their pet shop was only a front but I believe differently. I say their stealing was only an entertainment. Some guys like to go out to ball games or bars, maybe chase girls. Jerr and Walt preferred to bust into people's homes. To each their own. I don't condone thievery, but I'll say this about them, they never cleaned anybody out, they weren't greedy. Today both of them are in chronic care. People think they were always senile and incontinent, but I know better. Was a time when they were fast-thinking buddies who never shit their pants on the job once, when plenty of other men would've.

Now I have to tell you about Mr. Macaroni. There are a lot of people involved in why I don't have my pass to the Smithsonian Institute. His real name was not Macaroni, of course, but I knew about him only through Jerr and Walt, and they named everybody after food. I was Mr. Hot Dog, because I was a nice guy, the All-American do-nothing. The cop on the beat was Constable Zucchini, because he could screw you anytime he wished, and because his favorite color was green: cash: kickbacks. The banker was Mr. Tomato because his wife was Whada Tomato. They called Luis Luis, because he'd break their backs singlehanded if ever they called him Mr. Refried Bean.

Mr. Macaroni was their supplier. You say that today and people think you're talking drugs. Marijuana, heroin, cocaine. I'm not talking about drugs. I'm old, don't forget. I'm not dead, but I'm old. No, Mr. Macaroni supplied them with dogs and cats, puppy terriers and collies and furry wee kittens, budgies and hamsters, now and then a parrot or a fluffy white rabbit. Eastertime they sold baby chicks dyed yellow or purple which would be dead within two hours. Mr. Macaroni did not deal dope, he bartered happiness.

One day he wrote up Jerr and Walt's order and then he said, "Psssssst!"

"What?" said Jerry.

"You got a speech impediment, wop?" Walter asked.

"Psssssssssst!" Mr. Macaroni repeated. He signalled Jerr and Walt to come deeper into the store. No one else was around so they didn't know why he was whispering, especially if all he wanted to do was to sell them a bunny. Walter and Jerry exchanged smiles. They caught on. Obviously, Mr. Macaroni wanted to buy a T.V. set, and they had just received an R.C.A. Victor the night before.

But they were wrong. Mr. Macaroni already had a T.V., a Westinghouse. "Psssssst!" he said.

"Piss on you too!" said Walter.

"I've got something for you," Mr. Macaroni hinted.

"What?" asked Jerry.

"A kinkajou," Mr. Macaroni revealed.

Jerr and Walt looked at one another. "What the hell do we want with a kinky Jew?" Walter wanted to know.

Chantelle laughed, bringing me out of my reading. I smiled too, although that seemed to offend her. She did not appreciate having her spirits uplifted. She preferred the sullen defeat of her rebellion. I was breaking through her crust, however, the laugh a chink in her armor, which was the only encouragement I needed. I read on.

"No no no," Mr. Macaroni persisted. "You don't pronounce it *kink*, you spell it that way but you say it *king*: *king-a-jou*."

"So you have a King-ada-Jews. Christ? What do we want with Him?"

"No no no." Mr. Macaroni was sweating. He was an Italian but unaccustomed to crime. He had never met the Godfather though he probably went to see the movie when it came out. I did. "I have a kinkajou. It's a South American animal. Came in last week. It's worth a mint. I thought you fellows might be able to move it for me."

"Move it? From where to where? How heavy is it?"

"It's just a small animal. I meant sell it for me. You see, fellows, ah, they're not exactly, ah, legal. The uptown dealers in New York won't touch it. Kinkajous aren't allowed out of their own countries and they're not allowed into ours. You know how it is. We can't buy and sell certain wild animals."

Jerr and Walt observed him closely. "Do you mean, Mr. Macaroni," (that's what they called him to his face) "that you want us to commit a *crime*?"

"Pssssssst!" Mr. Macaroni said, and he gestured to the two men to follow him into the recesses of the storage room. They left the jerboas and the Chihuahuas behind, entering the zone of the electric hot plates and diamond rings. Once Mr. Macaroni felt that they were properly insulated against the inquisitive eyes and ears of the outside world, he said, "Yes."

"Why didn't you say so?" said Jerry. "Sure, we'll be glad to be your fence. Hey, while you're back here, how would you like a string of pearls for the little woman? Maybe a ruby choker for your dog?"

Jerry and Walter made major preparations for the arrival of the kinkajou. They assumed, considering its illegality and Macaroni's desperation, that it was roughly the size of a gorilla with the personality of a hyena. They figured they'd be selling it on the black market to a zoo. They made space for it in the store by having a sale on hi-fi's.

What arrived was the cutest, cuddliest, sweetest pet they'd ever come across. Had they not paid five hundred dollars for it ("Money back guaranteed," Macaroni had promised), they'd probably have kept him for themselves. Jerry named him Kinky and Walter knew on first sight that he'd fetch a grand, easy.

And he did. Kinky was purchased by a hairdresser in Greenwich Village. He wanted a gimmick to set his salon apart from the others and figured that Kinky would enliven his social life as well. Kinky was nothing if not adorable, a conversation piece, an attention-grabber. Cousin to the raccoon with the

temperament of a monkey, a kinkajou can hang from its pre-
hensile tail like a possum, curl up in your lap like a cat, greet
you at the door like a doting puppy, and keep you awake
nights like a new-born child. In short, a creature of love.
Kinkajous are night critters, something Jerr and Walt neglected
to mention when they delivered Kinky to Mr. Lemon Meringue Pie.

Mr. Pie gushed his adoration and showed off Kinky to Mr.
Watermelon, his three-hundred-pound houseguest. The two
men squealed and hugged each other in justified terror as
Kinky bounded off the grand piano and swung from the chan-
delier, emitting playful cries. Jerr surveyed the furniture. Walt
opened a few drawers. Jerr whispered to Walter, "Are you
thinking what I'm thinking?"

"The jewelry and the paintings are primo."

"Plus we get to rescue Kinky from these perverts."

"We'll wait for the check to pass first. Do it next week."

Jerr received payment and paused at the door before Mr. Pie
shut him out. "Do you know what you call a faggot — excuse
me, a homosexual gentleman — who has sex with a fat man?"

Jerry was like that, irreverent. I guess you have to be to be a
thief. Mr. Pie returned an icy stare and said coldly, "No.
What?"

"A punishment for gluttons. Oh-ho! Get it?"

Mr. Pie slammed the door in his face.

Jerr and Walt had a busy agenda that day. They crossed back
to Jersey and in Hoboken heisted fifty-two suits from a gentleman's haberdashery. The local police were not sporting about
that sort of thing and the two buddies had to make a hair-rais-
ing getaway. They were good thieves at night but as daylight
bandits they left a lot to be desired. Fired on. Bullets stung
their van. What a chase! The next day they drove the vehicle
into Luis's garage for bodywork and a new paint job: "Any
color, Luis, just different."

Kinky survived little more than a week in New York City. A

big hit at artists' parties, girls kitchy-cooed over him and young men wearing silk rainbows positively crooned to the creature. Everybody, including the weirdos, loved Kinky and he wasn't the least bit discriminating: he loved everyone in return. Unfortunately, he didn't do much for the hair salon, preferring to sleep all day, and return on his investment had been one of Mr. Meringue Pie's essential requirements. And then one night he was out partying with Kinky and Mr. Watermelon and when they returned home their paintings had been removed from the walls and their treasures confiscated from their drawers. Mr. Pie fell into a rage and in the heat of his tantrum he swatted Kinky.

Mr. Pie had forgotten that Kinky was not a dog or a cat, although he exhibited many of the attributes of those pets. Kinky was a wild animal. He leapt onto Mr. Pie's neck and bit him in the shoulder. Bit, I said, not nipped. Bit him so hard that when he jumped off his wailing master one of his front teeth remained imbedded in Mr. Pie's flesh and bone.

Jerry and Walter had been upset that their raid on Mr. Pie's apartments had not returned Kinky to them. It had been a lucrative adventure otherwise, even if they did have to rent a truck. They were walking on air. So that when Mr. Pie sashayed into their pet shop several days later, they were surprised and more than a little chagrined. What had gone wrong? They never expected to be caught, and had no patience with anyone accusing them of theft.

In a blue funk, Mr. Pie made no sense. His shoulder was wrapped in bandages and he ranted and raved about taking umpteen needles for rabies. "The authorities want Kinky put down but I want my money back, dammit!"

Walter let Kinky sit on his head.

Jerr said, "You got your nerve, faggot."

"What did you call me?"

"He's damaged goods! What's the idea of pulling out his

front tooth? How would you like your teeth bashed in to match?"

"Now listen here!"

"Get out of my store, get out of town, before I call the S.P.C.A. and have you arrested for cruelty to animals."

"Oh, for heaven's sake!" Mr. Pie lisped.

"Out. Scram. Take a hike."

Mr. Pie did as he was told, and Jerr and Walt had their kinkajou back, a collection of the finest modern art to be found in New Jersey, enough rocks to open a jewelry store, and the profit from Kinky's sale besides. They would soon discover that their windfall had been opportune.

"Luis! We don't have that kind of money!"

"I'm no charity case, gringo. I do a good job, beeg job. Mucho work, mucho money."

"Listen, you taco-faced enchilada –" Jerr forgot himself momentarily.

"What you call me, gringo?" Luis's mechanic's hands, perpetually bloodied and caked in oil, were as powerful as wrenches.

Walter intervened. "Maybe we can make a deal, Luis. The bill's kind of steep."

"Bullet holes cost mucho money to feex."

"I understand. Look. Maybe we can trade. You want a T.V.? Four T.V.'s? I know. I got just the thing for you. How would you like a new suit for every week of the year? Fifty-two suits."

"I heard about those suits." Luis passed on the local gossip. "Everyone of them has bullet holes. No thank you, señor. I accept cash."

"Luis," Jerr spoke up.

"What you want, gringo?"

"How would you like a kinkajou?"

"A what?"

"A kinkajou. From South America. It's practically a Latin pet. Understands Spanish. You need some friendship in your life."

Jerry was right about that. Luis was a workaholic, and aside from pestering the girls who came to his garage, some of whom required an oil change on a weekly basis, and except also for the occasional fling with a married woman, he lived alone. One look at Kinky and he struck the deal. Those big eyes. That soft woolly fur. The critter stole his heart.

But — in life, there is always a but — kinkajous are night creatures. They have fingers like pickpockets. Kinky would escape his cage in the garage at night and tinker with the cars. He'd throw mufflers off the wall where they were stored. He especially enjoyed hiding Luis's tools and flushing spare parts down the toilet. He'd take carburetors apart.

Every morning Luis would wake up early and come into the garage to build a better cage. Every night Kinky would escape and wreck the place. I came in one morning to pick up my car and Luis was banging away at Kinky's cage, banging and howling at the same time, he was a madman, beside himself, gone berserk.

"Luis! Luis! What's the matter?"

He turned, glaring at me. An idiot. "Meester Bum-kissed?"

"Blumquist. Yes, Luis? What is it?" The man was panting like he had run ten miles. And this was in the old days before people did that sort of thing.

"I want to geeve you a Spanish dog."

I took a look at the little mutt. Those big, frightened eyes, gazing lovingly at me. I lost my head and my heart both. "I'll take him, Luis," I said.

And so Kinky the Kinkajou became a part of my family. The best years of my family, I might add. My children were young then and they enjoyed our pet as much as did my wife and I. Beverly is gone now, though she was young and zesty once, and until her death I can honestly say that nothing saddened me more than what became of Kinky.

We had him for about two years. No more than that. I built a cage the size of a bedroom for him in the basement. He escaped out of there, a regular Houdini. I rebuilt it, and built a cage outside the first cage. That took him about three weeks to figure out and we found him in the kitchen, playing with knives. So I reconstructed the first two cages and then caged the basement. Kinky still found a way out, evacuating the basement through the air ducts, and we discovered him at the corner park, on the swings.

The next thing I had to do was seal the house, and that kept him indoors for a while. He broke out of there one night by going up the chimney. You might not believe it, but in those days we had raccoons in Hackensack, and they did not take kindly to their third-world immigrant cousin. They tore Kinky apart. He hobbled home and we dispatched him to an out-of-town vet, who wanted to know, "Why's he covered in soot?" And, after he had cleaned him up: "What the heck is it?"

Our pet survived.

We were extremely diligent with our locks and keys, concerned for Kinky's safety. I'm convinced that Kinky had a good life among us, our main regret being that we slept at night while he did whirligigs on his trapeze. He had the run of the house during the day, though for him that usually meant curling up in a closet and going to sleep. Evenings were the best time. He'd play with the children, keeping them out of my hair, then I'd take him for a stroll out-of-doors. He loved the attention of neighbors and climbing trees.

A sad, wintry morning then, when my youngest, Timmy, shook me awake. "Kinky's gone. Kinky's gone, Daddy." I had put him in his cage, all right, but must have left the key in the lock. He was loose on the world.

Kinky never came home. Weeks passed with no report. I

drove around in my cab looking for him, thinking he'd make an appearance at a playground. The evenings, damn, they were the worst, trying to cheer up the children. Then the local newspaper ran a story about a strange animal that had been mauled by a pack of dogs. The dogcatcher had brought him into the veterinary's, but the animal's chances of survival were slim. "It's a kinkajou," the vet announced. "There aren't any in North America. It's a miracle! How it found its way up here is anybody's guess." The newspaper invited anyone claiming ownership to visit the pound, adding that the keeping of wild animals was in violation of a city ordinance, and that the police intended to press charges.

Some invitation.

Kinky died.

That should have been the end of it. Yet the spirit of that creature prevails. Rutgers University asked to examine the body. The dogcatcher consented, and told reporters that he intended to turn the kinkajou over to a taxidermist when the animal was returned to him. Imagine his surprise — but don't feel sorry for the dumbbell; I don't — when he received a box in the mail with no kinkajou inside. Only his bones wrapped in white tissues. A haphazard jumble. This news also made the newspaper, with the dogcatcher expressing his moral indignation.

Here comes the Smithsonian Institute, one more buzzard in search of a cadaver. They took the bones in exchange for a lifetime's pass for Hackensack's dogcatcher which to this day has never been used. The scientists at the Institute were very clever; they glued Kinky's bones back together again and put him on display. He looked like the miniature skeleton of a dinosaur. Pedantic children *still* cry out, "Look, Mommy, it's a baby brontosaurus!" He doesn't look at all like the fun-loving, nutty bundle of joy he once was.

That would be the end of my story except that the bones disappeared one day. The authorities were baffled. They refused to pay the ransom demands of the insidious kidnappers. So I went down to Jerry and Walter's pet shop, and requested a particular pet. "About yea big. Preferably skinny. In fact, let's say it has no skin at all. A long tail, also with no fur on it. Would you have anything like that? I'll pay a hundred bucks."

"Is it okay if it's not breathing?"

"Of course."

The two buddies, who are now in chronic care, God bless them, gave me back the kinkajou. A hundred bucks I paid and do I have a lifetime pass to the Smithsonian? Nooooooo-oo. I put Kinky in a locker in a bus depot and mailed the Institute the key. Every year I visit, sometimes twice, sometimes three times, and recall the old days when I and my family were young.

To foil kidnappers, Kinky is now kept in a glass cage.

I wouldn't bet against him escaping again.

A museum can't hold him. Bones or no bones, he'll always be a living kinkajou to me.

On this cuckoo tale Chantelle's life hinged.

Certainly the life of her child.

I was pondering, or at least feeling the resonance, of my father's trumped-up tale about the kinkajou. Why Hazel would disparage it was plain to me, also why its religious-allegorical nature had endeared the story to the nuns. Perhaps that was the fable's true worth: everyone received it differently. Though I found the sentiment cloying and (only a little) self-pitying, my reaction to *Kinkajou* was that it fairly and succinctly represented the story of my life.

Probably my father's too.

Chantelle struggled from the bed, pushing herself forward as though eight months pregnant and not the invisible six weeks. "I showed the others," she said. "I might as well show you."

"Show me what?"

"The trick with my eyes." She walked across to her purse perched on the dresser.

"What do you mean?" I asked.

Foraging through the contents, she extracted a small tobacco tin. "Your father was on to me, you know. He was an old carny, he knew every trick in the book."

"Trick?"

"He never gave me away, mind. I guess because of his native carnival allegiance. You don't tell secrets. He stayed on my back though, trying to coax me into coming clean, into taking the world seriously. Maybe . . . maybe he's finally succeeded."

She screwed the cap off her tin. Spilled something out into her palm and placed the tin on the dresser. "This works best when the lights are off, tambourines are beating, voices chant, and everyone's eyes are closed. Manipulating the audience is a magician's first order of business." Walking with her hands cupped together, Chantelle returned to the bed and lay down.

"You remember," she continued, "that night when you burst in on me, Maundy Thursday, and Gaby booted you out? When she came back into the room she caught me. She saw how I did it. My trick with my eyes. That destroyed her illusions, and without illusions she went off the deep end. She couldn't cope. Couldn't even confront me with the facts, I suppose because she'd have to own up to her own ridiculous gullibility. She had the poison in her travel kit — I mean, doesn't that tell you something? Originally she brought it along to ease your father behind the veil. But she kept it with her. She never disposed of it. She kept the poison *handy*. I say that means she was flirting with the idea of using it all along, and was just looking for a good excuse. Me, I was her excuse. She did herself in. Preferred taking her secret to the grave than living with the truth above ground."

"Chantelle, what exactly are you talking about?"

A tiny, jelly-like marble, red, rolled around on her palm. "Your father would be glad that we met, Kyle. You're one of his tricks, one of his ploys to wiggle inside me, make me confess. I was your dad's pet project. He used to say, 'I'm going to rehabilitate you, girl, and dying won't stop me.' He wanted to reform me. He understood that I had to do what I did. I'm no charlatan. I hope that maybe you'll understand that too. Unlike the others. It's a lot to ask, but it's all that I can hope for from a friend.

"See, Kyle, I learned my tricks growing up. Improved them

every year. Every year I was punished in the convent for sacrilege. I measured my success by the number and size of the welts blooming on my behind. A nun would have to sit with me overnight, putting cold compresses on my swollen rear, saying, 'Why do you *do* it, Chantelle?' As if I had any idea. As if I had a choice. I became so good at it they couldn't punish me any more, they only suspected me, and eventually they found a way to kick me out.

"And I still kept on. Each Easter I'd commemorate, with that ceremony, what had happened to my family, and what had happened to me weeks later. The two occurrences were linked for me. When I menstruated and accidentally smeared myself, I enjoyed all that attention, the nuns in awe of me and terrified, the medical staff solicitous and caring. I was scared too, but I revelled in their concern and in their fright and somehow it had something to do with my parents, I just didn't know what."

Chantelle's head jerked downward, her body whipped, the convulsion guided the heel of her hand across her left eye. She looked at me squarely. Then she winced, pressed her eyelids shut tightly, exerting great force through her shoulder and neck muscles as if trying to twist the jammed lid off a jar, and I heard a very faint *pop!* The moment she looked up again, a bright red tear ran down her cheek.

"Exposing me was not your father's method. He wanted me to save myself, more or less. He told me once that he planned to leave the inn to his son. When I came this year I knew I had to take you on, just to see what gives. You were your father's last and best trick — I had to find out whether you were for real, a threat, or a practical joke. For the record, I guess that I was his trick too, intended to be of some use to you. I don't know."

"All your talk about faith," I muttered.

"Every word true. That my eyes didn't bleed for real makes no difference. On other people they do bleed for real. It's like communion. Because the blood is a nondescript Burgundy doesn't make the ritual any less significant."

"You were deceiving your friends! Constructing illusions about yourself!"

"I needed the framework to hold myself together. How else could I survive? As for the others, it's only what they believe that counts." Chantelle pushed her hands through her hair from front to back, the nails plowing the scalp. "It's funny, hearing you read *Kinkajou*, how different it sounds now. Maybe because you're you and not your father, but I was thinking while I was listening that *I'm* the one who's different. It's like the question is not whether God is alive or dead, but whether God is alive or dead in *me*, in you, in all of us. That's what counts. So before I would listen and it was the story of Christ, coming with love and generosity, being savaged, then being reduced to a museum-piece. But His love lives on, pierces through all that. But listening to it just now, the story says something different. That you get what you get in this world, and the lucky ones are those who can still feel regret. The story's not different. I guess I am."

"*Kinkajou* made me think about my old friend, Cindy, being humiliated as a bag of bones in the trunk of my car. That's so . . . sad for me. But, like in the story, what counts is that the love hangs together, in a special way it transcends the savagery." She made a gesture with her lips to indicate that yes, she knew that, but she was not willing to sanction such a code for the moment.

All she said was, "Poor Gaby," remembering her own lost friend.

I stood up. Walked around. Chantelle's red tear stained her cheek. What an actress she had been. I needed to know, "Why did you bleed one day early?"

"I told you. I had to take you on. If I'd waited a day, the Sisters would have found a way to neutralize you. At the very least they would have posted guards. I wanted to draw you into the bedroom, Kyle. I wanted to sucker you. I wanted you to witness my act for yourself. See what you were made of. Let you know what you were up against. And anyway, this is how I make friends. I bleed for people and they adore me, at least until the flow stops." She sniffed a little and rubbed her nose. "Besides that, I was preparing to change things. Shake a few doubts out of the trees and let them scamper loose. You see, I was preparing to pull back. I was wearying of the charade."

"You were trying to help yourself," I noted.

"I beg your pardon?"

"Killing my father shook a few doubts of your own loose. You were forced to start taking yourself seriously — your madness seriously. Forget the serendipity."

"Kyle—"

"Think about it." While she was doing that my thoughts skimmed along a different tangent. "Maybe this is your way of cutting out," I specified.

"Come again?"

"Demonstrating to everyone that it was always an act. When maybe it isn't. Maybe this is your way of breaking free of the obligations, severing the bonds. Next Easter, Chantelle, what will you do? Go public? Or sequester yourself?"

"Don't be ridiculous. Where would I have learnt a trick like that otherwise?"

"Here. From my father. He knew every trick in the book, you said. Was he your teacher? Was he giving you a way out?"

Folding her legs beneath her, she clamped her hands on her knees. "We'll just have to wait and see," she breezed. "Who knows? Maybe I'll be giving birth next Easter. Then again, maybe I won't."

"Is that part of it too? Have sex, get pregnant, have an abortion. Do whatever's necessary to infuriate your God so that He'll leave you alone. About the baby —"

"Goodnight, Kyle. I want to rest. I have a long drive ahead of me in the morning."

"Don't throw me out now."

"What I hope you understand is, what's behind it all comes from the same source. That's what your father understood, that's why he never condemned me. My hope for God was always sincere. Likewise my rejection. That's what those . . ." Her eyes misted over as she searched for the appropriate description. ". . . *friends*, so called, can't get through their thick skulls. *I'm* why they came together in the first place, *I'm* why they've hung in there through the years. Now they want out. Just because my secret's been exposed. What's happened to our commitment to each other? Our love? Your father was more faithful, Kyle. He cared about me no matter what. The rest of them — screw them. I wash my hands of them. Now go, Kyle. Please."

I wanted to harangue her pride, brutalize her folly. At the same time, I longed to cushion the terrible loneliness she must be feeling, that sense of being betrayed by her friends. My father's seemed the wiser path, however, and I relented. I wonder if he had hated her as much as he had loved her, just like me. I moved next to Chantelle, and ever so lightly kissed her dry eye.

Early the next morning the nuns departed, each her separate way. Chantelle lugged her mammoth stuffed suitcase out to her car, having brought along the nuns' habits that none of them would ever wear again. That made me very sad. For she was leaving without friends, only the empty robes as reminders of her former affiliation with the self-declared nuns. Taking the robes with her seemed a hopeless ritual, as if she could not yet fathom that she was irrevocably severed from the past. That was still to come. Chantelle was on her own now, and what a weight that must be for someone in her circumstances.

I watched her from the eyrie of my window before descending for the hard job of saying good bye. She was waiting for me. We kissed each other on the cheek.

"Any decision?" I asked her. Gently.

"I'll have to decide," she answered. Only in her wavering could I rejoice. "Maybe I'll write."

"I'd like that."

"Or maybe I'll mail you a wee bundle wrapped in blankets."

"Always consider it an option. Only use a courier service."

Chantelle offered her hand. "Been nice knowing you, fellah."

I tapped my left breast before accepting the handshake. "You'll always be close to my heart."

A moment's silence only stirred our laughter at my remark. But we both knew I meant it. Chantelle climbed into her car and buckled up. She started the ignition. Gazing at her one last time as if searching her beleaguered psyche, I leaned against the car with my hands on the roof. She mouthed a "Good bye," smiled faintly, and the car backed up. I let go. I watched the Chevette dip and jump down the rough driveway. I waved. And Chantelle was gone.

Although she was not the last of her group to depart Toll House that morning, my heart welled with the inn's emptiness. My emotion stung too much; I took a long walk, wanting to keep alive and to accustom myself to my new life. I had no desire to sleep this one off.

In the warming sunshine I listened for bird song, and was treated to the lazy flight of grosbeaks. A troop of blue jays kicked up a ruckus in the underbrush. The trees were in their summer finery now, the leaves a deeper, richer hue, and as my walk progressed I removed my wind-breaker and strolled along the shady side of the road.

Horses grazed across the meadow. In that twinkling of light and shadow-play I knew that I would reopen the inn, if for no other reason than to see who'd come by. I would have to call the stables' operator, advise him to hire trail-riders. And I'd buzz Hazel, inform her that it was high time she got off her fanny and knuckled down to some serious work.

Luxuriating in the adrenalin of my new-found energy and conviction, I walked, wanting to make a go of it, to wake up once and for all and welcome a new day. I'll sing the call of the olive-sided flycatcher to my guests

quick-three-beers

and play them riffs on my dulcimer. Send them back to the hard-core world of bones and blood, jobs and bills, replenished and slightly out of kilter. Give them a wacky view of what we possibly can be.

Excited, I twice broke into headlong sprints as I dashed down the mountainside. My Bengal Lancer's charge took me past the signs to Toll House.

HALT!

I retreated, staring at them.

PAY

TOLL

I had to chuckle to myself. I elected not only to keep the inn's name as is, but to maintain the nonsensical signs as well. To whomever might inquire about them, I'd repeat one of my father's crazy rejoinders, "Never yet met the man who didn't have to pay the price." And I'd add, "Woman either," in case that was not understood.

On certain nights, when the wind blows loud and menacing, when the floors creak and the shutters bang, I shall read Kinky's story to them. Or I'll relate the tale of how I came to be the proprietor of the Toll House Inn. And if I recite the tale differently each time, alter or embellish a detail or two, who is there to prove me wrong? Who is to say that I'm not closer to the truth this time than last? If anyone disputes my version, I'll whistle the migration melody of the ruby-crowned kinglet, and let the fowl of the air discuss it.

Look! There! Do you see! On that birch — a redbreasted nuthatch giving full throat to its morning praise.

Though I was tempted, I did not give the PAY TOLL sign a swift kick in its gluteus, as Franklin D. Ryder had been compelled to do. Nor did I blast the HALT! sign with a shotgun, which had been the reply of an aggrieved, anonymous, and perplexed hunter. Rather, I patted each sign on the back, and added a few stones to the base. The signs were the upright representations of my father. My . . . pop. And like a god who is dead, or who perhaps never existed at all, or who has merely gone missing for a while, it was uncanny how he was right about just about everything, and wrong about nothing at all.

Let the signs stand.

The End.

More Great Titles from M&S Paperbacks...

FINAL APPROACH
by Spencer Dunmore
Final Approach spans the horizons of adventure with its dramatic tales of heroism, romance, and camaraderie. Taking the reader from 1911 to 1942 to the present, it will appeal to veterans, aviation buffs and lovers of good fiction.
0-7710-2922-5 $5.95

FASTYNGANGE
by Tim Wynne-Jones
"Wynne-Jones guides us with sure feet over the many bridges between this world and imaginary others . . . *Fastyngange* is a strange and delightful hybrid." - *The Ottawa Citizen*
0-7710-9032-3 $5.95

COPPERMINE JOURNEY
by Farley Mowat
The epic story of hardship, perseverance and courage, based on the extensive journals of Samuel Hearne, who explored the more than 250,000 square miles stretching north across the continent, one of the most forbidding territories in the world.
0-7710-6690-2 $4.95   Includes maps

ALONG THE SHORE
Tales by the Sea
by L.M. Montgomery
The sea forms the beguiling setting to sixteen previously unpublished tales of humour, adventure, tragedy, and romance.
0-7710-6170-6 $4.95

LETTERS OF A BUSINESSMAN TO HIS DAUGHTER
by G. Kingsley Ward
"Gems that both men and women will find useful" - *Financial Times*
0-7710-8803-5 $4.95